MW00459832

ONE LAST

ALASKA AIR ONE RESCUE | BOOK FOUR

STAND

ONE LAST

ALASKA AIR ONE RESCUE | BOOK FOUR

STAND

SUSAN MAY WARREN

Revell

a division of Baker Publishing Group
Grand Rapids, Michigan

© 2024 by Susan May Warren

Published by Revell
a division of Baker Publishing Group
Grand Rapids, Michigan
RevellBooks.com

Printed in the United States of America

All rights reserved. No part of this publication may be reproduced or transmitted in any form or by any means without written permission of the publisher.

Library of Congress Cataloging-in-Publication Data
Names: Warren, Susan May, 1966- author.
Title: One last stand / Susan May Warren.
Description: Grand Rapids, Michigan : Revell, a division of Baker
  Publishing Group, 2024. | Series: Alaska Air One Rescue ; #4 | Summary:
  "When Air One Rescue pilot London Brooks finds herself falsely accused,
  her reputation tarnished, and her life in danger, she has no choice but
  to plunge back into the treacherous world of espionage she left behind.
  Shep Watson already saved London's life once-and he'll do everything in
  his power to bring her back home"-- Provided by publisher.
Identifiers: LCCN 2024009898 | ISBN 9780800745509 (paperback) |
  ISBN 9780800746476 (casebound)
Subjects: LCGFT: Christian fiction. | Romance fiction. | Novels.
Classification: LCC PS3623.A865 O56 2024 | DDC 813/.6--dc23/eng/20240229
LC record available at https://lccn.loc.gov/2024009898

This book is a work of fiction. Names, characters, places, and incidents are either products of the author's imagination or used fictitiously. Any similarity to actual people, organizations, and/or events is purely coincidental.

Scripture quotations are also taken from the Holy Bible, New International Version®, NIV®. Copyright© 1973, 1978, 1984, 2011 by Biblica, Inc®. Used by permission of Zondervan. All rights reserved worldwide.

For more information about Susan May Warren, please access the author's website at the following address: www.susanmaywarren.com.

Published in the United States of America.
Cover design by Emilie Haney, www.eahcreative.com

24 25 26 27 28 29 30   7 6 5 4 3 2 1

For Your glory, Lord

ONE

THE ONLY SUPERPOWER HE'D EVER LONGED for was flying. To lift off this earth, untangle himself from this life with its griefs and responsibilities and broken hopes—even the constant whirring of his brain—and soar.

The sky today arched a brilliant, endless blue over Mt. Alyeska, the sun's rays glistening upon a pristine plain of powder-fresh snow that had dropped over the ski resort and sifted into the Teacup Bowl. He stood at the headwall of the Alyeska Chute, his skis pointed just over the edge, the angle into the bowl so steep that, yes, he could spread his arms and simply lift off.

"You're not serious." Oaken Fox stood a ways back, wearing skis and leaning on his poles. In his silver helmet, wearing goggles, a scarf, and a ski suit, no one would know that the country music star had just taken to the slopes today after a three-week tour in the lower forty-eight.

Maybe he'd returned to keep Shep from spiraling into darkness. Oaken and his girlfriend, Boo, had shown up on his doorstep last night with a pizza and plans for today's ski trip.

But even the blue sky and bright sunlight couldn't seem to break through the hover of grief.

How could London be gone? He simply couldn't wrap his brain around it . . .

So maybe he just needed to fly . . .

Oaken skied over. "I did mention I grew up in South Dakota, right? Not a hill to be found."

Boo joined them. She wore a lime-green one-piece ski suit and a matching helmet. No one would lose her on the slopes.

Below them, in the bowl, sat all of Alyeska ski resort, and from here Shep could make out the upper tram terminal along with the ski-patrol shack and first-aid center. Below that, runs fanned out over the mountain in all directions, bordered by a forest of mountain hemlock, spruce and Douglas fir, and way too many tree wells for out-of-control skiers to plunge into headfirst.

And then, of course, freeze to death.

He shook the thought away. Not today. Today was for freedom, flying . . . forgetting.

"Tell me again why we had to go all the way to the top?" Boo said. "Plenty of decent skiing below this ridge of terror. Don't look at me as I'm snowplowing my way down. I just need someone to catch me at the bottom when I turn into a snowball of doom."

"You'll be fine." Shep pointed to a ridge below, a razorback, with a groomed slope in the valley that twisted its way to the bottom. "The sun is on the snow there—no shadows—and it's a shorter chute into the bowl. Take the High Traverse to the Center Ridge run and it turns into a blue square."

"As opposed to the double black diamonds that surround us," Oaken said. "I'm with Boo on this, Shep. I don't know about you, but Boo and I are among the bunny-hill aficionados."

"Hardly. I've seen you both ski. Just plan your route and take it easy." He gestured to the chutes that dropped from the headwall into a massive bowl of powder.

Okay, yes, he could admit that it all looked like an avalanche just waiting to happen. But probably not yet, this early in the season. The snowfall hadn't been so great as to layer up the seracs or create the shifting planes that could lead to a lethal slide.

Still . . . "I'll go last to pick up any debris from a yard sale," said Shep, grinning.

"Funny," Oaken said. "Just promise to dig me out before the paparazzi find me if I end up face down in the snow." He looked at Boo. "C'mon, babe. We'll do this together."

She pushed off and they traversed the headwall to the nearby chute.

Shep breathed in the crisp air, bright and biting in his lungs. He closed his eyes, taking in the whisper of the wind, the slight rattle of the gondola in the distance. He'd talked one of his ski-patrol pals into driving them up to the top, Boo and Oaken all thumbs-up until they saw the drop, the snow that gathered around jutting boulders and along the cliffside.

He opened his eyes, feeling the silence build inside him, the adrenaline burning. He glanced over at Boo and Oaken—both of them had lied to him more than a little. Boo had attacked the wall straight down, finding air off a small cliff, landing, and then completing a beautiful line down to the High Traverse.

Oaken followed, avoiding the cliff, cutting short turns until the slope opened up and he glided down to Boo.

Shep let out a breath he hadn't realized he'd been holding. Last thing he wanted was to lead his cohorts into disaster.

Boo raised her pole, and he waved back.

Now to the cliff in front of him. A fairly narrow passage dropped some twenty feet into a thick pillow of powder, and from that, the slope veered nearly straight down some twenty more feet until it started to flatten.

Yeah, time to fly.

He pushed off, lifted his skis from the edge, and found air as he fell. Held his arms out, just for balance—and maybe wings—then landed, spring in his knees, and moved into a sharp turn to slow himself just a little, then eased up and widened it out.

Wind buzzed in his ears, powder drifting up to feather upon his helmet, his goggles, his jacket. Skiing in loose, thigh-deep snow required more leg strength than edge, and he kept his form tight, his speed high, his line wide enough to stay in control. He felt his spirit, at least for a moment, soar. The grief left his chest.

The grip on his soul released.

Breathe.

He focused on his rhythm, keeping his legs together, centering over his skis, letting the swish overtake him. One right move at a time.

He slowed as he neared Boo and Oaken, then stopped, managing not to spray them with snow, and laughed.

Laughed.

Oh, it felt like a betrayal. He swallowed it back, fast.

Boo gave him a tight-lipped smile, nodding.

"Okay, when you said you 'did some skiing,' you left out that you were some sort of powder master," Oaken said. "Seriously—you look like a big-mountain freeriding world champion. Like that guy from Mercy Falls—Gage Watson."

Shep nodded and let a real grin out. "Yep."

Never mind that Gage was his cousin and that for a while he'd followed in Gage's footsteps. Until the accident.

Until responsibility had caught up to him.

"Shep is on ski patrol here in the winter," Boo said, glancing at Oaken. "He gets to ski for free."

"In between scraping people off the hill," Shep said. He didn't mention that he hadn't signed up this year.

Or the fact that the only reason he'd tagged along today, like a third wheel, was to give himself something to do while his realtor opened up his house to potential buyers. A private sale for now.

He didn't want to tell the Air One Rescue team until the purchase agreement was inked and he couldn't change his mind.

"Okay, that's enough daredevil for me today," Boo said. "I'm headed down to the blue runs and maybe all the way to the bottom for some hot cocoa."

"I think I'll take a leisurely ride through the trees," Shep said. "See you at the bottom."

He pushed off, heading across the lower traverse, crossing the ridge over to the north face and down Picnic Rock toward the Big Dipper, a thinned but wooded black diamond run. He was passing through a narrow chute between the trees called Spider Bite, the heavily wooded off-boundary section of tree-skiing to his left, when he spotted a flash of silver.

He slowed, then skirted to the edge of the run and stopped, peering into the woods.

Oh no.

Skis protruded, just barely, from the bushy branches of a mountain hemlock.

Shep unsnapped his bindings, set his skis upright, then tromped into the forest, grabbing tree limbs as the snow tried to suck him in to his thighs.

"Hey!" he shouted.

No reply. The skier had hit the tree, evidenced by the broken branches, and then tried to break their fall—headfirst—into the well around the tree. They now lay wedged into the space under the branches that formed a well around the tree, only their red jacket and silver ski pants showing.

Slowly suffocating.

He found solid footing, grabbed a couple branches, then dropped to his knees, leaning into the well. "Hey, you okay?"

No sound. *Please, God,* let him not be too late. He grabbed his walkie even as he started to paw at the snow. "Ski Patrol, this is Shep Watson. I'm just off Spider Bite in the off-boundary area—

there's a skier trapped in an SIS hazard. I'm going to start to dig him out—send help."

He pocketed the walkie even as he heard the senior patroller confirm, and pulled off the backpack he carried for exactly this reason. Pulling out the small handheld shovel, he dove in, digging out from the side of the well. "I'm coming—just hang on."

He tunneled in from the side, creating a bigger opening, then dropped his shovel and pulled out the soft snow with his hands, not wanting to take out a chunk of flesh with the edge of his shovel.

"C'mon, stay alive—"

Don't think about the darkness, the feeling of suffocation, the sense of aloneness that can sweep over a person—

He uncovered a shoulder, spotted movement—*hallelujah*—and followed the arm down, found a helmet. Maybe they'd found a pocket of air—

He cleared out the snow, and there, at the base of the tree, a space of air. And then—

"Help!" The voice lifted—a female. She started to wriggle. The snow had trapped her arms behind her, so she was unable to leverage them to push herself free.

Terrible way to die.

"I got ya," he said, trying to pull her up, but the position wedged her tight. He would need to get in with her—

Shouting sounded behind him. Over his shoulder, he spotted Oaken and Boo fighting toward him through the snow and trees.

"For a second, we thought it was *you* trapped in the trees," Oaken said as he fell to his knees opposite the woman and also began to dig.

"Careful not to cave in more snow on her," Shep said and handed him the shovel. "And don't get crazy with the shovel—you don't want to break bones."

He handed his radio to Boo, who stepped back to check on patrol status.

Oaken raked back more snow, and Shep freed her shoulders. A long blonde ponytail snaked out the back of her helmet.

Shep climbed down into the well, nearly to his hips in depth. "Ma'am, did you hit your head?"

"No—no—" She started to cry.

He'd prefer to put a C collar on her, but she might be going into shock, hyperventilating, so he slid an arm under her, around her shoulders. Oaken got in on the other side, did the same.

"Boo, stabilize her legs," he said. "On three."

They pulled her up, heaving until her body came free of the hole, some five feet deep.

The woman rolled over, gasping. She still wore her goggles and a helmet, but with her blonde hair unraveled from her braid, she looked like—

His breath caught. *No* . . . It couldn't be.

And he knew—he'd seen her body, after all—that London was dead. The facts confirmed it—her car found in a nearby lake, her body mutilated but still the same frame, height, and weight. Most of all, the terrible emptiness in his soul. So yes, even if his heart didn't want to believe it, facts were facts.

Yet this woman lying in the snow, breathing hard, maybe crying, had brought him right back to the what-ifs.

What if the body wasn't London's?

What if she'd reactivated what he knew was a clandestine past with some interesting skills he'd never suspected and . . . what? Faked her death?

Let it go. Let her *go.*

Words he'd been dodging for the better part of a month.

Oaken had unhooked the woman's skis, retrieved her poles.

Okay, so he was desperate, but as Boo, the team EMT, leaned over her and moved her goggles off to check her vision, he hoped—

Nope. Midtwenties, freckles on her face, brown eyes. Not London.

Ski patrollers had arrived with a sled, one of them trekking out to their position.

"Get a collar on her," Shep said, and reached for it as the first patroller handed him the bag.

He snapped it on, leaning over her.

She grabbed his jacket. "Thank you."

"You know this area is off-limits, right?" Shep said.

"Easy there, bro," Boo said softly.

Right. He blew out a breath, studying her face as she let go of his coat. "Anything broken?"

"I don't think so. And I didn't mean to ski in here—" Her eyes filled again, her face reddened from cold and tears. "I took the wrong run and was trying to take a shortcut back to the inter-mediate slopes. I wasn't going fast, but my ski caught, and down I went. I tried to grab branches to stop myself, but the snow just came down over me. . . ."

Her breath caught, and *aw, just loosen up, like Boo said.* Clearly, memory had a grip on him, turning him into a jerk.

He gave her a small nod, his gaze softening at her fear.

"I don't know how you saw me, but . . . if you hadn't—" She hiccoughed. "Thank you."

He had to look away, then he blew out a breath, found a smile for her, and nodded. "You must have angels watching out for you. And you're welcome." He then stepped back as the patrollers closed in—a new crew for this season. "She probably needs an X-ray."

"Thanks," said one, the name badge on his orange ski jacket reading Bowman. He directed others to bring in a sled.

Boo and Oaken carried her gear out to where more patrollers sat, ready to ski her down the hill.

Shep stared at the tree well. Any longer and it might have become a tomb. His throat thickened, but he shook away the grip of what-ifs and headed back out to the run.

Boo and Oaken waited for him, already in their skis.

"I thought you were going to take the blue runs."

"And let you call us pansies?" Oaken said. "Please. Besides, we weren't sure if you'd just . . . I don't know. Ski off the edge of the planet, never to be seen again."

He blinked at them.

"You're not fooling anyone, Shep. We know you put your town-house up for sale—I have the same realtor."

Boo leaned on her poles. "You're really leaving?"

So much for his secrets. "Maybe." He swallowed. "Probably. But don't tell Moose yet, okay? I just . . . I'm not ready . . ."

"To tell him that his number-one rescue tech is leaving during the time that he might very well be losing his company?" Boo raised an eyebrow.

Yeah, that. He pursed his lips.

Boo's voice fell. "Listen, Shep. We all grieve London. She was my roommate. I miss our chats, the way I'd spot her in the yard, working out—even our late-night conversations about faith. If I know anything about London, it's that she was a woman of faith—and she'd want us to be rejoicing that she's in heaven."

Her words stripped him. "*Rejoicing?* Boo—she was *murdered.* And somewhere out there is the person who killed her. And . . ."

And he was supposed to have protected her.

His one task when recruiting her for the Air One Rescue team had been to keep her safe.

So not only had losing her taken him apart . . . he wanted to hurt the man he saw in the mirror every dark and brutal morning.

The shadows had returned, the darkness seeping back into his pores. "The dead-last thing I feel like doing is rejoicing."

He snapped back into his skis. "I think I'm done for the day. Thanks, guys. Try not to break any bones."

Then he pushed off, leaving them behind as he tore down the slope.

Not flying at all.

The longer she stayed, the more danger she brought to his doorstep.

Maybe.

Or perhaps she simply couldn't say goodbye.

But really, how did someone say goodbye to the one person who'd saved her life not only physically but also by bringing to life something long dead inside her. . . .

Something very near to hope.

The ski hill glistened under the fading sunlight, and even at this unusually early start to the season, cars jammed the parking lot. Mostly locals this late in the year, despite being a weekend. London sat in her cold car in the parking lot, wishing she could join everyone on the slopes. The memory of skiing with Shep last year—the rush of heat as they'd flown down the slopes together—in truth, she'd loved him even then.

She just hadn't wanted to admit it.

Shep returned, looking tired, and shoved his skis onto the roof of his Tahoe.

Of course, he looked amazing. Lean, strong, a hero even if he didn't know it. He sat and pulled off his ski boots, putting on leather mukluks, then stripped off his jacket to only a thermal shirt that outlined his toned body, still wearing his suspendered ski pants and a stocking cap over his dark hair, the faintest hint of whiskers on his chin.

How cruel was it that the vivid and terribly wonderful memory of his arms around her, of him kissing her, swept through her and took hold?

She should have told him she loved him long, long ago.

As in a decade back, maybe, but for sure a month ago when he'd tried to step over the line of friendship.

Ghosts. Ghosts of past lives stole her future.

Trapping her in the regrets.

"Really, Laney, it's time." The voice in her earpiece, the one with a slightly Italian accent, sounded more compassionate than her true personality. Ziggy Mattucci had scared London to her bones the first time she'd met her, but that might have been because Zig had been holding a pugil stick, padded up and facing her in a ten-by-ten ring.

Ready to ring her bell.

So yeah, the softness of her trainer's voice betrayed how long London had let this final goodbye linger.

"If no one has come after him by now, I think your secret is safe."

"Which one? The one where I'm supposed to be dead? Or the one where the Russians have found me—how, I have no idea—and will stop at nothing to get their money back? Which one is the one I should be most afraid of, Ziggy? Because in my gut, I know—just *know*—that they'll figure out that I'm alive . . . and then everyone I love will be in danger."

Love. She drew in her breath at the word. *Okay, whatever.* Maybe admitting it to Ziggy would be the only way to release this terrible clench in her heart.

Fine. She loved Shep Watson. Mistake number one.

Mistake number two was probably thinking that she could escape and start over.

Again.

"Do whatever you have to do to say goodbye, and I expect you on the next plane to Switzerland—"

"I already told you, Zig. Those days are over. I'm *not* coming back." She picked up her necklace, running her thumb along the etchings of the simple paddle pendant she wore around her neck.

"We'll see."

Silence.

"Fine." Ziggy's voice held a softer edge, turning into her mentor, maybe even a friend. "But you *are* leaving Anchorage. If they found you there once, they can find you again."

"We don't even know who hired—"

"I'm working on it. In the meantime, I'd be much happier if you were back at the mansion—"

"No. That life is done. I'm not that person anymore."

"This life is who you are."

She drew in a breath.

"Don't make me come back there."

London's mouth tightened. "I didn't need you the first time."

A laugh, small, that had nothing to do with humor and everything to do with reality. "Maybe not. Keep in touch. I need to know where you land. And, Laney . . . *assurgo*."

Right. "Assurgo."

Ziggy hung up.

The word echoed in London's mind. The Black Swan motto— *Stand up and soar.*

She sighed. No, she was in this alone.

Now, she got out and stretched as Shep piled the rest of his gear into the back end of his SUV. Just two rows over, but he didn't have a hope of recognizing her with her long black wig, sunglasses, knit cap, and white puffer jacket, Uggs.

She looked like a snow bunny, and as he turned her direction, she made to wave at someone behind him, blowing that imaginary someone a kiss.

Her heart burned as he turned away.

Yeah, maybe it was time to say goodbye.

He got into his Tahoe, and she waited until he'd pulled out, a couple other cars behind him, before she followed. She knew the way to his townhouse—down the road and up the highway from the ski hill. A gorgeous modern townhome that he'd self-remodeled a couple years ago, before she got here.

She'd seen the realtor come and go, twice, and it had knotted her gut.

Don't run, Shep.

Right. Pot, meet kettle. But he had a life here. Or he had. Until she'd so perfectly destroyed it.

They crossed the bridge over Glacier Creek, a tourist way-stop, where a family had stopped in their ski gear to snap the glorious view of the setting sun off Mt. Alyeska with its deep runnels and sharp ridges, soaring peaks against the deep-blue sky.

She'd really hoped to hide here forever.

His Tahoe continued south to the highway, then north some fifteen minutes, and finally turned into a subdivision with a line of townhomes built into a mountainside overlooking the sound. Down here, closer to sea level, the snow hadn't lingered, just lightly dusting the yards. Winter had come early, the days growing shorter, dusky at four p.m.

Shep parked in his driveway, and when his motion-sensor light blinked on, she drove past, up the road, where she turned and headed back down again to park in the shadows.

Another long, cold night where panic drove her to scrutinize every movement.

"Really, Laney, it's time."

Her heart lodged in her chest as he closed his garage door. Then she pulled up her phone and opened the app.

Yep, she'd turned full-out stalker, watching him climb the stairs to his main floor dressed in his stocking feet and long johns. He went into the kitchen, and she lost him from view—her camera only caught the main area, which included the front door and the sliding door out to his deck. Any more and she couldn't justify invading his privacy.

Whatever. She despised the lies she told herself in this version of her life.

He returned into view with a mug of hot cocoa. Climbed onto a stool and stared into the mug.

Just stared.

Ah. And here he'd stay, probably. Unmoving in the darkness. For hours.

Sometimes he powered up his gas fireplace. Watched television—he loved old John Wayne movies.

And then he'd go to bed. All in the darkness.

Always Mr. Calm, Mr. Suffer in Silence, Mr. Tuck Away His Emotions. Until, of course, a month ago, when he'd told her he wanted more. And even then he'd been patient. Kind.

Mistake number three: letting him love her.

Letting herself believe in a happy ending.

She didn't turn on the heat, preferring the cold.

She deserved the cold.

Lights flickered on, peeking around the window shades of nearby townhomes. She ducked down in her car—a very used Ford Bronco she'd purchased with cash—when a couple neighbors returned home.

Still Shep sat there, in darkness, even after he'd finished his drink.

Maybe Ziggy was right. Why would someone come after Shep? He had no connection to her except being her friend.

More than a friend.

And maybe that's why her gut had remained in knots since the moment she and Ziggy had pushed her Subaru into the lake, the dead body of a stranger inside. Because London just couldn't dodge the sense that . . .

Well, the Russian mob wasn't exactly above tracking down someone she cared about to flush her out.

Maybe she should grab Shep and run.

What, like he was a puppy?

She leaned her head back on her seat, took a breath. Closed her eyes.

For a second, just like every time, the memory of the attack lurched back to her.

The assassin's blow had come from behind her. If it hadn't been for the reflection in the sliding-door window—

She'd dodged, whirled, caught the woman's wrist and slammed it into the wall, jarring loose the club.

Thank you, Ziggy, for the muscle memory.

The woman threw a fist at her, but London dodged it. The second punch caught her though, and the woman shook out of her hold, rolled out, and came back with a knife.

Yeah, well, London too. She'd grabbed the butcher's knife from the block, breathing hard, bracing.

No one came out of a knife fight uncut.

The woman was lean, about London's build, blonde hair snaking out of a black stocking cap. She dressed like an assassin, in all black, and moved slowly, circling. London circled with her, and that's when she spotted another woman outside on the porch.

One, maybe, but she was out of practice and—

The door opened, her attacker turned as if surprised, and right then, a shot—just a whoosh and ping—from a silencer.

It hit the woman center mass with a thunk.

Vest. But the attacker dropped, and then the second woman—she also wore black, her dark hair back—jumped on her.

She put her hands to the attacker's throat.

The first woman struggled, fighting.

London drew in a breath, the reality of the quiet moment seeping into her. No, no this couldn't be—"Don't kill her!"

The second woman looked up, and recognition shuddered through London. "*Ziggy.*"

"She's with the Orphans."

And that froze London to the spot as she watched the assassin's body still.

Her heartbeat punched her. *No, no—*

Finally, Ziggy got up. "You okay?"

No. Not even a little. She nodded. Then, "How—"

"I got a message from a friend who heard from Raisa Yukachova, the head of the Orphans, that someone put a hit out on you. We need to go. But first, you need to die."

London knew how she meant it, but still . . .

She was tired of dying.

Maybe she'd hesitated, too, because a hint of rare compassion flashed in Ziggy's dark eyes. "Now. We need to throw off the trail before they send another."

Right.

So London packed while Ziggy took care of the nasty business of changing the woman's clothes, deforming her face, taking off her fingertips. London had been out of the business too long, apparently—well, had never really been *in* that business—but seeing the woman's mutilated body as Ziggy shoved her into the back of London's Crosstrek had sent London to the bushes to be sick.

Ziggy waited for her by the car, holding keys. "This life is over."

London snatched the keys from her, acid in her throat. Then she drove the car to the lake. They put the woman in the driver's seat, then together, pushed the car in.

And then, London ran.

The last thing she wanted was to watch as her team found "her" body, so she'd stayed in Ziggy's motel room while Ziggy watched and confirmed London's death.

Then London had the row of her life with the woman who'd taught her everything.

I'm not leaving until I know he's safe.

Maybe she should have said, *I'm not leaving.* Full stop. Because after a month, she still didn't know how . . . well, how to tell him goodbye.

"Do whatever you have to do to say goodbye."

What if . . . what if she didn't have to? What if . . .

She opened her eyes and looked at her phone. He'd left the kitchen, and she switched screens. He had climbed up the stairs to his lofted bedroom, the darkness pitch around him, although the wan light from the rising moon in the big great-room windows betrayed his form.

She could sneak in and . . . at least tell him the truth. All of it, starting with the day he'd saved her life. He deserved that much, at least. Then, yes, she'd leave.

He'd keep her secret; she knew it in the depths of her soul. Shep was good at keeping secrets—after all, he'd lied to her for the better part of a year, and now, *oops*, tears brimmed her eyes. She'd forgiven him for that—but at the time, she'd been a little too hypocritical.

Or just afraid that he knew everything.

But he hadn't probed, hadn't said anything about the lies she'd told him. Instead, he'd kept showing up. Holding on to her.

No wonder she couldn't let go.

Maybe he deserved a real goodbye—

Movement flickered across one of the outside views on her phone, and she clicked on the window. It opened.

Nothing in the grainy picture—but she'd seen a shadow, she knew it.

From the glove box, she pulled out the tiny Glock Gen5, G47, a nine mil that should do the job—a parting gift from Ziggy. London hadn't asked any questions.

She'd already shed her white jacket, wearing just her black thermal shirt, and now she turned her hat black side out and slid out of the car, no dome light.

She crept down the street, in the shadows along the ditch.

Crossed over to Shep's driveway, dodging the motion-detector lights.

In her car, her phone would be pinging desperately.

She circled around to the back and then crouched near his deck—jutting from the side, visible from the road for anyone else who might be watching. A grill under a tarp sat against the far edge, a sofa and a couple of outdoor chairs situated for a perfect view of the sound.

Movement. Something small—so not an assassin from the Orphans, unless they now employed seven-year-olds. But something...

Her body froze when a dog crept out from behind the grill. A garbage can with a lid had been knocked over, and now the dog sniffed near it. Found a bone and dragged it away, settling on the deck for a good gnaw. A bigger dog, black and skinny, its bones protruding from its body, poor thing.

Wait. She had some beef jerky in the car, a stakeout treat.

She backed away, worked her way back to her car, and retrieved the rest of the bag of jerky. Then she returned, her gun tucked into her belt, and crept up to the deck.

The dog looked up. Whined.

So, not an angry dog, just scared.

"It's okay, buddy." She crouched near the stairs and held out a piece of jerky. The animal had shifted back into the shadows near the grill, trapped as she stood at the only exit.

"C'mere. It's okay."

The dog's eyes glowed gold in the darkness. She tossed the jerky toward him. It didn't go very far, but the animal didn't move.

Aw. "C'mon, sweetie. I'm not going to hurt you." She pulled out another piece of jerky and then crept up onto the deck. She held the jerky out. "C'mon... it's okay."

The dog considered her, then hunkered down, submissive.

She took another step toward him.

He strained his neck and took the jerky from her.

Settled down to gnaw at it.

"You're just hungry." She took out another piece of jerky and stood up.

Just like that, light bathed the porch. Rookie mistake. She spotted the motion detector light, set high enough to detect a human but not an animal.

Dropping the jerky, she took off around the back of the house, alongside the driveway, and then back into her car.

Right then, he stepped out of his townhouse onto the side deck, into the light.

So he hadn't been asleep. Just staring into the darkness. Again.

He crouched and, as her throat thickened, picked up her dropped jerky. Looked out into the night.

She sank down, even though her car sat hooded in darkness.

Now, tell him now.

But then Shep turned to the dog and fed it. He disappeared into the house and came out with a bowl of water and what looked like steak. As she watched, Shep coaxed the animal into his arms.

Wow, she loved this man.

She couldn't, just couldn't, break his heart again.

More—and the thought struck her like a blade to the heart—if she went inside, told him she was alive . . . well, how was *she* supposed to tear herself away?

No. If she went in there, she stayed.

And that's when she really put his life in danger.

He picked up the dog, and the animal lifted its snout to lick his chin. Then, again, he stared out into the night.

In the light, she could make out his tight jaw, the emotion in his eyes.

Her breath turned to glue in her chest. Her eyes burned.

And she couldn't help but put her hand to the window.

Goodbye, Shep.

He sighed and disappeared into the house.

London put her car into gear, and slowly, finally, pulled away from the curb.

TWO

THIS HANDSOME GUY WAS JUST STANDING ON your deck?" The question came from Anchorage detective Flynn Turnquist, who crouched in the lobby of the Tooth, the headquarters for the Air One Rescue team, located at Merrill Field on the north side of Anchorage. Her hands rubbed the floppy black ears of his visitor slash new roommate, and the dog leaned its head to one side and groaned, something deep and happy emanating from the inside.

"Yeah," Shep said, setting the coffeepot back into the maker and coming around the giant island that separated the kitchen from the main area—a long table where they held conferences, and a seating area complete with worn leather furniture and a table in the center, all facing a flatscreen television. When the team wasn't working out, training, or tending to their equipment, they watched a lot of *MacGyver* and *Magnum, P.I.* Moose loved the old shows, and he'd made a convert out of all of them.

With the advent of the season's first snowfall, the tourist season had died down, and with it, their callouts, although hunting season had begun. Still, that left more time for workouts, training, and downtime.

That would end with the first real blizzard, however.

He couldn't wait for something to take his mind off London.

"The light went on outside, and I wasn't sleeping, so I got up and found him," Shep said as he walked over to Flynn. "He was eating some beef jerky. He'd gotten into my trash. I had a T-bone steak the other night for dinner and set the bone outside . . ."

"Poor guy. He was hungry."

"And thirsty. Drank about a gallon, then went for the eternal drinking fountain in the bathroom. I shut that down. He slept in my laundry room." He crouched beside the dog. "After I gave him a bath."

"He's pretty," said Axel from where he sat at the table, scrolling through his phone. "What kind is he?"

"I dunno. Sort of looks like a black lab."

"Except for this brown patch here," said Flynn, indicating the fur on his chest. "And his snout is too narrow. Doberman, all the way."

"Maybe a mixed breed," said Shep. "Anyway, he's a good dog. He didn't whine once, and when I told him to lie down, he immediately obeyed me. I'm going to take him into a shelter and see if he's chipped."

"What if he's not? Are you going to keep him?" Flynn stood up. She wore her auburn hair back, a pair of leggings tucked into boots, an oversized tunic. Makeup. Maybe they'd come from morning worship. Since she'd saved the life of Axel Mulligan, Moose's brother, and they'd begun dating, they'd started attending a local church.

Two years and Shep still hadn't found a place to worship.

Hadn't really looked, honestly, so that was on him.

"I can't—"

Axel looked over at Shep, frowned.

"—imagine that he doesn't have an owner." The last thing Shep wanted was to let the team know, well, that he was running away. Or maybe just trying to move on, forget.

Start over.

Right. As if. He'd given his stupid heart away to London Brooks long ago, and frankly, he didn't have a hope of getting it back.

Flynn got up. "I love dogs."

"Maybe you can take him." Shep didn't know why he'd said that—just, well, maybe the dog had nudged into a nook or cranny of his heart.

"No . . . no. I am way too busy for a dog." She looked at Axel. "I can barely keep a boyfriend."

"I'll sleep on your porch if I have to," Axel said, winking. He glanced at Shep, and Shep remembered a recent conversation about Axel hoping to propose after he'd found a place to live that wasn't his brother's basement.

Flynn walked over to Axel to peer over his shoulder. "Find anything?"

"Everything is too expensive or too run-down or in a bad neighborhood or . . . I don't know. I don't like anything."

"Spoken like a man who has a massive flatscreen and a live-in chef who cooks him steaks every Friday night."

"A crabby, bossy chef who also collects rent from me and tells me to turn off the lights every time I come upstairs." He glanced at Shep. "Besides, as soon as Tillie and Hazel get back from Florida, I think Moose has *plans*."

That made sense. Moose had been in love with Tillie from back when she was just his favorite waitress at the Skyport Diner. Felt weird to think of Tillie like that now.

Now she'd blown them all away with her background as a US Marine, an MMA fighter, and two-time champion of the Iron Maiden competition.

With a daughter.

"That's a lot to consider—taking on an instant family," Shep said. "Lots of hidden land mines there."

"Can't plan for every contingency, Shep," Axel said. "Where's the fun in that?"

Shep shrugged. "It's better than following your impulses. Like leaping onto a sinking ship without an exit strategy. . . ."

Axel glanced at Flynn. "I dunno. That seemed to turn out all right."

Shep shook his head, refrained from rolling his eyes. But *okay, maybe.*

He just never wanted to live life that unhinged, thank you. People who thought ahead didn't end up in over their heads, out of control and, well, in a tree facedown.

He'd taken Flynn's place, petting the dog. "What are you looking for?"

"A house. A condo. A townhome. Anything. I need to get out of my brother's basement."

"Says his girlfriend." Flynn looked over at Shep and winked.

Shep gave them a smile and got up. "Need something to drink while I work out, buddy?" He walked over to the cupboard, found a bowl, filled it, and then brought it over to the entry, where he set it on the floor.

The dog walked over, looked at the bowl. And obviously wasn't thrilled, because he stuck his wet snout into Shep's hand and nudged it.

"Oh, I see how it is." He'd found some cheese sticks in his refrigerator this morning, in lieu of dog food, and must have created a monster. Now he pulled out his last string cheese packet from his bag.

"You need to give that animal real food."

"He loves string cheese." He knelt and fed him, breaking the cheese into pieces.

"Methinks someone is in a better place today," Flynn said quietly.

Shep looked at her, the words a hot sliver through him. *Oh, maybe*. But he wasn't sure he liked it. "I'm going to work out."

"Shep—"

He stopped on his way to the locker room. Met her eyes. "I'll always be ten feet underwater, dragging her frozen, broken body out of her car. Always be the guy who knows that the last thing she knew was terror. So no, I'm not in a better place. I'm—" He took a breath. *Stuck*. He was stuck. "Just . . . unless you have an update from the Anchorage PD, just leave it, Flynn."

She sighed, shook her head. "No update."

"Perfect."

"Moose said you two have history. Do you know her parents? Do they know?"

He ran a hand across his mouth. "I don't know. I met them, a long time ago. They live overseas—I'm not sure where. I did call my father—thought he might be able to find them—but my call went to voice mail." Of course. "They travel a lot, so . . ."

In fact, he hadn't talked to his parents since before London's death. Not that they connected a lot, with them on the road. But still . . . sometimes he wondered if he might be an afterthought.

No, not sometimes. Always.

"I'll try and track them down," he said now to Flynn. "But without confirmation, I'm not sure what to tell them."

Flynn gave him a frown, a hue of sadness in her eyes. "Are you still holding out hope . . ."

He drew in a breath. Then, "No. No hope." He brushed past her, into the locker room.

Pulling off his boots and jeans, he put on shorts. Okay, maybe he'd been a little cold. Because it did help to have someone—or *something*—to take his mind off . . .

Aw, and now he was back on the deck, his feet freezing, his heartbeat pounding as he stared out into the darkness. Because for a moment there, last night, when the light flickered on, he'd thought—wildly hoped—that maybe . . . no, really, he knew it couldn't be—but maybe London might be standing on his deck. Alive. With a crazy story. He didn't care what it was—he'd pull her into his arms and bypass all the just-friends nonsense and kiss her.

His slammed locker resounded through the room. His mood had evidently fouled when he emerged.

The HQ was empty, except for the dog—which he should probably name—so Axel and Flynn had most likely gone to look at a house.

Shep headed to the back, where Moose, their boss and founder, had built a weight room. He turned on the television and found it still on the National Geographic channel, so someone had been watching reruns of the crazy survival show they'd filmed six months ago. For some reason, the rookie training of Oaken Fox as he'd joined the Air One Rescue team had hit a chord with fans, and the channel had already rerun their full six episodes twice.

An episode of *Locked Up Abroad* came on now, and while he picked up the jump rope and warmed up with a hundred hits, he watched the story of a woman who'd smuggled drugs into Italy, gotten arrested, and been imprisoned for five years.

Yeah, that sounded unfun.

He finished his kettlebell routine just as the show finished. Then he cooled down with more jumping rope.

He found the dog lying near the door, its head on its paws, watching as he turned off the television. "I'll bet you didn't like getting locked up either, huh?"

The dog got up, followed him down the hallway, then climbed onto the leather sofa as Shep headed into the locker room.

Moose would love that.

Shep showered and changed clothes, Moose on his mind. He should probably tell him . . .

Maybe Axel could buy his townhome. Then Shep could get

in his Tahoe and head back to Montana and start his entire life over again.

Maybe he had crawled out of the dark place today, into the bleak, gray, barren plain ahead.

Moose sat on the sofa, his hand on the dog's head, when Shep emerged from the locker room.

"Oh, uh, sorry, boss."

"This your dog?"

"No. Yes.... I don't know. He showed up on my deck last night."

"Nice dog. Calming." Moose stood up. "Listen. Tillie's coming back into town tomorrow, so I need to talk to you about something."

Aw, he knew about the townhouse. "Okay, listen, I know—"

"I need you to take over the training schedule."

Oh.

"I know—I hate asking, Shep. But you're the only one who I trust to get it done."

He meant now that London was gone.

"We've gone a month without anything, and with winter upon us, we could use some snow training—avalanche rescue, snowmobile skills, maybe ice rescues. You can simulate some of that at the Shed. Feel free to reach out to any of the climbing gyms around and see where we can set up for an ice rescue. I think PEAK Sports Center has an ice-climbing sim we could use. And ask your pals with the ski patrol if we can get on the slopes and simulate an avalanche rescue."

Shep swallowed, his throat tight.

"I'm sorry, Shep. I hate to ask you, and I know this is the last thing you want to do ..." Moose hesitated, then, "No one is going to forget her, Shep. I promise. But we have to keep moving forward, and my plate is full. I don't want to drop the ball, and with Axel trying to buy a house ... well, I thought, too, maybe it would be good for you to ..."

Yeah, he got it. *Stay busy.*

As if his brain would ever not be caught in the clench of grief, the spiral of what-ifs. But in Moose's mind, being busy might help.

"It's okay. I'll put something together." Maybe this was the last thing he could do for Moose since he'd be leaving him another man down.

Moose gave him a tight smile and put his hand on Shep's shoulder. Squeezed. "Maybe it's time to think about a memorial service."

Shep shrugged the big man's hand away. "I'll put that schedule together." He moved past him toward the door. "C'mon . . . Shadow."

The dog got up and followed him out the door.

Huh.

He put down a blanket in the backseat of the Tahoe, and Shadow bounded in, rounded a couple times to nest, then lay down. Sighed.

"Me too, pal." The dog did bring unexpected comfort. He ran his hand over the dog's snout, and Shadow's tail thumped.

He closed the door, got into the front, and then headed toward the Alaska Animal Rescue shelter.

As he pulled up, barking lifted from the building, located between a furniture store and a residential care facility. Maybe they had a run in the back.

Behind him, Shadow sat up, ears perked. *Oops,* he hadn't brought a leash. Shep got out and headed inside, where a woman sat at a desk, her dark hair pulled back. She didn't look up at him.

"I found a dog."

"Mm-hmm."

"He doesn't have a collar."

"Bring him in. Leashes are hanging by the door." She pointed to a rack of orange leads.

"I was hoping you might scan him and see if he has a chip."

"Sure. We can do that." No other signs of life.

Ho-kay. He grabbed a lead and headed outside, opened the car door. Shadow looked at him, panting.

"It's okay, pal," he said, not quite believing himself as he made a loop and put it over the dog's head. Then he stepped back. "Come."

Shadow got up and hopped out.

Sat beside him.

"Sorry, pal. We have to go in there."

He took a step, and for the first time, Shadow didn't budge, just emitted a whine.

"Hey, listen, we're just going to see if you have a family, okay? This is a good thing."

Shadow looked at him, and something in his eyes made Shep crouch in front of him. "I won't leave you there. Really."

The dog considered him for a moment, then suddenly slurped his chin. *Oh—*

Shadow got up, and when Shep moved toward the building, the dog heeled. *Yeah, good dog.*

They went inside, and Shadow's ears pricked forward. He sat, panting hard as Shep stood in front of the desk.

Somebody was stressed out.

"I'll send someone out to get him," said the woman. She wore a nametag—Nora.

He leaned on the counter. "Listen, Nora, I know you're busy. And the last thing you want is a guy coming in here needing help with his stray dog. But see . . . I think this dog actually belongs to someone. And I keep thinking about a little girl who lost her best friend and is really scared and worried, and I'm thinking, I'll bet you'd like to get this guy back to his family as much as I would."

She looked up at him, raised an eyebrow.

"I just want to get him scanned. Then"—he looked at Shadow, who stared up at him with those big brown eyes—"I'll take him home with me."

Not forever. Just until they found his home.

"Fine." Nora picked up a small handheld scanner. She came around the desk, through the swinging doors, and felt around Shadow's neck. She scanned him and looked at the readout.

"Yeah, he's in the system. Let me look him up."

She returned to her computer. Typed in the number on her scanner. "Okay, says that he's from Minnesota. No one has listed him as missing, but there's quite a bit of information on him—says he's a legit companion dog for people with PTSD."

No wonder he was so well trained. "He has an owner?"

"Yes. We can try to contact him. And you're welcome to leave him here until we do."

He looked at Shadow, back at Nora. "No, I made a promise. But I'll leave my information."

She handed him a Post-it note and a pen. He wrote down the information, then handed it to her. "Does he have a name?"

"Yeah. It's Caspian."

Cool name.

"Okay, Caspian, let's go home."

Caspian thumped his tail and got up, leaning into Shep.

He couldn't help but smile. Okay, yes, maybe he was in a different place. Temporarily.

They got into the car, and he made a stop at a pet store, loading up on food, a collar and a leash, bowls, a tug toy, and a plush bed, even a couple dog cookies.

Set him back a crisp three hundred smackers. But Caspian happily gnawed on the bone in the back seat as they returned to his townhome, the sun dropping into the sea to the west, behind the ragged mountains. It was nearly dark by the time he turned onto his street, despite the before-dinner hour.

He'd fry up a steak and share it with Casp, and . . . *Oh brother,* maybe they were made for each other. Two lost, sad bachelors without their people.

The driveway lights didn't flicker on as he drove into the darkness of his double garage. *Weird*. But he opened his car door, then the back door, and Caspian jumped out.

He dropped the dog's leash as he opened up the back end, shouldering the food bag, grabbing the other loot.

Caspian stood by the front of the car, whining.

"I know you're hungry. Everything is going to be fine." And somehow he sort of felt it—the sense that things would be . . . maybe not fine, but . . . better than yesterday.

Today he didn't plan on sitting at his counter in the dark, staring at his cold cocoa, trying just to breathe.

He headed toward the garage door, where Caspian was still whining, although only now did he notice that the dog stood staring away from the door, at the car.

"What? Did we leave something behind? I got your cookie, buddy."

He set the food bag down on the step and reached for the doorknob.

Caspian growled.

He turned and spotted the dog in the wan light, his fangs pulled back, snarling—

What?

Then spray—it hit the dog's face. He yelped, and Shep dropped the shopping bags as a man emerged from the darkness.

The spray hit him too, full in the face. He shouted, hands over his face.

A push, a trip, and he went down. He barely got his hands in front of him before he hit the floor.

Definitely didn't get his hand underneath the arm that viced his neck or the other that tightened behind it. He struggled, his eyes burning, his shouts cut short—

And then he went from sorta bad to wretched as darkness closed around him to the sound of Caspian crying.

It simply looked too suspicious for her to show up for her flight carrying only a toothbrush. London rolled a black sweatshirt, a pair of socks, extra underwear, a few more toiletries, and some leggings into a ball, securing the extra passports and cash inside and putting it all into her go-bag. The sum total of her life, which she'd grabbed from her house the day she'd walked away from the life she loved.

The life she wanted.

She opened the British passport, the edges frayed, a few stamps inside, and stared at the picture. A much younger version of herself, although she still had two years on the passport before it expired. And a name she'd tucked away, hoping to never use it again.

Laney Steele.

Always better to hold on to a piece of truth, something that she could remember.

But Laney was dead, or was trying to be, so she shoved that into her backpack bundle and pulled out a different version, the one she'd used to travel to the United States a year ago, issued by the United States.

This passport read *Delaney Brooks*. Her given name. Maybe it was time to return to herself, the beginning.

She tucked that into her crossbody bag.

Outside her second-story bedroom—an Airbnb condo rental— the sun had just started to rise, gilding the sound with gold, a frost covering the bare red alder trees in the yard. She'd liked this place—reminded her a bit of the rental cottage that she'd shared with Boo. Although it didn't have Boo's company, didn't have someone to talk to at the end of the day to make her feel less alone, more like a woman with a future.

She'd liked that woman.

Her phone buzzed on the bed and she picked it up. Ziggy, texting her.

> Ziggy
> Please tell me you're leaving.

She sighed.

> London
> Yes. Heading south. Going to buy a boat.

It felt like the safest idea—get lost in the blue, keep the Petrovs off her tail.

> Ziggy
> You sure you don't want to come back?

The text blinked a moment, and she stared at it. *No.* Because if she couldn't have the Air One team, she didn't want . . . well, maybe the Black Swans had been a family of sorts. But clearly, family cost her. So

> London
> No.

A moment, then

> Ziggy
> Text me when you land.

Whatever. She set the phone down, headed to the bathroom, pulled her hair back, worked on a stocking cap—it had a tiny hole in the back for her ponytail—then grabbed her toothbrush and added it to her crossbody bag.

She felt like the female, real-life version of Reacher.

Not how she'd hoped this restart might end. Wow, she was tired of dying, resurrecting as a new version of herself.

Too many versions.

Especially since this one had in it everything she'd . . .

Well, no use wishing for the happy ending that'd probably never belonged to her. She'd made her choices.

Picking up her phone, she added it to her crossbody bag, then grabbed her backpack and headed out to her Bronco. She'd already vacuumed out the inside, hopefully scrubbing it clean of any DNA, but she'd give it another once-over at the airport, then ditch it.

She absolutely would not drive by his house on her way to the airport. Not only was it in the opposite direction—so that helped—but she'd said her goodbyes.

Said. Her. Goodbyes.

Her throat thickened as she pulled out of the driveway of the condo unit.

Her flight left in three hours.

A layer of ice skimmed the road, the traffic slow as she edged out onto Hickel Parkway, toward the Anchorage International Airport.

Somewhere ahead, in the distance, a low siren whined, although as she looked into her rearview mirror, she didn't see police or an ambulance.

Ahead of her, the mountainscape to the north rose brilliant white, the sun glistening on the peaks. Her chest tightened. She'd miss this—the view, the rugged allure of the last frontier, the freedom.

The team.

She'd miss the smell of the black spruce and Siberian fir trees, the gorgeous sweep of the golden yellows of the poplar and paper birch against the deep-green conifers of the foothills, the contrast of the deep blue against the white granite peaks. The crisp breeze off the sound, and the deep indigo of the water in summer. Yes,

Switzerland had its alpine beauty, but nothing like the sea-and-peak contrast of Alaska.

She could have lived here forever.

Okay, breathe. Calm down. She'd said goodbye before . . .

The whining continued, and as it persisted . . . *Wait.* It came from her crossbody bag. She turned off the highway and pulled into a Starbucks. Unzipping her bag, she pulled out her phone.

A missed call from Ziggy, but she'd ignore it. Probably just hounding her to get on the plane.

The surveillance app popped up, already open, and she studied the four screens—two outside cameras, two inside cameras. No movement inside—it looked like Shep had left for the day. But on the deck, the dog lay outside the sliding glass door.

Whining.

Right—the siren. She opened the window. The dog seemed distressed, its face matted, its eyes watery. It kept wiping a paw over its snout.

She flicked to the inside of the house. Strange for Shep to leave the dog outside, especially in pain.

The house was quiet.

He could be on a callout . . .

Aw. Something buzzed inside her. But if she circled back, she might miss her flight.

As if that mattered.

She turned her Bronco around, got on Highway 1 and took it south, the phone propped on the dash.

The dog sat up once, barked, as if upping his game, but Shep didn't let it in.

She turned onto his road and gave the townhome a drive-by. The garage door was closed, the place quiet save for the suffering dog on the deck.

The buzzing inside her deepened. *Fine.* She'd just pull in.

Getting out in the driveway, she grabbed her bag of beef jerky, then rounded the house to the side deck. The dog sat up, whined, and she held out the jerky.

"Hey there, buddy. What's the deal?"

His tail thumped, and she came closer, holding out the treat. The dog sniffed, then gently took it from her fingers. She crouched and examined his eyes as he gnawed at the jerky.

Reddened, the area around his snout matted. And a capsaicin smell—not unlike pepper spray—emanated from him.

He'd been maced. Or maybe bear-sprayed. She ran a hand over his head. "Poor guy."

No way Shep had done this. Which meant . . . "Stay put, big guy." She left him another piece of jerky, then returned to the garage, found the entry box, and keyed in the code.

The garage door opened.

Shep's car sat in the middle of the two-stall space. She walked inside and noted that the light hadn't flickered on.

A bag of dog food sat by the inside door beside bags of pet supplies. *Huh.*

She tried the inside door—unlocked—and, okay, here went nothing—she let herself in.

If he was here—in the shower or something—she was about to blow apart his world. But she'd considered it yesterday, and . . .

Oh boy.

But she refrained from calling out his name, just in case he *was* home and might suffer some sort of heart attack at seeing her. As she climbed the stairs to the main floor, however, the place seemed eerily vacant. Just the hum of the refrigerator and the quiet rumble of the furnace.

The sink was dry, so he hadn't made coffee.

She unlocked the sliding door and let the dog inside. "Let's get those eyes cleaned." Finding a cloth, she wet it, then sat on the floor and washed the dog's eyes. "What happened here, bud?"

The dog's tail thumped on the floor.

Shep had evidently decided to keep him, which meant that he wouldn't have left him alone outside, even during a callout.

And his car was here. But if the Air One team had spun up, Oaken Fox might have joined them, picking up Shep on his way into Anchorage.

The silence jammed inside her, however, along with the slow tightening of her gut.

She got up, retrieved the bag of dog food and the shopping bags, then opened the food and filled one of the new bowls with breakfast, another with water. The dog wolfed it down as she went upstairs just to make sure Shep wasn't . . . *what—dead on his bathroom floor?*

Maybe, because she took a deep breath as she opened the door, and blew it out when she found the room empty.

She returned to his bedroom and stopped at the picture on his bedside. He must have pulled it from his phone, because it seemed like a selfie—her and Shep last year, skiing one of the big bowls of Alyeska, grinning into the camera.

Not a hint of trouble, of fear, of foreboding in her smile.

The doorbell rang.

She jerked, then headed to the upstairs window and peered out. A dark-haired woman stood on the stoop, wearing Ugg slippers and a flannel overshirt, her head bare, hands in her pockets.

Probably *not* an assassin. Still, London debated, then headed downstairs to open the door. Because her car sat in the driveway, and if she didn't answer, maybe that would lead to more doorbell ringing and maybe even an uptick in concern. Could end with police on the doorstep—and maybe that was her worst-case-scenario tendency kicking in, but it had kept her alive for five years, so . . .

She opened the door. The woman had turned away, staring out into the day, and now whirled around. Petite, with Filipino features and a warm smile that dimmed a little and turned into a frown as she stared at London. "Oh, hi. Um, is Shep here?"

And London didn't know why the sight of her put a prick in her side. "No."

"Oh. Okay, um—I'm his neighbor—" She pointed to the townhome next door, deck side. "I noticed a dog on his deck and wanted to come over and see if he was okay."

"The dog, or Shep?"

She frowned. "Shep. Because I've lived here for six months, and I don't remember him having a dog, but . . . anyway, I'm Jasmine." She held out her hand. "And you're the girlfriend."

London's eyes widened. "What?"

"I've seen you here a few times—although I thought you had an orange Subaru."

"It was . . . in an accident." But, *really?* Who knew their neighbor that well?

"Our decks face each other, and a few times we shared conversation while we drank coffee. He never called you his girlfriend, but . . . you're on his rescue team, right?" She gave a wry smile. "He has a photo of the team in his great room."

Right. A team shot taken by Moose a year ago after a callout. One that she'd made him promise not to put on the website.

"Okay, well, I just wanted to see if Shep was okay. He's such a nice guy—fixed my faucet once when it leaked. Oh, good, you brought the dog in."

She leaned in. The dog had gotten up, walked across the room. Jasmine edged toward him, and what was London supposed to do? Hip-check her out the door, shut it, and run?

"Would you like to come in?" But the question was moot because Jasmine was already inside and crouching in front of the dog.

"Oh, what a sweet dog. What's his name?"

Oh, um . . . "Lewie."

"Hey, Lewie," Jasmine said, and the dog's tail wagged, and he lay down, letting her pet him. So, not a watchdog.

"You're not in the reality show."

Right. That stupid show. Thankfully, Moose had kept his word and forbidden the producers from broadcasting her picture across the universe.

"They cut out all my scenes. It was really about Oaken Fox anyway."

Jasmine stood up. "Have you been on the team long?"

"Just a year."

Jasmine frowned. "For some reason I thought Shep said you were old friends."

How much had he told this woman about them? *Sheesh*—he knew her past, or at least enough to keep her secret.

Although, maybe that had been his way of . . . *what? Protecting her?* Always better to hold on to a piece of truth. "Yeah. We knew each other as kids—our extended families lived in the same town. We met when we were both visiting and went to the same summer camp."

So long ago she should have forgotten that. Except Shep Watson had always been a little hard to forget. And the world was so terribly small. They'd met again in, of all places, an avalanche in Switzerland. *"I thought that was you—and couldn't help but follow you down . . ."* His words, spoken in the darkness of their prison, trying to keep them both awake as hypothermia set in.

The beginning of the death of Laney Steele.

"And then you ended up here," Jasmine said. The dog had rolled over and given up all dignity by exposing its underbelly, its tongue hanging out of its mouth. Jasmine scratched his belly with both hands.

"Shep reached out—I was working overseas and needed a change," London said. Again, true, but oh, such a skim over the top. But she didn't owe Jasmine any information.

Jasmine got up. "Do you know when he'll be back? I actually was hoping that he'd come over and help me hang my new television set."

Right.

And now she got it—the probe. The girlfriend question. The dig into her background. Jasmine had her sights on Shep.

The prick in her side deepened, cut into her heart. But what right did she have to hold on to him? This Jasmine woman was . . . nice. The kind of nice woman that Shep deserved. "I don't know. But maybe . . . leave him a note?"

After all, London could hardly deliver that information. And it occurred to her then that maybe he was out running. He usually exercised in the weight room at the Tooth. So yeah, she needed to skedaddle.

"Oh, good idea, thanks."

London walked over to the kitchen, pulled out a drawer—she'd seen him pull pens and Post-its from it—and found paper and a pen.

Turned.

Jasmine had picked up an envelope from the island. "Who is Ziggy?"

London froze.

Jasmine handed her the envelope. Handwriting, in crisp, European-style script, on the back. *Ziggy will know where to find me. Get the card. Can't wait to see you. T.*

London stared at it. Managed to keep her hand from shaking.

No. No . . . But her insides curdled as she reread the message even as Jasmine scribbled out a note to Shep.

This couldn't be right—

"You okay?"

London looked up.

"You look like . . . okay, I know this sounds weird, but like you've seen a ghost."

"Oh, um . . ." *Yes, most definitely a ghost.* "No. I just realized that I'm late for a birthday party."

46

As in her own. The rebirth of Laney Steele. "I'm meeting Shep there, and I totally forgot."

Jasmine's smile tightened. "Right."

And then . . . "Um, do you have . . . I mean . . . I'm not sure when we'll be back." She glanced at the dog. "Do you think—"

"You want me to check in on Lewie?"

"I—"

"I have the code. I just didn't use it. But sure." She patted the dog's head. "I'm so glad that Shep has a friend. I get a little worried about him—especially lately." She looked up. "He's seemed pretty down. I thought you two had broken up."

I bet you did.

And London didn't know why—because really, she had no business saying it, but she couldn't help the words. "No. Shep and I are soulmates. Always have been, always will be."

Because it was always better to hold on to a piece of truth.

She let Jasmine out, then locked the door and pulled out her phone.

Her voice shook just a little as Ziggy answered.

"Yes," Ziggy said without greeting, blowing apart London's world. "Tomas is alive. And he has Shep. And if you want him back, you'll need to break into Pike's office and get that card key."

She closed her eyes. So much for saying goodbye to Laney Steele.

THREE

THE PLACE HAD ONE WINDOW, SUNLIGHT slanting in through shuttered blinds, the smell of bacon frying, and as Shep opened his eyes, following the stripes of light on the wooden floor, he spotted a man in a tiny L-shaped kitchen.

His captor. Maybe. Possibly.

Weirdly. Because the man wasn't dressed like a thug—he wore a pair of snow pants, a black turtleneck under a patterned ski sweater, a wool hat, and insulated hiking boots. A down jacket hung on a hook by the door. He hummed as he cracked a couple eggs into a cast-iron pan.

So, what, his host was Ken the Mountaineer?

Except the jangle of a cuff around Shep's wrist, securing him to the arm of a sofa, suggested something not quite so convivial.

His eyes burned, and a scratch roughened his throat from the acid of the bear spray. Or maybe the residue of his attacker's arm around his throat. Hard to believe the lean guy—maybe five foot ten, a hundred sixty pounds soaking wet—could so easily wrestle him to the ground.

Hence, the bear spray.

The room held sparse wooden furniture with homemade cushions, and a tiny Formica-topped metal table pushed against the wall in the kitchen.

He glanced at his wrist and put his other hand on the clasp, just to see if he could move it.

The sound of his movement turned the man at the stove. "Ah, you're awake. I feared I'd doused you with too bloody much . . . but you kept breathing, so that boded well." He spoke with a hint of a European accent. Sounded almost Russian, without the brr of the vowels, but his English bore a hint of a British accent—although most second-language English speakers in Europe spoke the King's English

"Boded well?" His voice sounded raked. "Who are you? And more importantly, where is my *dog*?" He didn't know why Caspian came to mind, as if sitting right there in the forefront. Maybe because his last clear memory included poor Caspian crying out. "You didn't have to hurt him."

"He's fine." The man picked up a towel and wiped his hands while eggs sizzled and popped behind him on the gas range. "I let him out of the garage before I closed it."

"It gets below freezing at night!"

"He's a dog. How do you like your eggs?"

Shep's mouth opened.

"No preference? Okay, then I'm going to scramble them." He turned back to the stove.

"What is going on?" He worked the cuff again. "Why—"

"We'll get it sorted." The man scooped the eggs out and put them in a bowl. Added a scrap of bacon. "Sorry, no coffee. I could offer you a cuppa."

Tea? What—

The man walked over and set the bowl at the edge of the sofa, just within Shep's reach if he extended his hand. His stomach decided to betray him and growled.

"What time is it?" Shep asked.

"Nearly noon. I expect to hear from Laney by tonight, so don't fuss. Cooperate and you'll be back home in a few hours."

The words had nothing for him. "Who's Laney?"

"Oh, sorry, pal. Da. I think she's going by . . . what is it?—oh, yes, *London*."

Shep's entire body chilled as he stared at the man. Clean-shaven, green eyes, sharp features, almost Slavic, so yes, maybe Russian. "London?"

The man checked his watch. "She should have received my message by now. It might be a little longer—I'm not sure where she's hiding the key, if it's not on her."

Shep ignored the eggs, suddenly not hungry. "It's going to take a lot longer than you think, *mate*. I don't know what's going on here, but London is"—he drew in a breath, growled out the word—"dead. So if you're trying to, I don't know, enact some sort of revenge or leverage or whatever you have in your head . . . it's over, pal."

The man had sat at the small table, picking up a cup of tea. Now he looked at Shep and laughed.

Laughed.

It shuddered through Shep, and he turned at once brittle and hot.

Especially when the man smiled. "She's not dead."

No. "I saw her body."

The man took a sip of tea, put it down. "You saw *a* body."

He refused the terrible, wild spurt of lethal hope. "It was her—her build, her hair—"

"The woman you saw was a member of a group of assassins called Odin—a Russian word that means 'one.' In English, they call themselves the Orphans. Your girl, London—Laney, as I know her—killed her and set up the woman's body to divert her escape."

Shep just . . . well, the information simply wouldn't settle into him. "No. That's not . . . I mean . . ." And yes, he knew she'd had a different life before she came to Alaska. Knew also that it'd involved clandestine skills, but *murder* . . . "No. London wouldn't kill anyone."

"But Laney Steele would." The man winked.

Shep just stared at him. "You don't know her. Didn't know her. She wasn't—"

"I think you're the one who didn't know her." He set down his cup again. Picked up a paper napkin and wiped his mouth. Folded it on the table. "I'm the one who knew her. The real version of your friend London. Laney Steele, Black Swan, spy . . . and my fiancée."

Every cell in Shep's body simply shut down. *Her fiancé?* "But you're . . . *dead*."

Tomas made a sound of wry humor, maybe, but shook his head. "No. She just left me for dead. And I've made a good go of it, but . . . well . . ." He pursed his lips. "I'm not the only one looking for her. And this is why I know that Laney is not *actually* dead. What I'm not sure about is if she is still in Anchorage. So indeed, this is a bit of a long shot. But I'm willing to take a gamble. After all, she owes me, and she knows it. And . . . for the record, I do believe she really does care for you."

Shep looked away.

"At least, the woman you know does. What does she call herself? London? Interesting." He sighed. "I'm not sure that the woman I know as Laney Steele knows how to love. But she is good—*very good*—at her game. So we'll just sit tight and wait. And we'll see who is dead and who isn't."

They'd be waiting for a ghost. Because despite the man's words, it *had* been over a month. And if London were alive, she would have told him instead of letting Shep believe . . .

Not even this Laney person could be that cruel.

"She's dead, buddy. Let me go and I'll walk away."

"No eggs for you, then?" Tomas got up. "They're getting cold, and you're being quite rude."

Wow, Shep had never in his life wanted to hurt someone the way he wanted to wrap his hands—

Breathe. He wasn't that guy. Had *never* been that guy, and that was the problem, really. Why he lived in Alaska, worked on an SAR crew instead of... well, instead of the other offer he'd gotten.

"So, you're Tomas, then."

The man had started for the bowl of eggs and now stopped. "She told you about me."

Shep lifted a shoulder.

"Interesting. I would have thought... I suppose she would since you were there, weren't you? On the mountain. In the avalanche. And maybe she hoped I was dead, so telling you that..." He shook his head. "Oh, Laney. Pitiful."

Tomas set the egg bowl on the counter and Shep swallowed just a smidgen of regret. His stomach probably couldn't handle it anyway, although suddenly his SERE instructor sneaked into his head. *"Eat when you can."*

Oops. But while Sergeant Hogan was here, Shep started to listen. *"Survive. Evade. Resist. Escape."*

Apparently, he'd jumped right to the end of class.

But still—three of the A's stuck in his head. *Attitude. Adaptability. Awareness.*

The best chance for escape happened in the first forty-eight hours. He'd already ticked off a good chunk of that, and clearly Tomas knew to immobilize him by knocking him unconscious. But now ... *"Betray an emotional breaking point, and throw your captor off guard."*

Which meant roleplay submission. He blew out a breath, looked away even as he surveyed the window, the door.

Tomas pulled out a crumpled pack of cigarettes and lit one,

holding it between his lips as he spoke. "It's okay. Oy—she even got the jump on me. I didn't see it coming."

Shep sighed, maybe a little too much, but . . .

Smoke spiraled out of Tomas's mouth, the cigarette held between his finger and thumb, cupped in his hand, the bead of red hidden. "Laney is a Black Swan. Never forget that."

Wind stirred the curtains at the window—the frame had a gap.

"Fact is, she played you too. Not sure why, but she always has a mission."

Shep's jaw tightened, but he looked over at Tomas and didn't have to pretend the confusion. "I have no idea what you're talking about."

"Like I said, she's very good at her game." Another drag, more smoke. "Truth is, I never really thought she loved me. Even though she said it. Deep inside, I knew it was exactly that—a very delicious game."

He smiled, and Shep swallowed back bile.

Tomas laughed. "Yeah, that's how I felt when I saw her with you the first time. Same old Laney, flirting, stirring that flame inside. She's a real sparrow."

This couldn't be the same person. London was . . . well, she was a woman of honor, chaste, a woman of faith and morals.

Tomas blew out smoke. "All I want is the key. You can have what's left of her."

Shep knew better than to reply. But his gaze flashed to the lighter on the table beside the pack of Chesterfields.

Tomas had moved to the chair closer, sat on it now, his ankle propped on his knee. "She'll try to rescue you before she hands over the key, so we'll need to fix that."

"What key?" he asked, just to buy himself time.

The window casing looked flimsy at best. London *wasn't* coming—he knew that much—and as soon as Tomas figured that out . . .

Well, chances were that Shep wasn't walking away from this with a handshake and an apology.

"Oh, just a little bank key, so to speak. To an encrypted . . . box, let's say." Tomas drew in another drag. "It contains money she stole from me—well, not me, per se. The Russian mob. Which, of course, they think I stole, so that's an inconvenience. But we'll get it sorted."

The Russian mob? The question must have shown on Shep's face.

"Oh, so much you don't know, my boy. The Black Swans are a group of operatives, all female, trained in the art of deception, infiltration, burglary, and all sorts of other techniques that make them highly desired and rather exclusive in their choice of clients, including the US government. Laney's mission was to break into the . . . let's say, bank account of the Petrov Bratva and steal their money."

"Why?" *Shoot.* He shouldn't have asked, but he'd noticed the gas burner contained a flicker, as if it hadn't quite shut off.

"Because they were funding terrorism—some of their own, some to outfits like the Boko Haram, ISIS, Hezbollah, Hamas . . . all the big players, and some smaller ones too."

"How do you . . . Never mind. I don't care."

Tomas smiled, snuffed out his cigarette. "Because I used to work for the Bratva. Accounting. And of course, back then I was younger and weaker, and Laney was beautiful and very, *very* good. And now they want their money, or they want me dead. And Laney is going to fix that."

"She's not coming, man. So just let me go and let's be done with this."

"You think I'm going to kill you."

Shep refused a response.

Tomas shook his head. "I'm not going to kill you, Shep. You're far too valuable to me for that."

Shep glanced around the room, searching for something—a pin, a paperclip, a piece of wire—but nothing.

Tomas looked at his watch again. Stood up. "Two hours until nightfall. I suppose I need to get ready."

Ready?

And all sorts of questions stirred inside Shep.

Except . . . "If you're leaving, how about those eggs?"

"Hmm." Tomas considered him. Then nodded and set the bowl and a fork down at the end of the sofa. "This will all be over in a jiff." He walked away. Stood at the door, looked at Shep. "You'll see."

Shep couldn't stop the shake of his head.

"Really. Sit tight and watch. You'll see that your London is very much alive."

And for a second—a very long, brutal second—Shep wished Tomas were right. That somehow London—or Laney, or whoever she was—would show up out of the night, alive and beautiful, and he didn't care in the least—well, mostly not—what she'd gotten herself into.

He just wanted her alive.

And maybe—a close second—in his arms. But he'd be okay with just alive.

Then Tomas grabbed his jacket and a small backpack and left, the door closing with a soft click and a bolt turning.

Time to escape.

Maybe she should have dressed warmer.

London crouched in the woods, just below Moose's massive timber home, darkness seeping out of the two-story picture windows off his deck, the place quiet, eerie, and maybe a little haunted by the memory of a man she'd known as Hawkeye.

Behind her, the Knik River rushed, gray and frigid, lethal chunks of forming ice jockeying their way downstream. A mist lifted into the night and slid under her black thermal shirt, her gloves. She wore the wool hat too, boots, a small notebook in her pocket, along with her night-vis monocular, and she held a KA-BAR. She couldn't believe she'd left so many of her tools behind, but frankly, she'd left a lot of herself behind when she'd followed Ziggy that night over a month ago.

She'd really had no desire to retrieve her bag of Laney's goodies. She'd had to swing by her old digs, wait for Boo to leave, sneak in, and retrieve them from her bedroom.

But here she was, back in the game.

For now.

Boo hadn't touched her belongings. She didn't blame her—who packed up their dead roommate's things? Maybe Boo had been waiting for Shep to make that move.

London's throat tightened.

Please, Tomas, don't hurt him.

She'd hiked in from where she'd parked, a mile downstream, in a closed-for-the-season glamping campground. The soggy riverbank pressed moisture into her boots, and her feet chilled despite the wool socks.

She shivered. But this would be over soon. She'd driven past the Tooth and seen both Axel's and Moose's trucks parked in the lot, along with Boo's Rogue. Flynn would be at work, a detective in the Anchorage Police Department. And Oaken was probably in his studio.

All clear.

London stepped out from behind the trio of birch trees and sneaked toward the house. Hawkeye had been a zealot for security—she remembered that from her first go-round with this place. Nearly got caught by Moose coming out onto his deck. But over the past year, she'd mapped it, knew how to dodge the lights all the way to the root cellar located in a shelter that also contained Moose's supply of firewood.

Funny that he'd never figured out that this root cellar, located some twenty feet from his house, actually led to a space under the house, Hawkeye's nest. Which meant it'd ended up being a genius place to hide the bio card.

Then again, Moose didn't seem to spend a lot of time in his yard. Mostly sat on the deck, or grilled steaks, or hung out at Air One, so . . .

Or maybe he knew and simply hadn't said anything.

She scooted into the shadows under the shelter, waited behind the wood, but the house stayed quiet. A heartbeat, then she opened the root cellar and descended the wooden stairs to the earthen floor.

Empty, smelling of dirt and age. Maybe once upon a time, homesteaders had stored their potatoes and dairy and anything they wanted to keep safe for winter here. In the daylight, standing on Moose's deck, she could make out the remains of a foundation, so her guess was it might have been dug under the floor of a homesteader's house.

Now, Moose's beautiful timber home—a mansion, really—stood overlooking the river, imperious and oblivious to the control center inside.

She headed to a built-in bookshelf and pressed a latch, and the shelf jerked. She had to wrestle it open, and it shook a little, but behind it was a metal door with a push-button mechanical code. Seven numbers. She pulled out her notebook, paged it open, and shone her phone light on it, then pressed the numbers in the correct order and the door unlatched.

The door refused to budge, probably age and disuse rendering the hinges stiff. She put her shoulder against it and finally moved it, the squeal raising the tiny hairs on her neck. But it came open enough for her to squeeze inside. Then she pulled the shelf tight against the opening and pressed the door closed—again, putting her weight behind it.

Pitch darkness, except for her phone light. She ran her hand over the cement walls and found the switch. Turned it on.

Lights illuminated a cement tunnel that went all the way to the house, another metal door on the other end.

What Moose didn't know—probably—was that he could arrive home and discover her sitting in his sauna room or even watching television in the basement without having touched a lock on his doors.

The place reeked of moisture, despite the attempts at sealing it, the bunker moldy and damp. She hustled down the twenty or so feet toward the far door, same mechanical lock, same code, and then let herself inside the safe room.

Moose had an office upstairs with a couple built-in flatscreens that showed exactly the same pictures that these screens displayed. However, his security setup didn't include satellite coverage of the Black Swan mansion slash fortress in Switzerland. Or a dedicated satellite communication line from what looked like a defunct massive satellite near the shore.

Moose had once mentioned taking it out, but London had quietly shut him down, mentioning disposal costs. The guy pinched pennies like no one she knew.

Now she turned on the computers, and the screens came to life, fed by the electricity from the house. She turned on the satellite link to the mansion too, then sat down in the desk chair as Ziggy's face appeared on the screen.

"What took you so long?" Her voice came through the speakers.

"I had to pick up the code and . . . some things. Where is Shep?"

"Tomas sent me coordinates. Said to come alone."

"He's going to try to kill me."

"Probably. Or maybe he just wants his money."

"Not his money. The Bratva's money."

"And now your money."

"It was never my money. I'm just holding it."

Ziggy's mouth made a tight line. "Okay."

London tried to read her mentor's dark eyes. "Did you know?"

Ziggy frowned.

"That Tomas was alive?"

Ziggy's shoulders rose and fell. "Yes. We found him after you left but decided not to tell you."

"Might have been helpful." She didn't bother to tame the sarcasm.

Ziggy didn't bite. "I know he was a mark, but I also know you had feelings for him. And we needed him dead."

"Why is that always your go-to? Can't people simply . . . disappear?"

"Only to be found again? The people they left behind kidnapped, tortured, and killed?"

To put a fine point on it. *Ouch*. London's voice lowered. "Tomas had no one but me."

Ziggy's too. "Listen. We tried. We put him into our own WITSEC program. The Petrovs still found him."

Of course they did. They had tentacles and covert operatives around the world. Even in the US government. "And now what—Tomas wants the money so he can disappear?"

Ziggy sighed. "I don't know. But even if he has the bio card, he doesn't have the seed phrase, right?"

London nodded, pointed to her head. "Twenty-two random words, in specific order."

"Okay then. Get the key. Find Tomas. End this."

She stilled. "Ziggy—"

"You want him coming after you again?"

"I have a rule—"

"Your rule nearly got you killed! And let a rogue CIA agent run free to terrorize America. You know how much damage Alan

Martin has done to your country? He betrayed your country, helped the Petrovs nearly murder your president—twice—sent a plague of smallpox into your nation, and most recently, tried to start a war between Russia and America!" Ziggy took a breath, but barely, her voice cutting low. "If you had killed him that day on the mountain—"

"I didn't know."

"You should have known. You read the situation—"

"It's done. And I nearly died that day." Never mind that, yes, she'd panicked seeing her CIA contact dead.

Maybe she wasn't cut out to be a Swan. It wasn't the first time she'd had that thought.

"You had the chance to kill him, and you walked away."

"With the money—that counts for something. I cut off their funds."

"Yeah, well, it looks like they haven't forgotten. And maybe they're using Tomas to get to you."

"Tomas wouldn't betray me."

"You're so naïve. Everyone betrays everyone." From inside the mansion, in the massive office, Ziggy shook her head.

Not everyone. "Shep wouldn't."

"He lied to you about why he brought you here."

"He told me the truth. It just took . . . time."

"And this is your problem, London. You trust too easily."

She drew in a breath. "It's better than believing everyone is trying to kill you."

"Really?" Ziggy leaned into the screen. "You're alive because *I* believe that."

Right.

Maybe she wore that truth in her expression because Ziggy leaned back, her tone softening. "Okay, I get it. Tomas is a friend. Fine. Find out what is really going on . . . and then we'll see."

Yeah, right. She knew exactly what Ziggy meant by *we'll see.*

"I'm going to get the bio card. Send me the pin."

"Remember your training. Once a Swan, always a Swan."

That's what she'd been trying to forget. "I'll be in touch."

She disconnected the feed, then got up and headed over to a safe built into the cement bunker. Pulling out her notebook, she keyed in the twenty-one-digit number, then pressed her thumb to the display.

The door unlatched.

Inside, along with a stack of other manila envelopes, sat a letter-sized envelope with a bio card along with a piece of paper inside. The twenty-two-word-long seed code. Just in case she forgot it. Her backup, should her memory fail her.

She left the code in the envelope but grabbed the bio card and shoved it into the leg pocket on her cargo pants. Then she rooted through the envelopes, found her ID packet, and took that also.

Because if she was going to disappear, she'd need to destroy all that was Laney Steele.

Then she closed the safe and locked it.

The monitors to the house had clicked on, and she peered at them, searching for movement. The driveway remained empty, the garage door closed, the backyard barren, and no lights flickered on in the house.

So far, so good.

She shut off the computers, then opened the metal door and headed back down the pitch-black hallway, her light bouncing through the space.

She reached the other doorway. A latch on the other side fused to the metal door, rust bleeding down around that. She hadn't noticed that before. She put her hand on it, tried to tug it open, but the door wouldn't budge.

She pulled on the handle again, harder—

It screamed as it popped off, the door shuddering, and she stumbled back with the force of it, nearly fell. *What—*

She returned to the door, shining her light over it.

The rivets at the top of the handle bled red, weakened by rain or whatever moisture had wicked in. Not surprising—this was Alaska—but now what?

She'd have to sneak out through the house. Preferably before anyone returned home. She ran down the tunnel toward the other door, keyed in the code, and thankfully, it opened, no problem.

Back inside the safe room, she found the door to enter the house. No rust. She punched in the code, same as the office door, and the lock disengaged.

She wrenched the door open.

Metal stairs leading up, no light. She shone her phone on them and climbed up. At the top, at the end of a small landing, stood another door, this one unsecured. Maybe she should close the door at the bottom, but frankly, she didn't want to be stuck in the middle in case this door didn't want to budge.

She pulled the door open without a fight.

Inside, another door, this one covered in insulated foam, and she guessed it led to the sauna.

Moose never even suspected.

She pushed it open.

The sauna room sat adjacent to a space that held a hot tub. And beyond that, through windows, the basement rec room, with the pool table and massive flatscreen.

All dark.

She let out a breath, then pushed through the sauna, closing the metal door. She'd leave the office door open, but with the sauna door closed, who would know?

She closed the sauna door, heard it latch, and crept out of the room.

Just through the basement walkout, and she'd be into the yard and down to her car and—

"Gotcha!"

The light flickered on and she whirled around.

Axel stood there, holding a cast-iron pan, his eyes wide.

Behind him, Flynn held her Glock, maybe just a little more lethal, but still, the pan in Axel's grip looked menacing enough.

"It's just me." She put up her hands.

Axel stared at her, blinked. Didn't move.

"Put the pan down, Axel." London said.

He lowered it, and it dropped out of his hand onto the floor. "*London?*"

"Hi," she said.

Silence, then, "*Hi?* That's what you've got?" His eyes darkened.

Then Flynn, who'd tucked her gun away, shoved past him and threw her arms around London. "Oh my gosh—I can't believe it. I can't..."

London hugged her back, her gaze on Axel, who still hadn't moved. Maybe not even breathed.

Flynn pushed away, held London's arms. Stared at her. "Are you okay? What happened? How are you—oh my gosh, wait until Shep finds out!" Her eyes widened. "Wait—does he know?"

Aw. "It's a long story. And shoot—maybe you should just... turn off the lights and pretend you didn't see me—"

"*Hear* you," Axel said, his voice sounding a little strange. "There was this terrible sound, sort of a whine, and we thought it was an animal, and then we heard movement in the sauna, and I thought maybe, I don't know... maybe a bear?"

"You were going to take out a bear with a frying pan?"

Axel's eyes narrowed. "Okay, so maybe a small bear."

A moment of silence. And then she laughed. And oh, it felt so terribly, wonderfully whole and right and good—and, "I'm so sorry. I shouldn't have lied to you all—I really am sorry. But it's a really long story, and if I tell you, then... people could get hurt."

Axel seemed to breathe then. And finally, he reached out and pulled her to himself. They'd never been terribly close, but they were friends, and suddenly, maybe, family.

She hugged him back, wishing he were Shep and that this were over.

Axel pushed her away, met her eyes. "Maybe you haven't noticed, but we're a rescue team. We specialize in hurt."

Oh.

She glanced at Flynn, who put a hand over her mouth as if trying not to laugh at Axel's statement.

Axel let her go. "Okay, fine, that didn't come out quite like I hoped, but you get it, right?"

London nodded. "Yeah. I get it. But . . . okay, are you sure? Because if you say yes, then right now, your life changes, or at least, what you know about me changes, and maybe that won't affect you at all, but . . . it could, and—"

"Yes," Flynn said. "We're sure. Do not go out into the dark and disappear again. No one has been okay since they pulled your body—or not your body, as it turns out—from Jewel Lake. We're barely breathing, and if you leave again . . . Yes, whatever is going on, London, we're in."

London cocked her head.

"At least give us a chance to be in."

London drew in a breath. Oh, this was a bad, very bad idea. But weirdly, her eyes burned, and maybe, at least for a moment, she needed her Air One team. Especially if she hoped to rescue Shep.

Even if, at the end, they didn't see the London they knew, but someone else.

A version of herself that she'd been trying to forget. But now, someone she clearly needed.

"Let's go upstairs, but I don't have a lot of time."

How she'd missed the upstairs lights, she didn't know. Maybe they'd come in while she'd been struggling with the door, because groceries sat in plastic bags on the island in the kitchen. *Dinner.* Her stomach growled, betraying her completely.

She'd eat *after* she rescued Shep.

"Okay, start at the beginning," Axel said, setting the cast-iron pan on the stove.

"I don't think we have time for that. How about if I start at the epic moment where we have about an hour to save Shep's life?"

Flynn froze, along with Axel. And at that moment, the front door swung open.

And now *London* froze as in through the front door ran a little girl, age seven, her hair in braids, and behind her, Moose Mulligan, carrying a Moana suitcase along with another bag. He set them in the entryway, then held the door open for the little girl's mother, Tillie, who stepped into the foyer, shivering.

"Oh, I forgot how cold Alaska is. Can we please go back to Florida?"

Moose laughed, and then the little girl, Hazel, ran over to Axel and hugged him. Then turned to London and also hugged her.

Oh. Uh. But London crouched down and hugged her back because, well, it was Hazel.

And then all the air in the room seemed to evaporate as she looked up and spotted Moose staring at her, his eyes wide, his mouth opening.

She swallowed.

"London," he said, the name barely whispering out of him. "*London!*"

"Hey, boss." She stood up.

Tillie had toed off her boots and hung up her coat and now came in, her dark hair back. "Hey, London. Axe. Flynn."

Flynn gave her a hug, but her gaze stayed on London.

Moose came down the hall, still wearing his coat, his shoes. "London. What the—*what is going on?*"

Tillie let Flynn go, looked at Moose, back to London, and frowned. "So, uh, what did I miss?"

"London died and you didn't tell me?"

So, this wasn't quite going the way Moose had hoped. He'd asked Axel to pick up groceries, maybe a pie from the Skyport Diner for dessert, and had planned a steak dinner. They'd put Hazel to bed together, and then Flynn had driven home and he'd gotten rid of his brother to his downstairs lair—yes, the guy needed to move out, pronto. Now Moose could finally sit down with Tillie and ask.

Not pop the Big Question, but ask . . . were they heading that way? And if so, when? And how long was enough time before they could start the life he'd been dreaming about since the day he'd met her—okay, maybe sometime after that, but certainly since he'd kissed her, and definitely after he'd met and fallen in love with her seven-year-old adopted daughter, Hazel, and helped disentangle them both from a man who'd claimed to be Hazel's father.

Which left him, Moose thought, free and clear to line up and fill in the gap.

Maybe. In time.

Soon, he hoped.

"I really can't believe you kept the accident from me," Tillie said now, opening her suitcase with more oomph than needed.

Okay, so the showdown in the kitchen probably hadn't helped his plans at all. What he'd like to do was erase the last fifteen minutes, start over, and shut Axel up when Tillie asked, *What did I miss?*

No—no—shoot. Because Axel and his smart mouth had answered, "A lot. Like London's body being found in her submerged Subaru, cold and frozen, as in dead."

Moose had wanted, right then, to reach out and clamp his

hand over his kid brother's mouth and say ix-nay on the ead-day. Because Hazel's eyes widened, at which point London saved the day, turning and laughing with an, "Uncle Axel is just kidding. I'm alive and fine, see?" And then she'd high-fived Hazel, who'd high-fived her back.

Then Hazel had bounded upstairs to the guest room to draw a bath in his jetted guest-room jacuzzi, something she'd been talking about for weeks and nonstop on the drive home from Ted Stevens Airport.

So, yeah, that had given him a moment to say to Tillie, "It's a long story, but true. We did find a body, about a month ago, in Jewel Lake, in London's car, that looked like London—we thought it was London. Except, she'd been beaten, her fingertips were gone, and—"

"Seriously." Tillie's tone had shut him down. "You've known for a *month* that your copilot and fellow rescue team member was *dead*—"

"Not dead," Axel had said.

Moose glared at him.

Tillie held up a hand. "Presumed dead, and you all were grieving and you never, not once, mentioned it?" She stared at Moose. "Do you think I'm so fragile that I can't handle the truth?"

"Not the truth," said Axel.

"Shut up, Axel. It's not funny." Flynn's voice. "No one likes to be lied to."

And that statement had sort of shut down everyone.

Silence.

Finally, "Sorry," London said. "I have reasons."

He'd bet she did, but his priority was Tillie, his beautiful, strong Tillie who had just, finally, sorted out custody of Hazel and needed *anything* but a crisis right now.

"This isn't on you," Tillie said to London, her gaze on Moose.

"It sort of is—" Moose said.

Tillie's gaze stayed hard on his. *Fine*. He looked at London. "London, I don't care about your reasons right now. Instead, I'm going to trust you and say—okay. I'm glad you're alive, and we'll sort this out as soon as—"

"I'm going to unpack." Tillie had turned then and walked down the hall, grabbing her monstrously heavy bag. And sure, as a former marine, Iron Maiden champion, and most importantly, a waitress, she had guns, but not on Moose's watch. So he'd run down the hall after her, taken the handle, and met her eyes.

"Fine," she'd said and let him carry it upstairs. She'd grabbed Hazel's bag and followed him up. And then shut the door behind the both of them. Which meant that, yes, he was in trouble.

Now, staring at her, he schooled his voice and responded to her accusation. "I *don't* think you're fragile. Are you serious? Please. And I know you can handle the truth. But you've also been handling a lot of emotional bombs over the last month, with the charges and the case against Rigger, all the depositions you've given, the custody battle, not to mention getting to know your father again, so . . . yeah. I kept London's death from you. Frankly, all of us weren't even sure that . . . well, the body hasn't been conclusively identified. The face was beaten, the fingers cut off. Seriously, Shep lost it at the crime scene—"

"*Shep* found her?" Tillie had calmed a little, and now, in the silence, they heard singing from the bathroom.

Hazel. "How Far I'll Go" from Moana.

Tillie smiled, her eyes warming despite her anger. "She loves your tub."

"I love her."

And maybe now was the time—

"And Shep loves London. I can't imagine finding your body, mutilated . . ." She stepped toward him, put her hands on his chest. "He must have been destroyed."

"A little. No, a lot. He's been quiet. I gave him London's job of putting the training schedule together. I was trying to keep him busy."

"And what do the police say?"

"No sign of a struggle at her and Boo's house. And no sign of her killer—no DNA, nothing. It was a complete shock—Shep had seen her the night before and sent her home before an ice storm hit. The next day, they found the car in the lake."

"So terrible." Tillie's eyes filled. She closed them.

Oh, she was so . . . amazing. Strong and beautiful, and he put a hand to her cheek to catch a tear that edged out of her eye. "I'm sorry I didn't tell you."

She opened her eyes, the anger gone. "I forgive you," she said softly, then shook her head. "Poor Shep. I'd lose it if I lost"—she swallowed—"you."

Her words warmed him through. "Me too."

And of course he kissed her. Pressed his lips to hers, and she was willing and soft and sort of melted into him.

Wow, he loved this woman.

She tasted of coffee from her plane ride and had lost some weight, maybe, from stress, but she slid her arms around his body, holding on. He wanted to deepen his kiss, his hunger for her rising through him, but . . . well, not yet.

It was probably a good thing when she pushed herself away. "My daughter is in the next room, and your friends are in crisis downstairs, and . . . I should go home."

"Not tonight. I want to make sure you're safe and . . . I don't know. I'm still looking over my shoulder a little."

She stepped away. Sighed. "Me too. So okay, I'll stay—for tonight. And I'll let you feed me."

"I asked Axel to buy pie."

"Of course you did." She sat down on the bed. "So, how is Shep?"

"Not great. It feels strange that London wouldn't have told him she was alive."

"Reasons, she said."

"And I want to hear them. But Shep and she . . . they have history. They survived a trauma together in Switzerland a few years ago, and . . . I don't know. That feels cruel—to be alive and not tell the people you love."

She nodded, her mouth tight, and looked away.

"Oh, Til, I wasn't referring to you and your dad or—"

She held up a hand. "I didn't know my dad was alive, and he didn't know where to find me. It's all good."

Right. And she'd spent the last month fixing that deep wound between them.

"But . . . do you think London faked her death?"

"Clearly."

"So why now? Why come back *now*?"

He had nothing.

"Go downstairs. I'm going to find some clean pajamas for my daughter." She smiled. "Feels good to officially call her that."

"Yeah." Then he leaned down and kissed her forehead. Somehow refrained from saying, "I look forward to that day too."

He left her in the bedroom and headed downstairs.

Axel was on his phone, searching a map.

Flynn was texting.

London was pacing, looking at her watch.

"Okay, London. Please tell me. . . . How are you back from the dead?"

FOUR

THEY DIDN'T HAVE TIME FOR THE WHOLE EX-planation, but London had to give them *something*.

Moose stood at the end of the counter, Flynn and Axel also still standing, and she glanced at her watch. Darkness outside said that she had maybe an hour before Tomas expected her.

She'd already given Axel and Flynn the short version—*A man from my past has kidnapped Shep, and I need to get him back.* Then she'd checked her phone and forwarded Ziggy's pin to Axel, who was looking at the map when Moose came down the stairs.

She looked at Moose, repeated herself, and ended with, "I never intended for Shep to get hurt."

"Of course you didn't," Moose said.

Of course she didn't.

She didn't know why his words reached in like a steadying hand. Still. "But I feared it. Which is why I stuck around." She sank down on the stool. "I don't think Tomas will actually kill him—he wasn't that guy when I knew him."

"Your former fiancé? The one who is supposed to be dead?"

Moose said. He was unrolling a topo map onto the island. "Axel, you got a location for that pin?"

Axel looked at the map, then his phone.

"Yes," London said to Moose's question. "But actually, he wasn't really my fiancé—that was our cover story. He really started out as a mark—and that part is a longer story, but let's just say that before I got my gig at Air One, I had a much different job."

Silence.

"More of an international gig—"

"Cut the lies, London. Just say it. You were a spy." Axel narrowed his eyes.

Ah, Dark and Angry Axel from the basement was back.

She turned to him. "Not a spy. A highly trained agent in a group called the Black Swans."

"The Black what?" said Flynn, who was texting on her phone.

"Swans. It's a covert organization of women for hire in certain sensitive operations. Like infiltrating terrorist organizations to dismantle them from the inside out. In this case, the Russian mob. And please don't call the police, Flynn."

More silence. Flynn put down her phone. Then, "You speak Russian?"

"*Da.* And French and Italian. A little Mandarin. I can understand more, even if I can't speak them. My mom was a diplomat—I lived in eight different countries growing up. And I attended a European boarding school in my later years, so I was exposed to many different languages. My accent is a crazy mix of American, from my parents, and the influences around me."

"Where'd you learn to fly planes and helicopters?" Moose had tacked down the map with salt and pepper shakers, a coffee mug, and a butter dish.

"Got my pilot's license when I was seventeen one summer in America. Added the chopper cert during my sophomore year in college. Listen, I'll give you the entire story after I meet with Tomas."

"What does he want from you?" This from Flynn, who turned her phone over when it buzzed. London eyed her.

"It's just Dawson. I only asked where he was."

Dawson, Moose's cousin and Flynn's partner. Maybe wouldn't hurt to have backup. But not the AK police.

Too many questions, starting with, well, her non-death.

"Tomas and I stole money from the Russian Bratva—the mob. I hid the money in a crypto wallet to protect it from any terror organizations or even the CIA—just to be sure. Then I went to meet my handler—and discovered that he'd been killed by a rogue agent named Alan Martin. We tried to get away, got separated, and then the avalanche happened—"

"The one that you and Shep were in," Axel said as he looked up from where he studied the map.

"Yes. And that's another story, but I thought Tomas had died, so I ran. I didn't know who to trust. So I went to Nigeria and hid. And that's where I met Colt Kingston."

"Colt?" Axel said. "You know Colt Kingston?"

"Yes. Sort of. He was on base with a security team from Jones, Inc., doing personal security for a doctor. I worked for a missionary outfit, flying."

"You said you were a missionary when I hired you. Was that a lie?" Moose gave her a hard look.

She swallowed. "After the avalanche, I had a bit of a ... let's say a spiritual awakening. I joined the missionary group and wanted to leave the Swans behind. So no. But. . ." She sighed. "But the Swans tracked me down and asked me to keep an eye on some groups associated with the Boko Haram—"

Axel's eyebrow went up.

"Wasn't Colt kidnapped in Nigeria?" Moose said, glancing up from the map.

"Yes. And when he was, I told Ziggy, my mentor slash handler. She told a guy she worked with named Roy, who told a friend of his, Pete Sutton, who called his boss, Logan Thorne. He somehow got word to Colt's family and—anyway, Logan thought I was made, so he asked Colt to get me out of Nigeria. And that's when Colt called Shep. And Shep called you."

"How does Colt know Shep?" Moose said, now standing with his arms crossed, as if trying to dissect her story for lies.

No lies. Just misguided hope that she'd escaped her past.

"The military, I think. You'll have to ask him." *After he's safe.* "You figured out where they are yet, Axel?"

He motioned Flynn over. "Working on it."

"Why did Colt call Shep?" Moose asked.

Oh, shoot. She'd sort of wanted to leave out the bit where Shep had been spying on her—not spying, protecting her—for the past year, per Colt's request. "I don't know. I guess he knew we were friends, but . . . huh. Anyway, that's how I ended up here."

"Small world," Moose said, running his finger along a ridgeline on the map.

She didn't want to tell him how small—at least, not now. "I don't know how Tomas found me, but he wants the bio card to the crypto wallet where I stashed the money."

"If you have a crypto wallet, why can't you simply access it over the internet and transfer the money?" said Axel.

"It's a high-security cold storage wallet, and it can only be accessed through a bio card created from my DNA and eye scan. The bio card holds my data, so technically, if someone has that and the seed code, they can access my wallet."

"What's a seed code?" asked Axel.

"It's twenty-two random words in a specific order that unlocks the wallet."

"Is that why someone tried to kill you?" Flynn said.

"I don't know. But right now, I don't care. Tomas took Shep

and asked for the bio card, and I'm going to give it to him." Her hand went to her necklace, her thumb running along the pendant, a habit she should probably break. It only made her look weak.

"And then he gets the money?" Axel said, shaking his head.

"No. Of course not. He still needs the seed code. And that brings us to . . ."

"Here," Moose said, and put his finger on the map, a point between Eagle River and Wasilla, in an enclave of mountains. "It's an old hunting cabin near the Rabbit Lake trailhead. Looks like there's a service road that runs back to it."

She looked at the terrain map. "Lots of mountains."

"Lots of cover. Tomas know how to shoot?"

"Tomas is clearly not just the accountant I thought he was, so I'm going to say yes to that. I'll go in expecting the worst because, honestly, I'm not sure what I'm walking into."

"What *we're* walking into," Moose said quietly.

She looked at him, and right then, it hit her.

They were with her.

She didn't know why that sank in, found her bones, fortified her. "Are you sure?"

"You should have told us from the beginning, but yes," Moose said.

Her mouth tightened. "Listen, Tomas might not be alone—"

"Agreed. So that's why we're going to be smart about this. You and Flynn head to the cabin. I'll go to the Tooth and get the chopper. We'll run reconnaissance over the area, and if you get into trouble, we can swoop in and help."

Right.

"And in case this does go south"—he pointed to the terrain and a blue line at the base of a mountain—"this is the Rabbit River—not a small one, but it has a hiking path, and right here is a falls. Should you end up on foot, follow the river. I'll pick you up at this lookout area above the falls."

"How big are the falls?" Flynn asked.

"Not big—thirty feet maybe. And this time of year, it's not running strong. But it's cold, so don't go in."

London looked at Flynn. "I don't think—"

"I'm going."

London drew in a breath. The last thing she wanted—*please*—was for someone to die because of her. "We need to move, then, because Tomas is waiting."

Hazel had come to the top of the stairs, wearing pajamas, her hair wet. "Are you leaving, Uncle Moose?"

He looked up. "I'll be back in a couple hours. I'll see you in the morning, pumpkin."

She grinned, and Tillie appeared, her mouth grim. So maybe she'd heard them talking. But she met London's eyes and nodded. *Be safe*, she mouthed.

Just like that, London knew it would be okay. Tomas, she could handle—she knew him. And if that's all who was waiting for her, then she had high hopes she could hand over the bio card without bloodshed.

The sky had started to sift snow from the darkness as she climbed into her Bronco, Flynn beside her. Moose got into his SUV with Axel, and she followed them out of the driveway.

"So, sort of like Sydney Bristow?"

London looked over at Flynn. "Not even a little. First, yes, I have hand-to-hand combat skills, but put a three-hundred-pound man against me, and I can at best inflict enough damage to run."

Flynn smiled. "Yeah, I get that. Body weight almost always wins."

"But I can handle myself. Mostly, however, our tactics were in the area of infiltration and subterfuge."

"Recruited in college?"

They turned onto the highway.

"First year of university, actually. I went to school in Lauchtenland, roomed with a woman named Pippa. She left for the Marines about the same time I left to join the Swans. I've never felt like I had a country—yes, I'm American, but I grew up mostly overseas—so being a Swan gave me a place, a purpose. Maybe even a sorority."

"Who is this Russian group?"

"The Petrov Bratva?" She turned on the windshield wipers as the snow dampened her windshield. She followed Moose's red taillights, the darkness encompassing, no stars out.

Could be tricky trying to find Tomas if he'd set up an ambush for her.

"They're a faction of the Russian mob, headed by General Arkady Petrov, who sits in the Russian parliament. They've been at work for years trying to draw the US into a war—first by attempting an assassination of our president, then by trying to infect the happiest place on earth with the smallpox virus, and most recently, an attempt to bomb a NATO-affiliated country. They sponsor terror throughout the world, and my job was to break into their crypto wallet and change the code, making their funds inaccessible."

She got off the highway and took the bypass through Anchorage, south, leaving Moose to continue on to the Tooth.

"Tomas was the accountant, this branch led by a man named Drago Petrov, and I knew if I could get close to Tomas, then I could get the seed code. I also needed the bio card, which I already mentioned is encrypted with a bio lock. I knew Tomas had access to it, because he was the one who transferred money in and out of the crypto exchange."

"Where they can change money into different currencies."

She glanced at Flynn, impressed. The woman wore a thick jacket, sturdy boots, a wool cap—prepared for the Alaskan winter. Then again, she'd originally worked on a police force in Minnesota, so she knew how to brave the weather. Her auburn hair poked out of the back of her hat, her profile serious.

She'd have made a good Swan.

"Tomas had his own reasons for wanting to extricate himself from the Petrovs, and I turned him. He called me his fiancée, and I got close to Drago. We didn't trust that they couldn't hack the lock we put on the account, so I created my own bio card and transferred the money into my account before I met with my handler."

She got back on the highway. "The meet was set up in Switzerland at a mountain resort in Zermatt, but when I got to the chalet, I found my handler, Mick Brown, dead, and in his stead, a different man claiming that Brown was a double agent. Something inside me said it was a lie. I'd left Tomas behind, intending to get him later and figure out our next move, and all I thought was—run. So I did, and that's when the mountain blew apart. I managed to get to a smaller chalet, higher on the mountain, but the slide took out the main lodge of the resort, killing twenty people. Tomas was never found, and after I was found, I ran. And left him behind."

The service road led east, and she cut her beams to high. The snow had lessened, was melting on the dirt pack, and here, not much had accumulated. She slowed.

"I am sure he thinks I ran away with the money, but I haven't touched it. It's still in the account." She sighed as the night pressed in around them, the trees arching above, just the beams cutting a swath into the bush. "When I came here, I'd hoped this was all behind me."

"It will be after you settle this. But aren't you worried the Russians have found you?"

"I'm not sure they know it was me—Tomas was the one who worked for them, was the inside man who accessed the money. But . . . yes. Of course."

Flynn had been holding her phone and now zoomed in. "Just up the road here, there's another road, probably the drive into the cabin."

"We should leave the Bronco here and hike in. How far is it?"

"Three hundred yards, maybe? What's the plan?"

London glanced at Flynn. "I think I go in, you stay behind, watch my back. He just wants the bio card."

"What about the seed code?"

"I wrote down a code with the card." She patted her pantleg pocket. "But it's not right, and the minute he tries it, it will lock the account."

"And he'll come back."

"I'll be ready for him." And the solution Ziggy had suggested flashed in her head.

No. She'd never killed anyone and never would.

Maybe Flynn read her mind, because she turned to London as they pulled over. "If he hurts you or Shep . . . I'm not letting him get away." She grabbed one of the walkies that Moose had given them.

London nodded, then turned off the car and grabbed the other walkie. Slid the KA-BAR into her belt.

Then she went around to the back and took out her Glock and the night-vis monocular from her backpack.

She handed Flynn the night-vis. "Keep an eye on me." Her own eyes would adjust to the darkness, and really, Tomas wouldn't just shoot her. Probably.

She had left him for dead, however, so . . .

A film of snow covered the road. She turned on her phone and used it to guide her. If Tomas was watching from the trees, it didn't matter—she needed him to know she was here and cooperating.

Please, don't let him have hurt Shep.

The driveway led through the forest, the woods silent, the snow sifting gently from the heavens. If only things had gone down differently, she could be sitting in her cute bungalow in front of a fire. Maybe with Shep, sharing a pizza, playing a game of Scrabble.

The thought tightened her chest.

Things had been good—so good—for over a year here in Alaska. Made her believe in happy endings, even.

She should have known better.

The cabin sat in a clearing, small rough-hewn logs stacked together with chinking between them. It sat in darkness, a small SUV parked in front of it, covered in a thin layer of snow.

She wanted to call out, but maybe Tomas was waiting for her inside—which made sense. Still, she paused and inhaled a shaky breath.

Okay, here went nothing—

The cabin exploded.

She threw herself onto the ground, her face in the snow, her hands over her head. Debris rained down into the yard. The fire roared, thundering, heat and light a fireball into the sky.

She pushed herself to her knees, staring at the furnace. It lit up the entire forest, the flames engulfing the house.

The windows of the SUV had shattered, the roof pummeled by fireballs of debris, which now burned in the yard.

Shep. No—oh no . . . no, no . . . no—

Shep!

Her knees buckled, and she hit the ground, her hand on a tree.

No.

Then, in the light of the fire, she spotted a figure—just an outline—but it fled into the forest.

And right then, Ziggy's words hardened in her heart.

Tomas had to die.

His plan had worked better than he'd expected.

Shep paused only a moment at the edge of the clearing to watch as the cabin burned, the flames so hot he ducked down, his hand over his face.

Hopefully Tomas wasn't in the area, standing too close. The last thing he wanted was to kill someone. But now maybe Tomas might think he'd expired in the fire, and this lie he'd told himself about London being alive might die with it.

It didn't matter—Shep knew the truth, and he wasn't waiting around for Tomas to return empty-handed and maybe unravel in a very lethal, anger-induced temper tantrum.

So yeah, he'd used the fork to free himself from the cuffs, then turned on the gas, leaving the stove unlit, but the pilot light that wouldn't turn off would be sufficient to add oomph to the explosion. Then he'd jimmied open the window, climbed out, flashed the lighter and dropped it inside, closed the window again to keep the fumes inside, and run. The scant amount of air from the window delayed the flash—just a few seconds, but long enough for him to dive into the brush. Roll, protect his head, then get up and run.

Now he whirled around and, using the light from the blaze, took off through the forest. Away was the only direction in his head. Maybe later, after he'd trekked far enough, hunkered down, and survived the night, he'd sort out his bearings and find his way back to civilization. But without moonlight, he could be heading straight over the edge of a cliff.

And wouldn't that be fun?

Still, anywhere—even a broken leg at the bottom of a cliff, but *free*—seemed a thousand times better than shackled to the sofa waiting to die.

He held his hands up to protect his face as the forest grew darker, the light from the blaze dimming. Still, the flames reached above the tree line and dented the night enough for him to keep from running into trees or earning a slap in the face from an errant limb.

He kept trekking, listening. The fire thundered behind him, but ahead, a whoosh, something louder—maybe a river. Which meant even in the darkness, the world might open up enough for him to see. And all rivers headed to the sea, so that seemed the right direction.

He followed the rush of the river, slowing as the darkness consumed him, plowing through the bushy arms of mountain hemlock and black spruce, his feet wet in the soggy loam of the forest floor.

Branches breaking. He stiffened as the thumps of footfalls broke through the clutter of the forest, the wash of the river, and—

Shoot. Tomas was a hound dog with a bone.

Shep took off, pushing harder through the trees, toward a glimmer of light in the darkness. It helped that the clouds had jockeyed open, a wan amount of moonlight sneaking through.

He caught himself seconds before he careened right over the edge of the riverbank, jerking back just in time.

Not a far drop, from what he could tell, but—

Footsteps, faster now, and he turned.

His pursuer tackled him flat-out in a flying run.

It blew them both out above the river, and for a second they hung there in space, the frothy tangle of whitewater below.

Then they dropped, splashing down, hitting the river with such force it knocked out Shep's breath.

The frigid water jerked Tomas's grip.

Shep's feet hit bottom, the cold nearly stopping his heart, but he jammed his elbow back and hit Tomas. The man broke away, and Shep pushed to the surface.

The current grabbed him and wrestled him downstream, the cold in his brain, his cells, colliding with his reflexes. He slammed against boulders, the pain sharp and bright, his body numbing, and in the darkness, he was a pin ball.

He got a glimpse once of Tomas, also fighting to stay afloat, but still crazily hard after him. What was his problem?

Shep flopped in the water, turning, his legs rubber as he tried to kick to shore.

Then, the thunder. *Oh no . . .* because despite the darkness, in his bones he knew—

Waterfall.

Aw—so he'd take it back. Give him the cabin and a fighting chance with Tomas. Water choked him, running over his face, into his eyes, his mouth. He turned, tried to kick, but he could barely feel his body. The fact that when he hit rock it didn't break his bones like before probably wasn't a good thing. Mostly because he couldn't feel it, so who knew what damage he might really have.

Maybe God would be merciful and he'd die before he went over—

Nope. The current grabbed him, spun him, rolled him over and over. Then—lights. They shone down over the falls, the water, and he looked up to see—what? A *chopper.* Maybe the Air One chopper—which seemed crazy, but . . .

Then the door opened, and in the opening stood a form—Axel. He had hooked onto the line, appeared about to go in the water—

The current grabbed Shep and sent him over.

The dump of water gobbled him whole, pummeled him, pushed him to the rocky bottom. His feet scrubbed and he pushed hard, surging up, and popped out of the froth, gasping.

The chopper hovered above the falls and he waved his hand—"Axel!"

But the roar ate his words, and the current again grabbed him, spun him. He fought it, turning, and in the glow of the spotlight, glimpsed Tomas shooting out, dropping hard.

The chopper rose up, the light washing away from him toward the churn of the water.

No—he was over here!

But maybe they'd lost him, had gone back to search.

Shep rolled to his stomach. *Swim.* Swim and get away, and then the team could pick him up. His arms might be moving—he couldn't tell. But here, the current calmed a little, not quite as rampant. He had nothing left, so he rolled onto his back, feet out, and rode the river, glancing back to the tumult of the falls.

No Tomas, so maybe . . .

No. He didn't wish death on anyone. . . .

Overhead, the moonlight pierced the clouds, turning the river silvery, the forest skeletal, the chopper still upstream.

His body had numbed now, and he started to shake, his core temp dropping. The current roughened, his eyes blinded. He coughed water—there wasn't a hope he'd survive another plunge.

Then, up ahead, on a rock outcropping, he spotted a downed tree across the water.

Please, hands, work.

He reached out for the branch—more of a log, really, with a few remaining bushy arms. He missed the first branch, the trunk rolling past his frozen hand, but just as he passed under it, a miracle. The tree shifted, and a branch caught him in its V.

He turned and threw both arms around the space, hugging the trunk. Sorta. Maybe. But the river pushed him into the curve of the branches, pinned him there.

He clasped his hands, barely feeling them, and tried to hold on, kicking, angling for balance. The tree had been in the water for a while, much of it bare with a tangle of branches, but maybe not so long that it had turned brittle, because it held his weight.

But he couldn't haul himself up on it.

And the water wanted him, the rapids tugging him. His grip loosened—

"I got you!"

He looked up, searched for the voice, tried to make out the person in the darkness, but his rescuer wore night-vision goggles. The man leaned out from the rock, one foot on the log, and grabbed Shep's jacket. Then he grabbed Shep's wrist and hauled him out of the water, onto the log. He kept hold of his jacket and helped Shep work back to the shoreline.

Shep dropped onto the rocky embankment, drew his arms

around himself, and started to tremble. No, he'd call this shaking. Violent shaking, his teeth rattling, his body out of control.

"I know, mate. It's cold, and now you blew up our shelter, so we're in a fix."

*No. What—no—*Shep opened his eyes, stared up at the man. *Tomas?* But he still wore NVGs, so—

The man stood up then and hustled back out to the tree. Shep rolled over as the voice lifted over the rush. "I got you, lovely. Don't fret."

Then his rescuer hauled another person from the water. Sopping wet, wearing a wool cap, boots, a thin shirt. Shep made out . . . curves?

His attacker?

The man who could be Tomas pulled the woman to the boulder and dropped her next to Shep, behind him.

Shep rolled over, his body breaking apart with the cold, but who—

Then the man took off his goggles. "Told you she wasn't dead, mate."

Wait—*what?*

The woman was trying to get to her knees, and now Tomas—yep, the jerk had saved him—knelt and helped her, unzipping his jacket and putting it around her shoulders.

Then who'd nearly drowned him?

The woman looked at Shep, and even in the dusty light, he could make out her features, her eyes, that set of her mouth.

No . . . no . . . he must already be dead, because—it couldn't be.

He'd thought he couldn't turn any more brittle, but when she sighed and opened her mouth, he simply shattered. London. *London.*

"Shep. Are you okay?" She crawled over to him, put her hand on his chest as if to confirm his heartbeat.

He just stared, because despite the shouting inside, his mouth opened but no words came.

"He's sliding into hypothermia," said London, her own voice breaking with cold. "He needs a blanket, and we need to get him someplace warm."

"How about the cabin the bloke just blew up?"

Shep looked at Tomas, back to London.

Tomas didn't look in the least surprised to see her, which made *Shep* the chump among them.

Maybe he wasn't as cold as he thought. "I'm fine," he finally roughed out. Not even a little, but . . . yes, hours ago, he'd dreamed of this moment, of seeing her again, telling her that he loved her, that he was sorry he'd waited too long to tell her, that if he could do it all over again . . .

Instead, "You lied to me."

London looked at him, and her mouth opened. Then closed. "I can explain."

"You *lied* to me!"

Overhead, a light skimmed the surface of the river, the thunder of the chopper drowning out her words, the turbulence of the river. Shep spotted Axel again at the door, now waving.

Then behind them, as the chopper rose, a shout. "Freeze, right there. Don't move!"

Flynn Turnquist emerged from the woods, holding a gun trained on Tomas. A night-vision monocular hung from a lanyard around her neck. As she stepped out onto the rock, she looked at London. "You okay?"

Shep blinked at her. *What?* Not undone and shaken to her core that London was in fact not dead on a slab in the Anchorage morgue?

And then it clicked.

Somehow, London had alerted Air One to his kidnapping, sent them in for rescue. Which meant *they all knew.*

His chest burned, which might not be better than feeling noth-ing. In fact, maybe he'd take numb again, because he couldn't even look at London as Flynn motioned Tomas to his knees.

"Point of order, I rescued them from the river."

"Shut up, Tomas," London said.

"I wasn't going to hurt him—I just needed your attention."

"You've got it. But now I'm also mad." She moved over to him to pat him down. "He's not armed," she said to Flynn.

"Can I put my arms down?"

Flynn shook her head. "Just . . . stay there."

Overhead, Axel lowered down a basket.

London moved over to Shep again. "Are you okay?"

He just stared at her. Then he rolled and, still shaking, pushed himself up. He rocked on his feet, and Flynn moved in to grab his jacket.

He tore away from her, his gaze hard. "You knew. All this time, you *knew*."

She shook her head, but he didn't believe her. After all, she was with the police department. He'd always suspected something . . . not right. After all, how did it take thirty days to figure out that the body they'd pulled from the lake wasn't London's?

He reached up to guide the basket to the ground.

"You go first, Shep," said Flynn.

"No. London goes first. Then Tomas, because if he tries to run, I'm stopping him. And I don't trust London not to run."

He met her eyes then and didn't care even a little about the hurt in them. "Get in the basket."

She drew in a breath, then obeyed, visibly shivering.

Axel brought the basket up, then sent it back down, and Tomas got in.

"I hope London can handle him if he causes trouble in the chopper," Flynn said, looking up.

He didn't know what side London was on at the moment. "Axel

is there." Still, he wasn't sure, and appreciated the way Axel grabbed the man out, manhandling him a little.

The basket came down empty. "You're next."

"You're freezing."

"You have a gun."

She got in.

By the time the basket came down for him, he nearly fell into it. Axel winched him up, helped him onto the deck, and Flynn was there with a thermal blanket. Axel pulled in the basket and shut the door. "Let's go, Moose."

Shep leaned back, shaking, drawing the blanket to himself, staring at London, who sat beside Tomas.

Her dead fiancé.

And despite the heat that tried to find him, to steel the trembling inside, there wasn't a hope of putting his shattered world back together.

FIVE

SHEP HAD THE TERRIBLE SENSE THAT HE didn't know this woman. At all.

At least, not the woman who sat in the Tooth, having showered, changed into the clean, warm leggings and pullover still stashed in her locker from over a month ago when she was, well, you know, *still alive.*

Now she looked mostly alive, if a little wrecked and maybe angry, as she sat wrapped in a blanket in one of the leather chairs in the main room. Flynn sat in the other.

Tomas sat also, on the sofa, uncuffed, which felt a little unfair, but with Axel and Flynn on him, maybe secure enough.

And then there was Moose, standing sentry between him and the door, arms folded, legs spread, immovable, as if trying to hold them all together.

He, for one, felt in pieces. Shep had showered, found the feeling in his toes and limbs again, his body core heating, his heart still beating with a painful sharpness, a byproduct of the thirty-minute flight and the last hour heating up, his thoughts turning every breath to razors.

For a month, London had been alive and had deliberately let him grieve. Suffer. *Sheesh,* he'd been ready to sell his townhouse, move to Montana, quit the life he loved.

He'd mourned her, deep into his soul, nightmares slicking through him like knives as night after night he replayed pulling her body from the car.

Her *mutilated* body.

He didn't even know where to begin to ask how that had happened. So yeah, this wasn't the London he'd thought he knew. And maybe that hurt most of all.

"How long have you all known?" he said now as he came over, holding a cup of hot cocoa poured from the teapot of boiling water on the stove. He didn't look at London, directed the question at Flynn, then Axel, and finally Moose.

"Just a couple hours, Shep," Flynn said. "Really."

His mouth tightened, and he pulled out a chair at the table, unable to sit with the group.

"We found her at Moose's house, sneaking—"

"I wasn't sneaking, and I'm sitting right here. I can tell him—tell you all. And I guess it starts there—with the fact that under Moose's house is the headquarters for the Black Swans, or at least, it was up until Hawkeye died."

Moose blinked, looking nonplussed. "*What?*"

She drew up her legs, pulled the blanket around herself. "Pike Maguire, the guy who gave you the house, was a former CIA operative. He ran a number of shell companies to disguise himself as a businessman, but when he got out of the CIA, he started the Black Swans as a way to operate outside the purview of the US government but with some of the same skills."

"Like getting close to people like me," Tomas said, his mouth tight.

"Please. You're hardly innocent in all this." She narrowed her eyes at him.

Shep looked away, his chest knotting at their history. Okay, yes, he sort of wanted London's entire story to start at that moment when they'd been trapped together in the chalet in Zermatt.

Or earlier, years earlier, one summer in Montana.

Clearly, he'd been lying to himself too. He might be sick.

"Darling, I'll say it again, I wasn't going to hurt him," Tomas said.

"You pepper-sprayed him, dosed him, and handcuffed him to a sofa."

That, she'd probably gotten from Moose, who'd followed Shep into the locker room and quietly asked if they should be going to the ER instead.

"I'm fine," he said now, again, his gaze going to London.

She tried to meet it, but he looked away, out the window, to the darkness.

Where, for such a long time, he'd lived.

Maybe now wasn't any better.

"When Pike died," London continued, "I was in the middle of my mission. My orders were to secure the funds from the Bratva, then hand over their bio card to the CIA. Between Pike's death and my handover, a rogue faction of the CIA got wind of our operation. I already told you all that a rogue agent killed my contact and how I escaped. What you don't know is that my coming here was all planned. Maybe by the Swans, maybe another group, I don't know, but it's no coincidence."

No, it wasn't. This part of the story, at least, Shep knew. Because he'd been the one to orchestrate it.

The rest, however . . . His jaw tightened as she continued.

"When I got here, Ziggy, my handler, reached out and told me how to secure the bio card in Pike's vault."

"*Under my house?*" Moose said. "Seriously?"

"Well, yes."

Moose just shook his head. "I always thought the guy was just super paranoid."

"Who tried to kill you?" Shep asked. Enough about the stupid past, and maybe the last thing he wanted was for the team to know that he'd actually been keeping watch over her since she'd arrived.

Great job at that, Shep.

"A hired assassin from Europe. I don't know why or who sent her. Ziggy's been trying to figure that out ever since she found out and intercepted her." She met his eyes now, and this time he didn't look away. "The assassin was waiting for me that night I got home from your place. I don't know if she was going to kill me—maybe—or just maybe take my eye and my fingers for identification—"

He didn't flinch at that—at least, not on the outside.

"But Ziggy showed up and killed her. And then . . . tried to make it seem like she was me. The plan was to slow down another attempt while she figured out who was behind the hit. I was supposed to leave with her but . . ." She blinked, her lips tight. "I was worried."

He refused to release his grip on the hot ball inside, even as she reached up and wiped a hand across her cheek. "I know you all were grieving. But I thought it was safer if you didn't know—"

"Safer for who? You?" Shep ground out.

Moose gave him a look.

He met it. "Just to clarify, I was kidnapped, so just wondering if maybe I was misunderstanding exactly who she meant."

Her mouth tightened. "Yes, me. And you. Because I feared *exactly* this happening." She looked at Tomas. "Although I can admit, the last person I expected to show up was you."

"Never stop looking over your shoulder, love."

Her eyes narrowed.

Shep set down his mug.

Moose shot him another look. Shep ignored him. He wasn't

a violent man, but sitting here with Tomas . . . there was only so much they could expect from him.

Now he looked at London. "Who did you think is hunting you?"

"Drago Petrov, maybe? But I'm not sure he knows that I took the money or that I'm even alive. And for the life of me, I can't figure out how they—or anyone, for that matter"—she looked again at Tomas—"found me."

"It wasn't so hard," Tomas said. "After all, your boy Shep made the news after surviving the avalanche, especially since so many had perished."

Shep stilled. *Wait*—

"And then he popped up again in that reality show." Tomas smiled at him. "As soon as I saw his face, I knew . . . if you were alive, you'd be with him."

Oh no.

Moose winced, shook his head. "That stupid show."

"Wait—why?" Shep said. "I mean . . . you were dead. How did you even know—"

"She carried your picture. In a locket, around her neck. She took it off for the op, but I found it. You were younger, but . . ." He looked over at her. "It was in her belongings, back at our hotel. It wasn't hard to scan, to age with AI."

He had nothing. Especially since London appeared stricken.

A picture . . . *Wait.* He caught her gaze. "From Glacier Peaks Wilderness Camp?"

She swallowed. "I never thought . . ."

He shook his head, not knowing what to do with that information.

"A woman never forgets her first love," Tomas said. "Right, Laney?"

"We weren't . . ." Shep started, but saw her expression.

Huh.

And, "Laney?"

"Oh, sorry. *London*. So cute."

London looked like *she'd* like to do violence. "What's your game here, Tomas? You had to know I wasn't going to give you the seed code, even if I did give you the bio card. Which, by the way, is destroyed, thanks to the river."

Something about Tomas's story, a question that was yet unformed, lodged deep inside Shep. But Tomas answered her before Shep could get his fingers around it.

"I need you, Laney."

She raised an eyebrow.

He sighed. "Of course the Petrov Bratva found me. And they want their money back."

"Then let's hide you again."

"Yes, well, it's not that tidy, I'm afraid. See, they know you hid it in Montelena. Which, conveniently, is where your parents are stationed, right? My guess is that is how you got in and were able to set up your wallet."

Shep knew that look. Tomas had bull's-eyed it.

"Where?" Flynn said.

London got up, wore the blanket like a cape as she walked to the kitchen. "My mother is the US Ambassador in a very small but very powerful country near Italy and Austria named Montelena. It's the Switzerland of cryptocurrency." She grabbed the kettle and filled it with water. "About twenty years ago, Montelena had a terrible earthquake. Took out the capital city. And the king there—they have a constitutional monarchy—rebuilt it into a fortress. Impenetrable, it has its own dedicated, unhackable satellite and is where the billionaires in the world park their crypto." She spooned chocolate powder into a cup. "Yes, it's also a hotbed of criminal activity, but Montelena has developed their own crypto tokens, called Cryptex, which are backed by their gold supply, so they're incorruptible. As is their exchange system. All users' names are scrambled, all transactions deconstructed and stored on thousands of blockchains. Anything that passes through Montelena as Cryptex is untraceable." She poured hot water into her mug.

"I don't know much about cryptocurrency," said Flynn, "but I know that Bitcoin is traceable."

London turned, blew on her cocoa. "It is. Which is why so much of it goes through a crypto exchange and is changed into Cryptex. And a Cryptex account can only be accessed by the bio key, which I mentioned before."

"Hence, why I need my former fiancée's help to get into the wallet," Tomas said.

Shep tightened his hold on his cocoa mug. If the man called her that one more time . . .

"Which, of course, is a big, loud *not on your life*," said London. "I'm sorry, Tomas, but Drago and his ilk can't be given two hundred million dollars."

Shep's eyes widened.

"And maybe it's worth even more now—I don't know. But . . ."

"They'll kill me." Tomas's voice had softened.

"We'll hide you."

Shep frowned.

"The Black Swans," she said, probably seeing his frown.

And she probably didn't mean for the words to send a fresh spear through him, either. She wasn't planning on staying.

"I knew you'd say that," Tomas said. "So before you go thinking I'm going to take the money and run off to Argentina, or maybe the Seychelles, my plan was to destroy the wallet."

She set her mug on the island. "You can't destroy a wallet. You can only lose the login. Which I've done."

"No. It only takes your eye scan and your DNA to get another card. Easily obtained by a successful assassin."

Flynn drew a breath. Nodded. "That makes sense."

"They still need the seed code."

"And how hard is that to get, with the right amount of water-boarding?"

Shep's throat tightened. He looked at London.

"But you could corrupt it."

Silence.

Tomas leaned forward. "I've been working on a program that would launch a distributed denial-of-service attack on the nodes of the blockchain network, corrupting the integrity of the block-chain. From there, we could attack the blockchain's consensus mechanism and interfere with the validation process for transactions. Which would mean false confirmation and—"

"In English, please," Axel said.

"It means that suddenly no one trusts each other. They all think they're stealing, or corrupting the crypto, and then terrorist groups are fighting each other," Flynn said. "Brilliant."

"So you're saying . . ." London said, leaning a hip against the island, "give the money back, but upload this program. And then sit back and watch the players destroy themselves?"

Tomas nodded.

She stared at him, and Shep could see her wheels turning.

This London, the clever one, he knew.

But not the woman who then nodded. "That means going to Montelena and getting a new bio card, uploading the program, then transferring the money to Drago's account, virus attached." A small smile creased her face. "That could work. Then we sit back and watch the Bratva crumble."

Wait—who was "we"?

"I'm in." London said.

Shep found his feet. "You must be joking."

All eyes landed on him. London's breath caught.

"Over my dead body are you going to leave with this . . . *jerk*— and give two hundred million dollars back to an international terrorist. Have you lost your mind? Who even are you?"

London's mouth opened.

"London, think for one long second. They find out that you attached a virus to their money and it's not just these Russians you're running from but *every other terrorist organization in the world.* Next time we find your body mutilated with the fingers cut off, it won't be some nameless assassin. It'll be you. And maybe even Tomas, if he's not actually in league with this Drago guy—"

"The Petrovs murdered my family, so . . . go boil your head, mate."

Shep just looked at him, then at Moose, and then, *oh, wow*—he couldn't stop himself from laughing. "What did you say to me?"

Tomas hit his feet. His eyes sharp.

London stepped between them. "Sit down, Tomas." She turned to Shep. "Tomas was my mark because I knew how much he hated the Petrovs. He's Abkhazian by birth, and the Russians . . . they attacked his village."

"My mother was shot in front of me, and my sister . . . they took her. I heard her screaming as they assaulted me. I woke up in a Petrov prison—the Russians *sold* me to the Bratva. So yes, you can just sod off."

Shep raised an eyebrow. Then he looked at London. "Do whatever you want. I have a dog I need to go home and feed."

"The dog is fine. Your neighbor Jasmine is taking care of him." London said the name weirdly, as if . . .

His mouth tweaked up. "Jasmine, huh?"

She narrowed her eyes at him.

"Good. She makes the best bibingka." He met her gaze.

She shook her head, her eyes glossy.

Wow, he was a liar. But the room had gone quiet—terribly, brutally quiet. He looked at Moose, then Axel. "I'm going to need a ride home."

Moose nodded.

Then Shep turned and headed to the locker room, his chest burning.

And all he heard was, "Let him go, Laney."

No, he didn't know this woman. Not at all. Still, as he walked into the warm and a-little-steamy locker room, he braced his hand on the wall of locker doors.

How . . . what . . . He didn't know how to sort out—

"I'm sorry, Shep."

He looked over. London had come into the room, the door closing softly behind her. She leaned against the wall, her hands behind her.

"I'm sorry I lied to you."

She did look sorry, her eyes soft, a swallow after her words.

He wanted to round on her, to shout, but he drew in a breath. Schooled his voice. "Why?"

"Why?" She frowned at him. "Because of the very thing—"

"Why didn't you trust me?" He took a step toward her. "Why didn't you come to me? I would have kept your secret—you *know* that."

Her voice fell, turned quiet and small. "I do."

He stared at her, his heart in his throat, his eyes suddenly burning. "I was . . . eviscerated when you died. Absolutely lost. London, I *mourned* you. I mourned you as if—" As if she were his *wife*. That hit him then. Yes, his wife, a part of himself. He found other words, however. "As if I'd lost a piece of myself." His jaw tightened, his voice roughening. A tear edged his eye, and he wiped it away with a fierce swipe. "And the *way* you died. It . . . took me apart. London. What you did to me was *cruel*."

Her eyes had filled. "I know. I saw you suffering, and . . ." She closed her mouth, shook her head, her voice breaking. "I know. But . . . I just thought it might be easier because I . . . I knew I had to leave—"

"Easier to think you were dead instead of just . . . *walking away from me*? Sheesh, London. How fragile do you think I am?"

"Not fragile! Kind and protective and . . . and . . . it wasn't about you; it was me."

He recoiled. "Oh, please. That's just beautiful."

"Shep—"

"Save it. Now you're just being patronizing—" He turned away.

She grabbed his arm. "I didn't want to leave you! I couldn't say goodbye, okay? I've been . . . watching you. Making sure that . . . well, that this, today, didn't happen. Except never did I think that Tomas might be the one to grab you, but . . . yeah, I *did* fear something bad happening. But I also feared never—" Her voice dropped, so low it turned into a whisper. "Never seeing you again."

No. He refused to be moved. His gaze hardened. "You walked away from me at least twice before, London. Laney. Whatever you want to call yourself."

A flash of something flickered in her eyes. "Laney is not me. London is the real me—"

"London is a nickname I gave you because of your accent," he said quietly. "And because Delaney didn't seem to fit with the fifteen-year-old tomboy I met at summer camp so many years ago. So I guess I'm to blame for all the subterfuge and lies."

"No!" She closed her eyes, looked away.

Silence pulsed between them. She looked wrung out, her blonde hair in strings, and for a second, all he wanted to was reach out, pull her to himself. Hold her until everything was back to right and normal.

He balled his hands into fists, just kept breathing.

"Okay, I can see that there's no fixing this." She drew in a shuttered breath. "I should go." She turned to leave.

And it was that—the final goodbye flashing in front of him, accompanied by a terrible rush of pain through his body—that made him grab her arm. Pull her back to him.

"No," he said roughly, his eyes on hers.

"No?"

"No." A beat, during which his gaze roamed her face. Her eyes widened, her mouth parted—and then he kissed her. Mostly impulse, but the vortex of everything—the pain, the horror, the regret, the disbelief, and the longing—ignited everything inside and simply took hold. He curled his hand behind her neck and . . . dove in. Perhaps rougher than he meant to, but it all poured out, right there, as he practically consumed her.

Maybe he'd scared her, because she put her hands on his arms. But then they slid around his waist and she pulled him to herself, tight, all in as she kissed him back.

All in, as if she, perhaps, had been waiting, longing for this moment also.

Oh, London.

She tasted of hot cocoa and smelled of shampoo and soap and fit as perfectly in his arms as he'd always imagined, and he didn't have a prayer of slowing down. Of letting his common sense take over, of pulling them back to the just-friends cliffside they'd once navigated.

Not just friends ever—at least for him.

And when she softened her mouth and let it open, let him deepen his kiss, he thought—*maybe not for her either.*

London. Beautiful, brave, and amazing London.

Alive.

He groaned with the fresh memory of his grief and put his arm around her neck, his other around her waist, tightening his hold on her. *I love you.* The words hung in the back of his throat, clogged his chest. But the thought shook through him, heat encompassing his entire body as he slowed. He finally lifted his head, meeting her beautiful eyes. Because that was the answer to this entire thing, wasn't it? He loved this woman, even if he realized that maybe he didn't exactly know her.

But he would. Because he wasn't going to lose her again, no matter what it cost him.

Her breath emerged a little uneven. "Oh," she said. "Well. Um . . ."

"I should have done that a lot sooner."

She caught her lower lip. "I have to go to Montelena. With Tomas."

He stilled. And then he had to know. "Tomas—are you . . . He's your ex-fiancé—"

"It was part of the game. But I do need to go back and end this."

He drew in a breath, then braced his hand on the wall behind her. Bent his head. "I know." Then he pushed away, his eyes still on hers. "But like I said, you're not going anywhere."

Her mouth opened. Closed. She shook her head. "Shep—"

"Not without me."

A beat, and then she cringed. "I don't—"

"Stop protecting me. I am not losing you again, London. I'm tired of people walking out of my life without a backward glance. So whether you like it or not, I'm your shadow, or your watchdog, or your partner—whatever. I may not be some James Bond, but just *try* to shake me."

She leaned her head back, considered him. "That's real cute."

"Yeah, well, if you think I'm going to let you trolley off with Tomas, even if he is a fake fiancé—"

"Trolley off? Really?"

"Really," he said, not smiling.

She smiled then, something sweet. "I knew kissing you would be trouble."

"How's that?" he said, stepping closer again, bracing his hand over her shoulder, touching her face.

"Because I'm actually considering saying yes."

"Consider the fact that you don't have a choice."

"So. Bossy." But her voice had fallen.

He leaned down, but she put her hand on his chest. "If this is going to work, maybe we should nix the kissing in Montelena."

He arched an eyebrow.

"I mean it, Shep. With you all nice smelling and handsome and tasting like chocolate . . . I can't think straight. And Drago Petrov wants me dead . . . so I have to stay on my game. Aw, and I can tell by your smile that was the wrong thing to say."

"Completely." And he pressed his mouth to hers.

He didn't know how long he kissed her, taking his time, the disbelief washing away, the terrible clench of his chest loosing, the last thirty days fading to shadow, but a knock brought his head up, and then Axel opened the door.

"Yep, that's what we thought. After the shouting was over . . ."

"Go. Away."

Axel held up his hand. "There's someone here to see London."

London, who, until six hours ago, was, um, *dead*?

"Who knows you're alive?" He asked as she ducked under his arms. "Hey, wait—" He reached out to catch her, but she'd stepped out of his reach.

Of course.

But, hello, maybe it was one of those orphans—

"London, stop!"

A man, dark-blond hair, lean, wearing a leather jacket and gloves, dressed in black jeans and hiking boots, stood in the lobby of the Tooth. "Hi," he said. "We've never met, but my name is York Newgate."

Shep came up to stand behind London. No one else looked worried, but he put a hand on her shoulder. Like . . . what?

He didn't have the first clue how to protect this woman.

"I know this is the middle of the night, but I got here as fast as I could," York said.

"I don't understand," London said.

"Ziggy sent me."

More silence.

"Apparently you need a ride across the pond?"

London didn't know who she was. Not ten thousand feet over the Alps of Switzerland, in a Learjet 36, with her ex-fiancé sitting in the seats behind her, cuffed despite her protests. (Although, he had kidnapped Shep. And bear-sprayed him. And tranq'd him. And *please, please* let him not be duping her into some kind of ambush.)

She wasn't London—she'd blown that persona apart. She saw the way the Air One team looked at her, questions behind their tight smiles.

And she wasn't Laney. Or didn't want to be.

Or at least, she thought so.

Maybe she was Shep's . . . what? Girlfriend? Maybe, yes, because large in her mind, over and over, played her painfully eager and out-of-bounds response to him kissing her.

Hel-*lo*. That had been a big yes before she really got her brains around it all. Just an impulse and a hooyah, and what did that say about what was really buried inside her heart? What had Tomas said—a woman never forgets her first love?

Although it hadn't been until the moment Shep walked up to her, put his hand around her neck, and kissed her—really kissed her, like he'd broken open pieces of his heart to let her in—that she'd dived in and embraced it.

Yep. First love.

Beside her, Shep sat on the Learjet's sofa, his eyes closed, clearly still tired, yesterday's events worn in the fatigue on his face. He'd shaved and showered after getting home and had slept until noon, but he'd been back to the Tooth by four p.m.

And of course, he'd put himself back together. Jeans, sweater, hiking boots, a wool hat, jacket, and satchel. *Have woodsman, will travel.*

All the way over the ocean and to the small country of Montelena. She looked out the window. *Welcome back, Laney Steele.*

Oy vey.

"Ziggy is a little creepy." Shep opened an eye and looked at her. She curled up on the opposite end of the couch, her knees drawn up, her arms folded, like she might suddenly spring from the plane.

Maybe.

"You think? And apparently she has the ability to pick up the phone and send us a private jet from across the world."

"The plane and the pilot are rented, from Seattle," York said from the seat on the other side of the aisle. He'd spent most of the flight with his eyes closed, and Shep had assumed he was asleep. Apparently not.

"Where did you meet her?" he asked London, lowering his voice.

"She was my trainer with the Black Swans, years ago. Then my handler. Now, I don't know . . . my boss?"

"I thought Moose was your boss."

Right. But Moose was *London's* boss.

Moose gave her a tight smile, as if he'd read her mind.

"Is Ziggy an assassin?"

She shrugged. Nodded. "When she has to be."

"I see." His mouth made a tight line.

"I've never killed anyone," she said softly. "Just so you know."

"No one except yourself."

Oh. Right.

"How'd it go with Boo?"

She lifted a shoulder. "I'm a coward. I didn't go home."

"You didn't tell Boo?"

"I didn't know what to say. Flynn is going to tell her."

"London."

She sighed. "I ... I know. But it would be another couple hours of explanations and ... I was hoping it could wait until I got back."

Shep gave her a slow smile. "So, you're coming back."

It was the first time, really, that she'd said it aloud. But that life had suddenly started to sift through her hands, and she didn't know if she could get it back.

But that kiss ...

He touched her hand. "London, everything is going to be fine."

"You've never met the Petrov Bratva." Her jaw tightened, and when he drew in a breath, she wished she hadn't said that. "I just don't want you to get hurt."

"I'm not completely helpless."

Right. She had forgotten about his time in the military.

"And it seems like you have some, um, *skills*."

"The Black Swans aren't military. We're mostly a surveillance-gathering organization, although sometimes we're tapped to acquire something sensitive or to procure information."

"So, thievery and torture too."

"What? No. Like ... attending diplomatic functions and sneaking into an office to snap a few clandestine pictures. Or maybe making friends with the girlfriend of a known gun smuggler to discover his next buy."

"Just that."

She sighed. "It sounds more exciting than it was. Mostly, it was sitting at café tables, a microphone aimed toward our mark, listening, eating a croissant and drinking tea."

"Mm-hmm. In three different languages."

"Keeps it interesting." She smiled at him. Then she unfolded her legs and put them on his lap.

Like they might be a couple?

Maybe, because he massaged her feet.

"I could get used to this."

"What, Learjets and foot rubs?"

"You knowing my life."

His strong hands stopped, just holding her feet. "I don't know your life, London."

Her mouth opened, and he held up a hand. "I knew you were an operative of some sort—Colt told me that much. But . . . honestly, I didn't know what to think. And maybe I didn't want to."

Oh. "And now?"

"And now, I think that I'm very much interested in how the fifteen-year-old girl with freckles and braids that I met at Glacier Peaks Wilderness Camp with her cousins Sam and Pete ended up leaping tall buildings."

"I only jump from them."

His eyes widened.

"Just the once. With Tom Cruise. *Mission: Impossible III.*"

A beat.

She smiled.

"You're very cute," he said.

"I'm glad you think so."

"Okay, so after you left me brokenhearted in Montana at the age of fifteen—"

"I did not leave you brokenhearted. We were just friends."

"That's what you thought. You were this exotic, cool girl who lived around the world—"

"And you were this hot guy who lived in a motorhome, was an amazing skier and climber, and could swim better than me."

"I *was* a better swimmer." He winked. And *wow,* he was still devastatingly hot.

"Yeah, your sister could beat you, though. I liked Jacey. You never talk about her."

Weirdly, he seemed to jerk, almost stiffen at her words. Then he drew in a breath and nodded.

Huh. So, not a topic he wanted to talk about.

"Okay, so after camp, I know you traveled with your cousin

Gage, skiing. And then joined the military—another thing you don't talk about much."

"Not much to say." He leaned his head back. "Food was bad, I made a few friends, and I was really cold most of the time."

"That's what happens when you join a mountain unit."

He smiled, although it seemed tight, and for a moment, secrets hid in his eyes.

Maybe she didn't know Shep as well as she thought, either. "Why did you leave the military?"

He considered her for a moment. Then, "I broke a couple ribs in the avalanche—"

"I remember."

"Right, well, my contract expired, and I just . . . I decided I didn't want to live that life. Always moving. Never landing. I spent my childhood doing that. I didn't want to live the rest of my life hauling a rucksack."

"I thought you had such an exotic childhood, your parents ski bums."

"They both worked as patrollers most of the time. My dad was also a street preacher and an evangelist. He went where God called him. I guess that was the point of the motorhome."

Outside, the clouds had parted. Below, the spires of the Swiss Alps rose, white and brutal, into the blue sky.

"I do feel like I should clear up something." He stopped massaging her feet. "You once said to me that you knew I had skills. . . ." He sighed. "I was a medic in the Tenth. And then attached to Colt's Ranger team for my last year. I don't have . . . well, I've never killed someone and would like to keep it that way. I'm not a man of violence and don't want to be."

"I don't think going to my bank will require any hand-to-hand combat. Unless they get stingy with the Dum Dums."

"Dum Dums?"

"You know, those suckers they hand out to kids?"

One side of his mouth lifted, his blue eyes catching hers, and for a second, she was back at The Kiss. At the feel of his arms around her, the taste—*oh boy*. She swallowed. "I didn't know you were attached to the Rangers."

"Yeah. We trained with them in some alpine settings—which is how I met Colt. He was a ranger, and we actually went through a blizzard together in a snow cave. After spending a year with them, I knew it wasn't a life I wanted. I was made to save lives, not take them."

There was more to that story; she knew it in her bones. And for the first time, she realized they'd spent most of the last year sharing movie preferences, making dinner, and training together. But his life, he kept guarded.

Maybe she didn't know him at all.

His strong hands worked her feet. "So, why did you join the Black Swans?"

Deflecting. *Sheesh,* she should pay attention a little more. Hard to do when he looked at her with those blue eyes, though, and a voice that always made its way under her skin to turn it warm.

"I guess I just . . . I liked the idea of doing something . . . extraordinary."

"Your parents are international diplomats. That's pretty extraordinary."

"My mom is the diplomat. My dad is an international lawyer. And he advises her. But yeah, it was . . . okay. I didn't have a lot of friends—hard to do that when everyone you bring home has to be vetted. And we moved a lot. I was mostly friends with the bodyguards, or even the kids of other attachés."

"Sounds lonely."

"A little. But my parents tried to get me involved in sport clubs. I took dance class and tae kwon do, gymnastics and swimming club. . . . anything to help me feel connected, I think. I spent the longest time in Russia. We also lived in Paris, and then Berlin, a year in Rome. . . ."

"All the really boring places, then."

"We even went to Taiwan for a while. We finally ended in a small country called Lauchtenland, where I met my best friend, Pippa. She and I attended post-secondary together, a sort of prep school. We roomed together in our first year of university, but it wasn't for Pippa—she wanted to be a royal guard, so she joined the Lauchtenland military. And about that time, I was approached by Pike to join the Black Swans. It sounded . . . well, sort of cool. *Mission: Impossible*, you know? So . . . I signed on and went through the most grueling four years I'd ever known."

"Ziggy as your trainer."

"Yes. She has her own interesting past, but she's not cold, or even cruel. She's just . . . resolute, I guess. Does what she has to in order to get the job done."

His mouth tightened and he nodded.

She glanced over at Tomas, who now had his eyes closed, leaning against the side of the plane. Turned back to Shep and cut her voice low. "Listen, I know that Tomas keeps calling me Laney, but you have to know, Shep—I'm not that person anymore. I'm just going to get another bio card. Because Tomas is right—the Bratva would keep coming for me. But if I give the money back and they think it's stolen from them by another terrorist organization . . ."

His gaze met hers. "This could backfire, badly."

And for some reason, his voice, his words, pierced her, deep inside.

Backfire. Yes. And Shep could get hurt.

Aw . . . shoot.

See, this was why Ziggy forbade personal relationships for Swans.

"Promise me that no matter what happens, you'll listen to me. And *trust* me."

He frowned.

She leaned up, grabbed his hand. "Promise me."

"I promise. I mean, I do trust you—and I do listen."

But he wasn't hearing her. "I don't want—I can't... please don't get hurt. I couldn't bear it."

His smile fell and he swallowed. "I will do everything I can to keep you—and myself—safe."

But something about his expression seemed almost... haunted.

She nodded, however, then leaned back and looked out the window. A ridge of tall mountains rose from the deep valleys. And just like that, his words, spoken to her inside a snow tomb three years ago, spiraled back to her.

"You're not in this alone, London."

Yeah, well, maybe she should be. Her jaw tightened.

The pilot came over the loudspeaker and announced their descent into Luciella International Airport in the capital city of Montelena.

She spotted the small country, landlocked and surrounded on all sides by tall, forbidding peaks, the country itself the size of neighboring Liechtenstein. The capital city—the only city—sat in the middle of the valley, still green, a paradise with a palace that reminded her of crazy Ludwig's Neuschwanstein Castle in Bavaria, seated on a mountain overlooking the city.

"Are you at all concerned that Tomas could be setting you up?"

She looked back at Shep, his mouth a tight line as he glanced at Tomas, now rising, looking out the window.

"Maybe. I don't know how the rogue agent got wind of the handoff with my CIA contact that day in Zermatt, so anything is possible." She drew in a breath. "I guess we'll just have to be prepared for anything."

He stilled then, and she frowned at him. "What?"

Shep leaned over, his voice low. "I need to tell you something. It's about that day on the mountain."

The day he'd appeared out of nowhere, barreling back into her life. The day he'd saved her life by pulling her into a chalet, protecting her from an avalanche. The day that'd led to three days of keeping her alive.

He grimaced. "I think my Ranger team was sent there to kill you."

He felt like a man waiting for the guillotine. And stripped nearly naked at that.

Moose stood up from the wooden bench in the hallway, unable to take one more second of sitting. Waiting for his life to end—or perhaps begin.

Inside the double doors of the courtroom of Nesbitt Courthouse in Anchorage, a judge deliberated Moose's future.

"What does it mean to have a motion for a directed verdict?" This from Tillie.

Sweet of Tillie to come to court with him today and sit here for hours while the prosecution dismantled his life. She wore a pair of dress pants and a sweater, her dark hair down, and just being able to glance over at her from the defendant's table and see her nod, so much trust in her eyes—yeah, he couldn't wait to marry this woman.

Get on with his life.

If, after all this, he had a life to get on with.

Six hours of testimony, evidence, and probing in front of a jury of his peers. And no, he wasn't a criminal—this was his civil trial. But not only had his policies, his decision making, and his past experiences been stripped open, but frankly, it'd had him reliving the entire nightmare over and over.

A callout to search for five women in a bridal party who'd gone missing in a snowstorm. All but the bride had been found—and she'd been murdered by a serial killer. So technically not his fault. But the bride's father, Harry Benton, had sued him anyway, alleging he'd given up the search too early.

Maybe he had. Or not. *Sheesh,* now his own brain waged a trial against him.

"Okay, the machine was out of Snickers, but I did score you a Three Musketeers bar and a Diet Coke. Oh wait, that's for me. I got you some bread and water."

Moose turned at the voice, scowling. "What?"

Axel was walking down the hall, holding goodies from the vending machine. "You look like you're a prisoner. Calm down, bro. This is going to go your way; I feel it." He handed Moose a granola bar and a bottled water. "Upgrade." Then he gave Tillie a bag of Sun Chips. "As you requested."

"Thanks, Axel," Tillie said, opening the chips. She had stayed seated while Moose prowled the hallway outside the chambers. "Sure is taking a long time. I don't know much about the law, but this feels like an easy win. The defense has nothing—"

"They have their hurt and pain," said Axel, unwrapping his candy bar. "Which, in this world today, seems to be enough reason to take people to court, even if they did nothing wrong." He bit into the candy bar.

"Yes, but even the coroner testified that Grace Benton was most likely dead when you paused the search. I mean, c'mon, it was a blizzard. Sending the Air One team back out into that snow would have been irresponsible—even lethal." She took a bite of chip. "I have to admit, Ridge is a great lawyer, getting Mike Grizz on the stand to talk about exposure and hypothermia and how dangerous it is to keep searching when people are exhausted. You saved lives that day, Moose." She gave him a smile that had the power to save his sorry life.

He had had a ring designed at a local jeweler's—just needed to pick it up. And figure out when to propose. *Sheesh,* at this rate, he'd pull over in a parking lot on the way home and take a knee.

"Yeah, but losing someone haunts you, and Benton's trying to park his blame somewhere," Axel said.

"He could try doing it without destroying the rescue team that saves so many lives—"

Moose held up a hand. "Listen. I hate that Grace Benton died. I hate that we couldn't find her while she was still alive—although, like the coroner said, maybe she'd already been shot by the Midnight Sun Killer, so who knows? I do know that it's a terrible balance—saving the lives of others and protecting the people who have volunteered to put their lives on the line. Believe me when I say I lie in bed some nights and replay that rescue, wondering if I did the right thing."

"You did," Axel said.

Tillie nodded.

"Your testimony was rather passionate, Axel. I'm not sure it helped."

"Oh, it helped." He finished his candy bar. "The jury hung on my every word. I'll bet that's why Ridge made a motion for a directed verdict—because he knew that there was no legally sufficient evidence for the jury to reach a conclusion and it was just wasting all their time."

"You memorize that?"

"Wrote it down." He tossed the soda can into the trash, a three-pointer.

"Maybe he just wanted to get you off the stand before you told any more stories that might make the jury think I'm reckless. I cannot believe you told them the story of the crash on Denali, with you hanging off the line."

"Bro. It was to show how committed you are to saving people—you performed an incredible maneuver to get those guys off the serac on Peter's Ridge—"

"And nearly killed you and them in the process."

"Aw, what's a little snow burn? You going to eat that granola bar?"

"Have at it." He gave it to Axel, who opened it.

"Listen, Moose, no matter what happens, you're a great leader and an amazing rescue pilot, and everyone on the team knows that you're not reckless. You might push your limits, but if you can save someone, you will. You just couldn't in this case. And Benton and that other guy—who is he?"

"The victim's fiancé," said Moose. "I think his name is Liam Grant."

"Right. Benton and Grant just need to accept that she's gone and start healing."

Silence as a couple people walked by. Moose looked away and cut his voice down. "This is all my fault for letting that reality show take so much footage. It feels like every time I turn on the television, I can catch an episode. And social media hasn't helped. The show made me look like I made a choice to leave her out there to die. I can see why Harry Benton just can't move on."

"He lost his oldest daughter," Axel said. "So I get that."

"But Moose and the team saved his daughter Caroline." This from Tillie. "And that show provided funding for all the rescues this summer."

And with her words, yesterday's events stirred inside Moose.

London was *alive*.

Still trying to get his head around that.

But, "Shep was abducted and nearly killed because of that show. And you, Tillie—Rigger would have never found you if it weren't—"

"Stop." She had stepped up to him, put her hands on his chest. She smelled good, and he got stuck on her gaze, those brown eyes tipped with gold around the iris, so much love in them he nearly reached out and pulled her to himself. Left the building without looking back.

Tillie's voice grounded him. "This is not your fault. *None* of it is your fault. You do what you can with the wisdom you have at the time. Now, breathe. From what you said, Shep and London are going to be fine. And Benton's civil suit will fail—"

The door to the courtroom opened, and Ridge White stepped out. He'd slicked up today in a suit and tie, and he looked terribly like Bradley Cooper might be presenting his case. Which could be a good thing, if the jury were all women, but no, the jury was a mix of middle-aged women, older men, and a few younger men who'd been pulled out of their jobs. And the judge—a middle-aged man who had a reputation for letting the people decide.

People who probably thought that rescuers were superhuman and who had seen too many fictional television shows where the impossible happened.

"The judge is ready with his decision." Ridge held open the door, his face betraying nothing of prophecy either way. Probably better to brace Moose for the inevitable.

Moose filed inside, followed by Axel and Tillie, who took the row behind the defendant's table. Ridge motioned him to stand as the judge was announced and came into the chamber.

The jury hadn't returned.

Moose glanced at Ridge, who raised an eyebrow. A hint of a smile tugged at his lips.

Across the room, Benton and Grant also stood. Grant folded his arms, his legs planted, a picture of triumph. Benton ran some kind of construction company in Illinois. Fit and wealthy, he seemed confident of his win in the way he looked over at Moose.

Moose turned his attention to the judge, who called the court to order, then directed them to sit.

He glanced at Tillie, who gave him a tight smile, a nod.

"Ladies and gentlemen, the court will now address the motion for a directed verdict."

Please, God, vindicate me. It felt like a psalm of David. *"Vindicate me, Lord, for I have led a blameless life; I have trusted in the Lord and have not faltered. Test me, Lord, and try me, examine my heart and my mind; for I have always been mindful of your unfailing love and have lived in reliance on your faithfulness."*

Okay, maybe not *always* in reliance on God's faithfulness, and he hadn't always not faltered, but . . . he was trying.

"In a civil case, the burden of proof rests with the plaintiff. It is their responsibility to establish their claims by a preponderance of the evidence. However, throughout this trial, I have observed significant gaps and inconsistencies in the plaintiff's case. The evidence presented has failed to provide a compelling and persuasive basis for finding in favor of the plaintiff."

Moose held his breath.

"Furthermore, the defense has effectively challenged the credibility of the key witnesses presented by the plaintiff. Through their cross-examinations, they have revealed contradictions and weaknesses in the testimonies, casting doubt on the reliability of the plaintiff's evidence. The defense has also presented counter-evidence and arguments that undermine the plaintiff's claims."

Please, God.

"Considering these factors, it is my opinion that a reasonable jury, properly instructed, would not find in favor of the plaintiff based on the evidence presented. The plaintiff has not met their burden of proof, and the evidence falls short of establishing their claims."

Moose looked at Ridge, who didn't meet his eyes, kept his focus on the judge.

Right. Don't celebrate yet, but—

"Therefore, I hereby grant the motion for a directed verdict in favor of the defendant. The plaintiff's claims are dismissed, and the defendant is relieved of any liability."

Moose's breath rushed out, his chest unknotting.

"Additionally, in light of the circumstances surrounding this case, I find it appropriate to exercise my discretion and order the plaintiff to pay all of the defendant's legal fees. The plaintiff initiated this lawsuit, and their failure to meet the burden of proof has resulted in unnecessary costs and expenses incurred by the defendant."

Moose's mouth dropped open.

"Therefore, I hereby direct the plaintiff to pay all of the defendant's reasonable and necessary legal fees incurred in the defense of this case. This includes attorney fees, court costs, and any other related expenses. The jury is dismissed and court is adjourned." His gavel came down.

Adjourned. Fees paid. Claim dismissed.

Moose put both hands on the table and closed his eyes even as outrage erupted from the plaintiff's table.

But he breathed in fresh air, and as he turned, Tillie came around and launched herself into his arms. He caught her up, and he just soaked in her embrace, the sense of tomorrow, and everything big and beautiful in front of them.

She pushed away from him, caught his face in her hands. "See! I told you—you did nothing wrong!"

"Nothing?"

The voice made him look up. Moose stepped in front of Tillie and even moved her a little behind him.

Harry Benton had come over, his lawyer's hand on his arm. Ridge stepped between them. "Mr. Benton—"

"He let her die. Freezing, bleeding, scared, and alone—he let her die out there!" His voice shook, his eyes reddened, and Moose just couldn't retort.

Not with the man in so much pain.

Instead, he swallowed, and his words emerged soft. "I'm so sorry for your loss."

"He did nothing wrong," Tillie said, stepping out from behind him, but Moose caught her hand.

Benton narrowed his eyes at her, then back to Moose. "You think this is over. But it will never be. Someday you'll know what it's like to lose someone you love and stand by helpless to stop it."

He blinked at the man. *What—*

"Is that a threat?" Axel said, sidling up to Moose.

Benton's lawyer pushed him away, but Grant kept his eyes on Moose as they headed out of the courtroom.

"Ignore them," Ridge said. He turned and shook Moose's hand. "It's over."

"Thanks, Ridge," Moose said, ripping his gaze away from the closing door. He put his arm around Tillie. *Over.*

On to the future.

He walked outside with Tillie and Axel, onto the city street, and stood in front of two snow-covered totem poles, the traffic sparse as dusk began to settle.

"Pie?" Tillie said. "Hazel is with Grandma Roz."

"I'm out," Axel said. "I need to catch up with Flynn. We're going to look at a condo." Axel twirled his key on his finger and lifted a hand before he turned to walk down the street.

Moose breathed out, turned to Tillie. "I might have something else in mind."

Her eyes widened.

"But maybe, yes, let's start with pie."

SIX

DESPITE THE SECURITY DETAIL THAT MET THEM
at the airport, the tall gates that cordoned off the US Embassy,
and the guards that stood by the doors of her family home,
the entire situation had Shep's gut in a knot.

"What do you mean your Ranger team was sent to kill me?"

Her question still hung in his head, the way her eyes had widened, the quick look at York and Tomas.

They'd started to descend for the landing, and maybe then hadn't been exactly the right time to tell her the entire story, but he couldn't escape the idea that the entire mission, from the very moment when he and the Ranger team had arrived at the meet in Zermatt three years ago, supposedly to safeguard the exchange, had been a setup. *Especially* when he'd spotted London.

He couldn't shake the sense, also, that someone had determined that *he* should be there.

"We were sent to protect a man named Alan Martin, a CIA agent who was apprehending a rogue agent, a man named Mick Brown."

"No—he wasn't . . . I mean . . . I don't think so . . ." London said. "Mick was my handler."

"I know. We saw Alan kill him."

She just stared at him, her beautiful blue eyes wide.

"We weren't on site at the time—the guys on overwatch saw the whole thing go down. Colt and a couple of the guys were taking position when Alan slit his throat, then took his place for your meet. I was positioned downslope, watching. And that's when I saw you."

The landing gear had gone down. "I knew something wasn't right—even when you were fifteen, you were a patriot. I couldn't believe that you would betray your country, so I told Colt and his team lead that I knew you. That you weren't rogue."

"They were supposed to take me into custody?"

"Yes. Or prevent you from leaving."

Her mouth had opened. "You stopped them."

"I told them I'd intercept and find out what was happening."

"I always thought it was so . . . crazy . . . that you ended up in that chalet with me—" London said.

"I saw you ski down, went to follow you, and I don't know what triggered the slide, but no, it wasn't a coincidence."

Although, even as he'd said it—how was it *him* that ended up on that mountain that day?

"That's the part that sits like a burr inside me. Because if I hadn't been there, you would have been at least apprehended. Maybe even killed."

The thought turned him cold every time he thought about it.

As it was, they'd survived the avalanche, and three days later, Colt had dug them out, and during the rescue chaos, London had vanished.

"The rogue agent turned out to Alan Martin," he said. "But I didn't find that out until Colt tracked me down in Montana a couple years ago."

London nodded, as if she might be putting the pieces together. "But that's why Colt wanted you to keep an eye on me . . . to make sure I didn't have a connection with Martin."

And suddenly, just like that, it made sense. Yes. Because if Martin knew London had survived, then . . .

He'd find her and finish her.

The plane landed, and his gut tightened, and no, he didn't like this little excursion, not at all.

They had stepped back in time in this storybook city of Luciella with red-roofed houses, cobblestone streets, and a massive central square cathedral with tall black Gothic spires. A river ran through the city, a drawbridge connecting the two halves. One side, the city center, held municipal buildings and a university, along with a political district with a row of embassies all at the foot of a castle on a hill.

"That's the Palazzo Reale del Sole," London said, seated beside him. York and Tomas rode in the SUV behind them. "It has Romanesque, Gothic, and Byzantine influences, with those tall turrets and towers. From the tallest tower, you can see the entire city." She pointed to a tower jutting from the keep, the ten-story bulk of the castle.

"You've been up there?"

"There are a number of state events every year, and I was visiting my parents for one of them. Prince Luka showed me around."

Prince Luka. He raised an eyebrow.

"Don't worry. He's only allowed to marry a royal. They have a hereditary, constitutional monarchy, and King Maximillian is the chief of state as well as the king, so there are *rules*."

She pointed out a large cobblestone square with an expansive fountain in the middle, surrounded by a five-story building with flags listing in the breeze, balconies, and a black slate roof. "That's the Montelenan gymnasium."

"A gym? Wow, that's a big place—"

"No," she laughed. "A gymnasium. It's a secondary school. Like a college. And over there is the Ministers Building, for the minister of state. And that gate there leads to Old Town, this quaint area of shops and homes that date back to the tenth century. The central square has a massive Christmas market every year, starting in early November, with a giant tree that they cut from the mountains."

"Lots to choose from," Shep said, eyeing the alpine peaks that surrounded the city.

She laughed again, and maybe the darkness had lifted slightly from her eyes.

"The Cryptex complex is located on the far side of the palace, inside the mountain."

"Inside?"

"Yes. There is a giant satellite dish built into the mountain—you can't see it from here, but remember the giant satellite dish in the Bond movie *GoldenEye*?"

"I didn't grow up with television."

"It was the Pierce Brosnan era of Bond movies. Anyway, this dish is just a little smaller but still sits in a crater at the top of the mountain. It's what provides the massive satellite coverage and networking for the Cryptex compound, as well as security. You can't fly over it, either, so no one really knows about it—although you can see it from space."

They had pulled up to the American Embassy now, the US flag waving from the gated entrances, two guards on either side. Their driver showed his pass, and the wrought-iron gates opened. Inside, a creamy-white building rose in a center compound, a black roof and a round window at the apex of the front of the building. Smaller buildings cordoned off the compound from the streets around it.

"Montelena is a mishmash of influences. It used to be part of Austria, then Switzerland tried to grab it, and then finally Italy, to the south. But they secured their independence after the First

World War and have hung on to it since. Are you ready to meet my parents?"

She had stiffened a little next to him, and he glanced at her. She swallowed, and for the first time ever, the woman appeared as if she wanted to wriggle out of her skin.

"I met your parents years ago—"

"You met holiday Sofia and Mitch Brooks. This is Chief of Mission, Madam Ambassador Sofia Brooks and her husband."

Oh.

Their security had gotten out and opened the door, and Shep stepped out to bright blue skies and the smell of early winter in the air. Snow glistened on the high peaks, but down in the valley, the temperature seemed in the midfifties, and the strangest urge to explore the area swept through him. Probably his mother's restless genes coming to life in a new place.

"Delaney!"

A woman floated down the front steps. Blonde like her daughter, she wore her hair short, with gold earrings, a necklace, a wide-collared white blouse, black dress pants, heels. She walked straight over to London and pulled her into a hug.

Behind her, a man emerged from the double doors. Dark hair, blue eyes, tall. He seemed almost regal, despite his relaxed, almost convivial expression, like he stored his thoughts and let them brew before letting them escape.

Indeed, these were not the flannel-and-jeans tourists he'd met ever so briefly in Montana.

London let her mother go and turned to her father. "Dad."

He embraced her. "Sweetheart."

Her mother stepped up to Shep.

"Madam Ambassador," he said. "Shep Watson."

"I remember you, Shep," she said, and as he frowned, she gave him a hug.

Huh.

"Call me Sofia." She stepped back, patted his arm.

Her father, too, came over, held out his hand. "Shep. I am going to hear the story of how you've ended up in Montelena with my daughter, right?"

He gripped the man's hand, gave a tight nod. "Yes, sir."

"Mitch."

"Right."

"I hope you're hungry," Sofia said. "Our chef makes the most amazing schnitzel and fried potatoes."

He checked his watch, and then didn't have a clue what time it might be.

Behind them, Tomas and York had gotten out of their car, and Mitch walked up to them, shook York's hand, and remanded Tomas into the custody of his security. Mitch and York walked off together, so that was interesting, but Shep followed London into the embassy.

Oops, former *palace,* given the travertine tile, the columns that bordered an inner entrance to an open area that, once upon a time, might have been a receiving courtyard. Steps led to an expansive meeting room with deep-blue velvet sofas, a massive Turkish carpet, gold brocade draperies at the soaring windows, and a number of small conversation areas around glass tables.

They walked through the reception area, then through double doors at one end to an enormous dining room. A fresco of angels and alps and clouds adorned the ceiling, with more gold brocade draperies at the windows. The long oak table could hold thirty or more.

"In through here," said Sofia and took them farther into the house, down a corridor, and finally into a smaller area, probably once regal apartments, but here, in a room that could still hold a small convention, was a sitting and dining area.

"My offices are just adjacent, but this is where we meet with many of our guests," Sofia said, gesturing to the gold-and-blue sofas. A beautiful black Steinway piano sat in the sun in an alcove. A smaller table, with space for maybe ten, was set with four plates. A gloved attendant was pouring water into a pitcher. Sofia spoke to him in . . . Montelenan? Sounded Italian, of course, what with the border so close.

He nodded and left the room through a back door.

London had wandered to the window, staring out. "I love this view of Mount Aleksandar. It's so . . . impressive."

He joined her, staring up at the granite spires, snowcapped and lethal.

"Just on the other side of those mountains is a ski area. It's probably not open yet."

"The higher runs are," said Sofia. She'd pulled out her phone, started to text. "And you're just in time for a blizzard. King Maximillian is quite worried that the Octavia Gala will have to be postponed." She looked up. "I do hope you're staying long enough to attend."

Shep raised an eyebrow. "A ball?"

"Oh, it's a glorious event. It coincides with Queen Isabella's birthday and is a true royal ball." She tucked away her phone. "Your father is on his way. The ball is this weekend. I'm sure we can find something for you both to wear."

The attendant came back in and set another place at the table right about the time York and Mitch came into the room.

"Darling. Do you remember York Newgate? He was in Russia when we were there."

"York. Oh, it's been years. How are you?" Sofia came over, gave him a two-kiss greeting.

"Good. I live in Washington State with my wife and daughter and our one-year-old son."

The staff had brought out lunch, dinner, *whatever,* in white stoneware, and Sofia gestured to the table. She sat at one end, Mitch at the other, and Shep sat by London.

The whole thing felt like a spy movie—so maybe they were in a Bond flick, complete with hidden motives and super-secret devices and people hiding guns under the table.

"So, how are your parents?" Sofia asked as she passed London the fried schnitzel. Shep's stomach betrayed him, growling. His last memory of food was somewhere over Quebec when they'd stopped to refuel and grabbed breakfast.

"Good. Mostly." Well, as good as they could be, given their grief. But maybe the Ambassador didn't know—London certainly didn't. So he didn't give any more.

"Are they still travelling in that '74 Winnebago Brave?" This from Mitch. "Your dad had overhauled the engine a couple times, if I remember."

"It finally died while they were in Canada. During the height of ski season, of course, so they rented a chalet and finished the season." Oh, this schnitzel nearly melted in his mouth, the potatoes creamy, garlicky, fried in olive oil. "Dad suggested sticking around, but Mom loves to travel, so they upgraded to a '98 Fleetwood Tioga with an overcab bunk. It's a 29-footer, so bigger than the one I grew up in. I don't know where they are right now."

"And your sister?" Sofia asked, reaching for the salad, what looked like cabbage and carrots and corn, all doused in a cream sauce.

He took in a breath. So they didn't know.

"Sofia," Mitch said softly. "I mentioned the accident, right?"

Everyone stilled.

Sofia looked at Mitch and set down the salad. Looked at Shep. "I forgot. I'm so sorry, Shep."

His chest tightened.

"What happened to Jacey?" London said now, looking at him.

"She was in a skiing accident," Shep said quietly.

She drew in her breath.

"She died."

"Oh, Shep, I'm sorry." She touched her hand to his under the table. Then she took it when he didn't respond, and, oh well, he squeezed back. It did seem to loosen the unexpected clench in his chest.

"When you're a backwoods skier and like to ski alone, that can happen. She was found by some other skiers. She'd hit a tree, went into a tree well face-first and suffocated." He stared at his half-eaten schnitzel, no longer hungry. He left out the rest because, well, the words spoken aloud could tear him apart. The memory found him anyway. *No, Jace, I'm not going with you today.*

London was looking at him. He took a drink of water, set it down.

"So, what have you been doing since we last saw you?" Sofia said, forcing a smile.

He forced one back. "Since I was sixteen? Um—"

"He toured with his cousin Gage."

"I remember him," Mitch said. "Amazing snowboarder."

"Yes," Shep said. "He joined a rescue team in Montana, and I ended up there too, after a little stint in the military."

"What branch?" This from York.

"Army. Tenth Mountain Division. I was a medic."

"And now you work in Alaska with Delaney," Sofia said. "Small world."

Very small. He nodded.

"Well, we're glad to see you. When Delaney called and said she wanted to visit, we had no idea she was bringing an entourage." Sofia wiped her mouth, set her napkin on her plate. "How did you meet York?"

"Work friends," York said.

"Really," Mitch said.

"Actually, I need to access the crypto wallet I set up last time I was here," London said. "I lost my bio card."

"You need to submit a request at least twenty-four hours in advance to even make an appointment, and then it takes a few days to get the new card," said Sofia. "I can ask my secretary to assist you."

"How did you lose your bio card?"

"It went into a river." She had finished her food, now took a drink of water.

Silence.

"It's a long story," said Shep. He still couldn't figure out why she'd chased him, but the plunge into the river had meant bye-bye, bio card.

"And that other man you brought with you? The one in hand-cuffs?"

"He's with me, Mother. He is . . . let's call him a courier."

Her mother cast a look at Shep, then back to her. "I thought you were working in Alaska. You're not still doing translation work for that international security group, are you?"

Shep glanced at Sofia, then to London, who made a face. "No, Mother. I still live in Anchorage—part of Air One Rescue. But York had a plane headed this way, so I hopped a ride. And Tomas is with him."

Wow, she lied so well, so easily—it sent a cold thread through Shep. Although, if you broke apart the facts, then yes, that seemed mostly accurate. So a lie made up of truths.

"He's secured in guest quarters upstairs," York said.

"I'll have the staff bring him some food." Sofia gestured to the nearby attendant and spoke again in Italian.

A knock, and a woman entered. "Madam Ambassador, the Minister of Arts is here for your two o'clock appointment."

"Very good." Sofia got up. "I'm helping King Maximillian with some seating arrangements for the gala. I'll be back. In the meantime, Louis will show you to your guest quarters." She put her hand on London's shoulder, bent down, and air-kissed her cheek. "I'm so delighted you're here."

Then she left the room.

"I think I'll take that food to Tomas," said York and also got up.

"I seriously hope I get the blue room," said London, and winked at Shep. "It has a view of the palace."

Her father laughed. "Delaney always wanted to be a princess. The problem of growing up on the edge of power. You see the elegance and even live it, but you're not ever quite royal." He pushed out his chair. "Let me show you your rooms."

Shep followed him and London from the room, down the hallway, and up a set of stairs with a wide stone railing, two flights to a private residence. A wide hallway, set in parquet wood, with pictures of the ambassador and her husband with dignitaries hung from the walls. They passed a magnificent sitting area with creamy-white velvet sofas and a picture-window view of the palace, and then Mitch opened a door on that same side. "The blue room, princess."

London stuck her head in. "Perfect." Over her shoulder, Shep spotted her sad and lonely backpack, the sum of her belongings after fleeing for her life, sitting on the wide king-size canopy bed. A curved, tufted white sofa sat in front of a hearth, and light streamed in the high leaded windows onto a round writing table with chairs.

"And Shep, you're across the hall." Mitch opened up Shep's room, and he found his view of the city, the cobblestone courtyard, the red-roofed houses, the mountains looming large and imposing in the distance. Also a king-size bed, his duffel bag a lump in the middle, the frame of the bed in dark walnut with spires at the four corners, and a dark-green brocade cover. Leather cigar chairs were parked in front of a similar hearth, and a heavy walnut wardrobe stood against one wall. "It's said that this was where King Aleksandar was kept under house arrest during the occupation of the Germans in the First World War. It's where he decided that, from then on, they would be a neutral nation."

"I saw quite a few guards at the airport."

"It takes a security force to stay neutral." Mitch had come in behind him, closing the door. "And there's the issue of Cryptex. It's Montelena's primary source of income. It cannot be compromised."

Shep nodded, noticed the closed door, the way Mitch stood with his arms folded.

"Sir?"

"I need to know, Shep. Are you still on mission?"

London had naturally walked over to the window. She'd lived in so many embassy apartments, a few houses, a few rental flats, but none, not even her apartment in Port Fressa, Lauchtenland, had had a view as grand as this view of the castle on the mountainside.

Not ever quite royal.

She'd never wanted to be royal. Not really. Didn't want to be trapped in that life. But sometimes she wondered what it might be like to live with so much . . . *attention.*

Still, the castle always intrigued her, perched right on the edge of a cliff, towers on either end of a white stone wall, a winding cobblestone drive leading up to an arched gate.

On her last visit, Prince Luka had pointed out a few hiking paths up the mountain for better views of the castle. Maybe she'd take a hike with Shep while they waited for her appointment.

She walked over to the bed and opened her backpack, pulled out her cell phone. She'd left it off for the trip and now it powered up. Putting in her EarPods, she dialed Ziggy's number.

"Tell me you're in Montelena," said Ziggy. She sounded like she stood outside somewhere, maybe in the rain.

"Yes."

"And you have the bio card?"

"No. I have to get an appointment. And even after that, it's a seventy-two-hour wait to get the card. That puts me at Friday."

"I don't like this, but okay. And you brought Tomas?"

"Yes. He's under York's custody. Thanks for the lift, by the way."

"York knows the Orphans and speaks Russian and has history with the Petrovs. Use him if you need him. He will deliver Tomas to the Swans after you are done with him."

She froze, staring at the cold hearth. The room held a chill.

"No. What? What will you—"

"Calm down. Tomas needs to be rehidden. We will help him secure new papers and disappear."

Oh. That. Right. "Sorry."

"Take a breath, London. You can trust me. And, by the way, yourself. You know what you are doing."

Did she? Because over the past month, she'd felt so far out of her element—

"To be clear, this is it. My last mission. I am going back to Alaska Air One after this. With"—she swallowed—"Shep."

"Are you sure he wants you?"

The question knifed through her, turning her a little hollow. "What?"

"You are a much different woman than the one he thought you were. Perhaps—"

"I'm not a much different woman. I'm London Brooks."

"You will need to be Laney Steele if you hope to succeed in your mission."

She shook her head.

"And then maybe you will see that you are—"

"I know who I am."

"Do you? Because *you* came to us. Twice. Even after trying to leave. You have the heart of a Black Swan."

"Really? What is that?" She had found the remote control for the hearth, now converted to gas, and turned it on. It whooshed to life, the flames flickering orange and yellow. She sat on the curved sofa.

"A black swan is rare yet creates a great impact. A black swan can change the world with its courage and bravery."

"I've read that black swans are bad luck."

"You make your own luck, Laney."

"I finish this, and I walk away."

"With your mountain man?"

She glanced at the door. She'd sort of expected him to come over after he'd gotten settled.

"He was the one from the avalanche?"

She lay down, staring at the ornate ceiling with the medallion around the chandelier. "Yes. He practically tackled me, skis and all, into the chalet—a one-room building with a kitchen and bathroom. The avalanche hit us, and I'm not sure how, but he sort of threw me into the bathtub—this deep claw-foot affair—then the whole chalet exploded with snow. Terrifying. He started on top of me, to protect me, but ended up under the tub in a pocket there. I heard him shouting, and then he shoveled out a space for his hand. I saw it and we got him free and into the tub. We were in this pocket. Shep figured the vent to the fan had come down but kept an access to air. Anyway, that's where we stayed for three days while his friends tried to find us."

"And he never said why he was there?"

"He's a skier, and he loves big snow—I thought maybe . . . but . . ."

"Lucky he was there."

"Yeah. Real lucky." She hadn't really thought about that before—the fact that Shep, the one man she'd pined for, had showed up on the mountain to save her life.

Okay, she had thought about it, but she'd dismissed it as a crazy coincidence.

What if it *hadn't* been a coincidence?

"Did you know that Shep was assigned to watch over me?"

Silence. "By whom?"

"Colt Kingston."

A beat. "He works for the Caleb Group, a sort of off-books, behind-the-scenes, get-'er-done organization created by the current president. Not sure why they'd want to keep an eye on you, but—well, my friend Roy works for them."

"Shep isn't a spy."

"People are not what they seem."

"Shep is. What you see is what you get. And that's who I need. Who I want."

More silence.

"Listen, I'm over Ruslan. It was a long time ago. And Tomas wasn't real. And Shep . . . he is both real and heroic. And . . . he's here with me."

She could almost see Ziggy's expression, those dark eyes widening, then the frown. "You brought him to Montelena?"

"He refused to stay behind."

"He will only compromise you."

"I know what I'm doing—"

"You won't be happy until you are true to the person you were made to be."

Oh. And who exactly was that? She had nothing to fill the silence.

A knock sounded at the door.

"Listen. I'll check in when I have the bio card." She pressed End before Ziggy could argue with her. Got up.

Her mother stood in the hallway.

London glanced across the hall at Shep's closed door as her mother, all grins, pushed into her room. "Okay, we only have three days, but that's enough. Let me take a look at you."

London stepped back even as her mom caught her arms.

"You're too skinny. And you need a haircut. And your eyes—" She stepped up. "It seems you're not getting enough sleep."

"Mother. I'm fine." London walked over to the fire, turned down the heat.

"Okay then, I'm only going to ask once." She took a breath. "Does he know?"

London rounded.

Madam Ambassador Sofia stood hands on hips, giving her a look that could throw a bomb into world peace.

"Know what?"

"Don't give me that. I know about your *international translation* job."

"My . . ."

"I know you were a Black Swan, darling."

She blinked.

"Please. First, you disappear for three years, sending me random postcards from exotic places, working for that commerce company, and then you move to Nigeria and fly planes into the bush of Africa?"

"It was a great job."

"There are terrorists in Nigeria! I read the news. And I get the action reports. Kidnappings all the time. Just two years ago, a doctor and two aid workers were kidnapped—"

"I know. And they survived, by the way."

Her mother blinked at her. "Were you involved in that?"

She folded her arms. "I was burned because of it."

"Oh dear."

"Yes. But that's over."

"Over?" Her mother braced her hands on the sofa. "Are you going to stand there and tell me that a member of the Orphans didn't try to *kill* you a month ago?"

Her mouth opened.

"I have a wide net, darling."

London sank back onto the sofa. "How long have you known about the Swans?"

Her mother walked over to her. Sat on the other end of the sofa. "Let's just say that Pike Maguire asked me before he approached you. I told him that you'd have to decide for yourself."

"You knew Hawkeye?"

"Back when I was a junior foreign service officer in Russia. Actually, the Swans were partly my idea. I realized we had a need for specially trained women to . . ."

"Acquire information in clandestine ways?"

"It's sounds more tawdry than it is."

"I know, Mother."

"Yes, well, I've stayed out of it, mostly, but yes, I have kept updated on your life. Since you never call."

"This is a little more invasive than installing a location tracker on my phone."

"Don't be dramatic. I know you're good at your job, Delaney. But these Orphans—they are serious. What happened?"

"What do you think happened?"

Her mother drew in a breath. "Oh no . . . you didn't—"

"Ziggy took care of it."

Her mother closed her eyes, just for a moment, and now who was being dramatic? Then, "Right. Good. Well, now that you're here, you're safe. Montelena is quite secure. But that doesn't answer my question, does it?" She leaned forward. "Shep."

Shep.

"He knows about the Black Swans, yes."

Another indrawn breath from her mother. "And?"

"And . . . it doesn't matter, because after this, I'm done." She got up, walked over to the hearth.

"Back to Alaska?"

"Yes."

"I like Shep Watson. I do. But, Delaney. Really. He's so . . . woodsy."

"He's a search and rescue tech. And a good one."

"He doesn't understand your lifestyle."

Oh please. "I wasn't aware that I had a lifestyle, Mother."

"Prince Luka has asked about you more than once—"

"Stop. I'm not interested in Prince Luka—"

"He might be interested in you."

She held up her hand. "First, you know he can't marry anyone but a royal—"

"They changed the law in Lauchtenland. I think for the right woman—"

"I am not here to catch a prince. I . . . just need a new bio card."

Her mother made a face, something genuine in her eyes. "I would just like to have you close."

Oh. She came back to the sofa, sat. "I miss you too."

Her mother touched her hand. "We have drama because we are so much alike. We're both trying to change the world, just in our own way."

"I'm done trying to change the world, Mother. It's a bad place with bad people, and there's nothing I can do about it."

She gave her mother's hand a squeeze, started to pull away, but her mother grabbed it. "I know Ruslan's death still haunts you. That his betrayal still wounds you. That you feel to blame—"

"I was eighteen years old, naïve and stupid."

"You were in love."

Her mouth tightened. "Yeah, well, he used me and someone died, so—"

"You couldn't have known he was KGB."

She looked away. "Okay, so yes, I might have trust issues." She looked at her mother. "But not Shep. He would never betray me."

"If you don't trust him, he'll never have the chance."

She blinked a moment, then. "What is that supposed to mean?"

"When did you tell him you were a Black Swan?"

Oh. "Yesterday."

"And yet you spent a year with him. I think you love him, London, because the truth is we can only be betrayed if our heart is involved. And you don't give away your heart without giving away pieces of yourself . . . which means letting him inside to the real you."

London stared at her. "He knows the real me."

"Okay." Her mother held up her hands. "I believe you."

Oh, Mother. For a diplomat, she sure knew how to stir up conflict. "What do you want from me?"

"I want you to be happy. To find a man who sets your heart on fire. With whom every day is a new adventure. And who makes you feel adored. Like a princess."

"Enough with the princess—that was . . . I was a *child*."

"Of course. And now you are a Black Swan. My worry isn't that Shep will betray you, but . . ."

A beat.

"What?"

"I'm worried that you will betray him."

London's mouth opened. "Seriously?"

"Yes. Because—well, because you're a Black Swan."

"What's that supposed to mean?"

"Just that you're . . . impulsive, and . . . well, you yearn for impact, a life out of the ordinary."

What—had her mother and Ziggy had a coaching call?

"And who taught me that, Madam Ambassador?"

Her mother held up a hand. "Like I said, we are a lot alike. The difference is that I have found a man who is willing to walk into the unexpected with me."

London's jaw tightened. "I am happy. I've been in love with Shep since that day he held me on rappel as I climbed up the tower back at Glacier Peaks Wilderness Camp. He held me for two hours that day, and . . . frankly, he's still holding me."

The thought brought her up, stilled her.

Shep had always been there.

And yet, her mother was right—she had lied to him. Starting in the chalet, all the way to yesterday. And if Tomas hadn't kidnapped him . . .

Shep would have never known the truth.

Her chest knotted.

"I just don't want you to settle for anyone less than the man you're supposed to be with." Her mother stood up. "Please tell me that you will attend the ball?" She offered the faintest of smiles.

Aw, "When is it?"

"Friday night."

She'd hoped to be out of the country by then. Still, if things went south, this would give her a reason to stay in country without raising eyebrows. "Maybe. We'll see."

Her mother smiled. "Prince Luka will be surprised to see you."

"Mother! That wasn't a yes. But if I go, I'm going with *Shep*."

"Nothing like a little jealousy to put a fire under a man. Or a prince."

"For the love, it's like I'm not here. You cannot arrange a marriage for me—align the kingdoms with a royal match. I'm not even royal."

"Laws are changing every day, honey." Sofia got up and kissed London on the cheek. "You'll see. A royal ball is magical—you just might find that you end up in a place you never imagined."

She only wanted to end up in Shep's arms, thank you.

Oh, and she'd add the caveat that she didn't want anyone to die because of her in the process. That was her happy ending.

"I'll find you just the dress." Her mother got up and headed to the door. Stopped, her hand on the knob. "I like Shep. I truly do. I hope he turns out to be all you hope for."

"He already has."

Her mother gave a slow nod, her mouth pinched. "Whatever you say, Delaney." She shut the door behind her.

And her mother wondered why London had loved attending boarding school during her high school years.

Still, weirdly, Shep's voice filtered through her head, stuck there. *"I may not be some James Bond . . ."*

Yeah, well, she didn't want him to be either.

And he wouldn't need to be. *Everybody just calm down.*

She'd get her bio card, go to a ball, infect the Russian mob with an internet virus, and resume her life in Alaska.

No problem.

SEVEN

"ON MISSION, SIR?" SHEP HAD STOPPED AT the window and now turned at Mitch's question. "What do you mean, 'on mission'?"

Now Mitch walked into the room, clasped his hands on the back of one of the leather chairs. Inhaled, exhaled, pursed his lips.

"What's going on?"

"How much do you know about your orders that day in Zermatt?"

"My orders? Um, they were just . . . orders. I don't understand the question." And then . . . *Wait one doggone second.* "How do you know about Zermatt?"

"Sit down, Shep."

"I'll stand."

"Fine." Mitch went around and sat in the chair.

Ho-kay. Shep sat on the other, in front of the silent hearth. The lunch had started to settle like a clump in his stomach, and fatigue pressed over him. It felt like he'd been up all night and was walking into morning without a cup of coffee, fuzzy-headed and

140

bloated. Like a hangover, maybe, although he'd never experienced one of those.

Frankly, he'd never been the guy to let himself wander outside the boundary lines.

"I know my daughter is a member of the Black Swans."

Shep just blinked at him.

"And I know you know also, because York filled me in. Said you two talked about it on the plane, so I'm not revealing anything."

Shep's mouth tightened. "How long have you known?"

"I worked with a man named Pike Maguire to set up the Swans. And when he died, I took over."

"You're the director of the Black Swans? Does London know this?"

"Why do you call her London?"

"It's a nickname. From summer camp—she had a cute sort of British accent, so . . ."

"Charming."

He had a feeling that it might not be. Still. "She likes it."

Her father made a sound, deep in his throat. *Sheesh.* Shep understood why parents might not have liked the ski-bum version of him as a teenager, but hello, today he had a home, a decent job, and . . . "I get that maybe you disagree with her quitting the Swans—not sure why, as it's dangerous—but—"

Mitch held up a hand. "You don't know Delaney like I do. It's not up to me whether she quits the Swans. But I do care if she lives or dies."

"On this we can agree."

"Which is exactly why I sent you on the mountain that day."

He sent . . . "What—wait. That was a Ranger operation. And we were there to protect the CIA operative—who I think turned out to be a rogue agent."

"A man named Alan Martin. At the time, he was just forming his faction inside the walls of the CIA, and he was the one who ordered your operation. But I had intel that suggested a double-cross, and when I heard that they wanted to send a Ranger team to 'protect the operative'"—he used finger quotes for that last phrase—"I feared that something—or someone—might get caught in the crossfire. My only hope was you."

Shep blinked at him. "Me?"

"I knew that if you saw Delaney, you'd stop any attempt to eliminate her, so I spoke to the right people, and your Ranger team was tasked with the mission."

"I was a medic. I had no command authority—"

"I know you were in the military, and I remember the climbing story from camp. You're dependable, Shep. In fact, I think it's your greatest trait, and of course, your Achilles' heel. And I knew you'd do anything to stop an attempt on her life." He nodded. "And you did."

"I . . . yes, okay, I saw her that day—couldn't believe it, really—and I did convince my team to stand down, but then we almost died together in an avalanche—"

"From where I sit, you kept her alive."

Shep had nothing.

"You got her to safety, kept her alive in that chalet, and frankly, I think you're still on that mission."

What? "Listen, I'm here because—"

"Love."

"It's not a mission to love someone." It might be quite the declaration, but he didn't care.

"Isn't it? I think it takes great commitment and capacity to love someone. Especially in Laney's line of work."

"She's out of that."

"Pardon me, but wasn't she dead for the last month?"

A breath, then, "How do you know about that?"

Her father cocked his head. "Really?"

Right. And then . . . "Wait. You were behind Colt's asking me to watch over her in Alaska—even the invitation to bring her there?"

"I knew the moment I picked her up from summer camp. I saw it in your eyes. And it's still there—in your eyes and your words. You love my daughter."

Fine. "And you used that to manipulate me."

"I used that to protect her."

Shep's mouth tightened.

"I called you to the mission, even if you didn't know it. Because I could count on you."

Shep looked away, out the window, to the city nestled under the rugged protection of the mountains.

"And I knew, given your losses, that you wouldn't let her run off into danger."

Shep looked at him.

"Like your sister, Jacey."

Aw. But . . . "What do you know about that?"

Mitch held up a hand. "I'll bet your worst nightmare is thinking of her alone, freezing to death."

Shep stilled. "You don't pull your punches, do you?"

"Just being honest."

He leaned up. "Fine. Yes. That is a recurring nightmare, thank you so much."

"And I would guess, given how close you and your sister were, that she normally didn't ski alone."

Shep drew in a breath. "No." His jaw tightened. "We were supposed to go out together that day, but I had promised to fill in for another instructor at the ski school. I asked her to wait for me, but she got a free ride with a couple of other heli-skiers . . ." He ran his hand over his mouth. "She was always a little impulsive that way. Didn't like to have to wait for anything. Or anyone."

"I'll bet you resented that."

Shep glanced at him. "No. I knew that's how she was. Like my mother. She always wanted the next new, fun thing. The next great adventure."

"And you're not like that?"

He met Mitch's eyes. "No. That's why I got out of the military. I get enough adventure trying to extract people out of trouble. I don't need to create it." He leaned forward, ran his hands down his face. Wow, fatigue had crept up on him. Then he looked at Mitch. "I don't want a life where I don't know if I—or the person I love—will come home. I saw what that did to my parents when Jacey died, and I don't want to live that way."

"Maybe loving Laney requires living that way."

"Or maybe that was someone else, from the past."

"The past has found her." Mitch sighed. "Can I be frank with you?"

"If this isn't frank, then I'm bracing myself."

Mitch smiled. "I can see why she likes you."

Shep didn't smile.

"I think she's in over her head. I think that Tomas is not to be trusted—"

"You think? My eyes are still burning."

Mitch frowned.

"Never mind. Yes, I agree. Tomas is up to something."

"We're testing to see if the crypto virus is real. But Ziggy still hasn't figured out who took the contract out on Delaney—"

"Wasn't it Drago Petrov?"

"Maybe. Probably. But someone else could have picked it up—"

"So someone is still after her."

"Montelena is known for its security—it has to be with all the cryptocurrency it handles every day. The exchange here has to be hackerproof. But outside these walls . . ."

Still on mission. The words reverberated through him.

Mitch sighed, got up, and walked to the window. "When I married Sofia, I knew she wanted a life overseas. She'd started her early days as an ESL teacher and had already lived in Japan and Nepal and Taiwan. She loved . . . an extraordinary life. And I knew that loving her meant giving up what I would call the standard American dream." He drew in a breath, turned. "But I can honestly say that God knew me better than I knew myself. I've found great purpose in my life in the shadows of Sofia's aspirations, and the reward is much greater than the cost."

Now, in the silence, Mitch met his eyes. "I believe that God put you on that mountain, even with my directive, to save her life. And maybe that's why you're still in her life. Because like it or not, Shep, you've been given a mission, and yours isn't to ask why. You can only accept, or walk away."

Aw. "I don't know what you want from me. I'm not a Ranger; I'm a medic. I don't kill people or . . . whatever."

"Keep her alive. Bring her home. That's what you do, right?"

His mouth tightened.

"She can do the rest."

That's sort of what he was afraid of, and now a cold thread zipped through him.

Mitch walked back over, stood in front of the hearth. "God sometimes gives the hardest tasks to the ones he can count on the most. And if it was easy and didn't require all of us, then we wouldn't need God to complete it."

Shep swallowed. "I didn't realize you were a man of faith."

"The world is not a safe place. It requires faith to keep the fears at bay." He gave Shep a smile. "So, I ask again. Are you still on mission?"

Maybe it wasn't the best day for a hike, but she had to get out of the embassy.

"My mother bought no less than thirteen dresses, and she had me trying them on all day. We finally got into a row. I don't know why I feel like I'm thirteen as soon as she walks into the room."

London pulled her wool hat over her ears, the wind on the higher slope of Mt. Lucielle whipping down from the taller peaks to find them as they wound along the hiking path.

Even from here, the view fanned out over the city, the deep-blue river dissecting the two banks of the city, the tall spire of St. Andrew's Cathedral crisp against the fresh snowfall of the faraway peaks. A wonderland that seemed trapped in time.

Above them, the castle walls loomed tall and impenetrable. No wonder this place had held out against invaders for so many years, with its stone walls and parapets for archers.

Behind her, Shep had stopped, putting up his collar. He'd shaved, his dark hair sticking out from under the cuff of his wool hat, and wore his red Air One jacket, as if he'd forgotten that here, he was just a tourist.

Or . . . well, she didn't know what to call him. Friend? Boyfriend? She had sort of staked a claim to her mother yesterday, but he'd done nothing yesterday to confirm it. No more foot rubs, no hand holding . . .

It had started a small twinge inside her. *He knows the real m*e.

No, he knew *London*. And she . . . well, she wasn't real, was she? And maybe, just maybe, he'd started to figure that out.

She kept going up the path. Maybe they just needed to get away from the suffocating craziness of the embassy, find their way back to Shep and London.

And that kiss.

"My mother and Jacey used to go round and round. Jacey wanted her freedom, and my mom feared that freedom would get her killed."

Oh.

"It was just because she loved Jacey so fiercely. It was fear. It makes people hold tighter than they need to."

A quietness hung between them, but she didn't want to read into it.

Aw, there she went, reading into it. Because perhaps he'd been holding tighter out of fear too. And maybe he'd started to regret that.

"Your father gave me a walking tour of Luciella, along with a history. Ask me anything about the reign of King Maximillian, or better yet, the entire history of the house of Ribaldi," he said, changing the subject and not at all adding fuel to her spiraling. "Did you know that King Aleksandar helped with the partisan underground in the Second World War, secreting downed airmen out of Austria and Liechtenstein?"

"I thought they were neutral."

"They were under the protection of Switzerland, like Liechtenstein, so technically. But according to your father, the castle has secret tunnels that run through the mountain down to the valley, where people hid or even escaped through. They'd hide in boats that took them down the river into the Adriatic Sea."

They'd reached a small overlook, and she walked over, staring down into the valley that ran into the village. Small houses with red or black roofs dotted the mountainside all the way down to the cluster of white and yellow stucco homes in the city. And the other way—"Look! You can see the backside of Lucielle ski area from here." She pointed to the snow-covered bowl, bordered by furry white trees. "I'll bet you'd like to ski that."

"Not with that headed my way." He pointed to a dark cloud shadowing the mountain. "That says rain. And any higher, ice."

She turned to him. "Wanna hike down?" He stood less than a foot away, and she saw his eyes roam her face.

Maybe he would—

"Nope. I'd rather be out here in the rain, with you."

Oh, sweet. So, hello, just stop the crazy. No, he didn't reach for her, give her one of those soul-baring kisses, but . . .

Aw, and now her mother walked back into her head. *"My worry isn't that Shep will betray you but that you will betray him."*

Right. Because she'd dragged him halfway across the world into a life he clearly didn't want. Except, *not* dragged him, because he'd insisted on following her, but maybe—of course it was—out of fear . . . so . . .

"You okay?" he asked. "You're really quiet. Jet-lagged?"

Oh. "Yes, maybe a little. But I was just thinking about the last time I went hiking around a castle." *What? Where did that come from?* Still, it sat in the back of her head, the idea that there were parts of her he didn't really know. "When I was thirteen, my parents and I took a month off and went on a castle tour. We visited every castle in Germany, Austria, and Switzerland. We even visited Schloss Lichtenstein—which, by the way, is in Germany, not Liechtenstein. It was more like a hunting hangout than a castle, but it was on the side of this mountain." She stopped, looked up. They stood along the backside of the castle now, on a balcony overlooking the impossible route of attack. "Many castles, I guess, are on the sides of mountains or at the top. Always on the lookout for trouble."

"Or always a place to run to."

She glanced at him. "Hadn't thought about that."

"Your father said that back in 1013, when this castle was first built, they installed a postern gate, and it was used numerous times by people fleeing from danger."

"What's a postern gate?"

He looked up at the massive granite wall. "It's a small back door, sometimes in a really obscure location, that can't be easily accessed by an army. It's even too small for a horse. It allows the castle to be regarrisoned if it's under siege, to send messages out to other people, and in the event of being overtaken, the family or whoever can use it to escape."

He walked past her, still looking up. "It wasn't without its dangers, however. A traitor could open the gate and let marauders in, and if they could overwhelm the guards at the main gate, they could let the horde in."

"That would be bad."

He glanced at her. Smiled. "Gotta watch for the invading horde."

She realized she was completely overthinking this. A month ago, they'd been just friends, just stepping over the threshold of something more.

Aw, shoot. Maybe the kiss had just been an emotional moment for him. Sneaking in, like a marauder.

Yes, probably. Frankly, she'd been emotional too. It wasn't every day that she came back from the dead.

"Your dad said it was just a story, but I thought maybe the back-side of a mountain would be a good place for a postern gate."

She blew out a breath, caught up to him, said, "My parents are castle buffs, so I've seen castles from Germany to Austria to France and every country in between. I think France has the most impressive castles, but the most beautiful one was crazy Ludwig's in Bavaria."

"The *Chitty Chitty Bang Bang* castle?"

She frowned. "If you're referring to Neuschwanstein, then yes."

"I've only seen the movie."

"Out of the two hundred rooms, only fourteen are finished. The rest of the castle is empty. He only lived in it for a hundred and seventy-two days before he was committed for being crazy."

"Sounds like an amazing trip."

"Yeah. It was just . . . just me and my parents." She shoved her hands into her pockets. "I had them all to myself. I started calling myself Princess Delaney."

"Your Royal Highness."

"Cute. I'll bet you saw a lot of the US countryside in your family's Winnebago, right?"

They turned on the trail, up a switchback, and he looked up. "Where are we headed?"

"The trailhead ends at a waterfall on the backside of the mountain." She shivered as wind stirred the fir trees along the trail, the clouds moving in overhead.

"Okay. The rain will probably hold off. That cloud isn't moving quickly. And my family didn't travel. We just parked—at one ski resort, then another."

She turned up the collar on her jacket. "I thought you lived in a motorhome to see the world."

"We lived in a motorhome because my parents were ski bums."

"Right. I remember you saying that now."

"But during the summer, my dad turned into a sort of evangelist. We parked in resort towns, and Dad was busy witnessing on street corners while Mom worked in coffee shops or at local diners. In the winter, they worked as patrollers. They'd met as ski bums, got saved along the way, and decided that God had called them to a vagabond, John the Baptist kind of life."

Oh. She went silent.

"Maybe that came out negative . . ." He looked at her. "I love my parents. They're free spirits, and they encouraged us to be the same. Maybe too much." He gave a wry smile. "Sometimes I feel a little forgotten by them. And honestly, growing up, their lifestyle wasn't . . . wasn't exactly stable. Dad was always fixing the stupid RV, and sometimes we'd spend weeks at a hookup in some grassy roadside waystation while my dad worked on people's cars, just for gas money. If we got lucky, there'd be a pool or something nearby. When I got old enough, my parents started to send Jacey and me to summer camp in Glacier Park—mostly because it was paid for by Gage's parents. But I loved it. Same place for six weeks."

"I remember," she said. "That's where you learned to climb."

"Yeah. And obviously the skiing was a part of my life."

"Some people would be envious."

"It's never fun to be poor."

"But your parents, your sister—you were all together. You couldn't avoid each other."

He glanced at her. She hadn't meant to argue. "Seriously. Sometimes I didn't see my parents for months, with all their travels and my boarding school."

He paused then. "Yes. I did have that. My father lived by the will of the Lord, which often felt only as far as his gas tank would take him, but he did love us. And they loved Jesus. He lived by the mantra of Romans 12:18—'If it is possible, as far as it depends on you, live at peace with everyone.'"

And suddenly Shep's words about not wanting to be a man of violence returned to her. His father had rubbed off.

"We had a simple life. No television. We were outside a lot. But my dad did spend time with us. When we were little, we'd curl up in our bunks—he'd built them into the Winnebago—and he'd read us his favorite books, like *Where the Red Fern Grows*—"

"Oh no, I can't even bear that one."

"I cried for days."

She looked at him, and he smiled, winked.

And *oh,* she just wanted to step up to him, pull him down to her—

No. Just keep walking.

"And *Charlotte's Web.*"

"What was wrong with your father?"

He laughed. "And *The Velveteen Rabbit.*"

"*C'mon!*"

"*The Adventures of Tom Sawyer?*"

"Better."

"*The Phantom Tollbooth.*"

"There we go."

"The Chronicles of Narnia."

"He's forgiven."

151

"*The Mouse and the Motorcycle.*"

"I still think if I make the noises, it'll go," she said, then made the *brr* noise.

He laughed, and *oh,* it fueled her soul, deep and delicious and rumbly in her bones.

"Right?" he said. "I spent hours trying to make that happen with an old dirt bike my dad found. My favorite adventure, however, was *The Call of the Wild.* Maybe that's why I love Alaska. And I loved Buck, the dog, and all the ways he touched people's lives."

Now, that explained a lot. And *oh no,* now her heart started to swell.

"My dad always wanted me to join him. You know, share the gospel, rescue people from darkness. I think he was always a little disappointed in me."

Seriously?

"Anyway, yeah, we were poor, but we were happy and warm, and it was an adventure. But I'm over adventures. I'd prefer to read about them, thank you. There and back again." He gave her a look then, his mouth tight.

"There and back again?"

"*The Hobbit?* My family was obsessed with J. R. R. Tolkien. I read *The Hobbit* and *The Lord of the Rings* until the spines broke in my books. But I never needed to go on my own quest to save the world."

"Right."

But now that feeling was back. And *shoot,* she just had to— "Shep, are we ... are we ... okay?"

They'd reached the backside of the mountain, higher now, with a look into the valley below. The gondola from the resort still ran up the mountain, a few of the cars swinging on the cables. The sky had turned mottled, the wind now whooshing through the trees. She hadn't really realized the change in weather ...

"What do you mean?"

She faced him. "I mean . . . why haven't you kissed me again?" *Oh,* her stupid mouth. It said all the wrong things sometimes. Maybe she *was* thirteen.

Even *his* eyes widened. "What?"

Too late to take it back. "You haven't . . . Okay. I know this sounds weird, but . . . maybe that was just a moment. And if it was, then . . . it's fine. Really. I mean, I was emotional too, and maybe we're going to be just friends, but—"

"Are you kidding me?"

Her mouth opened.

"I've been wanting to kiss you for the last forty-eight hours, but . . . you said maybe we shouldn't kiss again. And there's . . . this." He spread out his hands to the intense alpine scenery and the valley below, with the river that dissected it. Then he turned back to her. "I wasn't sure you wanted—"

"Oh, I know what I want." Then she stepped up to him, put her hands on his jacket, and rose on her tiptoes. "I'm very sure about that."

He smiled then, slow and perfect, and when his gaze roamed her face, all the spiraling simply stopped. He bent—

The gunshot pinged the air, took off a piece of his jacket, hit a tree behind him.

Instinct had her tackling him, hooking a leg behind him, pushing.

She landed on top of him with an *oof* as he put his arms around her, of course cushioning her fall.

Another shot, and this time it hit the pathway ahead of them.

"What was that?" He pushed her off him, started up, but she scrambled to her feet, grabbing his hand.

"Run!"

She took off down the pathway, and he kept up, ducking with her as another shot barked in the air. "London! What is going on?"

"I don't know!" But *oh,* maybe she did.

Whoever had picked up her abandoned contract—so much for safety in Montelena—had found her.

And *Shep.*

The path headed downhill, and in the distance, a roar lifted.

"The falls—up ahead."

"To be clear, I don't want to go swimming again—"

Another shot. She ducked, then pulled him off the path, toward the sound of the falls. They cut through trees and scrambled over boulders until—

"Whoa!" He grabbed her back a moment before she took a header off the edge of a cliff. Below, some twenty feet, narrow, turbulent rapids led to a lethal drop, only mist rising in the expanse.

"Let's just think a second before we jump!"

She looked behind her at the rise of forest. "We're trapped."

"Maybe." He was staring upstream, to the source of the river. Another waterfall careened from a ledge some thirty feet up.

"What do you see?"

"Just . . . nothing, maybe. But . . . let's go." He pulled her with him upriver along the cliffside. They stayed low, behind boulders and trees, and behind them, the sky began to tremor.

"Rain is coming. That should hide us," he said, his voice solid. He'd gone into rescue mode.

They climbed to the next falls, these more narrow, misting in the darkening air. They fell into a pool before escaping downstream.

"Can you climb this?" He pointed to the not-quite-vertical granite face that bordered the falls, slicked with moss and water.

"Of course."

Then she was suddenly fifteen and back at camp, finding footholds, jamming her hand into crevasses. She worked her way up the face, not looking down, keeping her body away from the rock, making sure each hold worked before easing onto it. Even a thirty-foot fall, especially in this terrain, could be fatal.

And of course, if she fell she could take out Shep. He'd started up behind her, just a few feet below and a little to the side, as if he could catch her if she tumbled by him.

Maybe.

He'd turned dark and serious and a little bossy as he pointed out holds to her here and there.

"I do know how to climb there, Alex Honnold."

"Who's that?" he said, his voice roughened by effort.

"The guy in that terrifying documentary *Free Solo*."

"London, there are people shooting at us. Just climb."

She glanced over at him. "Sorry. Sheesh—"

"I'm more concerned that you're having a good time. Seriously?" He gestured and she turned back to the climb, spidering up to the top.

He came up beside her just as the sky opened up and spat on them.

"So this is a fun outing," she said.

He looked at her, breathing hard. The clouds had settled in, turning the entire mountain to shadow, and even in his red siren jacket, up here among the trees, probably they were hid—

He kissed her. Took her by the lapels, pulled her to himself, and kissed her. No, inhaled her. Fierce, and maybe fueled by desperation, or frustration, but he kissed her in just the same breathtaking, desperate way he had before. So maybe that first time hadn't been about the rush of emotion over her coming back from the dead, although someone *was* shooting—

It didn't matter. She wove her fists into his jacket and kissed him back, the rain on her face, his whiskers against her skin. He was the mountain, pulling her into his protection as he put his arms around her. A sound rumbled out of him and into her, taking her slowly apart.

Yeah, she'd definitely stopped spiraling.

He finally released her and met her eyes. "I hope that answers your question."

She blinked at him. *Question?* "Wait—*you* were the one with the questions."

"Was I?" Then he got up and pulled her with him. "C'mon. It's around here somewhere."

The granite wall was covered in vines and scrub brush, but he pushed the litter away and there in the wall hung a double wooden door, slightly rotted around the edges. "I thought so." Built like an old stable door, with a few fasteners holding the boards together and two rings hanging from the front, it seemed like it locked from the inside.

Except, the hinges faced outward, so . . .

"You take one ring; I'll try the other."

She grunted, with no success.

His side, however, moved, just slightly.

"I can't believe it isn't locked."

"It is. But the river has probably flooded over this area so many times the lock rusted through—see the hinges here?" He pointed to the red bloodying the wood. "Enough force and we can break the lock, or maybe just pull it free from the hinges."

"Maybe we should just go down the path."

His hand landed on her arm. "There's a shooter down there. Somewhere. We go that way, we walk right into them. I'll get my side open enough to wedge something inside like—oh, like a knife? That KA-BAR you carry?"

Her mouth opened. "I don't—"

"Please."

Fine. "I didn't bring it."

He looked at her. "What kind of supersecret covert operative are you?"

"The kind that thought she was out for a nice day trip with her boyfriend!"

He smiled then, and it touched his eyes, and despite the drizzle and the darkening sky, her entire world lit up, bright and perfect. *Oh boy.*

"I'll find a stick." She rooted around one of the trees. *Wait.* "I found something. It looks like one of the door fasteners. Still in good shape."

"Perfect. I'll heave open the door, you shove that into the space, and we'll use it like a lever."

It worked. He pulled, she pried, and the door lock broke off with age and flooding, flicking rust into the air. He opened his side. "It's a tunnel."

She stepped inside, the odor of must and dankness and the cool lick of a breeze from deep inside stirring something in her gut. "It's a *very dark* tunnel."

His hand curled around hers. "I got you."

Alrighty then.

He flicked on his phone light. Shone it against the walls of the cave.

"You're such a Boy Scout."

"I've been out in the bush enough times to know that you don't leave without a cell—or sat—phone. Let's go."

Maybe ten feet high at its tallest and five feet wide at its widest, the cave still bore the marks of pickaxes scraped into its sides. Shep closed the door behind them, just in case, and shone his light into the corridor. The darkness gobbled it up, but the beam shone far enough for them to walk a few feet, and a few feet more, and soon the sound of the waterfall lessened, their breaths and the scrape of footfalls the only noise.

"This is creepy," she said.

"Imagine it without the light."

"Thanks for that."

He touched his hand to her shoulder, warm and solid, and there was no one she'd rather be wandering around in the dark with.

He moved ahead of her then and led the way until they came to a set of wooden stairs. They took them down, then more and down again, maybe two hundred feet, and came out to a wider area. This part of the tunnel had been smoothed out, as if used regularly, wine casks stacked on their sides on one side of the rounded room.

Another tunnel led away, and he headed toward it, taking her hand. "I think there's a door up there." He shone his light on a towering arched door with a smaller door built into it.

And just like that an alarm screeched, lights flickered on, and a siren moaned, echoing through the chamber.

He winced, turned, and she spotted debate in his face.

Then the door at the end burst open, and she pulled him down to his knees and hit her own as her hands went up.

Armed guards ran into the corridor, shouting.

"Get down," she said, glancing at him. "Get way down, onto your face."

"What?"

"We've just breached the castle."

His eyes widened, and he put his head down.

"Don't shoot!" she shouted as a hand went onto her back, pushed her forward.

She turned and spotted Shep's tightened jaw as a guard also pushed him forward, knelt into his spine. "Don't fight them!"

He put his hands behind his back, something flickering in his eyes.

Her wrists were zip-cuffed too.

And then they were rolled over. She stared up into bright fluorescent lights at the face of a palace guard, and all she could think to say was, "I'd like to talk to Prince Luka."

Stop being a coward. What did Moose think was going to happen—that Tillie would say no to his marriage proposal? That somehow something catastrophic and horrible would happen if he finally embraced his happy ending?

Moose drove down the highway, the sun at twilight turning the mountains purple, the waters of the Knik Arm a deep blue, all of Alaska painted white. A beautiful night for the rest of his life to start.

And so what if their conversation over pie a few days ago, after the court hearing, hadn't gone quite like he'd planned? . . .

"Tillie, you're back!"

He should have known that the minute they walked back into the Skyport Diner, one of her former colleagues would recognize her. As it was, it was the rather unhelpful cook behind the order line who spotted her and came out to greet her. Lyle, king of the kitchen, if Moose remembered correctly. The guy still looked fresh out of the clink, short sleeves, wearing a hairnet, tats up his arms.

Lyle the Killer pulled Tillie into a hug. "Missed you, Steelrose."

She gave him a slug. "I'm not that anymore."

"Yeah, you'll always be my favorite Iron Maiden."

Moose tried not to roll his eyes.

She shook her head, then motioned for Moose to head over to their booth, the one by the window, where he'd spent the better part of a year or more pining for her, coming in late after rescues, ordering midnight fried chicken and pie just to have a chance to talk to her.

She knew how to make him feel that all would be right with the world.

She walked over to the pie case and helped herself to two slices of apple pie. After scooping ice cream onto each, she carried them over to the table and set one down in front of him. "Just like old times."

He caught her hand as she slid in across from him. "Better than old times. Because before, you never got to sit with me, really."

She smiled and pulled the pie over. "Yeah, well, I called and my manager said I could get my old job back. So enjoy it while you got it."

His eyes widened. But of course she'd go back to work. Still ... "I was ... thinking ..."

"Oh, this is good pie. I've missed it. Key lime is great, but there is nothing like a good Alaskan apple pie made with Haralson apples."

A waitress came over, and Moose didn't recognize her.

Tillie did. "So they moved you over to nights, Mandy?"

"Someone had to take your spot." Mandy was midtwenties, pretty, with short brown hair. "But now that you're back, I'm happy to get my night life back. My boyfriend hates my late-night shift."

Yeah, Moose too. Because sure, he worked any—and all—hours, but frankly, he'd prefer Tillie home at night, safe and—

And *wow,* that sounded a little more parochial than he meant. It was just that ... well, Benton had stuck in his head with *"Some-day you'll know what it's like to lose someone you love and stand by helpless to stop it."*

So he felt a little less than thrilled about Tillie putting her blue waitressing outfit back on and suiting up to serve midnight chicken.

And maybe he'd said that—*whoops*—as Mandy headed back to the kitchen, in the form of ... "Do you have to take the night shift? Wouldn't it be better for Hazel if you were home?"

Tillie's brows rose and she cocked her head at him. "As opposed to the schedule I've had for the past two years, with Hazel being tucked in by a grandmother who loves her?"

Right.

"The other alternative is that I don't get to drop Hazel off at school, or pick her up, and know that she's safe at home with Roz."

"I could drop her off."

He didn't know why he'd said that, really. Maybe he'd felt like the conversation he wanted to have—one that talked about their future, as in a permanent future—was slipping out of his fingers.

Admittedly, he'd reached out to grab it poorly. "Or you could come and live with me."

She just blinked at him. Opened her mouth. Closed it and—

"I didn't mean it like—" He put his fork down. "I meant as—"

"Slow your roll there, cowboy." She looked up as Mandy came over with coffee and set the cups down. Tillie smiled at her.

Then as Mandy walked away, she looked back at him, her smile vanishing. "I'm not going to live with you, Moose."

Oh. Just like that.

But, "Like I said, I didn't mean—"

"I know what you meant. But it's . . . we just moved back into our house. Hazel is thrilled to have her room back, and . . ." She shook her head. "Just give it some time."

He sighed. *Time.*

He hated time. Because as patient as he was with everything else, he just wanted it all . . . now. Tillie his wife. And Hazel his daughter. And . . .

Tille touched his hand. "Listen. It's been crazy, right? And . . . I do love you, Moose. But I need to figure out where we're going, me and Hazel . . ."

And he'd probably given her a crazy look, because she let go of his hand, drew back.

"Weirdly, I thought we both knew where you were going."

Wow, he'd assumed way, way too much.

Mandy came back to refill coffee that hadn't been touched.

"Can I get a box?" he said, his stomach now revolting at anything sweet.

Tillie sighed. "Moose, that's not what I meant."

"What did you mean?" His voice emerged gruffer than he wanted, but suddenly everything rushed over him—the trial, and the trauma with Tillie's ex, and even the worry for London and Shep—and his bones just felt heavy.

Frankly, he just wanted to start this entire year over.

"Just that—" Tillie started, hurt in her expression.

Great.

"I don't know. It's just so fast."

He held up a hand. "I get fast. What I don't get is . . . a different direction. I thought—" And he should just stop talking, because she stiffened.

"Just give me a minute to live in freedom, okay?"

Freedom. As if he might be *chaining* her to him. *Nice.*

Mandy returned with the box. He pulled out his wallet and handed Mandy a card.

She took it and went to the cash register.

"Don't you want time, now that the lawsuit is over, to figure out what's next?"

He looked at Tillie and just . . . yeah, fatigue had him laying it all out there. "I know what's next. You. You and Hazel. At least for me." He shook his head. "So I guess now's not the time to ask you to marry me."

He met her eyes, and she drew in a breath. Swallowed.

Way to go, Moose.

Mandy returned with the card. He took the slip and signed it. Handed it back. She glanced at Tillie and walked away.

Tillie's mouth had tightened. But still she didn't answer.

He got up. "I'll be in the truck." Five minutes passed as he sat in the cold cab, terribly afraid that this was the end. Staring out at the Alaskan sky, so dark but riddled with pinpricks of light, as if hope were trying to break through.

And then his driver's-side door opened and Tillie stood there, her eyes filled.

Aw. "I'm sor—"

She took his face in her hands and kissed him. Sure and deliberate. And she tasted like apple pie and coffee and all the hopes and dreams he had for them. Beauty and strength and compassion and everything this woman had become for him. Oh, he loved her, and he didn't care what might be going on—or that he didn't understand any of it, really—he just curled his hand behind her neck and kissed her back.

She didn't pull away, just stepped closer as he turned in his seat, tucked her into his embrace, and deepened his kiss under the blinking stars, giving her his tired, way-too-raw heart.

Yes. Yes, he'd wait for her.

She finally broke their kiss and touched her forehead to his before backing away and meeting his gaze. "You are what's next, Moose. I'm just trying to keep up."

"I can slow down."

She gave him a soft smile. "Don't slow down too much." She put her hands on his chest. "Truth is, you make me, and Hazel, feel safe, and I trust you. So ask me again."

"Right now?"

She gave him a look. "Maybe give me a day or two."

Fine. He'd give her as much time as she needed. As long as the answer was yes.

Which brought him to today, tonight. He *wouldn't* be a coward, despite the memory of the crash and burn. Although really, his first try hadn't been an actual, decent, official marriage proposal.

Next time, however, it would be perfect.

He turned off the highway toward her house in Eagle River, running the words through his brain.

Tillie, you are smart and amazing and beautiful—

No, he should start with her courage. Or maybe her compassionate heart. Or maybe the way she listened to him, calmed the terrible whirring constantly in his head.

Or perhaps, *I love you, Tillie. I would give my life for you, and Hazel....*

Aw. Maybe he'd just walk up to her, get down on one knee, and open up the ring box that he'd finally picked up from Kirchner

Jewelers yesterday. A gorgeous one-carat diamond in a white-gold band. The box sat in his console.

The radio played, and of course one of Oaken Fox's songs came on. He hummed to it, listening to the words.

But then you walked into my life, like a sunrise over fields.
I saw forever in your eyes, and all the past wounds healed.
Now I know, deep in my soul, I'm the luckiest guy alive,
For in your love, darlin', I've found my guiding light.

A little sappy, but maybe it was right.

He turned onto Eagle River road and, in the fading light, thought he spotted smoke, black and rising into the night. A chimney fire, probably—so many people in Alaska burned wood for heat.

He'd taken to lighting his fireplace every time he got home.

He checked his dash clock—they'd be at the restaurant early for their dinner reservations.

It wasn't until he turned onto her street that he saw the glow. Trees illuminated a blaze. *Oh no,* one of the houses on the street must have—

No.

He slammed his foot on the gas, then screeched to a halt in front of Tillie's house.

Tillie's *burning* house.

Flames engulfed the garage, the place an inferno, the front of the house still uneaten, smoke clogging the sky, and—he slammed his truck into Park and barreled out of it, sprinting into the yard, his feet plowing through the snowbank, then the caked snow. "Tillie!"

The front door remained closed, and her car sat in the driveway, melting under the heat, the flames from the garage licking out at it.

Please, God, she couldn't be in there—"*Tillie!*"

Someone had to have called 911, but he'd left his cell in the car. Now he lunged at the door, put his hand on the handle.

Yanked it back. Hot—which meant the fire was baking the house, ready to explode out if he opened the door.

But *Tillie was in there, with Hazel,* and—he pulled down his jacket sleeve to cover his hand, pulled the neck up, and—

"Moose!"

Her shout yanked him back, shuddering through him, and his legs nearly gave way as he turned and spotted Tillie running across the street.

He launched off the porch, stumbling through the snow.

She wore a bathrobe and Uggs, like she'd been getting ready to go out but had gotten derailed, and—

"Where's Hazel?" No way would she leave the house without her, but—

She caught him, her hands on his arms, pulling him away from the fire. "She's safe—she's safe—she's with Roz. Come away from there before the house—"

He heard it even as she said it, or maybe felt it, the tremor of heat and destruction. Instinct made him grab her and dive toward the snowbank, pull her down with him, his body over hers just as the house exploded, fire and debris raining down over them.

Covering his neck with his hand, he braced his body over hers, the snow cocooning him.

Behind them, the fire raged, an inferno.

"Are you okay?" she said as he rolled away from her.

He nodded, but he had no real answer as he dragged her away from the flames, into the street.

Behind them, in the distance, sirens wailed.

He stared at her house, the one she'd gutted and remodeled and called home. She turned and put her head into his chest.

He put his arms around her, holding her tight, standing in the street as a fire engine roared up. "It'll be okay, Tillie. It'll be okay."

EIGHT

PERFECT. SHEP HAD RESCUED LONDON RIGHT into a royal prison cell. Or rather, *ahem*, a *dungeon*.

Nice. They sat in a small concrete room in the bowels of the palace, a gate across the rough opening, an electric light illuminating the corridor. Next to him, London shivered in her wet clothing. He wanted to put his arm around her but could only lean against her, shoulder to shoulder, his hands secured behind him.

"So, I guess I didn't think this all the way through to the end. Sorry. When I saw the door in the rock—"

"Stop, Shep. There was a shooter behind us. Don't worry, Prince Luka will sort this out." She glanced at him, her face half obscured by the shadows. Dirt streaked her face, her hair sodden under her wool hat, but she could still make his heart stop in his chest, sweep the breath from him. *I hope that answers your question.*

Maybe he'd been talking to himself, because he *had* been the one harboring questions. And maybe now wasn't the time to think about a future, the life he'd hoped for them. Because the more he ventured into London's world, the less he saw of the woman he'd known for the last year and the more . . . well, the more she became a mystery.

Maybe her father had been right—Shep might be in love with the version of London he'd created.

He'd known she was a woman of action, of purpose, known she was into something, well, questionable, given her presence at the meet in Zermatt. So, *hello*, *someone* had been in denial.

But yes. He was still on mission, and her father's words back in the study yesterday reverberated through him. *"Keep her alive. Bring her home."*

Alive in the king's prison was at least better than dead in the rain on a mountain.

Except, "You don't think they'll draw and quarter us, do you?"

She laughed, looked at him. "It'll probably be the boiling oil."

"Nice. That's a great mental picture."

"Don't worry, Prince Luka is a friend."

He didn't like that mental picture either.

Footsteps, the shudder of metal against stone, and then a guard appeared. Spoke in Italian.

She looked at Shep and translated. "Prince Luka will see us."

"Hopefully not to chop off our heads."

"Just our ears."

"I think we should stop this game."

London smiled as the guard opened the door. She addressed him in Italian. He shook his head, took her by the arm, and helped her up.

"What was that?"

"I asked for the cuffs to come off."

Shep followed them out of the cell and down the hall. "Not for a second do I think you can't get out of these zip ties."

"Never hurts to try manners first."

Interesting.

The guard opened the door at the end of the hall.

"Besides, my mother is the ambassador. No need to start a squabble."

"We did break into the palace."

The guard directed them to an elevator, pressed the button, and then invited them inside when the doors opened.

They rose a number of levels, and the door opened to a hallway with a deep-blue carpet and gilded walls, with ornate molding around the windows, and gold wall sconces that held faux candles. Chandeliers dripped from the ceiling, and through the leaded glass, the village was dark.

Weird. Shouldn't lights be on in the village below?

They followed the guard down another hallway, then stopped at a door and knocked.

It opened, and another blue-uniformed guard looked at them, nodded, and stepped aside.

Shep glanced at the sword sheath hanging from the man's belt. Talk about playing the part.

The office bore all the vestiges of a royal space, from the deep-blue velvet draperies that framed two tall windows that overlooked the city, to a painting of some ancient ruler dressed in the deep blues and gold of the royal colors that overlooked the domain from between the windows.

A bookcase held trinkets—probably gifts from visiting dignitaries. Silver bowls, an ivory statue of an elephant, an intricate filigreed wooden sailing vessel, what looked like a totem pole, a glass vase, a couple lion bookends, even a Russian samovar and a nephrite egg.

An exquisite polished-walnut desk sat in front of the windows. A gold carved crest of Montelena inlaid the desk's paneled front, an elaborately carved trim twining along the top and sides. A couple tufted leather chairs faced the desk, and a matching executive chair pushed up behind it.

An office befitting a ruler.

And the ruler? Standing near the floor-to-ceiling bookcase, hands clasped, wearing a sweater, a pair of dress pants. He had a distinct Henry Cavillness about him—tall, broad-shouldered, a cleft chin, a chiseled jaw, dark eyes, a confidence in his expression, which now bore a slightly tweaked smile.

"Your Royal Highness," London said, and Shep just stopped and stared as she curtsied.

Prince Luka raised an eyebrow at Shep, who tightened his lips, then bobbed his head. *Whatever.*

London stood up, and Prince Luka directed his attention to her, his smile widening. "Delaney, darling, if anyone is permitted to break into my palace, it's you." Then he walked forward, his hands out, leaned over, and kissed one cheek, then the other. He glanced at his guard. "Uncuff her."

The man took out a clipper and relieved her of her cuffs.

Shep stood there watching as London ran her hands around her wrists, over the cuff marks. "Thanks. And sorry. We weren't trying to break in—someone tried to shoot us."

"What?" Prince Luka took her hand. "Are you okay?" He spoke fluent English, maybe because London had addressed him in English. *Manners.*

"Yes. Shep saw the door in the rock, and he—we—got it open and used the tunnel to escape."

Shep kept his gaze on Luka. *Um, cuffs, buddy?*

Apparently His Highness wasn't keen on freeing him. Still, the prince glanced at the guard and nodded.

A clip, and Shep was rubbing his wrists too.

"Now, again, someone was *shooting* at you?" The prince had a distinctly highbrow, almost British accent, perhaps with a small amount of eastern European thrown in, which only added to his royalness. "*Ma chérie,* that is disturbing." He took her hand and directed her to a chair.

Oh, and of course he spoke French.

Shep folded his arms, remained standing.

"Are you sure?"

"We're sure," Shep said, and Prince Luka looked at him.

"And this is?"

"Shep Watson, my . . . he's with me."

What happened to boyfriend? *Whatever.* He met Luka's gaze. "Where she goes, I go."

"Oh, I see," the prince said. "Very good. I will ask my security to look into it. In the meantime, let's get you out of those wet clothes."

Shep held up a hand. "I don't think that's necessary."

"Nonsense." Luka snapped his fingers, and the guard opened the door, spoke to someone in the hallway.

"Really, Your Highness—"

"Luka. We've played this game before, Delaney, and I won."

He did? Shep stilled. Especially when Luka's smile felt a little, *hello*, too warm. Too genuine. At least, when directed at London. *Oh, wait*—maybe he meant the first name, not the clothing change. *Sheesh, calm down.*

Still, Shep didn't like the man.

"Okay—Luka," London said. "I'm so sorry to have disturbed your security services, especially right in the middle of your gala preparations."

He waved a hand. "Oh, that is my mother's domain. I'm more undone by the fact that you are here, back in my country, without a word of warning. I need time to brace my heart for the possibility that you will break it again."

Shep rolled his eyes.

London smiled. "Yes, well, it was an impromptu trip. I have an appointment at Cryptex tomorrow to replace my bio card."

"Tomorrow?"

"The waiting period."

"You should have called me. You know I would do anything in my power for you." The door behind them opened, and in walked a steward holding two thick robes. Prince Luka reached out and took one, held it open for London.

She turned, slipping into it, pulling it around her and belting it.

Shep looked at the steward as he handed him the robe. *Sheesh,* he wasn't that cold. But, *okay, fine,* especially when London gave him a side-eye.

He felt like the Pillsbury Doughboy.

"Come with me, and we'll get your bio card taken care of. No reason for you to wait." Luka reached over and picked up the land-line phone on his desk. "But only on one condition."

"No more sneaking into the palace?"

He smiled. "Perhaps. But I was thinking more of a request—that you'll attend the ball tomorrow night." He glanced at Shep. "With your guest, of course."

He'd sort of hoped London had been kidding about the ball.

"Yes. Of course. My mother has already purchased dresses."

"Very good." His Highness turned to the phone and spoke Italian, waited a moment, then nodded and hung up. "You're all sorted. My guards will escort you to Cryptex. I'll make sure you have your card by tomorrow night at the ball."

A knock at the door. The guard opened it, and a man stuck his head in. Spoke again in Montelenan.

Shep should really pick up a few words, ASAP.

The prince nodded, and the man left.

"The electricity went out?" London said.

"With the storm, the entire city grid went out." And even as he spoke, lights flickered on in the darkness behind him, the city turning magical in the valley below.

"Does this happen a lot?" Shep asked.

Prince Luka glanced at him. Lifted a shoulder. "Occasionally. We're on an old grid. The palace has been updated, of course, but the earthquake of 2004 shook through eastern Europe. It even hit us here and destroyed much of our infrastructure. We're slowly replacing it, but our primary focus was rebuilding and fortifying Cryptex and the palace security. It appears we forgot the postern gate." He gave Shep a nod, almost a thank-you.

Hmm.

"My guards are waiting to take you to Cryptex. And then I will see you tomorrow night at the gala?" He walked to the door, held it open. "Please let me know if the palace can assist you in anything else." He lowered his voice. "Preferably not something criminal." Then he winked. At London. Who curtsied again.

"At least, not officially."

He chuckled, deep and resonant, and Shep had the crazy and completely inappropriate urge to deck him.

What. Ever.

They walked through the halls in their silly polar-bear robes, took an elevator down a couple levels, walked down a concrete tunnel, passed through a series of secure doors, then took another lift up to a main floor and into a marbled entryway with an inlaid travertine floor and a tall door with two large circular locks.

"Those locks are just for show," said London as the guard beside her keyed in numbers on a digital panel. The door slid to the side, and lights bloomed in another corridor. "You can access Cryptex through an external entry also." She pointed to a door on the other side of the entryway as they entered the tunnel. "But you still have to go through the same amount of security."

At the far end, a view through bars revealed a lobby. A guard stood sentry by the inner entrance, and a receptionist sat at the desk. "It's guarded twenty-four seven but is only open daylight hours. My guess is that Prince Luka asked someone to stay."

"He likes you," he said softly.

She glanced back at him. Smiled. "I'm taken."

Oh. Yes. Okay, see, calm down. But she did this spy thing a little too well.

The guard keyed in a long code, the gate opened, and they went inside. A simple white-oak built-in reception desk sat in front of a black granite wall, the words *Cryptex Bank* hanging in gold letters. The guard spoke to a receptionist—a slim woman, midforties, her blonde hair pulled back, wearing a blue uniform with a gold emblem on the jacket breast. Looked like a filigreed *C,* for Cryptex.

"Wait here. I'll be right back," said London.

"Not on your life."

She turned. "This is the most secure building in Europe. I'll be fine."

"I'm starting to think that my definition of secure and yours might be different."

But then she squeezed his hand and followed the woman to a nearby room, also unlocked with a thumbprint and a code, and there he stood, an idiot in his puffy white bathrobe, like he was on walkabout in a spa.

He shucked off the robe, his clothing now reasonably warm, although still soggy, and scanned the place. On the other side, a wall of vertical black wooden strips sat against glass, and beyond that, an array of slick-looking computer towers filled the room.

Could be the crypto-mining banks.

Another door led to an area beyond the granite wall, but it was also locked with the same lock system.

The sooner they dumped this virus and headed back to Alaska, the better. He didn't know the lay of this land, couldn't see around the corners of London's life to know what to expect next.

And then there was the ball. *Sheesh,* if his father could see him now. And of course, the old man walked into his head. *"Now all glory to God, who is able, through his mighty power at work within us, to accomplish infinitely more than we might ask or think."*

Huh. So maybe the old man would be a little impressed with him.

Although, the man had never been impressed with wealth or

power, so maybe not. *"People look at the outward appearance, but the Lord looks on the heart."*

Behind him, the barred gate buzzed open, and he turned to see a man walk in, dressed in a similar Cryptex uniform. He stood in the lobby, glanced at Shep.

Shep had never been so glad to be out of a bathrobe.

The door opened, and London came out, blinking hard. She closed her eyes as she came toward him. Her thumb pressed a piece of cotton against her middle finger. "They need blood for the DNA in the card and shoot air into your eye to dry it out." She blinked a few more times. "That's better."

The receptionist took her place behind the desk, and when the man flashed a bio card, she reached under her desk and buzzed him into the secure area, through the other door.

Meanwhile, London looked at the guard, spoke in Montelenan, and they exited the lobby, back to the tunnel. Shep had picked up his robe, and after another elevator ride and another walk down a corridor, they gave them to the guard, who escorted them out of a side entrance, to a courtyard outside the palace. Light sprayed down onto the cobblestones. A driveway led into the mountain, probably to the entrance of Cryptex. Stairs descended from the area, down the mountainside to the village.

Commoners once again.

At least it had stopped raining. He started for the stairs, but a horn beeped from a nearby parking area. An embassy SUV sat in the lot, and a door opened, the light shining from an inside dome. "Your ride, ma'am."

Oh.

"Prince Luka must have called the embassy," London said, a hint of chagrin in her voice.

It was better than the hike down the mountain, although he felt like a child being collected from the principal's office as he climbed inside the SUV.

They drove down the mountain, into the city, through the pools of light that splashed on the wettened streets, and finally through the embassy gates.

As they climbed out, Shep held out his hand to her. She took it.

"Prince Luka has nothing on you."

His mouth tightened at the edges. *Yeah, well,* it wasn't a competition.

Really.

They went inside and then upstairs and stopped by the private living area where Mitch and Ambassador Sofia sat on the sofas. The smell of dinner came from the nearby kitchen.

Mitch put down the paper he was reading. "Get caught in the storm?"

"Something like that," London said. "But I did get my Cryptex appointment, so you can cancel it. Oh, and we're going to the ball, Mother, so yes, I'll need one of those dresses."

Her mother smiled. "I knew you'd come around."

He waited for a retort from London, but she nodded and walked down the hall to her room.

He followed her. "You okay?"

She turned around. "Perfect. I was trying to figure out when and how to get into Cryptex to upload the virus. I caught the code the guard entered as he let us in, and it looks like you just need to press the buzzer under the desk to get into the inner rooms. Tomorrow night, after I get the bio card, we'll sneak in and upload the virus and be gone, and all this will be over."

"What about"—his voice lowered—"that assassin?"

She held up a finger. "Working on that." She smiled at him. "I can't wait to see what you look like in a tux."

"Wait, London—I don't dance."

"There's a time for everything." Then she rose up on her toes and kissed him. Quick but sweet and, *okay, fine.* Maybe he didn't need to worry about the stupid prince. As if he'd been worried. Which he definitely hadn't.

"I'm going to take a shower and warm up. See you at dinner?"

He nodded, then headed to his room. A chill clung to it, so he started the fire in the hearth, then headed to the bathroom, filled it with steam from the hot shower, and started to feel the ends of his fingers and toes again as he stood under the spray.

He came out of the bathroom dressed in a towel around his waist, the steam following him out, the bedroom warming.

And there, in one of the chairs, sat York. He wore black jeans and a dress shirt and now stood up.

"Um, maybe I'm confused. This is my room, right?"

"Sorry, mate. Of course, but . . . I need a word with you."

"Yeah, me too, *mate*. Did you know we were shot at out there in the woods? Your assassin group or whatever still has a hit out on London." And he couldn't believe he'd entered a world where those words not only emerged from his mouth but were comprehended and maybe even normal, because York just nodded.

Whatever. "They're going to keep coming, aren't they? Until you guys stop them."

"I don't know. I'm working on that."

Shep walked over to the wardrobe and grabbed fresh clothes, brought them to the bathroom. "If you're not here about the hit, what couldn't wait until dinner?" He dressed, then came out in a pair of jeans and his last clean shirt.

"I don't want to speak about this in front of London," said York, who had gotten up and paced to the window, keeping his voice low. Now he turned. "We're going to need your help delivering the virus into Cryptex."

Shep cocked his head. "I thought Tomas was going to do that."

"Yes, well, first—the virus Tomas created just might be a decoy. Our hacker, Coco, has tested it and is pretty sure it's actually an access device that allows a back-door entry into the crypto wallet of any account that touches London's wallet."

"Like the CIA?"

"Or any other group. If she were to send money into the exchange, it could be disseminated to all other accounts."

"They could hack into every other account."

"It seems that way."

"London said she didn't trust him. Clearly for good reason." His stomach growled. "So, what virus do you need uploaded?"

York pulled out a jump drive. "This one. We've been developing our own virus, and this one will follow the money too, but right back into the account of the Petrovs and then slowly corrupt it . . . and like the other, corrupt every organization that they touch."

"Not taking out just their terrorist money but the money of every terrorist network."

"Yes."

"Brilliant."

"So we'll actually defund them instead of just causing factions. Better, right?"

"Why don't you just switch it out, Tomas none the wiser."

York looked out the window, his hands in his pockets. Shep's gut tightened at the look on York's face.

"Because during the blackout, Tomas escaped."

Shep wanted to punch something. For a man who hated violence, his recent impulses irked him. Still. *Escaped.* "How?"

"The locks on the doors lost power. When the lights came back on, he was gone."

Shep shook his head. "London needs to know this."

"Of course. And we'll tell her of the new plan, but . . . just in case something happens, I'm giving you the virus."

"Something . . . *happens*? Could you be clearer?" He took the jump drive that York held out, closed it in his palm.

"Yes. Like . . . I don't know. Tomas waiting to apprehend her or—"

"Kill her?"

"We don't know his plan, so . . ." York shrugged.

"In that case, the last thing I'll be doing is uploading a virus. My job is to keep London alive and bring her home." And suddenly, he was very, very glad for that job description, *thank you*. "I am not a spy. I'm a rescue tech."

"And you were a soldier."

His mouth opened, closed. "I was a *medic*. I didn't even carry a weapon."

York considered him. "Just . . . hang on to the jump drive. And where London goes, you go. She can upload the virus. Leave finding Tomas to us."

He nodded, but as York let himself out of the room, and as Shep stared out through the dark pane of glass, he heard his father's voice, quoting some obscure psalm that seemed to live in his bones. *"The wicked draw their swords and string their bows to kill the poor and the oppressed, to slaughter those who do right."*

His hand closed around the jump drive.

So, he guessed he was going to a ball.

London didn't recognize herself.

Again.

Which probably boded well for tonight's events, but still . . . the woman who stood in the mirror's image seemed too . . . confidant. Too regal.

And not even a little fragmented and confused and at odds with the life she'd thought she loved. Because as she'd planned out tonight's heist, a terrible, familiar, and intoxicating buzz had started to simmer under her skin.

Laney Steele, rising like a Phoenix.

She blamed York, who'd pulled her aside after dinner last night with the news of Tomas's escape. York would attend the ball, on the alert for Tomas, then, when she was ready, help her break into Cryptex and upload the new and improved virus before she transferred the money back to the Petrov Bratva.

"I can ask Coco to hack into the electrical grid to the palace and temporarily shut it down. She's already mapped the route to Cryptex. The entire mountain is a Faraday cage and supported by generators powered by the water that runs through the mountain, so there's no way to break the lock, but she can disrupt power to the palace and distract the guards so you can get in. The hiccup can only last five minutes tops, which means we need to create another reason for the palace guards to leave their post to give you more time."

Shep had been a part of that conversation, listening, arms folded as if he hadn't liked any of it. "Just pull a fire alarm, right?" he'd said.

York had looked at him. "Brilliant."

Shep had raised an eyebrow as if he hadn't expected York's agreement.

"And while everyone is managing the alarm, you get into Cryptex, log into your account, and upload the virus."

"Just like that," London had said, and that's when the simmer had lit.

And hadn't left. Worse, it had grown as she'd picked a dress for tonight's ball, then let her mother's stylist do up her hair in a loose French twist. She'd applied some makeup—hadn't worn that in over two years—and a hint of lipstick, then slid into the gown. The neckline dropped in a steep V in front and back, the sleeves long and loose and gathered at the wrist in a satin cuff. No slit up the leg, and the tight bodice had no give, but the looser skirt meant she could hide a plastic night-vision scope.

She'd wanted to take that KA-BAR that Shep had joked about,

but on the off chance that she'd be wanded, she didn't want to risk it.

She had tucked the jump drive with the virus into a pocket at the apex of the front V, right under the pendant of her necklace, which had just enough metal to alert the wand, but not so much as to stop her, and wow, now she felt like a Swan.

An unpredictable, unexpected *Black* Swan.

She slipped into a pair of peep-toe mesh heels, sturdy enough to run in, added her gold pendant necklace and teardrop earrings, grabbed her purse with her cell phone and the speed dial straight to Ziggy, and stepped out into the hallway.

Shep was outside his room, standing at ease, his hands clasped in front of him, watching her door, dressed in a tuxedo that perfectly, devastatingly, outlined his wide mountain-man shoulders, those lumberjack arms, the jacket tailored to his trim waist, the pants fitting his strong skier's legs. He'd shaved, of course, and his dark hair appeared freshly trimmed.

"Are you wearing hair gel?"

"I do not want to talk about it." His gaze travelled down her, back up, and he offered a wry smile. "The only thing good about tonight is seeing you in that dress. However, I feel like I need to hand you my jacket."

"You're just used to seeing me in my red jumpsuit."

"Don't tell anyone, but I might like this better." He held out his elbow. "You look . . . breathtaking."

She slipped her hand through the crook of his arm. "And you're very princely."

"I'm a peasant in a monkey suit. This night can't end fast enough. And I did mention I can't dance, right?"

"Preacher's kid?"

"Two left feet."

"We'll see."

They took the elevator down to the embassy lobby, where her

parents waited along with York. Her mother wore a long cream A-line dress with sleeves that dripped lace to the floor. Diamonds sparkled at her neck. She met her daughter with an air kiss. "You look like you did at the Lauchtenland Rosengala when you were eighteen."

"Oh, for the love, Mother, really? That's the memory you bring up?"

"Sorry." A moment of strained silence, and Shep frowned at her. Maybe she didn't need to always jump to defense.

Fine. She met her mother's eyes with a *don't say a word* and said, "I have definitely put on some curves since then."

Her mother's expression relaxed, and she winked. "Indeed." Then she handed London a printed invitation, took her husband's arm, and they headed outside.

London followed with Shep and whispered over her shoulder. "My mother would like to set up a back-alley-handshake arranged marriage between me and Prince Luka."

"Of course she would," he said, nonplussed. He held open the door.

Outside, the stars twinkled against a deep velvet sky, the mountains outlined by the glow of the city. And above them on the hill, the palace glittered. Beyond the courtyard of the embassy, storefronts had stayed open, and buskers sang with their violin cases open as street vendors cooked up local cuisines.

A party for all.

Her mother and father got into the first limousine, and it pulled away.

"Can't we just stay here?" he said as the second limousine pulled up. "It smells amazing, like one of Moose's barbecues."

"That's the grilled cevapi—minced meat sausages of lamb, beef, and pork served on flatbread. Watch the sauce, though. It'll take off the roof of your mouth." The footman had opened her door, and she got in.

"Spoken from experience?" He followed her in.

"Oh, yes. I couldn't taste anything for two weeks." She folded her hand into his. It still felt weird to have him this close, this intimate, but . . .

But maybe this was what trusting—really trusting someone—felt like.

"We'll definitely have to get some pretzels later. They make them fresh every day, and they melt in your mouth."

"Keep going and we won't make it to the ball."

She laughed, and he looked down at her with a smile. "That's what I mourned the most."

She frowned.

"Your laughter. The idea that I'd never hear it again."

Her smile fell. "I really am sorry I put you through all that."

He nodded. "I am starting to understand. I think I have a little PTSD from being shot at yesterday."

Oh.

"Hey." He turned and touched her face. "I was kidding. It's not my first time being shot at. I think being arrested by the palace guards was more traumatizing. That was a first."

"And last, hopefully."

He met her eyes. "I know this mission is important. But I have my own mission, London. And that's to keep you alive and get you home. *That* is my goal."

Sweet. "Okay."

And, *aw,* he probably deserved to know the reason behind the look that had passed between her and her mother. She glanced at the driver, but he stared straight ahead. Schooling her voice, she said, "When I was eighteen, I was invited to the Rosengala, the Rose Ball of Queen Katherine of Lauchtenland. I wanted a date, so I invited a boy—a man—I'd met in Russia during our time there. He and I had corresponded for years after we lived there, and I thought he liked me. His name was Ruslan, and he stayed in the embassy residence. He ended up trying to plant a bug in my mother's office, so that ended our short romance pretty quickly."

"Seriously."

"He'd joined the KGB. Wanted to prove himself. I should have seen through it."

"You were eighteen."

"Yeah, well, when we found out, he tried to run and died in a shootout with one of the embassy guards, who was also fatally injured." She looked at Shep. "The guard had a wife and two kids and had just brought them over from America, so that was . . ." She looked away, her throat suddenly tight. "I'll never forget the way his wife looked at me. And no, she probably didn't know the details, but I did. . . ." She looked back at him. "I vowed never to let someone betray me again."

"Kind of a hard vow to keep."

"You only get betrayed if you trust." She looked up at him. "Don't betray me."

His mouth opened. Then it closed and his gaze met hers. "I would sooner lose my soul."

Oh. And see, this was why she needed him, trusted him, loved . . .

She swallowed. Because *oh,* did she love him, and please let this night end well so they could go back home to their lives.

Ziggy's words crawled into her head. *"You won't be happy until you are true to the person you were made to be."*

Tonight, she'd be Laney Steele for the last time.

They pulled up to a courtyard midway up the mountain, where the castle entrance road wound up and then under the first archway of the castle. It then rose to the next level and through another gate, then finally the third level and under a massive tower. Lights lined the path of the winding entrance, guards standing in full regalia outside each gate.

They entered the main courtyard, and the limo lined up behind her parents', drawing alongside a magnificent cathedral, also lit up, the ornate stained-glass windows splashing color out into the night.

"Do you know why every castle has a chapel inside it?" London asked.

"So that the sovereign of the land can go to his sovereigns and pray for protection."

She looked at him. "You did read a lot."

"And my sister and I made up a game one summer about knights and armies and kingdoms. Every kingdom has a hierarchy of power—and it's all about protection. From the serfs to the lords, to the barons or maybe earls who then pay tribute to the duke, who then owes homage to the prince or king of the land. The king has no one above him to seek protection from except God. Hence the chapel. The very wealthy kingdoms had a priest on staff, and if they were a large kingdom, they might even have a bishop on site, which could mean a visit from the Pope, but they'd need vineyards for that, to host a grand event. Usually gala events like this were used to keep an eye on all the other layers of nobility and remind them who was in charge." The limo had pulled up to the door. "They were also very good places for a royal assassination."

Seriously. "Homeschool pays off."

He laughed. "Probably more information than you needed."

Never. She just liked hearing his voice, really, the way he explained things. He was always so calm, so wise.

Yeah, Laney Steele for the last time.

He held out his hand as he slid out, and she took it. "For the record, we'll have no assassinations tonight, thank you."

"Perfect." He slid her hand into the crook of his arm.

They followed her parents into the castle, past enormous pots of lilies at the doors—probably freshly flown in from Greece or Italy. From inside, chamber music spilled, and as they entered, a uniformed butler handed London a program with a map of the grounds and the areas accessible to the guests. She studied her little map as they stood in the receiving line.

"Cryptex isn't on it," Shep said, looking over her shoulder.

"Shame."

He looked at her. "You're doing it again."

"What?"

He shook his head. "I'll tell you later." They'd come up to the entrance hall.

Shep gave their names to another steward, and London handed over their invitation, which the steward then handed to an aide. The receiving line led up to the line of royals, the entire Ribaldi family. Luka, the crown prince, stood next to his mother, looking every inch the royal catch.

And not even close to the man on her arm.

Shep leaned down, his voice in her ear. "Remind me who these people are."

The royal people? "Prince Alrick—youngest. Age twenty. At uni." He was the bookend to his oldest brother, his dark hair a little longer, but with that same confident, charming smile and a build that suggested he'd followed in Luka's stead and started rowing. "The redhead is Princess Madeline, age twenty-two and just finishing up university. I heard she wants to go into the military." They stepped up closer. "The next is Prince Rillian, who is a chopper pilot in the military." Light-brown hair, cut short, he took after his mother's side, the Austrian side, and always reminded her of a younger Maverick with his swagger, despite his European accent.

"I'd probably like him," Shep said.

"Yes. Except he's a bit of a headline maker with the ladies. And then there's Princess Victoria—she's a doctor." And every inch the woman that, once upon a time, London might have wanted to be. Put together, smart, regal.

"And you've met Crown Prince Luka."

His Highness might have heard her, because he glanced down the row between greetings and spotted her. She bowed her head.

Next to her, Shep drew in a breath and stiffened.

Her parents stepped up to their announcement and walked to the center for their greeting.

She tugged Shep down, spoke in his ear. "King Maximillian and Queen Isabella are at the end. Don't forget to bow, and don't go crazy—just nod your head. And it's Your Highness for the princes and princesses and Your Majesty for the king. We stand in front of the entire crew—and here we go."

She waited until they were announced, then walked to the center. She did a small curtsy and Shep bowed his head and King Maximillian smiled and then they were in.

"That wasn't so hard."

"I feel like I'm back in boot camp."

"Calm down. Let's get some food."

They entered a grand reception area with the house of Ribaldi's cursive *R* emblazoned on all of the tapestries that unfurled from the balconies' balustrades, standards hanging from the soaring marble fireplace.

"There's the buffet. I'm grabbing a shrimp crudités. Want one?"

"I'd rather eat my socks."

Wow. She glanced at him. He did seem strung a little tight. "You okay?"

"When are we going to sneak away?"

She glanced around her. "Ix-nay on the eaking-snay."

He frowned.

"Keep your voice down. After dinner, during the dance."

"I might throw up before then."

She patted his arm. "Try to find a plant."

They wandered into the halls, the designated areas, and surveyed the art, read some historical facts. He filled her in on some stories, evidence of him having done some googling. Then they found their assigned chairs in the dining hall. In total, maybe two hundred people stood at the two long tables, waiting for the king to adjourn them to sit.

They settled onto the plush blue-velvet chairs. Gloved waiters removed the cloches from their plates. "What are these?" Shep asked.

"Game hens, I think," she said, and yes, perfectly cooked, along with the lemon broccoli rabe. She dug in.

Shep hardly touched his food.

"It's really good," she said.

"I'll get a pizza back at the embassy."

"You wish," she said, but she didn't blame him. The first time she'd done a covert mission, she too had nearly thrown up. "Dessert—I think it's crème brûlée—then a speech and this is over."

He squeezed her hand under the table.

Right then, Prince Luka came over to her, his hand on her chair. "Delaney Brooks. You look ravishing tonight." He set his hand over hers on the table, and she felt a keycard press upon it. She turned her hand and took the bio card, secreted it back to the table.

She loved it when a plan came together.

"Good to see you too, Mr. Watson," Luka said.

"Your Highness," Shep said stiffly.

London met Luka's eyes. Yes, he was a handsome man, the kind a girl could fall for. If she weren't already taken.

"Save me a dance, chérie?"

She nodded, and he left them.

"You got it?" Shep asked, his gaze following the prince.

"I got it." She tucked the card into her dress.

Shep raised an eyebrow.

"Women have been hiding things in their cleavage for years."

"I'm not going to search you."

She stilled. "Did you just make a joke?"

He shook his head. "Not even a little." But he took her hand again. And now she fought the simmer under her skin, growing hotter, brighter, as the king finished his speech. She'd text York the signal, and he'd send it to Coco from where he was holed up—probably near the outer door to Cryptex—and then the game would begin.

A thousand years later, or maybe just twenty minutes, the guests adjourned and headed to the dance floor, where a small orchestra played a waltz.

"Does anyone know how to dance to this stuff?" Shep said.

"My parents do." She gestured to them on the dance floor. "But after the king and queen leave, they might drag out a DJ and play some real dance music for the young at heart."

"I hope this heist is over by then, and I can't believe that is coming out of my mouth."

She laughed. "Yes. Okay, ready for this?"

He looked at her. "Ready to become a criminal? Oh yeah, can't wait."

"I'm going to go to the washroom. There's a window in there that has good cell reception. I'll send York the signal, then come back out."

"I'll give you one minute after the lights go out. You don't come out, I'm coming in."

"Thanks for the warning."

His mouth pinched.

"You get a little uptight during missions."

"You're just now noticing that?"

"Calm down. This will be over before you can say—"

"Just go to the stupid bathroom."

He followed her down the hallway and then stood at the end of yet another hallway that led to the lavatories. The men's room was across the hall from the ladies' entrance.

She glanced at him, standing with his arms crossed, a fortress at the end of the hallway, a knight. Then he raised his chin and winked, and *yes, see*—everything was going to be just fine.

She slipped into the bathroom. A small antechamber with a bench formed a sort of lobby, and she walked through that to the expanse of the women's lavatory. A long row of sinks extended from the far wall on both sides of a long mirror, and on either side, stalls jutted out.

She walked to the far stall near the outside of the building, beneath the window, locked herself inside, and then pulled her phone from her purse.

She keyed in a text.

London

Go for Coco

Sent it.

A moment later, a text came back.

York

Coco in two.

Two minutes.

And then another five to get down the back stairs and through the hallway and over to Cryptex, key in the code, push through the door, key in the next code, and by that time, if the lights were on, she'd be in.

And uploading the corrupt code that would have terrorist agencies on the run.

Bam. Not bad for a last mission.

She pulled the night-vision monocular from her leg strap and dropped it into her purse. Then she stepped out of the stall, washed her hands, grabbed a cotton towel to wipe them, and then deposited the towel into the linen basket.

Women were walking in and out of the bathroom. She headed out and spotted Shep at the end of the hall. Met his eyes. Nodded.

He gave her a tight smile.

See, big guy, nothing to worry about.

The palace went dark. And here in the hallway, no ambient light eked in from the starlight outside. In fact, the corridor turned instantly to pitch.

No problem. She'd memorized the layout, and she opened her purse to grab the monocular—

A hand pressed against her mouth, a voice in her ear. "Don't fight me."

What?

Tomas.

She slung out an elbow, but he dodged her, and then a prick burned her neck.

That jerk—he'd—

No—no.

The drug hit her fast and hard, and she couldn't believe that this was happening right here, in front of Shep. She tried to call out, but people rushed by her, knocking her into the wall, women screaming in the darkness, and . . .

Tomas, you rat! She thrashed, trying to find purchase even as the darkness crept over her. *No—Shep!*

Tomas was moving her even as her limbs betrayed her, as the darkness closed in around her. Sirens sounded through the castle, blaring, reverberating off the rock and stone, brutal, and drowning her shouts—

Shep!

And then everything went black.

NINE

ONE MINUTE. WAIT ONE MINUTE. EXCEPT Shep had seen London just down the hallway, and—*sheesh,* ten seconds out of his sight and—

Forget this. He pulled out his phone and tapped on the flashlight.

Around him, people panicked under the darkness and the scream of the siren, rushing past him to find an exit, but he stood still, shining his light down the hallway to the bathrooms.

No London.

That didn't make sense.

He spotted a slew of gowned women, but none wore the deepblue V-necked dress that turned London into some kind of lady-in-waiting. He hadn't known what to do with the sense that he'd stepped into a world way over his head as they'd gotten into the limousine.

He stood in the tourniquet of his monkey suit and cast his light around him, that sense crashing over him again. No London, and . . . *shoot.* He knew, just knew, this would happen.

"London!" He raised his voice, but the siren gobbled it.

Maybe she'd already headed to Cryptex. He took off down the hallway toward the stairs, following the map imprinted in his head.

No guard at the top, so perhaps York's plan had worked. Shep raced down the stairs, then the next set to the ground floor, and found the glass corridor that led to the Cryptex entrance along with the external door to the palace.

According to York's timeline, York would be standing on the other side of the door, in the courtyard.

Shep grabbed the handle and opened the door.

York stood on the other side, looking at his phone. He glanced up. "They're trying to turn off the alarm, but Coco has hacked the system. We have maybe three minutes and then the entire system is reset." He glanced past Shep, frowned. "Where's London?"

"Not here," Shep snapped. "She was in the hallway before the blackout. I waited—she never came back to me."

"Maybe she's already at Cryptex." York pushed past him and ran down the glass hallway, Shep on his tail.

Please, please—

Darkness bled through the Cryptex door, and Shep looked inside the glass, through the entry to the lobby behind the barred gate. Just the eyes of the computers, glowing against the night.

"She can't get to the inner area without help," Shep said. "Someone has to hit the buzzer under the desk while she grabs the door."

York turned away. "She's not here."

Duh. Still, the words sliced through Shep. He wanted to put his hand through the glass door.

Instead, he blew out a breath. "Let's go back to the palace. I should have checked the bathroom."

York nodded, and Shep took off back down the corridor to the palace entrance, flew up the stairs.

The lights flickered on, the siren cutting off as soon as they reached the second level.

People stood in the hallways, their hands to their ears.

Shep slowed, strode past them down to the bathroom, paused only a moment, then, "Man on the floor!" He shoved his way into the bathroom.

The door banged against the wall. *Empty.* "London?"

He stalked down one side, searching for a closed door. Nothing. Repeated on the other side.

Turned and spotted himself in the mirror.

He looked like a man who would do violence.

York had followed him in. "Not here?"

"Not. Here." He rounded on York. "Now what?"

"We can't get into Cryptex without her card—"

"Forget the mission, York! She's in *trouble*." He kept his voice low. "Someone took her."

York's mouth tightened. He whirled around and headed back out into the hallway.

Palace guards stalked the hallways, requesting the guests to assemble in the great hall. *Fine*—Shep headed toward the ballroom. *Maybe*—

York followed him. "We need to talk to their security, see if we can get any footage—"

"You took that out, remember?" Shep didn't want to say it, but frankly, he'd hated their entire stupid plan.

Hated the entire gig, really. And sure, he was all for getting London away from this Russian mob, but . . .

Breathe.

London, I'm still on mission. I'll find you.

A number of the guests must have evacuated, because the crowd that assembled in the great hall was sparse. And no London.

Shep held in a word as Prince Luka took the dais. "Please, everyone, stay calm. There is no fire, simply a malfunction of our system. All is well—"

"York."

Shep looked over at the male American voice that called York's name. A man, maybe six foot or more, came through the crowd. He wore a suit, not a tuxedo, so maybe security instead of invited guest. Tawny brown hair cut military short, blue eyes, and bearing a fierce, almost military demeanor as he pushed through the crowd to York.

"Fraser Marshall. What are you doing here?" York held out his hand, met Fraser's with a quick shake, Fraser's other hand gripping York's arm.

"I'm here with Princess Imani and Creed. They're with Pippa." He lifted his chin, indicating someone across the room. Shep followed his gesture and spotted a woman standing in a dressy black suit, her dark hair back in a high bun, wearing an earpiece.

"I should have guessed," York said.

"Pippa thought she spotted her old roommate, London, across the room earlier, and then I saw you. Something's going down. What is it?"

"You know London?" Shep said, stepping up to the man.

"Shep Watson—this is Fraser Marshall. He's a former SEAL, now works security for the Royal House of Blue from Lauchtenland. Fraser—Shep. He's on the Alaska Air One Rescue team and is here with London, who is here visiting her parents. Her mother is the US Ambassador to Montelena."

Fraser shook Shep's hand. "I met your outfit last year during a rescue. Moose still at the helm over there?"

Shep nodded, but he was more interested in—"How do you know London?"

"She's Pippa's friend, really. Where is she?"

Pippa. Roommate. University. Her story came back to him.

"Bathroom," York said.

Shep turned to Fraser. "Actually, she went missing in the blackout."

Fraser frowned. "Missing?"

York held up his hand, but Shep was tired of the games. "Yes. And frankly—"

"She's not missing," York said, giving Shep a glare. "She just evacuated with the others."

Shep blinked at him, his mouth tightening. What was his game?

"We're about to leave too." Fraser raised an arm and gestured to Pippa, beckoning her over.

York had grabbed his phone, texting.

Hello, did no one get it? London. Was. Missing. With an assassin on her tail and—

York's hand grabbed his arm. He held up his phone. Shep read the text.

Coco
_____
I got the GPS on her phone. We're tracking her.

Shep stared at him and a terrible realization gripped him, brought him back to a conversation he'd had months ago with Colt Kingston, the man who had tasked Shep to watch London.

"You want someone to find her."

"No. But we do want someone to make a move. We've been trying to figure out who might be behind some events that happened globally. And she's the key to that."

Now he turned cold as he looked at York. "You *planned* this?"

York's mouth opened, then closed. "Let's talk outside."

Shep clamped his hand on York's wrist, tightened his grip, then pried York's hand from his arm. "I'm done with this."

He turned and pushed through the crowd as the music started up again, probably an attempt to return the world to some semblance of calm and order.

Like the ensemble playing on the deck of the Titanic as it sank into the sea.

"Shep!" York's voice, but he ignored it.

He spotted Prince Luka heading his direction through the crowd, but he was done with the bowing and the *Your Highness*es and the posturing.

He wanted London. Now.

Finding himself in the grand reception hall, Shep strode through it to the doors.

"Mr. Watson."

He slowed, turned.

"Is everything all right?" Luka came closer, frowned. "Where is Delaney?"

"Good question," Shep said as York pushed through the doors to the room, and behind him, his friend Fraser. "My girlfriend went missing in the chaos. I'm trying to find her."

Prince Luka seemed genuinely concerned, his brow tightening, his chest rising and falling. "You think something . . . untoward happened?"

"Untoward—yes, I think something *untoward* happened. I think she was kidnapped." He glared at York then, coming up to them.

"Let me get my security to look into this—"

"We'll find her, Your Highness," said York. Behind him, Pippa came in, along with a woman in a ballgown and a tall tuxedoed man with dark hair. The woman wore a small tiara in her black curly hair.

"I should know that if the Caleb Group is around, there's trouble." This from Pippa.

"The Caleb Group?" asked Prince Luka. "What is that?"

"It doesn't matter," Shep said. "Yes, you can help. Search the entire castle."

Prince Luka nodded.

"I'm going to see if she's outside." Shep stalked toward the door, hit the corridor, then pushed through to the entry yard.

The air held a crispness, the breath of snow, or rain, lacing the air. He noticed that York hadn't followed, so maybe he was staying behind to help search.

He breathed in, listening to the banging of his heartbeat.

And tasted the disappointment that she wasn't out here, waiting for him. A number of guests, however, stood shivering in the cold, waiting for limousines to fetch them. He scanned the group just to confirm, many of the guests now bundled in fur or wraps.

The cool air slicked through him, cooled the sweat that Shep hadn't realized he'd worked up, the one bead that dripped down his back.

London, where are you?

He lifted his gaze to the night sky, so many stars blinking down at him, a perfect thumbnail moon hanging over the faraway peaks. *Lord, please help me find her.*

How had whoever had taken her gotten her out of the castle? Except, this wasn't the only door—he knew that.

And then . . . *shoot*. The *tunnel*.

He ran a hand down his face.

York pushed out of the doors.

"Why are you not searching the castle?"

"We are—*they* are."

"You should try the tunnel."

York frowned. "Tunnel?"

"There's a secret tunnel into the castle. We used it yesterday to escape the assassin. Maybe they saw it, used it to get in—or out." He shook his head. "I cannot believe you used London as bait. Who are you after?"

York gestured away from the others, moved over to a space away from the awning, in the shadows.

"We knew that Drago Petrov was after her—of course he was. But we also hoped that Alan Martin would poke his head out. We lost him after—well, he tried to set off a bomb in Lauchtenland a year ago, and since then, we can't get a bead on him. We thought maybe getting London back on the grid—"

Shep lifted his hands, then clenched them, put them back at his sides. Turned away. *"If it is possible, as far as it depends on you, live at peace with everyone." Fine.* But *oh,* he wanted to put his fist into something. Or someone.

"Listen, we've got this—"

"Clearly you do *not* have this. I cannot believe that you . . . that at the very least you didn't tell us—tell *me*—of this possibility."

York exhaled hard, and his voice bore apology. "Yes. Agreed. But we had this one chance, and we didn't want anything to keep us from finding him."

Shep blinked at him. "What if they kill her?"

"They won't kill her." York met his gaze, and Shep wondered just who this man was and had been, because a steely look came into it. Lethal and cold. "They need her seed code to get into her account."

"They could hurt her to get it."

York didn't move. Then, "She's a Black Swan—"

"She's not a freakin' superhero! She's a human being who—" *Okay, breathe.* He'd let himself off his leash a little there and now reined it back in. "She's the woman I love."

"And I get that. Better than you think. But you have to know that she *does* know how to handle herself. She's tough—"

"Tough enough to be *tortured*?" Again, words he'd never thought he'd say. He had, however, cut his voice low.

York's eyes bore the truth.

"Oh my—" Shep held up his hands, then fisted them. It did no one any good for him to strangle the man. "Where is she? Has your tracker found her?"

York held up his phone and clicked on a link. A GPS screen opened, and he zoomed out. His jaw tightened.

"What?"

"It's looks like they're heading east. Which means they're in a chopper."

"What's east?" Shep reached for the phone. York yielded it, and he turned the view to satellite mode. Stilled.

"Mountains," York said. "All mountains."

Shep shoved the phone back into York's hands. Then he turned and walked down the stairs and across the courtyard, into the darkness.

Stood for a moment in the cold, just to get his head on right.

Then he pulled out his phone.

The line picked up on the second ring, and he hoped they weren't out on a call.

"Shep. Everything okay?"

Just hearing Moose's voice felt like a handshake, firm and solid.

"No. London's been kidnapped."

Silence. And he didn't know where Moose might be, but he dearly hoped he'd heard the question in Shep's statement.

"What do you need?"

"A chopper. My team. She's in the mountains, and I need to get her."

"Okay. Sit tight. I'll be in touch."

He hung up. He looked up at the dark sky, the stars. The cold needled through him as the wind began to blow.

But he didn't fear the cold.

No, he relished it to keep him sharp, focused.

And still on mission.

The last thing, the very last thing, Moose wanted to do was to fly halfway across the world and leave Tillie and Hazel alone.

Then again, the second to last thing he wanted to do was abandon Shep. And London. Poor Shep had sounded stripped and not a little wrecked, and Moose had never let a teammate hang out to dry, so . . .

"You have to go," Tillie said from where she sat at his island, drinking coffee. She wore a pair of yoga pants and a long sweatshirt, her dark hair pulled back, having just returned from dropping Hazel off at school.

Because they were all apparently trying to pretend that someone hadn't just tried to burn them to death.

She'd listened with a grim look as Moose spoke to Shep on speakerphone.

Now, Moose ran his hands down his face. *Aw,* he hated this. "We haven't gotten the fire report back yet. What if it was arson? What if someone is trying to kill you?"

"Like who, Moose? Rigger is dead."

"Like Harry Benton! He threatened me—and everyone I care about—at the courthouse."

A beat, then, "That's still playing in your head? C'mon, Moose, the guy was angry, not serious. Most likely, it was my ancient furnace finally giving up the ghost. They said the fire started in the garage."

"Which might be the easiest place for an arsonist to get in—"

"Just cool your jets." She slid off the stool, came over to him. *Oh,* he liked it when she put her hands on his chest, stepped up to him, into his orbit. The action always settled the swell of emotions swirling inside him.

Like anger. Or frustration.

Panic.

"You've let Harry Benton and his words win. He is long gone, back to Illinois. And Hazel and I are fine in your fortress here, so just . . . get on a plane already."

She and Hazel had moved back in, taking the two guest rooms, and with Axel still hanging out in the basement, a sort of permanent chaperone, it felt like everything might sort itself out.

He still hadn't come around to asking her again, or maybe for the first time, really, but he would. Soon. Now he wrapped his hands around her upper arms and met her beautiful brown eyes. "Maybe I'll call Oaken and see if he can come over."

"What's he going to do, hit Benton over the head with his guitar? I have more personal security skills in my pinky toe than he does in his entire toned, cover-model body. Seriously."

Probably, and that made him smile a little.

"There it is, the Moose smile that makes the whole world feel better. No wonder Shep called you." She looped her hands up around his neck. "He seems pretty freaked out. And that is *not* Shep. He doesn't unravel."

"No, he doesn't," he said. "But if you went missing . . . oh wait, you were. . . ."

She narrowed her eyes, and he leaned down, his lips just a whisper from hers. "And I unraveled."

"And then you found me." She lifted herself up to kiss him.

Technically, she'd found *him*, but he wasn't going to argue. Not when she tasted of coffee, smelled of something floral, maybe her shampoo, and felt so perfect and right in his arms. Like she'd always belonged.

Should always belong.

Tillie, please marry me.

The question lingered in his chest as she deepened her kiss.

Oh. Boy.

And yep, that's when his brother's footsteps sounded on the stairway from the basement.

Tillie let Moose go and stepped back just as the basement door opened.

"I knew it. As soon as Tillie moved in, it's like, 'What's around door number one? A little snoggin'?' You guys need to hang a sock on the doorknob or something."

"No sock needed," Moose said, and stepped away. "But maybe we should attach a bell to you."

"Yeah. *Meow. Meow.* Just marry her already." Axel came over to the fridge and opened it, grabbing the milk.

But Tillie had gone quiet, glancing at Moose, and he'd put a hand around his neck and . . . *shoot.* Bad timing, again.

Axel shut the fridge door. Glanced at the couple. "Something I'm missing?"

"Don't drink out of the carton. And Shep called. London's missing."

Axel set down the milk carton. "Again?"

"Really?" Tillie said. "Axel."

"I'm just saying, what is her deal? Talk about needing a bell." He reached for a glass in the cupboard.

"Shep said she's been kidnapped."

Axel set down the glass.

"Shep is freaking out," Tillie added.

Axel picked up the carton to pour. "Shep doesn't freak out. He might go all dark and scary inside, but he does not do freaking out."

Silence.

Axel looked at Moose. "Wow. It's really that serious?"

"Really."

He picked up the glass. "So, what, are we saddling up?"

Moose looked at Tillie, who'd folded her arms, staring at him. He sighed. "Yes."

Axel was mid-drink. He put the glass down. "Yes? I was sort of kidding. What, we're jumping a plane for . . . where's he at again?"

"Montelena. It's a country near Switzerland and northern Italy, south of Austria—"

Axel held up his hand. "Europe. Check. And we're supposed to do *what*?"

"Shep said they'd tracked her into the mountains, so . . ."

Axel closed up the milk carton. Put it back. Closed the fridge.

Turned. "Just so I got this right. We're flying over there so we can . . . sneak into the lair of an international terrorist and rescue a woman who is a little like the female version of James Bond. This is like calling in the Boy Scouts for a mission to help SEAL Team Six, but whatever. I'm in."

"Good. I have a couple favors I can call in and get a plane."

"A *private* plane?"

"Remember that favor I did last year—"

"The one where you flew into Russian airspace and dropped a couple hitchhikers out into midair to parachute into Kamchatka? The one where you broke a couple international laws and nearly got fired at by ground-to-air missiles? Yep, I remember that one."

"Thanks for that." He glanced at Tillie, whose eyes had widened. "Long story."

"Can't wait to hear it."

He turned to Axel. "I think I can get the same plane."

"Nice. Want me to call Boo?"

He looked at Tillie. "Yes. And Oaken. See if they'll both come over while we're gone."

Tillie sighed.

Axel glanced at her, back at Moose. "Oh, I see. We're still freaking about Tillie's house."

"Hello. It *exploded*."

Axel lifted his hand. "Not arguing. I talked with Flynn yesterday, and she says it's still an ongoing investigation. So yeah, maybe you want to call Dawson and see if he'll camp out here too."

"Not a bad idea."

Tille looked at Moose. "We're fine."

"Yeah, well, maybe I'm not." And *oops,* maybe he shouldn't have said that in front of Axel, but, "Every night I wake up with the nightmare of you inside that house, Tillie. Burning to death. If you hadn't smelled the gas and gotten out of the house, you might have been."

He walked over to her. Took her hands. "I just . . . I'm just trying to keep life from crumbling beneath us."

Then he pulled her to himself, wrapping his arms around her, holding her. Wanting to never let her go.

"I'll be packing," Axel said. "That's your ten-minute warning." He left them in the kitchen.

Tillie raised her head, met Moose's gaze. "It's going to be okay, Moose. I can take care of myself, and Hazel, and we will be here waiting when you get back."

Waiting for their tomorrow to start.

And maybe that was the problem. Every time he took a step, the world slid out from under him. How could he ask Tillie to marry him when he didn't know what kind of future he could give them?

"As long as you promise to come back."

He kissed her, slow and long and giving her every promise he could make.

Except the one he wanted.

And ten minutes later, he walked out the door with Axel, praying he wasn't making the worst mistake of his life.

London opened her eyes, stared at the creamy plastered ceiling, light filtering in through a small window too high for her to see out of, too small for her to climb through.

Aw, they'd brought her to Castle Petrus.

The twelfth-century fortress in the mountain on the edge of the Austrian-Italian border in the high Dolomite Alps, near Tyrol, Italy. Built into the mountain and seated on a narrow outcropping, it was accessible only via a tunnel through the rock. The castle itself sat one hundred and twenty-three meters from the valley floor, a sheer drop from the high window in her room, and it clung to a cave that contained passageways for escape.

But from the outside, impregnable.

Especially since she was still wearing her dress. Torn, the skirt ripped, the sequins torn off in areas, at least the sleeves were intact.

And she was barefoot, so that was uber fun.

The smells of the castle—aged wattle and daub, wood fires from ancient days, and even the scent of the high firred mountains around her—filtered through the thick walls.

She lay on the wooden floor of the room, the door closed, just the strip of light to ward off the chill, just her heartbeat as company. Her neck throbbed where Tomas had dosed her—and—

Shep.

She sat up, her pulse in her throat. *Please, don't let Tomas have . . .*

She closed her eyes. Reached inside. Steeled herself. Because she knew—just knew—that having Shep involved would only get him killed.

Please, God.

The door opened and she climbed to her feet as a brute of a man stood at the door. Six-foot-gigantic, he had the girth of a Brahman bull and held a taser. "*Davai.*"

"Let's go" in Russian, so . . . back to the Petrov Bratva, apparently.

She pressed back her hair, then pulled it out of the unraveled French knot, shook it out, and stepped into the persona of the only one who could save her.

Laney Steele.

Igor pushed her ahead of himself, and she walked down the hallway, the stone on one side, a worn brick floor beneath her feet, to a stairwell that curled down around the edge, the expanse in the middle falling down five stories. At the next story down, he pointed along a hallway, and she headed toward a large room with a massive stone hearth. Windows overlooked the valley below.

She didn't know why she expected to see Drago Petrov waiting for her. The very name had evoked in her the image of Ivan Drago, the Russian who'd fought Rocky in the fourth installment of the movie—thick, tall, spiky blond hair, indestructible. She'd never met Drago Petrov, but his reputation had built in her head enough to make her exhale when she spotted Tomas standing alone in the room, his hands in his pockets.

This room was attired like a ski lodge—a thick wool rug, a couple leather sofas, a worn coffee table, and a fire in the hearth—minus, of course, the ambience.

So, maybe the lair of a possessed king, like in *Lord of the Rings,* and *thank you very much, Shep,* for putting *The Hobbit* in her head. There, and maybe not back again.

Outside, it seemed winter had found this higher elevation, snow on the mountains as far as she could see.

"Where's Shep?" she said as she came into the room.

Tomas wore a pair of black jeans, a white woolen sweater, had shaved and cleaned up from his short-term captivity. Now he just frowned at her. "Shep? Why would we bring him?"

Oh. But she didn't exhale.

"Although, he and I do have unfinished business. Goodbyes we didn't say, so . . . perhaps you're right. That was a mistake. Next time, we'll make sure he joins us." He winked then and gestured to the sofa, as if they were on holiday.

"What's going on?" She sank onto the sofa. Igor came over to stand beside her. Probably held the taser on her, but she didn't look. "I thought we were working together."

"Until your people decided not to trust me."

She raised an eyebrow.

He held up a hand. "I know, I know, but it was a perfect plan. And then you had to go and create your own virus." He put a hand to his chest. "I'm hurt."

"You lied to us. Your virus was a heist."

"And it would have worked." He sighed. "It's okay. At least you have a fresh bio card." He pulled it out of his pocket. "Or I should say—I do."

Her mouth tightened around the edge, but she raised a shoulder.

"You won't get the seed code from me."

"Really." He tapped the card against his hand.

"Tomas, what do you want?"

"Besides the seed code? How about . . . justice? Or would it be called retribution?"

"For what?"

"Leaving me to die in Zermatt."

She leaned back. "So now what? Take the money and run? The Bratva will follow you."

"Oh, I know they will. Day and night, like a bad odor." He perched on the arm of the opposite sofa. "Almost like they're in my head."

She stared at him as he smiled. Slow and . . .

Wait. "Where's Drago Petrov?"

"It's hard to be the leader without any clout. And when all your money goes missing . . ." He raised a shoulder. "And when you have the money, you have the power."

She frowned.

"It's more of a position than a person."

No. "You killed him?"

"Not personally. But I knew people who wanted him dead. You don't count the Petrovs' money without knowing who they double-crossed."

He crossed his arms. "You're looking at the leader of the Drago Petrovs, yes. And I want my money back."

Her mouth opened. "You weren't . . . I mean—"

"Yes, darling. Drago Petrov died the day you stole his money. I thought it would be easy—blame it on you."

And suddenly, it all clicked. How Alan Martin had found them, betrayed them. And how Tomas had so easily "obtained" the seed code. And even why he'd stayed behind at the foot of the mountain in Zermatt.

He'd sent her up on the mountain for Alan to kill her. Maybe even serve her up as a trophy.

"You faked your own death. You weren't even *at* the chalet for the avalanche."

"No. Watching. And when you went missing . . . well, I went back for my money. The last thing I expected was for you to have already transferred it to your own wallet. Tricky, tricky girl."

See, there was a reason she hadn't told him about the transfer, she just hadn't known it.

"Why didn't you kill me when you first met me?"

"We needed to see who you were working for. And eliminate them. And it worked out better than I thought—or would have. Drago is a ghost, and I can walk in and out of any country I want, no questions asked. It's amazing what you can do when you're dead." He leaned forward. "Although, the key is to *stay* dead, darling."

Her mouth tightened. "You sent the Orphans after me."

He shrugged.

"You *betrayed* me."

"That's rich."

She looked away.

He got up, put his hands in his pockets. Smiled. "So, I'll start with manners. I'd like my money back, please."

"Seriously?"

He nodded to the man behind her, and Igor pressed the taser to her neck.

"Tomas—"

"You will give us the seed code, sweetheart. Because if you don't, you're not the only one who will suffer."

London's eyes widened as another version of Igor came into

the room, this time guiding a woman by the arm, her hands tied behind her back. Her long dark hair hung a little disheveled from a ponytail, and she wore all back—black leggings, black tunic, black boots.

"Ziggy!"

Blood pooled at the side of her mouth, her eye bruised, and she winced a little when the man shoved her down on the sofa beside London.

"What—"

"Sorry I've been incommunicado. Got tied up." She winked.

"What are you—" She turned to Tomas. "What is she doing here?"

"Your legendary Black Swan leader? Oh, she's been causing trouble for me for years. I thought it might be time to come to an agreement."

Ziggy narrowed her eyes at him. "What kind of agreement is that?"

"Oh, not with you, darling. Her." He nodded at London.

London stilled.

"You tell us the seed code or we beat her to death." He looked at Igor. Nodded.

Igor slapped Ziggy. She slammed into the cushions even as her foot came out and kicked her attacker in the knee. He stepped back, cursed, and rebounded, his fist pulled back.

London leaped up, threw herself in front of Ziggy. "Stop!"

A thousand volts hit her back, stiffened her body, and every muscle contracted. She fell to the floor, paralyzed, her breath shucked out.

"That's enough, Staz."

The volts instantly stopped, but her muscles refused to recover, and she lay immobilized, pain clogging her breaths, her brain.

Ziggy called him a name in some language London didn't know.

"You Black Swans are supposed to be invincible," said a voice.

She knew that voice. It nudged something deep in the back of her brain, but she couldn't . . . seem to . . .

Her breath came back with a whoosh, the paralysis shaking out of her limbs, which turned prickly and sharp. She lay on the floor, just breathing, fighting to get her strength back.

First rule of fighting: wait for an advantage. She'd been stupid, impulsive, and, well, so very London.

C'mon, Laney. Find your way back.

The man who'd spoken knelt down, and a hand pushed her over to her back.

And then she stared up at him.

A scar over his forehead, dark hair—she remembered thinking of him as handsome when she'd arrived at the chalet, before she knew he'd killed her handler. He wore a wool winter coat and a pair of leather gloves, and Ziggy breathed his name even as London tried to form it.

"Alan Martin. I should have known you were behind all this."

As London watched, he stood, looked at Ziggy. "Miss Mattucci. Lovely as always. And tenacious. Oh, and bloody. My goodness, I hope you don't lose a tooth."

He stepped back, and Ziggy's Igor hauled up London and set her down on the sofa again beside Ziggy.

Alan stepped back, reached out to shake Tomas's hand. "Sorry it took so long for me to get here. What did I miss?"

"I was just asking Laney for her seed code."

Alan took off his gloves, put them in his pocket. "Oh good. I hate to miss anything." He undid his jacket and sat on the opposite sofa. Folded his hands.

Tomas glanced at him, just a hint of a frown, then got up. "Are you sure we need to make this difficult?"

London froze. He wouldn't . . . She looked at Ziggy, her tight jaw, her dark eyes. And Ziggy looked back at her.

"Assurgo."

Stand up. But . . . even as she stared into Ziggy's eyes, she saw it. *Help was coming.*

She nodded, and Ziggy closed her eyes as if steeling herself.

And then everything inside London turned to ice when Alan Martin said, softly, "Proceed."

Igor took a step toward Ziggy.

London froze. And then—*nope. Not happening.*

Her body buzzed, still on fire from the taser, and fury flamed inside her. She dove at Igor, hand out, her palm slamming against his chin.

He fell back, just a little, enough for Ziggy to come alive. London heard—no, sensed—

the scuffle between Ziggy and Martin even as muscle memory kicked in.

She was bleeding from the mouth, barefoot, and dressed in rags, but inside her, Laney Steele raked to life.

Help was coming.

No. Help was here.

TEN

FELT WAY TOO MUCH LIKE SHEP WAS SITTING in the Air One chopper, flying over the mountains of Alaska, on his way to a rescue.

Except the Dolomite Alps seemed higher, more jagged, and between them, in the valleys, tiny snowcapped houses sat in pristine white storybook clusters.

But he *was* on his way to a rescue.

Shep sat on the deck of a chopper that Fraser—who'd turned out to be more useful than he'd expected—had managed to procure from some contact he had in the States, who had a contact in Italy who'd shown up with a twin-engine Airbus H145, which had had Moose salivating, despite his jet lag, as he walked around the machine at the private airport in Luciella.

Axel had shown up too, along with Boo—who flew into Shep's arms, tight around his neck. "Are you okay?"

Not even a little. He couldn't believe the nightmare was repeating itself. But maybe a little better than last time because, "Thanks for coming. We're going to get her back."

Boo nodded. "They tried to leave me behind, but . . . seriously,

I couldn't believe it when Flynn told me that London was alive. All this time. Alive."

"Yes. And I'd like to keep her that way." *Please, please, oh God, let her still be alive.* "And, um . . . she'll tell you everything when we find her."

See, his voice barely shook.

"She'd better."

It had been a desperate move to reach out to his Air One team, but they were all he had. He didn't trust York—not completely—and while he liked Fraser and Pippa, and even the royal they came attached to, he needed people he could trust.

He'd let Fraser and York do the shooting. He was here to find London, keep her safe, bring her home.

Mission accepted.

He'd barely slept, but his head had never felt more clear, the map he'd studied in the embassy embedded in his head. He'd run scenarios with Fraser and York while waiting for his team. Mitch had helped by pointing out landmarks, his face strained despite his cool demeanor. They'd follow a river through the mountains as they rose in elevation, then fly above a ridgeline of cliffs to a tiny village where her GPS pin had stopped moving.

Please let her be alive. He couldn't stop praying it.

"Coco, our hacker, says that the location is an old twelfth-century fortress. It's built into a mountain, with a sheer drop on the outside. Best route in might be through these tunnels." York had leaned over the map too, adding his thoughts.

"Best route in is down a static line and in through a window," Shep said. "Right into the room where they're holding her and then back out. Just like that." He kept his voice calm, but really—the sooner they were in and out, the better.

Unless she was hurt—*please, God, don't let her be hurt.*

"This is what we're dealing with, Shep. The high windows are too small for a person. There are some second-story windows that we could get in. Or, like I say again, through the tunnels."

"Which will probably be guarded." This from Fraser, who had sat in a nearby straight chair. Apparently, he was a former Navy SEAL, so again, Shep liked him. And especially when he stood up and looked at a grainy picture that someone had pulled off the internet and blown up, then laid out his plan. "I think a better choice would be to put down on this walkway." He ran his finger across a balcony that seemed to run the length of the castle, midway up. "And if we rig two lines, York and I go down, break through the windows, come in hard and fast, provide cover, and then Axel and Shep drop in and find London, get her home."

He'd glanced at York then, who'd nodded. "Yeah, okay."

"I'd really prefer to have Pippa on the line," Fraser had said, "but she needs to stay here with the princess. She's technically her secretary, but I don't trust Imani's protection to anyone else."

Whatever. Shep couldn't care a whit about some stupid princess.

"I'll get the tech you need," promised Mitch, and by the time Moose had arrived, they had the chopper loaded and ready for its pilot. Shep had even found medical supplies, a stretcher, and a survival pack aboard, so Fraser's friend's contact might be in the rescue business too.

They'd climbed aboard, and he'd noticed that Fraser and York had kitted up, wearing body armor, carrying weapons, the spec ops part of the team. The rest wore jackets and pants, and he'd wished for the safety of flight suits. They also wore European-style suspender harnesses, which he'd customized to fit. He'd already checked all of their webbing and the winch. Good to go.

Fraser had clipped two ropes into the brackets in the top inside edge of the door—their fast ropes, maybe. As they'd taken off, the duo had climbed into harnesses, added descenders, then hooked into the line.

Now they sat, weapons across their backs, buckled in.

Him too. He'd already fitted his harness on, as had Axel, and Boo would run the line. He didn't know the other chopper pilot—a male—who had climbed in front beside Moose. He wore sunglasses and seemed to know the terrain, so maybe a local.

Now, nearly twenty-four hours since the world had gone dark and London had been snatched from under his nose—twenty-four hours of wanting to throw up, to hit something, to take apart every choice he'd made since finding London alive—he soared over the mountains.

He should never have let her leave Alaska.

They'd left the valley, climbing into the altitudes, the occasional hunting cabin or sheep farm coming into view. A deep-blue lake sat in a pocket surrounded by whitened peaks, a small congregation of houses along the shoreline. A misty cloud hung to the east, and in the west, the falling sun cast deep, long shadows into the valleys.

According to their plan, they'd arrive onsite just as the sun set, hopefully also distracting London's captors from any clear shots at the chopper.

His entire body had turned cold with that comment, made by Moose, when York had briefed him on the details.

Which indicated, however, that his boss understood the gravity of their situation. Moose had been a military rescue pilot once upon a time, so he knew all about edge-of-the-spear ops.

There would be no Purple Hearts if the chopper went down.

Shep glanced at Moose at the helm. Wow, he didn't deserve these guys. The fact that they'd shown up . . .

Moose's voice came through the headset. "According to GPS, we're ten clicks away. I'll do a flyover, and then we can deploy if you guys are a go."

Fraser gave him a thumbs-up.

Interesting to see their brief reunion. Apparently Moose had plucked Fraser's brother out of the freezing Bering Sea last year. Shep hadn't gone on that op—Harrington, one of his buddies from the PEAK team in Montana, had been up visiting, and Moose had been trying to recruit him, so Moose had taken him out on the ride into the wild, churning lethal blue.

Shep had been thinking about reaching out to the PEAK guys, seeing if there might be a place for him—

"There it is," York said.

The castle seemed to grow out of the mountainside, backed up against a yawning cave, maybe seven levels in total including the two towers on each end. Black slate roofs, small windows, but along the walkway, larger leaded-glass windows suggested Fraser's plan might work. The setting sun had turned them golden, the entire place an imposing prison.

Fraser lowered a monocular. "I don't see any guards."

Moose pulled up over the mountain, and they got a good look at the depth of the cave. Snowpack covered the backside of the mountain, falling into lush green forest at the bottom that washed down to a valley, cordoned on every side with more high snow-layered peaks. About halfway down the slope, on a ridge, framed by a scattering of trees and surrounded by snow, a small clearing held an A-frame hunting cabin.

Below, in the valley, maybe thirty clicks in the distance, sat another red-roofed storybook village.

Moose angled the chopper around. "We'll go in from the top, take them by surprise. Get ready to go, and I'll bring you as close as I can."

Shep opened the door and clipped his lead to the bar on the top while he unhooked the line from the winch.

They flew over the top of the mountain. Fraser and York had also gotten up, holding on to their bottom rope with one gloved hand, the above-door bar with the other.

"It's been a while since I've fast-roped," York said.

Fraser looked at him.

The chopper moved over the fortress, descending, the walkway extending from the stone maybe ten feet deep and some fifty feet below.

Moose hovered the chopper. "Go."

"Out the door," Fraser said and turned. "Wait until we're clear!"

Shep knew how to do this, thank you.

Fraser moved down to the chopper skid, York next to him, then suddenly they were zipping down the line, the rope moving through their descenders. Moose held them at a hover, the specialized rotors of his Airbus allowing him to pull in closer to the mountain.

The men landed, unhooked, and then deployed into the house.

Just like that.

Shep hooked into the line.

"I'm right behind you," Axel said.

Shep turned and, just like Fraser, stepped out of the door, onto the skid, and then Boo was sending him down the line with the winch. Not quite as cool as the fast-roping, but it did the job, and his feet touched down on the stones of the balcony. He unhooked, then sent the line back up.

He didn't wait for Axel.

Fraser and York hadn't broken the windows, just pushed one open, and now he climbed inside too.

He entered a large room, a hearth on one side, a couple sofas, a carpet over the stone floor. Empty.

York stood near the chairs. "Blood over here."

Yeah, Shep didn't need to hear that.

Axel came in through the window.

York gestured to Fraser, and he took off down the hall.

"Stay behind us," Fraser said, and followed.

"Hurry up," Shep said, but hugged the wall until York gestured to him.

Fraser was already at a stairwell landing. "Up or down?"

"I'll go down," York said.

Fraser headed up, and Shep followed him. Axel went down with York.

A chill gathered on the next floor, emanating out of the brick floor and granite wall of the mountain. A series of closed doors ran down the hallway. Wooden and thick, with locks hanging from bulky hasps.

Fraser crept down the hall. He thumped on a door. "London?"

Nothing, and Shep went to the next one. "London! Are you in there?"

Down the hall, a voice. "Here!"

Shep ran toward it. Slammed his fist against the door. "London!"

A beat. "Shep?"

His knees nearly buckled.

"Stand back," Fraser said. He'd pulled out a long metal lever, like a fireplace poker. He must have picked it up along the way. He put it into the lock and pried it open with a snap.

Shep shoved past him into the room.

And then his knees *did* give out. London sat on the floor in her ball gown, although it had lost its magic, her knees up to herself, bruised and bloodied. And next to her, on the floor, a woman. A badly injured woman with dark hair, her face swollen, her eyes closed.

"Ziggy," Fraser said, his voice sounding a little wrecked as he knelt in front of her. "What happened?"

"A couple Igors," London said quietly. "But we hurt them back."

Shep couldn't listen to her anymore. He knelt on the other side of her, did a quick assessment of Ziggy. "Her arm looks broken, and—" She wore a black tunic and he raised it. "Bruising. So, internal bleeding, maybe broken ribs." He checked her eyes. "Pupils aren't fixed, so hopefully no brain damage."

"She just kept fighting, trying to take out Martin." London's voice bore an edge, and she looked . . . angry. Shep so wanted to pull her into his arms, but she looked . . . different.

And definitely not fragile.

Fraser got on the radio, updating York as Shep checked London. A bruise on her neck, one on her cheek, but otherwise—"Can you walk?"

"Yes." She pushed herself to her feet. "Let's go."

Huh. "Okay, let's go." Kneeling, he pulled Ziggy to himself, then scooped her up.

Axel had appeared at the door, breathing hard. "Oh my—who is this?"

"My . . . friend," said London as she pushed past him. But she tripped on the hem of her dress and nearly went down. Shep turned to catch her, a reflex, but Axel grabbed her arm first.

"You okay?"

"Dehydrated. But I'm fine."

Hardly. But he didn't want to argue. Not yet.

She looked at Shep. "They'll be back. We need to hurry." She gathered up her dress in one hand and headed down the hall, nearly running.

Get down the stairs, out to the balcony—

"Moose, we're going to need a Stryker basket," Axel said on his headset. "Boo, can you send it down?"

Shep scrambled down the stairs into the main room. York had beat them down, and Axel climbed out the window. Shep handed Ziggy to him.

Boo had sent down the basket, and Axel set Ziggy into it, clipping her in. The line zipped up with Axel and Ziggy attached.

Shep turned to London, and now, for the first time, grabbed her arms and really checked her, up and down. She held a bar in her hand, maybe the pry bar Fraser had used.

As if she'd needed a weapon.

"I'm okay, Shep."

219

Weirdly, she was.

But then she shook her head, drew in a breath. "But—"

Gunshots from down the hall—and really, the fact they'd gotten this far without any resistance seemed a miracle. Now, as Shep pulled London behind the sofa—or did she pull him?—Fraser turned and zeroed in on a man running down the hall.

Two shots, and the man crumpled midstride.

"Gotcha, Igor," said London, and Shep looked at her, the dark, angry, foreign expression.

More shots, and these came from outside, on the balcony. York fired back, and Shep grabbed London up and pulled her away from the window.

Outside, the chopper veered away, out of range.

Good boy, Moose.

Fraser had moved down the hallway, into the shadows, and York had taken a position on the balcony, also firing.

Shep yanked London down behind the other sofa.

"I saw this being not quite so epic," he said.

And then York came careening through the window. "Grenade!" He rolled into the hallway just as the entire balcony exploded. Shep threw himself over London as rock and metal and glass pelleted the room.

The chandelier shook in the ceiling and fell, crashing, as he covered their heads. A thousand tiny shards shattered through the room.

"We need to move," London said, and lifted her head.

He got up, but she scrambled to her feet faster and grabbed his hand, pulling up her silly dress with the other—"C'mon!"

She fled down the hallway where Fraser had gone, where York had already rolled to his feet. Below them, in the stairwell, gunfire pinged. And she headed *toward* it.

"What are you doing?" He reached to stop her, but she lit out across the landing. It turned into a walkway that faced an open cavern, and on the other side—the cave entrance. A black yawn in the rock.

The tunnels York loved so much.

Moose could pick them up on the other side.

"I'm headed into the caves," Shep said into his headphones.

London had already grabbed Shep's hand. She was breathing hard, didn't look so great.

"You okay?"

"You came for me."

Uh, yeah. "I did."

"Help is coming. I didn't believe her."

"Let's go!"

Behind him, another explosion destroyed the stairs, dust and wood and clutter clogging their escape.

Gunshots on the lower levels. *Please, God, keep Fraser and York alive.*

But he didn't look back as he and London ran into the darkness.

"Wait—wait!" *Shoot,* she didn't want to slow them down but—"I think I have a sliver."

He turned, frowned at her. "A what?"

London couldn't have let go of Shep's hand if she'd wanted to he gripped it so tight. And maybe she gripped it back just as tightly. She kept replaying the moment when he'd burst into the room.

She'd been so sure that Ziggy might die, right there next to her on the floor.

All of it had happened so fast—and now . . . now they were tromping through a cave, Shep's headlamp—the man was a Boy Scout, no matter what he said—leading the way. He didn't even seem rattled.

As usual.

He hadn't even, after the quick study of her exterior, tried to kiss her. Then again, the castle had been exploding around them.

Eight hundred fifty years of history, gone.

They'd climbed five or six flights of stairs into the passageway to the tunnel, the ceiling a good twenty feet over their heads, the floor muddy. The white limestone walls turned weirdly blue and translucent when Shep shone his light on them. The air hung like a damp sheet around them, and water trickled in the darkness. Their breath seemed to catch in the air, their voices swallowed by the expanse. They'd passed a giant lake in the recesses of the cave, so maybe mountain water fed the lake, which ran out under the castle.

She shivered. Her feet were ice. Still, she'd stepped on something back there, and now she had to get it out of the heel of her foot.

Shep's eyes widened as he knelt down in front of her and pulled up her dress. Just above her ankles, but enough—"You're barefoot!" He looked up at her, his eyes dark. "What were you *thinking*?"

She blinked at him. "When? When I was getting ready to go to the ball? Did you expect me to think, hey, you know, I might get kidnapped, I guess I'll wear my best wool socks and hiking boots? Of course I wore heels. I lost them when they took me."

"For the love, sit down."

He practically pulled her down onto a nearby rock. "And you don't have a sliver—your entire heel is cracked open and bleeding. It's probably full of bat guano and is going to get infected and fall off."

"You're in a good mood."

He looked up at her, his mouth tight. Stared at her for a moment, then breathed out. "Yes, yes, I am." Then he sat down next to her and unlaced his boots.

"What are you doing?"

"What does it look like?"

"I can't walk in your boots. They're too big—"

"Socks. I have wool socks. Because, you know . . . I think ahead before I go to a ball." He lifted a shoulder.

"Was that a joke? Are you trying to be funny right now?"

He smiled.

"You get kidnapped in your tux and see how you feel about it."

He looked back at her, something of horror in his eyes as he took in her flimsy dress. "I'm a complete jerk." He pulled off his boot, then his sock, then put his boot back on and did the same with the other.

Then he stood up, unzipped his jacket, and pulled it off, put that around her. Zipped it up, all the way past her chin. Met her eyes. "I am so sorry. I was so focused on getting us to the tunnel—"

"Hey. Me too. I wasn't even cold until now."

"You're such a liar."

He probably meant it to be funny, but suddenly, her throat tightened and she looked away. "I am. I am such a liar."

A beat, just the dripping of the water plinking around them. Oh, she couldn't look at him.

"Hey—what's going on here?"

"In the avalanche. If I'd told you then, then maybe . . . I don't know. Maybe we wouldn't be here, you know?"

"No. Too many what-ifs." He grabbed her foot and shoved his sock on it, pulling it up almost to her knee. Her feet still throbbed, but it helped.

He did that with the other foot too. "We were just trying to stay alive in that bathtub. Just trying to keep each other awake and lucid and find a way free. So . . . no what-iffing. We survived. That's all that matters."

Then he took her face in his hands and met her eyes. Even in the dim light, she saw the earnestness in them. "And the other lies . . . no more, right? You said that, and I believe you. And it's done. You're alive, and we're going home."

Right. She nodded.

"Okay. Now, your dress is going to make this tricky, but I'm going to carry you on my back."

"I can walk."

"You'll wreck my socks."

She narrowed her eyes.

He turned around. "Arms around my neck, put your legs through my harness straps, and Bob's your uncle."

"Who'd you learn that from?" She realized then that she still held the poker she'd grabbed as a weapon, and now shoved it behind her, into the belt at her back. Then she looped her arms around his neck, pulling up to his strong shoulders. She tried to get her legs into the harness, but yes, the dress prohibited her movements.

"Your friend Pippa. And this isn't going to work." He turned, and then, gripping the bottom of her dress, he ripped it. Did the same to the back. Then he tied the ends to themselves, making legs, of a sort. "Now try."

It worked. She shoved one leg into a harness strap, then the other.

He stood up as if she weighed nothing.

Wow, he was strong, and steady, and solid, and . . . She put her head down on his shoulder and held on as he started off.

His headlamp light cut through the darkness, and they came to stairs etched into the rock, leading up.

"This'll be fun."

"I can walk."

"Just hold on."

And up they went. He'd gone into rescuer mode. She hadn't realized how much she depended on that until now. How, in so many crisis moments of her life, *Shep had shown up.*

"You're not in this alone, London."

She didn't know why that voice strummed inside her, but it seemed to steel her. Turn her almost warm.

"I am still amazed that you were there."

"Where?" He grunted, one step at a time.

"The avalanche—you came out of nowhere, really, and—"

"Yeah, about that. Um, your dad said he pulled some strings to get my team up there."

A beat. "My dad?"

"Yeah."

"Why did he . . . why would he . . . What?"

Shep had stopped, breathing hard, his hand on the wall. "Uh, London, how much do you know about what your dad does?"

"He's a lawyer."

"Mm-hmm."

"What are you saying?"

He started moving again. "You two should talk. Anyway . . . he knew that if I saw you, then . . . there was no way I'd let anything happen to you."

Oh. She closed her eyes, set her face against his back, and fell into the rhythm of him climbing the stairs, his strong legs carrying her when she couldn't.

Oh, she loved this man. Had for so long she'd sort of forgotten what it felt like to realize it anew. And here he was, showing up for her again. In *Montelena.*

They finally reached the top, Shep breathing hard, his skin clammy. Another short tunnel wound out ahead, but from here, wind streamed in. He shone his light toward it.

"There's the opening on the other side."

She lifted her head. Some fifty meters away.

He adjusted her on his back, then headed toward the entrance. The air filtered in, fresh and crisp, and at the far entrance, they came out into snow. The milky way fanned out across snow-gilded mountains, the sky a deep blue, almost velvet, and so many stars tossed across the heavens, it seemed almost like . . .

"You don't see that kind of sky unless you're in Alaska," he said.

225

Home.

He pulled out his walkie. "Air One, this is Shep. Moose, come back."

It took a moment of scratch, but Moose's voice came through the line. "Sorry, Shep, I had to make the call—Ziggy isn't doing well and we were at bingo. I'm halfway back to Luciella. York and Fraser are hoofing it out on the other side of the mountain. Where are you?"

Shep sighed, his big shoulders moving.

Uh-oh. Even she could see their predicament. No place for the chopper to land, and the backside of the mountain had turned mostly white, with snow lifting off it. More, the wind had kicked up on this side of the valley.

But that wasn't the biggest issue. The rock over them jutted out, cutting off any deployment of a line.

But maybe it didn't matter anyway.

Shep finally keyed the mic. "We're on the backside of the mountain. It's all snow for about five hundred yards down and then . . . forest. And darkness."

Static, then, "Can you find a place to hunker down?"

Shep stared down the mountain. "Okay, when we scouted it the first time, I spotted an A-frame cabin. Sits on a ridge, about halfway down the mountain. We'll make it there and lay low until you grab us."

He clicked off the radio. "Good?"

"Good," she said. "I can eve—"

"Roger." Moose cut off and Shep clipped the walkie back onto his harness.

"Okay, princess, let's see if we can find our hotel."

"Shep, I know I'm getting heavy."

"For cryin' out loud, London. Don't you remember? I can hold you all day long."

Aw, he was referring to that moment back at camp, on belay.

"What I need is a pair of skis."

"Yeah."

"Maybe I can glissade."

"What—"

"But if I fall, we could both go headfirst down the mountain. And there are rocks." He'd taken off his headlamp, held it up for more of a view. "But it looks steep enough. I just need something to steer, and self-arrest."

"Like, a poker?"

He stilled. "What?"

She reached behind herself and pulled the metal bar from her waist. Brought it around front so he could see it. "I saw it on the floor when I tripped, and thought—weapon."

"And I see an ice axe. Maybe." He took it. "It has a sort of hook on it, so it could work." He looked down. "It's either that or we make camp in the cave and try to hike out in the morning."

"It's freezing in the cave, and we have nothing to make fire. . . . Do you really think you can find the cabin?"

"I think so. Or I could make us a snow cave. Remind me to tell you how I saved Colt's life in a snow cave during a blizzard."

"Apparently that's your MO."

He laughed. "I guess so."

"So that's what Colt meant by 'we're even' when he found us."

He'd been testing out the poker, holding it one hand, then the other. "When?"

"When his Ranger team dug us out of the cabin. He said—'Now we're even.'"

"Huh. Yeah, maybe. Okay, I think you'll have to go down on my lap."

"Say again?"

He had crouched. "Climb off and come around me."

She did so, stepping on the ground. The cold breath of the cave had made her socks damp, but now, stepping into the wet and snow, they turned downright soggy.

"You'd better find that cabin, or my feet just might freeze off."

"I'd prefer you with feet." He sat down on the snow, legs up, pushed off, and slid a ways, then he slammed the poker into the snow. "It'll turn me, but to stop us—" He rolled over and plunged the straight end into the snow, holding on. "Yep, this will work, but now let's talk about you."

He was born for this. The sense of it burst through her, took hold as he explained how he'd sit, legs flat, and she'd sit on his lap, her legs on top of his, her shoulders secured with the harness suspenders, "And if I suddenly stop and roll over, I won't crush you—but I'll need to dig my feet in, and you'll hold on to the straps with everything inside you. This will work, London."

She met his eyes. "I trust you."

He swallowed, and something hollow—maybe fear—entered his eyes. Then he blinked it away. "Okay."

He sat down and held his legs out, and she climbed onto his lap, put her arms through the harness suspenders.

Settled her legs on his.

"You gotta hold them there. Be strong. Don't scream."

"I don't scream."

"You should. Like when someone is, say, trying to kidnap you."

More joking? "Right."

"Craziest glissade ever. Okay, here goes."

He pushed them off into the snow. The fall was steep, but at first they didn't move.

Then, snow started to sift up at her, over the tops of his boots, dusting her face, her mouth. She closed her eyes, feeling them move faster. He slowed them down with his boots, his legs like timber below him. They bumped, faster, faster, his headlamp illuminating the snow flying at them like pellets.

He was a toboggan, and she clutched the harness and clamped her mouth shut.

Especially when their bodies lifted from the snow, took flight.

Then, suddenly, his arm went around her waist, and they were turning, scrubbing into the snow, sliding now on their sides, out of control.

She screamed.

"Roll!"

He pushed over her, and then, just like that, slammed the poker into the snow, his feet slamming into the hillside as they jerked, slid, and jerked again.

She collapsed in the snow. He hadn't crushed her, but the snow had found her face, her ears, throttled its way into her jacket. She'd lost a sock, and her legs were icicles.

But they hadn't died.

"You okay?" His voice, soft in her ear. And even in her frozen state, it had the power to light a fire through her.

But she'd need more than that. "I think so."

He caught her again around her waist and rolled over, him now in the snow, her on top. Snow cluttered his headlamp, but he cleaned it and then shone it around.

They'd traveled nearly all the way into the tree line.

"That was . . ."

"Terrifying." He pushed up. "I think the A-frame is that way. I was reviewing the map in my head and . . . yeah, see it? Through that stand of hemlock?"

She could barely make it out in the darkness, but it did seem like a structure.

"Back on my back, let's go."

"I can walk—"

"Please. For the sake of your feet, get on my back."

She climbed on, her legs through the harness again, and grimaced when he grunted.

But he handed her the poker, wrapped his arms around her knees, and started tromping through the knee-high snow. No wonder he had wanted to slide instead of walk.

They came to the trees, and he waited a moment, turning off his light.

No movement in the small cabin, sitting alone under the stars, surrounded by untouched snow.

"Okay, let's go."

He trudged out across the open space and up to the small cabin.

The roofline protected the wooden porch. He backed up to it and offloaded her, then climbed the stairs and went to the door.

It opened without struggle. He looked at her.

She shrugged and then, still holding the poker, followed him inside.

Darkness, but a stove with logs stacked nearby sat in the small room, a pipe directed outside. And on the other side of the room, a double bed. A small kitchen against the back wall held a vertical water tank, probably for fresh water from a nearby river, a bowl for a sink, and a small table.

Maybe a skier's cabin.

"I'll make a fire," she said.

"No, you sit. I'll make a fire."

She sat on the bed. It came without blankets, but after a moment, she looked under the bed. And there, in a plastic tub—a comforter and sheets. "This might even be one of those glamping B&Bs." She pulled out the comforter and wrapped it around herself.

Shep the Boy Scout had the fire glowing in a blink.

He stood up then and pulled off his harness, dropping it on the floor, and then he rubbed his shoulders.

"Sorry I'm so heavy."

He looked at her. "You're not heavy. But I am wondering if I need to put a tracker on you."

She stared at him a moment, then—"That's how you found me. My phone."

"York had someone in his organization hack you. So yes." He stirred the fire. And then, finally, looked at her. "What happened?"

She probably wouldn't tell him about her fight with Igor One, or Two, or the way Ziggy had fought Martin, relentless, even climbing onto his back, holding on with a choke hold until he nearly broke her ribs—or had—getting her off.

She remembered the poker, too—Tomas had used it to take Ziggy down and render her unconscious.

"I gave them the seed code."

He gave a nod. "You had to."

Maybe.

"But it wasn't the right code."

He sighed. "Of course not."

"The right code is twenty-two words, all in the correct order. And in case I forgot them"—she pulled out her necklace, the one with the Mandarin written on front and back—"they're here."

"On the necklace?" He touched the pendant and ran his thumb over the etchings.

"I learned rudimentary Mandarin when my family lived in Taiwan. The Hanzi—the symbols—are the words."

"Brilliant."

"It bought me time. They'll get locked out for twelve hours."

"So, we'll have twelve hours to get to Cryptex and attach the virus to your account."

"Yes. Ziggy said she thinks she knows why they want the money now."

"Not just for random nefarious plans?" He closed the door to the stove.

"She thinks the Petrovs want to buy a country."

He stood up, smacked off his hands. "A country. A little vacation country by the sea?"

She frowned. Who was this guy? "I doubt it. She says it's either that or some massive biological weapon . . ."

"Can't just go with a straight-up nuclear bomb, huh? Too boring."

"Are you okay?"

He sat down on the bed. Rubbed his hands over his face. Then he lay back and closed his eyes. "Next time you want to go to a ball, London, can we please stay home and eat pizza instead?"

She laughed.

"I just want to go home," he said.

Her laughter faded even as his breaths deepened.

So maybe now wasn't a great time to talk about the fact that suddenly, painfully, she'd realized that Ziggy was right.

Despite the horror, something had ignited inside her. A thirst for justice, maybe. And it felt like she'd also found the person she wanted to be.

She just wasn't sure that person belonged in Alaska.

ELEVEN

SHEP SPOTTED HER SOMEWHERE DOWN THE mountainside, a tiny orange speck between the trees, showering up powder as she turned, a flash of color, then gone again. Even in the dream, his heart pounded. Her name caught in his throat, although he tried to shout—"Jacey!"

But she wouldn't stop.

The allure of the out-of-boundary path kept her from looking back.

His bones still hurt from the fall, snow in his jacket, his skis buried. But he'd dug himself out, now stepped back into his skis.

His stupid sister should learn to wait. He could keep up—he'd just caught his edge in the deep powder. "Jacey! Wait!"

The wind rushed through his helmet, burning his ears, chapping his face, his feet frozen in his boots, his fingertips numb. Clouds had moved in, whisked up a fierce wind that sprinkled snow across his goggles and into his jacket. He shivered, then tucked and pointed his skis downhill, straight on, to bomb it, at least until he could catch up.

She was too far ahead—he couldn't see her anymore. And as he picked up speed, the wind whistled. Too fast. Too dangerous.

Out of control.

He tried to stand up straight, to ease back on the speed, but the powder trapped him. And the trees created an obstacle course ahead.

Go through, or turn and launch over the cliffside, off the trail—into the dark, bruised sky.

The trees would kill him. Below, he'd land in more soft, perfect powder. He pushed hard on his downhill leg, managed a turn, and cut sideways, still moving so fast he nearly sat back on his skis.

He heard his father's voice somewhere behind him, uphill, panicked. *"Slow down!"*

His heart thundered, the edge rising toward him—

Fall and break his speed, maybe catapult over anyway, or give it his all and fly—

Courage failed him. He wobbled, then sat down on his skis, throwing out his poles, dragging through the snow. Powder blinded him, the snow caught him, and he turned, circled, rolled. His skis snapped off and he heard a crack and—

He rolled to a stop in the snow.

For a second, everything stilled.

Then the pain in his leg shook through him and—

Screaming.

He sat up, just like that, in the bed.

Looked around, blinking, breathing hard.

"You screamed, not me."

The voice came from next to him, and he looked over to see London sitting on the bed, her knees pulled up to herself, wrapped in the comforter, her face illuminated by the flames of the still-flickering stove.

"I didn't know if I should wake you, but I was just about to.

Nightmare? Because you were breathing funny, and then you screamed and sat up."

"That was me?"

"Sounded terrible."

He scrubbed his hands down his face. "Yeah. A memory. I was thirteen and was following my sister down a back bowl. Snowbird, Utah, has some of the best skiing and heli-skiing, but my parents couldn't afford it. Jacey thirsted for some deep powder, so she decided to go off-boundary. Alta ski resort is right next door, and a high peak splits them—she took off onto the Alta side. It's steep and has a few trees, and cliffs, and she was a better skier than me. But I saw her leaving me . . . Anyway, I got in way over my head, fell, then got up and did something stupid and fell again—lost all my gear, broke my leg. They had to airlift me out. She made it all the way down without even realizing I was hurt."

"That's horrible."

"Yeah. But really, I knew better. My dad was on patrol that day at Snowbird, and he saw me—came after me. I could have died on that hill."

He got up, opened the stove. The A-frame had warmed, cozy inside. He'd radioed in to Moose with their location, and Moose had told him to sit tight until morning.

Shep just wanted to get off this mountain and back home. No more epic missions. He tossed in another log, then closed the stove.

"For a long time, I blamed Jacey. But the fact was, I had a choice. I didn't have to follow her."

"But it didn't feel like that at the time."

He stirred the fire to life. "No. She was the impulsive one. And I sort of thought that I was here to protect her."

"You were two years younger than her."

"It felt like I was older."

"Because you didn't do stupid things like skiing out of the boundary."

He nodded. "What can I say?—I'm a rule follower. It keeps people alive."

London's blonde hair had tumbled down around her face, and while she smiled up at him, he realized how very warm it was in the room. He'd fallen asleep on the bed without even thinking. Still, there was no other place to sit, so he sank down on the end of the bed.

"Seriously. Shep. Just—we shared a bathtub."

"That was different. We were trapped. And wearing snowsuits."

"I know." She smiled. "How about you just sit by me?"

"I can do that." He moved beside her. Put his arm around her. She leaned into him. And somehow, with the movement, the terrible knot that wound him up simply released.

Breathe. They'd made it halfway down the mountain, were both still alive and . . .

Closing his eyes, he leaned his head back against the wall.

"Is that how you got into rescue?"

He opened one eye. She rested her hand on his chest, turned a little toward him. He pulled the comforter around her.

"What do you mean?"

"Getting airlifted off the mountain?"

"Oh. Maybe. When I went into the Army, I knew I didn't want to be just infantry, but I wanted to be in the Tenth Mountain Division, so it felt right to be a medic. And then I ended up attached to a Ranger team, so—" He shook his head. "Got in a little over my head there too."

"That's why you got out?"

"Yes. I didn't want to live a life off grid, living one mission to the next, not sure if I'd make it home. I'm not afraid to die, but I wanted more. Something permanent, that grounded me. Someplace I could call home."

"A family," she said quietly.

"Yes. Someday, maybe. If God wills."

"That's living outside the boundary, isn't it?"

He frowned, said nothing.

She raised her head. "Faith. Believing in things you can't see."

Hmm. "Yes, faith is trusting what you don't see. But also trusting in someone who is faithful. You might not see what's ahead, but God does. I'd say that's living very much inside the boundary. The other way is just . . . chaos."

She nodded, then put her head down. "Remember that conversation we had in our snow cave?"

"A.k.a. the bathtub of doom? We had a lot of conversations, if I remember right."

"You told me a story about your cousin Gage. How he'd been blamed for the death of this guy who tried to ski with him."

"Yeah. Took him out of snowboarding for a while."

"But you said he told you something before you went into the military."

"Don't get shot?"

"No. That God has a reason for everything that happens. And that wherever you go, you can trust that he has a purpose. And maybe that you don't have to prove that you're worthy for God to save you. He already has."

He did remember that.

"That . . . stuck with me. Changed me. Made me realize that maybe . . . maybe I wasn't in charge of enacting justice."

He looked down at her. "You thought that?"

"A little." She took a breath. "When I was eleven years old, we were visiting London when a bomb exploded on our double-decker bus."

He sat up, pushed her off him. "What?"

She nodded. "It was just my mom, me, and . . . my little sister. She was six at the time."

Everything shucked out of him. "You had a *sister*?"

"Her name was Morgan. She was . . . perfect. Funny. She sang all

the time. Curly blonde hair. I was five years older, and I thought . . .
She just annoyed me. I'd spent five perfect years as an only child,
and here she was, causing trouble. I was such a jerk."

He said nothing.

"We were stopped at Tavistock Square, and I wanted to go to
the roof. I was hot—it was July—and the bus was really crowded.
It was just me and my mom and Morgan—we were going to meet
my father, who'd done some business for a local firm. The bus
stopped and I got up, and my mother told me to sit down, and I
had a fit right there, in the aisle. I headed up to the front, and Mom
followed me, maybe to grab me—I don't know. But as soon as we
got to the front, the world just—exploded. My mom had hold of
me, and we somehow landed on the sidewalk together, but . . . the
back of the bus was in flames." She swallowed. "They say everyone
in the back died instantly, but . . . my mom had a real rough go for
years after that. She put on a face, but . . ."

"Oh, London, I had no idea."

"I . . . I guess my impulsive temper tantrum saved my life and
my mother's life, but . . ."

"Your sister died."

"They kept it quiet. Out of the media. I don't even think she's
listed as one of the victims. Something about not wanting to make
it part of an international issue—but I wanted justice. I watched
the news relentlessly, and when they arrested the planners of the
attacks, I watched everything. But it was never really . . . put to
bed inside me."

He couldn't take his eyes off her. "All these years . . . you've let me
call you London. When . . . I mean, every time I said your name—"

"It reminded me that I survived. And that my life needed to
be about something. You calling me London made my life feel . . .
important."

"Is it why you joined the Black Swans?"

"Maybe. My justice meter ticks pretty high. But also . . . maybe

I felt a little like I needed to justify why I survived. I think maybe my mother has the same problem."

"You're the daughter who lived. She wants to do right by you—that makes sense, suddenly."

"Probably. But then I nearly died with you in Zermatt, and I thought . . . maybe I'd screwed up and God was giving me a second—or third—chance. And this time I didn't have to chase down evil or justify my existence."

"You don't."

She nodded, but something in her eyes tightened his gut. "That's why I walked away from it all and went to Nigeria. And I thought . . . I thought that was all behind me—I really did. But somehow, seeing Ziggy stand up to these thugs yesterday, and then I had this crazy sense of satisfaction handing them the wrong code . . ." Her jaw tightened. "I want to see the Bratva taken down, Alan Martin brought to justice."

"Of course."

"But the evil doesn't stop there."

And that statement had him by the throat. "What?"

"Listen." She put her hand on his chest, leaned up. "I can't stand by and watch as there are more terror attacks in the streets of London or Paris—"

"You're never going to stop bad people from doing bad things—"

"But I can try!"

He closed his mouth.

"All it takes for evil to triumph is for good men—or women—to do nothing. Someone has to stand against them."

He blew out a breath. "Yes. I know that quote. I just—" He touched her face. "I just can't bear the idea of something terrible happening to *you*."

She leaned against his hand. "Nothing terrible—"

He leaned up. "Are you kidding me? I walked into the room, saw the blood on Ziggy—and you—and it nearly blew me apart.

Imagine if that was you, London, getting life-flighted to Luciella."
He shook his head. "Please, London. Don't—"

"Ski out of the boundaries?"

"Yes! Yes. Because I'll just have to go after you—"

"No, you won't."

"Yes, I will. Because—" He shook his head, looked away, ground
his jaw. "Because that's how I'm built."

She looked at him then, her eyes wide. She swallowed. "I know."

A beat passed between them, raw and terrible and real, and then,
because the warmth of the chalet had found his bones, because
the comforter swaddled her and her golden hair tumbled down,
because she looked at him with those blue eyes that seemed to
contain more emotion than she could say, he leaned forward and
kissed her.

Maybe it started out as desperate, engulfing, but she came to
him, willing and sweet, her lips soft.

Yeah, this was why he shouldn't have scooted up on the bed,
because now he pulled her up against him, his arms around her,
holding her head in the crook of his elbow and deepening his kiss.

And yes, he was a Boy Scout, but he still let himself relish the
taste of her, the sense of time stopping. Her hair turned to silk
between his fingers, and she ran her hand around his waist, holding on. Slowly, the panic of the day seeped out of him. They'd
lived. She was here, right here with him, safe and whole, and he
felt it like never before, that right here, right now, he was home.
Or home enough, because he could nearly taste their future—the
family, the happy ending.

He finally lifted his head, his body starting to take over, and he
leaned away, blew out a breath. "Okay. We'll finish this. Then . . .
then . . . we go home."

She swallowed. Put her hand on his cheek. Then she pulled
down his head and kissed him again.

And only later, after he'd managed to slow them down and

bank the fire inside him, after she'd fallen asleep in his arms, did he realize that she hadn't said yes.

Go home. Maybe it could be exactly as Shep wanted.

Oh, he was a handsome man, especially in sleep. His dark lashes against his cheeks, his hand clutching her arm, holding on, even in his subconscious, like he might be afraid she'd run away.

She pushed up from the warmth between them—she was still wrapped in the comforter, like a cocoon, still wearing his jacket. He slept fully clothed on top of the bed.

"That's how I'm built."

Yes, every inch of him said rescuer. The man was a mountain—in frame, in force—and suddenly the memory of kissing him last night, the way he could make her feel safe, rose inside her.

"Okay. We'll finish this. Then . . . then . . . we go home."

Except, maybe Alaska didn't feel like home anymore.

Then again, nothing felt like home.

Nothing except Shep.

Dawn, with the glory of golds and reds, cascaded into the room, the light pouring in through the tall windows, onto the wooden floor. She guessed this was an Airbnb, because she discovered a welcome sign in Montelenan on the table. No internet, and according to the laminated page, the bathroom was an outhouse just off the porch. But the place also contained a hot tub and sauna, heated with an outside stove.

Snowshoes hung on the front wall, along with a map of the trails in the area.

The cabin contained a tiny kitchen, and she got up, wishing she still had both socks, and after stirring the fire back to life, she went over to the countertop and started to root through the cupboards.

A kettle, and she found a box of tea bags and another of hot cocoa packets.

She opened the front door to get snow. The air hung crisp and still in the morning, a slight wind stirring the snow from the trees. Looking up, she spotted the high exit of the tunnel.

She'd never forget, as long as she lived, the sense of flying down the mountain with Shep. A special kind of adrenaline. Addictive.

Closing the door, she came back inside and set the kettle of snow onto the stove.

Shep was awake. He had sat up, his hair standing nearly on end, sweetly tousled, and he looked over at her, blinking, then ran a hand down his face.

"Hey," she said.

"Hey."

"I found some hot cocoa. I think this place is an Airbnb."

He reached for his boots. "We'll have to find the owners and settle up." He laced up his boots. "Moose said he'd pick us up at first light."

He stood up into the pool of sunlight, a little gold reflecting off his dark hair, his eyes blue and rich in the light.

Then we go home.

Yes. Yes, that had to be the right answer. She didn't have anything to prove.

I just can't bear the idea of something terrible happening to you.

Her either.

The sense of it swept through her, and for a moment, she was back in the chalet in the avalanche, so many years ago, held in his arms, safe.

Loved.

And that was it. Shep was *love.* The truth swept through her, wrapped around her. Love was patient, love was kind. Love did not keep a record of wrongs. Love showed up, again and again....

"You okay?" He walked over to her, touched her face.

She leaned her hand into his touch. Here. Right here was home. "Yes."

Probably a good thing that the water on the stove had begun to boil, because really, suddenly, she wanted to sink into his arms. Which would do neither of them any good.

He'd been a gentleman last night, of course, but she'd heard the strain in his voice when he pushed her away, got up, stood outside in the cold for a moment before coming back and taking her—chastely—into his arms.

She'd met the man underneath all that calm exterior. Seen his heart. And the secret of that only stirred a desire inside.

So she walked over to the stove to grab the boiling kettle—using his coat sleeve to protect her hand—and pour water into the mugs.

The cocoa dissolved, piquing the air with the hint of chocolate. She handed him a mug and blew on her own.

He took a sip. "That's good." He set the cup down and reached for his stocking cap. "We need to get you out of that ridiculous dress."

Her eyes widened.

"I didn't mean that the way it sounded."

She laughed, then put her mug down and stepped up to him, put her arms around his neck. "Shep—you are the most honorable man I've ever met."

His gaze skimmed down her and back. "Not that honorable. Good thing Moose is picking us up this morning."

Yes, good thing.

And despite her bedraggled appearance, her ripped dress and one bulky wool sock, and the fact that she was grimy and smelly, he looked at her the same way he had when she'd walked down the embassy stairs before the ball.

Like she was beautiful. Rare. Unexpected.

A black swan.

She simply couldn't stop herself from rising up on her toes and kissing him. Chaste, sweet, terribly aware of how much she wanted to belong to him.

And to be all he needed too.

He touched her arms, held her there, then lifted his head, his eyes in hers.

I love you, Shep. She should have said it long ago. The words rose through her, took hold. She loved him for his faithfulness, for the fact that he never gave up, for being the one person who would come after her, always.

She opened her mouth to say it, but outside, thunder rumbled in the distance.

"Moose," he said. "Let's get off this mountain and go home."

"Yes," she said, because he was right. "Finish this. Go home."

She picked up her mug and finished her chocolate, then poured in the rest of the hot water and scrubbed out her cup. Rinsed it and did the same with his.

The roar had turned louder outside, then stopped.

Shep had folded up the blanket and doused the fire.

"They might have put down somewhere nearby," Shep said. And then he walked over and swept her up into his arms.

"Oh."

"I'll take it from here."

She looped her arms around his neck. "Okay."

Footsteps on the deck outside, and he went to the door and opened it.

Stilled.

She, too, froze.

"Cozy?" said Tomas. He wore a stocking cap and a snow jacket and held a gun. "Let's try that again."

And with his arms full, Shep couldn't do anything.

But she could.

She used Shep's body as leverage and kicked out at Tomas. Her foot hit him in the face, but it totally dislodged her from Shep's arms. Tumbling free, she fell, hit the deck.

Bounced up to scramble away. *Get the gun, get the gun—*

A shot cracked the air. She looked back to see Shep staggering back—

"No!" She launched herself at Tomas, but the snow, up to her knees, slowed her down.

"Listen. All you have to do is return what you took. Easy."

As Shep hit the door frame, Tomas turned the gun on her. "I see you, big man. You take one step and she's dead."

Out of the corner of her eye, she saw Shep right himself, the mountain he was.

"You're a terrorist, Tomas," she said. "Of course I'm not handing over the money!"

His mouth opened. Closed. "I'm a businessman."

Then he turned to Shep, and just like that, pulled the trigger.

She screamed.

Shep fell back, hands to his body, blood saturating his abdomen.

She ran to him, but Tomas grabbed her arm, yanked her back, shoving her out into the snow. *Stupid slippery sock—*

Shep.

Though he'd sagged against the cabin, he was still on his feet, and even as she watched, the man took two steps and launched himself at Tomas.

Big man, big tackle, and Tomas went down.

"London! Run!" Shep growled.

They rolled, and Tomas hit him in the gut with his elbow. A shout of pain, but Shep put an arm around Tomas's neck. Held on.

Tomas slammed his fist into Shep's head, then added the gun. Blood spurted from his wound, but still Shep held on. "Run!"

But the blood loss seemed to be loosening Shep's grip.

And, *sorry*—she hadn't trained for years under Ziggy to run away. Laney Steele didn't run.

Tomas scooted out of his hold, danced up, and pointed his gun at Shep. "You're in the way—"

London jumped him. Despite being clad in her flimsy dress, in a soggy sock. She brought him down into the snow, her legs around his neck, then slammed her fist into his ear.

He roared, punched her in the ribs, and her breath shucked out. He wrestled free, rounded, and she barely blocked a right hook. She shoved her full palm into his jaw, snapping his head back. Brought her fist around for a punch in his side.

He stumbled back but grabbed her wrist, yanked her in.

And shoved his gun under her chin.

She slapped away his wrist with her left hand.

The gun went off, right beside her ear, hot on her face, the bullet missing her. But the sound had her ears ringing, the percussion jerking her away, spinning her head. She stumbled back.

And he pounced on her. Took her down, her face to the ground, gun to the base of her skull, her arm back—submission hold.

"Stop!"

She spotted Shep on his feet, his hands up. Blood saturated his shirt.

His voice, however, cut down to something calm and easy despite the finest edge of pain. "Don't shoot, Tomas. Don't shoot."

"I just want the code."

And then, Shep nodded.

Wait—

What—no—

"It's on her necklace. The pendant. Written in Chinese."

"No!"

Tomas reached into her jacket, found the gold chain. Then he traced it around to the pendant. And snapped it from her neck.

"Clever."

Then she guessed he pocketed it because she heard a zip.

"You've got what you wanted—let her go."

Tomas looked at him, and she could guess Tomas's expression because Shep took a breath. "C'mon, Tomas—"

"Too many loose ends," Tomas said.

"What if it doesn't work?" Shep shouted.

Tomas hesitated.

And right then, a chopper flew over the trees, kicking up snow and ice, a whirlwind of chaos. Tomas jerked his arm up to protect himself—

She rolled, grabbed at the gun, and slammed her fist into Tomas's throat.

He fell away, and while she fought for footing, he scrambled up and away, toward the trees.

She turned to chase him, but Shep—he'd gone down on one knee.

And above them, the chopper circled again.

In the trees on the other side, a snowmobile fired up. She put a hand to her empty neck, then ran to Shep. He'd put one hand down, blood running down his head, into his collar, the snow reddening, melting.

She caught him. "Okay, just sit back. It'll be okay."

Beyond the trees, the snowmobile cut away, the noise drowned by the hovering chopper.

So much blood. The head wound wasn't deep, just a tear of flesh, but she couldn't find the gunshot in his abdomen. He held his hands over a wound to his side, his mouth tight, barely letting out a groan.

But she saw it in his eyes. "Hang on, Shep."

And then Axel was there on a line from the chopper, with a basket. He landed in the snow, ran over. "How bad is it?"

"Not bad," Shep ground out.

"It's bad," London said.

Her stomach threatened to give it up, but she focused on helping Shep into the basket.

On trying to forget his words—*It's on her necklace.*

And mostly, on the betrayal that burned a line straight through her.

After they'd tucked Shep into the chopper, Axel came down again for her and she climbed into the basket.

"Nice outfit."

"Get me off this mountain."

"Nice to see you too."

She looked away, numb, as Axel belted her in and as she watched Boo tend to Shep's abdominal wound. Blood sopped his shirt. The first bullet had nicked his head, just a flesh wound. She guessed that the second was embedded inside, given the way he grimaced, but even that seemed not critical, the way Boo had put a bandage over it and pressed his hand against it to hold it.

He leaned his head back, his face taut, and looked at her.

She stared out the window, unable to look at him, tracing the plume of the snowmobile as they lifted into the sky.

TWELVE

I T COULD HAVE BEEN WORSE."

Moose stood, arms folded, in the ER of the Luciella Medical Center. He appeared tired, not a little stress on his face. And Shep had a feeling it might not be all about scooping his bloodied body off a mountain.

"You okay, Moose? Everything okay in Alaska?"

"Yeah." Moose ran a hand behind his neck. "It's complicated. But . . . we'll sort it out."

Axel appeared, holding a skinny can of cola. Handed one to Moose. He wore a pair of cargo pants and a thermal shirt, having shucked off his jacket and hat in the tiny ER compartment where a nurse had parked Shep. Luciella didn't have its own chopper landing, so Moose had put down in a parking lot nearby. Then they'd shoved Shep into a waiting embassy car and trucked him over to the ER lot.

The hospital wasn't big—a three-story white building with the entrance to the ER under a pull-through at one end. Lime-green ceilings, modern yellow sofas in the lobby, and matching lime-green curtains hanging between ER gurneys.

Now Axel turned to Shep. "Tillie's house blew up."

The words didn't settle. "What?"

"Gas leak," Moose said and shot a look at Axel. "She and Hazel are with me."

"And I thought getting shot twice was bad. Poor Tillie."

"Yeah." Moose took a drink of soda.

Something seemed off, but Moose moved on with, "You're lucky this accountant doesn't have better aim. Could have taken out your kidney or gall bladder or even your liver."

"Right? Who gets shot without hitting any major organs?" Axel added.

"Skin is a major organ," Shep said. "And they had to fish out the bullet, so that was uber fun."

"Even that—the wound is, like, an inch deep," Axel said. He sat down in one of the molded plastic chairs in the tiny ER berth.

"In my *body*," Shep said. "Let's trade places, Axe."

Axel grinned, took a long swig of his soda. Crushed the can. "Nope."

He had also gotten three stitches in his head, so he felt a little like Frankenstein's monster. "Any sign of Tomas?"

"No. But Mitch is on it," Moose said.

"How's London? Is she done getting checked out?"

Axel glanced at Moose, a definite I-don't-want-to-tell-him expression on his face.

"What?" Shep sat up but closed an eye at the pinch in his side. Okay, so no sudden movements.

"She never came to the hospital."

What? Shep gripped the sides of the gurney, held himself up, but—"Never came . . . Oh." And now his chest burned. *Sheesh,* maybe he was hurt worse than he thought. He leaned back. "Okay. Maybe . . . I get that. Maybe her mother needed her."

"I don't think so." Axel said. "She was . . . different."

Different. Like she'd been at the fortress. A kind of different he didn't want to accept.

Axel tossed the can into a nearby garbage. "What happened back there? Because when I said, 'Hey, London, want to ride to the hospital with us?' her response was, 'Take care of Shep.' And I got a definite heave-ho kind of feeling from her. You two have a fight?"

A fight might have been less of a bomb to their relationship. "I had no choice."

Silence.

More silence.

"No choice about what?" Moose finally asked, his voice low.

"Tomas had her on the ground, the gun to her head—all he wanted was the seed code. So . . . I told him."

Moose didn't move.

"Do you mean the password to her supersecret crypto wallet with the billions of dollars in it that she risked her life—and Ziggy's—to protect?" Axel said.

"Yes," Shep snapped. "That one."

Axel held up a hand. "Just so we're clear."

"Did I mention the gun—to her *head*?"

Moose nodded. Blew out a breath.

Axel ran a hand behind his neck, but also nodded.

"Listen. He was going to kill her—"

"Not as long as they didn't have the seed code," Axel said.

Shep looked at him. "Really? And that's how you felt when the Midnight Sun Killer had a gun on Flynn? 'Hey, pal, let's *negotiate* for the life of the woman I love. Maybe share a beer—'"

Moose held up a hand. "Shep, calm down. No one is blaming you—"

"Are you kidding? *London* is blaming me." He reached for the IV port on his arm. "Get me a cotton swab."

Boo walked in right then. "Hey, what do you think you're doing?"

He must have worn something lethal in his expression, because she stopped cold.

Axel brushed past her, grabbed a cotton swab, and handed it to him.

Shep untaped his IV line.

"For Pete's sake, let me help," Boo said, and took over, pulling out his line, pressing the swab over the wound. "It'll bleed, so hold it there a minute."

He didn't have a minute. "She's going to do something stupid. Like go after the money."

Moose cocked his head. "C'mon. She's not that—"

"Impulsive? Brave? Determined?"

Moose held up his hands.

"Sheesh." He shook his head. "You'd think after what happened to Ziggy—" *Wait*. "How is Ziggy?"

"She was in ICU when we left," Boo said. "I just went up to check on her, and someone checked her out of the hospital."

Silence, again, in the room. "Who?"

"Dunno. The nurse said it was some guy. He came in with his own medical team and took her away."

More silence.

"York?" Shep asked.

"Who?" Boo said.

He shook his head. "Nobody." His feet hit the floor, and he reached for his coat. "I'm going to the embassy."

"Shep—" Moose stopped him with a hand on his arm. "We all have a flight out of here in a couple hours. You should be on it."

"I'm not leaving without London." He shook his arm away from Moose's grip. The movement shot heat through him, but they'd doused him with pain killers, so maybe he wasn't exactly all there. Still, "We'll be there."

"You sure you don't need help?" Axel said, but Shep held up a hand to him and Moose and Boo and even the nurse who ran down the hall after him. She said something in Montelenan, but he ignored it, came out into the lobby, and then pushed through the doors.

The castle sat on the hill, a fresh layer of snow dusting the parapets, the black gothic roofs. In the city below, the snow had turned to slush, cars splashing through it. The hospital sat blocks from the embassy, but he had the map in his head, thanks to the tour that London's father had given him, and he now set out for it, not hurting at all, thank you.

Except maybe his heart.

He shoved his hands into his pockets, head down, and stalked to his pounding heartbeat. *Let's get off this mountain and go home.*

His words, not hers. Maybe she'd never meant to return to Alaska with him. And maybe he was the jerk here for expecting that, but . . .

But he *knew* London. Or maybe he only knew *London.* The person she'd talked about last night, the one ignited by justice . . . *that* person he'd only gotten glimpses of.

Brutal and raw glimpses. Like the way she'd fought Tomas in the snow. And he'd nearly come unglued when Tomas hit her.

And when she hit him back. *What—*

And then there was—well, *everything.* Her tackling him into the river and running out of the fortress in her bare feet and glissading with him down a mountain and . . .

He'd never forget her the night of the ball, so beautiful she'd taken his breath away. Delaney Brooks.

But she had this other side, too, the Laney Steele side.

And maybe it wasn't fair of him to suppose she could only live as one version of herself.

Still—

He stopped at the gate. Looked at the guard. "I don't have ID, but call the ambassador."

"No need, sir. She's expecting you." The man buzzed him in.

Huh.

He came into the courtyard, wet with fresh, melted snow, and only then did he realize the nip in the air. A guard opened the door to him, and he went in, passed through the security checkpoint, and by the time he reached the stairs, Mitch stood there.

"She's in Sofia's office."

Shep nodded.

He put a hand out to stop Shep. "But you're supposed to be on a plane."

"Seriously. Take your hand off me."

A beat. Mitch lowered his hand. "Shep, this is bigger than you or your life in Alaska."

"It doesn't have to be!"

Mitch's jaw tightened.

"She nearly died!"

"I know."

"Shep?"

He looked up. She'd changed clothes, wearing a pair of black yoga pants and a black pullover, her hair back in a ponytail. No makeup, and even with the bruises and scrapes, she could still take his breath away.

In fact, he had to put his hand to the cool wall to keep his knees from buckling. Because clearly, she'd been crying.

He hadn't expected that.

"Can we talk?"

She nodded, her arms folded. He glanced at Mitch, to his pursed lips and disapproving expression, and then followed her.

Hello, someone needed to watch out for her, because it seemed that Mitch only saw the Black Swan in her.

And maybe Shep needed to see that *more*, but frankly, he saw *all* of her. The teenager who'd refused to give in, the woman who'd survived with him in an avalanche, the pilot who saved lives, and the woman who could fight in a ball gown.

And he loved her. All of her, even the parts he didn't recognize, the parts that stunned him, even scared him. That was the only thought that filled his brain, eclipsing all others as he followed her through the reception area to the inner office, the dining room where he'd eaten before.

He loved her, and he wouldn't apologize for betraying her, and if he had to do it all over again—

"You know millions might die." She'd closed the double doors, then turned, met his eyes.

Oh. So maybe she hadn't been crying over him. *Still.* "I didn't want *you* to die."

She drew in a long breath, then her mouth tightened and she nodded. "Yeah." She walked over to the Steinway, sat down on the bench. Played a few of the keys with one hand.

"London?"

"I know you did what you thought was right."

Words left him.

"I might have even made the same call for you." She lifted her left hand, played a harmony. "But I would have been wrong."

"No. Lives matter. People matter—"

"Yes." She met his gaze. "But I'd do anything to save my sister, or those people on the bus. Or in the subway station, or even the stadium in Paris years ago. Or how about 9/11, or any of the other attacks around the world? Aren't they worth one life—"

"Not *your* life!" *Aw,* he hadn't meant to roar, and maybe he'd left the man he was behind on the mountain too, but—"Not the life of the woman I love."

She took her hands off the keys. "London."

"Yes. *You,* London."

"What if I'm not—"

"Don't play that game. You can't separate yourself into partitions. Sure, you had a life as a spy. It makes you clever and tough. And you are a diplomat's daughter, so that makes you adaptable.

And you are Delaney, the girl who wanted to be a princess, so that makes you an optimist and a dreamer—and frankly, we need more of those. And yes, you're a rescue pilot too, so that makes you dependable and steady and the person we are all hoping will show up." And now he'd gotten a hand around his thundering heartbeat, schooled his voice. "You can't shut off any of those parts of you, London, because that is who you are. Who God made you to be—"

"And what about this part of me that can't let it go?" She stood up, a fire in those beautiful eyes. "The me that refuses to sit on the sidelines when life is blowing up around me? What about that part?"

He blinked at her. And then he got it. *Oh, no,* he *got* it. "You *like* this life."

She swallowed, but the truth stripped away the game on her face. *Oh.* And with it came a punch to his chest.

His voice fell. "No. You crave this life. Because even your life as a pilot has this—danger and the sense of living on the edge—"

"I was called to a mission, Shep—"

He took a step forward, hating the sudden panic that edged his voice. "Guess what—me too. My mission was to keep you alive and bring you home. Mission accomplished. Let's *go.*"

She held up a hand. "Mission *not* accomplished. The Bratva has the money! They're going to use it for terrible purposes—"

"And what, you're going to get it back?" He didn't have a hope of calming down. "You and who else? Ziggy is *gone*—she was taken from the hospital."

That stripped her. "What?"

"Some guy came in with a medical team and discharged her. And York isn't around, so my guess is he might be behind that."

Her voice dropped. "Or Roy, maybe."

"Who?"

"Never mind—" And then, right before his eyes, she rebounded.

"Listen. Okay, so yes, I'll just need to reach out to the other Black Swans—"

"*Listen* to yourself!" He put a hand to his forehead. "Your entire team came over here to rescue you, and you're just . . . diving back in?" He blew out a breath. "Let someone else do this, London. What about the Caleb Group? Their entire goal was to get a tracker on this Alan Martin guy. They can track him, go after the money—"

"No. It was my mission. I can't let this go, Shep."

He could almost hear the cracking inside, everything shattering inside him. "So this is it. You're going to just walk away, just like you did in Zermatt. No looking back."

Please, please, London—

A beat. Then, "It seems to me that you're the one walking away, Shep."

He couldn't breathe, the vice in his chest so tight. Still, what did she expect of him? "I told you the first day, I'm not a man of violence. I don't *want* this life—"

"It seems like you do. Because you keep showing up. Because like it or not, being with me is an adventure for you. You *like* rescuing me—"

"I like making sure you don't die! So yes, I show up—to keep you safe. To make sure your impulsive, foolish alter ego doesn't get you and everyone around you killed!"

Her eyes widened. And yeah, that wasn't completely fair.

But maybe parts of it were true too. And then it hit him. "I can't hold on to someone who doesn't want to be held." He took a step back, hating the words that burned out of him. "I'm such a fool."

She stared at him, then lifted her chin. "Maybe I should never have come back from the dead."

He managed to keep his voice even. "Maybe not." He backed away, his hand up, his painkillers clearly wearing off, because his entire body ached. "I'm not going to follow you anymore, London. This is me, letting go."

Then he turned and walked to the door.

Her father stood in the reception area. "Shep," he said. "Where are you going?"

"Mission's over, sir," he said. "I give up." He kept walking. But at the doorway to the foyer, he turned. "You should tell her the truth."

Her father turned, started after him, but Shep ignored him and kept moving into the foyer, out through the doors, into the courtyard, and through the gates.

Because he was going home.

This was not how the story was supposed to end.

London stood by the piano, listening to his footsteps fading away, still listening as he went down the stairs, then, when the sound died, she turned to walk to the window.

She watched him leave through the gate.

Shep.

She put her hand on her chest. Outside, the sky turned dour, pewter gray, the snow peeling softly down to melt into the sidewalk and cobblestones.

No.

Maybe I should never have come back from the dead.

She hadn't meant that—it'd just come out, and *shoot*, she was eighteen again, standing there in the bloody aftermath of Ruslan's betrayal.

"Are you okay?"

She turned at the familiar British voice, her mouth opening as Pippa Marshall, best friend and current secretary to one Princess Imani of Lauchtenland, came into the room. "Pippa!" She met her friend's hug.

Pippa wore a suit, of course, and heels, her dark hair back in a bun. But some of the tension lines in her face had softened, her bun not quite so tight.

"You look good," London said, scrabbling to find her voice. "Marriage suits you."

"It does," Pippa said. "I never thought . . . you know . . . me. Married."

"I was there. I signed the papers."

"I remember the covert operation."

London laughed. "Fraser thought sneaking you to the altar might be the only way."

"He knows me. And speaking of—was that Shep Watson I saw leaving the embassy? Your mother is meeting with the princess, and I came out to check on our flight back to Lauchtenland. He didn't look happy."

Oh. "Yeah. I uh, he uh . . . You know, it's probably my fault for thinking I could settle down, live in one place—"

"Oh, that's a lie." Pippa tugged her over to the sofa, pulled her down beside her. "Take it from someone who thought her only life was in protective services. There is more to you than being a"—she cut her voice low—"Black Swan."

London wished. "I don't know. The fact is, sometimes I don't know who I am. Part Swan, part pilot, part . . . dreamer, maybe?"

"Oh, the Princess Delaney thing."

"Silly."

"No. Listen. You're *all* of that, London."

"It sounds like an identity crisis to me."

"Really. You know who doesn't have an identity crisis?"

"You?"

"God."

London gave her a sideways look.

"Three persons in one Godhead. And yet perfectly expressed in different ways."

"I'm hardly the Almighty—"

"Be we're made in his image. Capable of being more than we think. Yes, you're a Swan, but you're also this amazing rescue pilot. And yes, you're gorgeous in a dress. I spotted you at the ball—couldn't believe it. And then when you were taken and Fraser—"

"I thought I saw him at the fortress. Is he okay?"

"Yes. He and his brother Creed are waiting for us at the hotel."

"He helped rescue me?"

"Of course he did." Pippa took her hand. "But it was Shep who put it all together."

Of course he did. *I show up—to keep you safe.*

Even when he'd been hiding the fact that he was protecting her, he'd done it for her. Holding on to her. Her jaw tightened. "Shep and I are over. He's tired of running after me."

"Oh, I highly doubt that. Just give the man some time." Pippa stood. "And maybe yourself some time, too, to figure out what you really want."

London walked her to the door. "I don't know that it's about what I want. You told me once that you were made for royal service."

Pippa laughed. "I think we all are. My orders simply changed. And perhaps yours have too." She air-kissed London's cheeks. "I need to run. Ring me now and again."

London's hand fell on the handle, and the door opened, and for a second—a crazy second—she thought, hoped, that Shep had turned around, returned to her.

But no.

Pippa startled. "Mr. Brooks, sir."

"Pippa," her father said.

London backed up as her father came into the room. She shot a look down the hallway right before he shut the door.

Pippa glanced back at her, waved.

But no Shep.

She looked at her father. And Shep's words from yesterday in the tunnel returned to her. *"London, how much do you know about what your dad does? You two should talk. He knew that if I saw you, then . . . there was no way I'd let anything happen to you."*

Backing up, she put her hand on the back of one of the blue sofas. He had gone to the table, pulled out a straight chair, and now sank into it. Crossed his legs. Blew out a breath, then nodded at her. "I saw Shep leave. He'll be back."

"I don't . . . I don't think so."

"He loves you."

Swallowing, she nodded. "But . . . he's angry."

"Of course he is. I tried to tell him, but he wouldn't believe me."

She stilled. "Tried to tell him what? What did you hear?" Because yes, her mother might know the truth but—

"Honey, you should sit down." He indicated the sofa.

She sat down at the far end.

"I know you're a Black Swan."

Oh. That. She exhaled. "Right. I figured, since Mother knew."

"No. I am the one who got you into the Swans."

She cocked her head. "What?"

He put his hand on the table, tapped it. Sighed. "Your mother thinks the Swans were her idea. But long before your mother was assigned to be a diplomat, I was recruited by the CIA."

And just in case the world was really shifting, she put her hand on the arm of the sofa and gripped it. "You—"

"Your mother doesn't know. *Shouldn't* know. But long before she was assigned to Moscow station, I worked with a man named Pike Maguire."

"You knew Hawkeye?"

"Yes. He had left the CIA but needed someone on the inside who could . . . let's say, point business his direction. And frankly, sometimes I needed"—he took a breath—"extra-curricular help."

"Dad. That means the Swans have been around—"

"Since you were a child. About two years before the bus you and your sister were riding on was bombed." His gaze hardened. "Did you ever wonder why all the other attacks were at tube stations and this random one hit a double-decker bus?"

"Not even once."

"Right. It was supposed to look random. But that was the work of someone who has been working from the inside for decades. A group of people who believe that perhaps war is better than peace and that if they can move pawns, they can topple kings."

"I don't understand."

"When the Cold War thawed, it meant problems for brokers of war, of course, and one of the biggest was a group in Russia—"

"The Petrov Bratva."

"Yes. Their leader, Arkady Petrov, was—and is—a general. Now a member of the Troika—"

"The three-headed leadership under the president of Russia."

"Indeed. And standing in the shadows of power. We believe he's been trying for a decade to pull America back into a war, and over the past five years, he's tried to assassinate our president, poison our country, and even nuke a small NATO-connected nation. And all with money they made in cryptocurrency mining in Abkhazia."

"Where Tomas is from. I know his story."

"Did you know that the Petrovs had built a massive crypto-mining operation there? They stole resources from the government to power their banks of computer mines. Last year, it was all dismantled in a raid."

"Cutting off their money."

"Yes."

"Which is why they turned to Drago Petrov to get back the money I took."

"Yes." He drew in a breath. "And you were one of the pawns."

"How?"

"Tomas. His backstory is real—the Petrovs killed his mother.

And took his sister. He thinks they took her to work in the crypto mines. But when they purchased him, they offered him a different future, and when he saw how much they made . . . He was a boy from a village without running water or electricity, and suddenly he's riding in Learjets and driving cigarette boats."

"Dad. He's the head of the Petrovs. He killed Drago."

"I know."

A beat. "When did *you* discover this? Because I only just found out."

"We had our suspicions, but he played the victim with us, so we weren't sure. And then we caught him on surveillance last night accessing your account. He used his own thumbprint, his eye, and his blood to access the Petrov account. *Drago's* account. Then he transferred everything into his crypto wallet."

She knew it, but still, his words were a knife. "It's gone?"

"All of it."

"Why didn't you arrest him?"

"Because he's not the one we want, Laney."

She blinked at him. "Wait—it's true? Shep said all you wanted was Alan Martin."

He made a fist on the table, and something flashed in his eyes. "Alan betrayed our country and is the mastermind behind too many terror attacks. Capturing him would lead to countless other connections and dismantle who knows how many terrorist networks."

And then it clicked. "That's why Ziggy was there. To capture Alan Martin."

"Ziggy is the best Black Swan operative I've ever seen or worked with."

"Was she caught intentionally?"

He drew in a breath.

"Dad, she nearly died—"

Silence. And then, "She accomplished her mission—"

"At what cost?" Somehow London had landed on her feet. "Dad!"

He held up a hand. "She's alive. And I knew she would be because . . . you were there. And now she's alive and recuperating in a safe place."

She stared at him. "You wanted me to be there."

"You're Laney Steele. Of course I did. And of course I knew that inside that Black Swan exterior is also the heart of a rescuer. You weren't going to let her die."

But . . .

"You don't think I haven't been watching this past year, do you? Who do you think sent Ziggy to save your life after Tomas took a hit out on you with the Orphans?"

She stilled. "Tomas did that?"

"He needed your eye and your fingers. But I couldn't let it get that far."

She had nothing for that.

"Yeah, well, now he has the money because he got the code anyway." She refused to think about *how*.

"Yes, but we can track it now. And Ziggy succeeded. She put a tracker on Alan Martin."

"How?"

"A bio patch. It was made with nanostructure to create micropores in the skin. It embedded in him a biochemical marker with RFID tags."

The memory of Ziggy holding onto Martin despite his violence flashed through her.

"We can track him, figure out what he and the Petrovs are up to."

"They buy terrorists!"

He held up a hand. "And we'll stop them."

We.

His gaze met hers. "This doesn't have to be a failed mission, Laney."

Words echoed inside her. *"Mission's over, sir."*

"Wait. What did Shep mean when he said the mission was over? He said it to you—"

"It's something I asked him to do."

A moment, and then it all slid into her. "You were the one who asked him to watch over me in Alaska."

He lifted a shoulder. "You're my princess. Of course I did."

She heard Shep again, in the cave. *"Your dad said he pulled some strings to get my team up there."*

At the time, her brain had been too tired to untangle what he meant, and weirdly, she'd thought he'd meant that her dad had somehow told Shep she'd be on that mountain. Sort of a "Hey, Shep, how are you? Did you know my daughter is skiing Zermatt today?" Except, that didn't make sense at all, because Shep had been on a Ranger team, and how had her dad known . . .

"Did you . . . You set up the meet in Zermatt?"

He nodded. "I knew that if you were there, then Martin would show up. And I needed evidence that he was rogue. But I had to figure out a way to justify it to the CIA, so I told them about a rogue agent—your handler—and asked them to send in the nearby Rangers unit, because they were already there, training."

"Shep said that his unit was there to kill me."

He swallowed. "You were to be apprehended. I would have gotten you out. Alan was the one who changed the orders."

"And yet you let me go up that mountain."

"You were . . . you were our operative."

His words dropped through her, down to her soul.

"You would have let me be *murdered* on that mountaintop. As it was, Shep and I nearly died."

He folded his hands in his lap. "It was out of control. And I had one desperate hope—to get the man who followed you around camp so many years ago and asked for your address and even wrote to you a half dozen times to go on that mission, see you, and . . . shut it down."

Silence. Just her heartbeat, a hammer against her chest.

"What if Shep hadn't seen me? What if he'd not been able to stop them? What if—"

"It's global terrorism, Laney. And . . . this is what you were ordered to do."

She blinked. "By *you*."

"By the *cause*."

His words shook her to her bones. "Dad. I'm your daughter. Your only remaining daughter. Isn't it enough that you lost one already?"

His jaw tightened, and even from here she could see the hit, how his eyes flashed with unshed emotions. Then he swallowed. "It was my fault she was on that bus. They wanted me. But I went in early that day, and . . ." He shook his head.

"And yet you'd sacrifice another daughter."

He looked back at her. "All it takes for evil to prosper—"

"Save it." She backed away from him. Stood by the piano. Folded her arms. "You may be bound by glorious purpose, but I am not."

Gone was the grief, a simple fury now in his eyes. "Your sister died because of terrorist groups like the ones Tomas funds."

"Shep nearly died because you used me to get close to your personal nemesis!"

He flinched.

She'd wounded him. But he rose, drew in a breath. "And now you have your own personal nemesis." He folded his arms. "Tomas."

Tomas. "He was a good man until I turned him."

"No, he *never* was, London. He killed the first Drago and took his place—which was possible because no one knew what Drago truly looked like. He took a trip to Montelena after the avalanche and got a new bio card. You double-crossed him by putting the crypto into the Cryptex wallet, but even so, he didn't want the

CIA to get it, so you played right into his hand. All he had to do was die in that avalanche and then, when the time was right, find you, come back and get the cash. He knew you'd never spend it."

"I might have."

"Not when you're held hostage by your *own* glorious purpose, whether you want to admit it or not. You can thank your mother for that."

Oh. But her mother's words hung in her mind. *"We have drama because we are so much alike. We're both trying to change the world, just in our own way."*

"I need to stop trying to change the world."

"You'd sooner stop breathing." He met her eyes. "You are who you are, Laney. And you can't change that." He took a step toward her. "Once a Black Swan, always—"

"I worshipped you," she said softly. "The way you supported Mom, moving with her career. All this time, you were running ops—running *me*—right under her nose."

"Your mother knew you were a Swan."

"I know. No wonder she wanted me to marry a prince. She probably thought he could protect me from all this."

"Please. You wanted to be a princess."

"No, I didn't. That was a fantasy. I just wanted to be important enough for someone to notice me."

She turned and headed toward the door.

"Where are you going?"

"I have no idea. But I'm not staying here."

"Delaney."

She turned as she opened the doors. Grabbed both handles to shut them behind her. "Oh, I think Princess Delaney left the castle a long, long time ago."

There was just enough old-fashioned inside Moose for the sight of Tillie wearing an apron, her hands dusted in flour as she came to the front door, to make him feel like a man coming home from war. Or maybe the daily war. And yes, he'd seen her in her waitress outfit plenty of times, but this was different.

This was her dressed in wool socks, leggings, and his black grilling apron, her hair back and messy, greeting him like a . . . well, a *wife* . . . as he came into the foyer and dropped his bag.

Okay, maybe not exactly like a wife because, with Hazel still at school, if she were his wife, he would have swooped her up despite the fatigue that coursed through his body and had a much different *hello, I missed you* than just the kiss he gave her at the door.

He put his arms around her, pulling her close, the events of the last two days raw and fresh in his mind, the reality that, just like that, the world could cave in on any of them. "Oh, I missed you," he nearly growled as he kissed her, at first softly, then as she held tighter, okay, maybe devouring her a little.

Enough was enough. *Tonight* he would ask her. Even if the world fell in and the sun stopped shining. Tonight.

Even that felt too long to wait, but he smelled like he'd been on a plane for twenty-some hours, and what he really needed was a shower, and maybe some shut-eye, but that was off the table until he'd also had some grub.

So he pulled away, met her beautiful eyes. "What are you making?"

"Pie."

Of course.

"I quit my job at the Skyport."

He blinked at her. "What?"

She sighed. "So, here's the thing." She caught her lip and . . . "I love you, Moose. And having you gone, and just thinking about London—and yeah, she's not dead, but for a while you all thought she was and everyone was just shattered, and I know how much

Shep is crazy about her, and why didn't they get together before this? But I'm just aware of how precious this life, every moment, is and . . . what am I so afraid of?"

Huh. But yes, what she said.

"I want to do more than serve pie. I want to help women defend themselves. I was an Iron Maiden, for Pete's sake—"

"Yeah, you were." His voice held a tiny growl.

She grinned. "I told them that when I applied for a job at the gym near Hazel's school. It's just part time, helping women in self-defense classes and boxing and other strength-training workouts, but they hired me on the spot."

"Smart move."

She drew in a breath. "They still haven't come back with the ruling on my house, so no insurance money yet . . . which means . . ."

"You're sticking around."

"Want a roommate?"

Oh, he wanted more than that, but he nodded, caught her face. Kissed her again. "Let me clean up, and then we'll have dinner and . . ." He raised an eyebrow.

"And?"

"Wait for it."

"Okay. I need to go get Hazel anyway." She pulled off her apron, hung it up, and grabbed her car keys.

He climbed the stairs, dropped his bag on the bed, and then scrubbed his hands over his face.

"Poor Shep. I know how much Shep is crazy about her." What had gone down between Shep and London, Moose didn't know, but Shep had seemed shuttered and quiet and dark the entire trip home. Something must have happened after his declaration that he wasn't leaving Montelena without her.

Moose got into the shower, and he emerged a little restored, shaved, put on a clean flannel shirt and a pair of jeans, and then opened his dresser drawer. The ring sat on top of his white undershirts. He pocketed the ring box, then came downstairs to the smell of something roasting.

The house was empty. He checked his watch. He'd been up there a while, maybe forty minutes. Long enough for her to get to Eagle River and back.

Axel hadn't followed him home from the airport, heading right over to Flynn's apartment, of course.

He walked over to the pie that sat on the counter. Of course she'd done an amazing job. It had a lattice top and fluted edges, and the thought of her here making him a pie undid him a little.

The crockpot simmered and he peered through the glass top lid to find a pot roast. *Well, look at that.*

The door opened, and he put the lid back on. "Hey, Tillie, nice job on—oh."

Axel had walked into the room carrying a plastic bag full of groceries, and behind him, Flynn. Something about the looks on their faces had him pausing.

And . . . *wait*—"Is . . . what's . . . nothing has happened to Tillie, right?"

Flynn still wore her badge on her belt, and he glanced at it and everything tightened inside him. "This isn't an . . . it's not an *official* visit, right?" *Please.* He put his hand on the counter.

Flynn's eyes widened. "What?" She looked at Axel, back to Moose. "Are you okay?"

"Tell me *Tillie* is okay."

Flynn blinked, her mouth opening. "I don't . . . I think . . . What? Was she not okay? Are we worried—"

Oh. He closed his eyes, running his hand across his face. "Okay. Sorry. I'm just a little paranoid these days."

"Hard not to be," Axel said as he set a grocery bag on the counter. "Listen, did you know that Shep had his condo on the market?"

So maybe that was what the look was about.

"Our realtor got ahold of it, and Flynn went to see it while we were out of town. It's nice. And she wanted to put an offer in, but just today, the realtor said he'd pulled it."

"Huh. I didn't know he was going to sell it. He totally redid it the year he got here. But . . . interesting. I knew he was restless after London 'died.'" He finger-quoted that last word. "Maybe he's decided to stick around."

"You think London will be back?" Flynn slid out a chair. "Axel said something went down between them in Montelena."

Where to start? "If you mean he saved her life and then somehow they broke up, then yes," Moose said, not sure where that came from. He glanced at his watch again. What was taking . . .

"Uncle Moose!"

He looked up as Hazel tore through the door, her arms out.

And behind her, Tillie, carrying Hazel's backpack.

See, paranoid. Sheesh.

Hazel wore a pink sweatshirt with a unicorn on the front, a pair of leggings, her hair up in pigtails, and launched herself at him.

He caught her up. "Hey there, pumpkin," he said and kissed her cheek before setting her down. "I missed you."

"I missed you more."

If his heart grew any larger, it wouldn't fit in his chest.

Tillie hung up her coat, took off her boots. "Hazel, what did I say—no boots on Uncle Moose's hardwood floor."

"Sorry, Mom." She came back to the door, and Tillie tousled her hair as she walked past her.

"You made a pot roast," Moose said, moving aside for her.

"You mean that piece of meat I dropped into the crockpot, slathered with salt and pepper and onion seasoning mix just like the internet said?" She leaned up to him. "I know you're the cook here, but let me try a little."

He put his arms around her. "I'll let you try a lot."

Outside, night had fallen, pressing against the sliding glass door.

Tillie set the oven to bake, probably for the pie, and grabbed some plates to set the table.

Axel and Flynn went downstairs.

Hazel took the remote, curled up on the leather sofa, and turned on the television over the fireplace.

And Moose simply drank it in. London was safe and Boo was happy, and yes, his brother was still in the basement, but he and Flynn were on the hunt, their tomorrows large and bright in front of them, and maybe Shep nursed a broken heart, but again, London was alive, which meant anything was possible.

Most of all, the woman of his dreams stood in his kitchen, tossing a salad like . . . well, not that she belonged there, but she belonged *here*, with him.

Because this was his life, one he didn't deserve, but God was good, so good. . . .

Now.

Maybe it wasn't a candlelit dinner with flowers and a violinist, but it felt perfect and natural and right.

"Tillie." He came up to her, took her hand. She turned to him.

"Yes, handsome?"

He grinned. And then he reached into his pocket and pulled out the box.

Tillie's eyes widened as he went down on one knee.

Hazel screamed.

Moose turned. Then hit his feet.

Hazel stood on the sofa, her fists clenched, took a breath, and screamed again.

"What—*what?*"

Tillie was right behind him, nearly pushing him out of the way to get to Hazel.

"I saw a face! Right there—in the glass. A face!" Hazel pointed to the sliding-glass door.

Moose took three steps, yanked it open, and barreled outside.

"Moose!" Tillie's voice, panicked, and maybe it wasn't the right move because, *yeah*—who knew what he could be walking into? But he was tired—way beyond tired—of disaster sneaking up on them, of the world fighting to keep them apart.

Tired of saboteurs and serial killers and drug thugs and even international terrorists attempting to blow apart his life, the lives of the members of his team.

So he stood on his deck in the freezing cold, in his bare feet, staring out at the tumbling river below, silvery in the darkness under a rising moon, the wind shifting through the trees, the rush of water rising to his thundering heartbeat.

Nothing. He saw *nothing*.

He turned, glanced at Hazel. "You saw someone here?"

She nodded.

"What did he look like?"

She bit her lip. "Scary."

He looked down at the snow, and sure, footprints littered the deck, but they could be anyone's—his or Axel's, or even Tillie's.

But just to be sure, he stepped out to the end of the deck and looked over.

No one running away from the house.

He stepped back inside and closed the door. Locked it.

"She's been having nightmares," Tillie said quietly over Hazel's head as she held her.

He put his hand on Hazel's back. "I get that."

"I saw him," Hazel said, leaning back. "I really saw him."

"I know, honey. But he's not here."

"I would never let anyone—whoever he is—hurt you, pumpkin," Moose said. In fact, he'd had it with waiting to step into that role permanently.

He walked over to the counter, grabbed the ring box, and came over to Tillie.

She set Hazel down on the sofa. "Moose."

"Just—wait for it." He got on one knee. Held the stupid ring box open. Looked at Tillie.

"Yes!" Hazel said.

Tillie smiled. But said nothing.

"I love you—I've loved you for a long time, I think. You and Hazel are my whole world. And yes, the world might drop out on us at any moment, but I'm gonna catch us. Or at least hold on to God while he catches us. I don't want to live one more moment without us being a family, so—"

"Yes, yes!" Hazel said, jumping on the sofa.

"Tillie Young, will you marry me?"

She smiled. "Sorry I made you wait so long."

He stood and grabbed her up and spun her around. Then, *wait*—he put her down. "You didn't say yes. Please say yes."

She parked her arms around his neck, smiled up at him. "Yes. Absolutely. Forever. I'll stand with you, Moose, and trust you, even try to hold you up if the world falls apart. I promise."

He kissed her, his hands cradling her face, keeping it chaste but still savoring her.

"Mom! The pie! The pie!"

He lifted his head and Hazel pointed at the oven, where smoke had gathered around the edges.

And as Tillie ran to the oven, opened it, and pulled out the pie—not burnt but deliciously done—he knew.

Nothing could hold him back from his happily ever after.

THIRTEEN

THE SNOWMOBILERS HAD MADE THE DISAS-
trous mistake of splitting up.

Shep sat in the bed of the Air One chopper, the night
falling around them, the belly lights illuminating the white for-
ested earth as he scanned for a man hiking the remote snow trail.

"Any sign of him?" Moose, through Shep's headphones.

"Just a bunch of caribou," he said. Their dark brown bodies
spotted a field they'd passed. With caribou, there had to be wolves,
and a guy walking alone in the Alaskan forest had about as much
chance against them as . . .

Well, as Shep had of trying to shake London out of his heart.

Yeah, bad analogy, but frankly, he had London on the brain, so
everything in the past five days since returning from Montelena
had been about her. About being *without* her, about walking away
from her, about finding footing in a life without her.

About his stupidity.

"He shouldn't have left her," he said now of the man, Willis
James, who'd abandoned his wife and their ten-year-old son on

the trail after a snowmobile crash that had broken the woman's leg and left both machines tangled.

They'd gotten the call from Winter Starr, a bush pilot who'd flown overhead earlier today and spotted the red jackets of the woman and her son. When they'd waved at her, she'd searched for a put-down place. When she couldn't find one, she'd done the next best thing.

Called Air One Rescue.

Shep had been dressed and out the door before Moose ended the call, five days of hanging out in his condo turning him antsy. He'd even tried to call his parents again. He could use words from his father, but again, the call went to voicemail. Figured. They were probably out on a slope somewhere.

He taught Caspian a few new tricks. He liked the dog, and after a call to the shelter, where they confirmed that the owner hadn't responded, he'd decided to keep him. Jasmine had done a decent job of taking care of him while Shep was gone. Apparently wanted to make that known to Shep, too, once he returned. He had a veritable smorgasbord of food in his fridge, each day a new offering.

Maybe he shouldn't have taken the listing down. But . . . he wasn't going to run. He had built a life here. Even without London.

Still, the place felt almost emptier than before, when he'd thought her gone forever.

Shep had driven into the Tooth almost on autopilot, and Moose took the crew out in the chopper—Boo, Shep, Axel. They found the mother and son shivering and nearly hypothermic in a partial snow cave that Shep had to admit wasn't a terrible construction. Better to have closed it off from the elements, but he made no criticism as Boo and Axel went down on a line, splinted the leg of the woman, then brought them both up in baskets.

Moose had flown them to the Copper Mountain clinic, then returned to search the trail for the husband.

Now, as twilight pressed in, shadows lengthening from the purple mountains in the north and west, the ground turning hazy, the chances of finding him before bingo on Moose's gas tanks . . .

And tonight's temps would drop to lethal below-zero digits.

"Put me on the ground, Moose. I have snowshoes—let me at least see if I can track him."

Moose said nothing.

"We can't even see footprints from up here. It hasn't snowed in the last twenty-four hours—if he went this way, I'll be able to see it. Besides, the trail diverges up ahead—maybe he took the other path."

"Fine. Sit tight—let me find a place to land."

Shep glanced at Axel, who wore a red jumpsuit, earphones. Not dressed for weather but for going out the door on a line, bringing up victims. Shep was the one who manned the open door, buffeted by the high winds, and he'd donned an extra jacket, a wool hat, and thermals under his jumpsuit. Besides . . . snow was his element.

As Moose found a wide space, Shep reached for his snowshoes, then clipped them on. Grabbed a headlamp, took off his helmet and fitted it over his hat, then took a handheld walkie and clipped it to the collar of his jacket.

"Do not get lost," Axel said as he opened the door.

"I'll turn on my GPS," Shep said as he landed in the snow. Here, a snowmobile trail had packed down the white into tiny ridges, and he ventured out from the chopper's ring of light, following the glow of his headlamp.

Do not get lost. He was in a perpetual state of lost, it seemed like. Or maybe two pieces of him were going in different directions.

Focus. London had made her choice. And he'd made his. He'd have to get his brain around that.

Now, he walked a hundred yards up the trail, scanning the ground for footprints. His feet crunched in the snow, and the farther away he got from the glow of the chopper, the darker the world became, just his tiny light illuminating his next steps.

Weirdly, his father's voice entered his head. *"Thy word is a lamp unto my feet, and a light unto my path."*

Around him, the wind lifted, and in the distance lingered the mourning howl of wolves.

"I am the light of the world. Whoever follows me will never walk in darkness, but will have the light of life."

"The Lord is my light and my salvation—whom shall I fear?"

There—he keyed his mic. "I see footsteps off the main path—looks like he followed a trail." Shep headed toward the path, a swath through the forest. And then saw why—

Ahead, in the darkness, a light flickered, a fire maybe, the glow scattering against tree trunks and into the night, winking out as it hit the clouds.

"I see a campfire. Maybe he hunkered down for the night." Not a bad idea, although if he'd had the means to camp, he would have stayed with his family.

Unless . . .

He followed the ebbing and glowing light, the darkness thickening behind him as his headlamp parted the forest. The smells of campfire burned into the breeze, and as he came up to it, he spotted a man crouched in front of another man, seated on the ground. A pack sat in the snow nearby.

The first man, dressed in a heavy winter coat, wearing a furry shapka, the flaps tied up on his head, held a Sierra cup, helping the second man drink it. The other man, wearing a red jacket, had lost his hat, his hair tipped with snow, his ears nearly white.

Willis James, his lost snowmobiler?

Fur man looked up at Shep. Nodded. "I was wondering when you'd get here."

What?

"I heard the chopper. I figured you were hunting our lost hiker here."

"I'm with Alaska Air One." He looked at the man on the ground, who was still struggling to drink. "Are you Willis James?"

The man looked up and dropped the cup. "My wife—"

"We have her. And your son."

Willis covered his face with his hands, shaking.

The man in the fur hat stood up. "I found him on the trail just up the way. He'd collapsed. I had to carry him to my camp—" He stepped forward, held out a mittened hand. "Judah."

Shep took it. "Shep."

Judah's long dark hair fell from the back of his hat, and he was tanned, as if he spent time out in the wild.

"What are you doing out here?" Shep asked Judah as he crouched next to Willis.

"Visiting a friend. He's got a cabin about a mile from here. I was walking on the trail when I spotted Willis here."

Only then did Shep see a pair of snowshoes parked on the ground near the fire.

"Always carry a Sierra cup and some flint with me," Judah said and winked. "Boy Scouts."

Of course, London stepped into his brain. He shook her away. "Good thing you happened along."

"God's path always takes you in the right direction."

Shep frowned, then stood up and radioed Moose.

"I'll send Axel your way with a litter," said Moose.

Meanwhile, Judah had put another log on the small campfire he'd built. It glowed in the darkness, the howl of the wolves still lifting in the breeze. "We can give you a ride back to your cabin," Shep said.

"Then I'd miss the beauty of the starry night," Judah said. "It's in the extreme darkness that the light shines the brightest."

Judah and his old man would make good friends. "And you're not afraid of getting lost?"

"You're only lost when you think you have a destination."

Oh boy. "Of course."

"My destination is simply to follow." He pointed to the sky, the swath of Milky Way. "There is enough light from the heavens to get me home."

Huh. Still, "I can't, in good conscience, leave you out here to freeze."

In the distance, he heard Axel's voice calling.

"Over here!" He turned back to Judah. "It's not safe."

"Safe is not a destination, Shep. It's a perspective. An understanding." He crouched in front of Willis, grabbed the Sierra cup. "Even when the world seems to be unraveling around you."

"Yeah, you can't think yourself safe there, pal."

Judah poured more hot water into the Sierra cup after adding another packet of cocoa. Now he handed it to Willis. "Drink. You'll be okay." Then he stood up. "Safety is about faith. Knowing that even if something goes terribly wrong, God still has you."

It was like talking to his old man.

"But you have to have faith. Without it, you can do everything right and still end up lost, right, Willis?"

The man looked up at him, holding his cup with both hands. They needed to get him to warmth, pronto. "I'm sorry. I just can't leave you out here."

"Because that is who you are." Judah had started to kick snow onto the fire. It sizzled in the flames. "You're a rescuer. That is your calling. Your mission."

The words settled inside him. *"Are you still on mission?"*

Axel came through the path, dragging the litter behind him like a sled. "Hey-ho." He frowned at the sight of Judah. "Who are you?"

"Judah. Lion," said the man, who held out his mittened hand to Axel. "Just a traveler. Let me help you get Willis into the basket."

Shep and Axel tucked Willis in—the man had gone dangerously quiet—and they packed him with a blanket, put a hat on him.

The fire had nearly died out, leaving just glowing embers.

"I'm going to say it one more time," Shep said, taking the other side of the sled handle. "Let us bring you home. Last chance."

"Not all those who wander are lost," said Judah. He winked. "Love that book. Take care of my friend Willis." He picked up a pack, shouldered it on, and headed out into the darkness, up the trail.

"Is he okay?" Axel said as he took the handle of the sled. "And what book?"

"*Lord of the Rings*. J. R. R. Tolkien. He wrote it about Aragorn, the ranger who roams Middle Earth. He wanders but is not lost because he knows his mission and his purpose. And follows it without being double-minded."

Axel pulled with him. "Double-minded?"

"Something my father used to say. Constantly being tossed by regrets or what-ifs . . ." Shep looked back. It seemed that the darkness and the forest had simply swallowed Judah.

They came out onto the path, the chopper's light pressing against the darkness, like a beacon. Willis roused, and only when they pulled up to the chopper did Shep realize that the man had started to weep. Again.

"It's okay, man," Shep said. "You're safe." He and Axel loaded Willis in, then he climbed in beside him as Boo took his vitals. Shep bundled him up more as Axel closed the door and Moose kicked up the rotors.

The man reached out, grabbed Shep's hand, his grip tight. "Thank you for not giving up."

Shep froze. Then nodded.

He sat back in the seat, donning his headphones as the chopper lifted off the ground into the night. *I give up.*

Aw. The words were a knife right into his chest.

"Are you still on mission?"

Oh no. He closed his eyes. *Stop.*

"Trust in the Lord with all your heart, do not depend on your own understanding. Seek his will in all you do, and he will show you which path to take."

Still his father, in his head. But maybe that was the one thing he'd forgotten in all this. He'd been trying to sort it all out with his own understanding, his own ways.

Below them, the forest had turned dark save for one small light, a cabin on a hill, not far from the trail.

"Are you still on mission?"

Fine. Yes. Because the one calling, the one path that felt right despite the route, had always been London.

Still was London.

And maybe—well, he was a rescuer. Her rescuer. *"You like rescuing me—"*

He did. He loved being the guy who made her smile, but it wasn't just about him swooping in to save her from Tomas—it was the way she laughed at his jokes and kept up with him when they were working out and even argued with him over a movie plot.

It was the way she made him believe that he was her hero.

Even though she was clearly able to take care of herself.

So yes. He *did* like rescuing her. Because somehow, in letting him, she rescued him right back. Made him into a man he wanted to be.

The kind of man who showed up.

And kept showing up.

He looked at Axel, and then, through the mic, said, "So, you still in the market for a condo?"

"You're missing Alaska."

London looked over from where she sat at a small bistro table, nursing a macchiato and reading a book. She put it face down on the table and looked up.

Oh. Prince Luka was attached to that male voice. She sat up, about to rise and curtsy, but he held out his hand. "We're in public, and this isn't a formal event, and all that is optional anyway until I'm crowned. But may I?" He gestured to the chair opposite her.

She nodded.

He picked up the book as he sat down. "*The Call of the Wild*."

"Recommended by a friend."

"Jack London. As I recall, it's about a dog and the people he saves."

"The dog is very loyal."

"Buck." He set the book down. "Ends up joining a wolf pack. You can take the dog out of the wild but not the wild from the dog."

"Or maybe he just made a choice. And thanks—now I don't need to finish it."

Prince Luka leaned back in the chair, crossed one leg over the other, folded his arms. He wore a simple white pullover sweater, dress pants. "No. Finish it. The journey—not the ending—is the point of the story. It's how the characters change and grow and become, right?" He winked.

Admittedly, he was a very handsome man. Dark hair that curled just slightly at his ears, tousled perfectly, and blue eyes that twinkled with charm. He bore a military frame, sturdy and lean, and she knew he'd served in some command position. Maybe search and rescue, which of course sounded right. After all, he was a prince. He even smelled good.

No wonder her mother hoped to throw her at him.

"I guess." She picked up the book and stuck her napkin into it as a page marker. "Maybe I'm just tired of the journey."

"You're not even halfway through the book."

She set the book down. "Do you ever get tired of being the prince?"

Silence. She looked up at him.

He seemed to be thinking through her words, gazing out to the mountains, to the castle on the ridge. Snow had fallen steadily for the last few days, finally sticking to the ground, turning the world, the city, white and sparkling.

"It's who I am. So while fatigue comes from the demands, the expectations, I can't change that."

Right. "What if you had a choice, though? To walk away. To be . . . common."

He laughed. "No one is common, Delaney. Each of us is royal. At least, if you are a believer in God's Word and a child of salvation. By His Word, we're all children of the King. Some of us just wear the crown on earth."

Right.

"Is this about the job offer?"

A beat. "How did you know about that?"

"I was the one who suggested it." He leaned forward. "You speak three languages, you know protocol, and frankly, you'd be a great asset to the office of the ambassador. Plus, you could travel with my envoy." His smile warmed in her direction. "Perhaps, in time . . ."

Oh. "Prince Luka—"

"Just Luka."

"I don't . . . I'm not . . ." She sighed. "I am not sure what I want."

"I see."

A waitress came over, curtsied, and then set his tea in front of him.

"Apparently she didn't get the memo," London said as he thanked her.

"If she wants to curtsy, then I respect that," he said. "Respect is different than require, right?" He took a sip of the tea, set the

284

cup back down. "I never want my countrymen to respect me out of fear but out of trust."

No wonder he was beloved.

"So you'll be turning down the offer?"

The look on his face could almost make a woman reconsider. But she just hadn't . . . it didn't feel . . .

"I suppose that makes sense. To be honest, I was surprised, during the weekly meeting with your mother, to hear that you were still here."

Of course he had a weekly meeting with her mother.

"I had heard that your friends left—and I thought you'd left with them."

"No. It seems as though my life in Alaska is . . . well, maybe I'm headed in a different direction."

"Hmm." He stirred his tea, then fished out the bag. "Indeed, I can almost see the Alaskan landscape in your expression."

No, he could see Shep in her expression, the longing for him, his devastating smile, his strong hands in hers, the sense that he was always there, behind her, beside her, in front of her. Her best friend.

Everything inside her simply ached.

Luka took a sip of tea, set it back in the saucer. "It's wild and untamed, correct?"

Oh, still talking about Alaska, because she'd hardly call Shep untamed.

Although, he'd kissed her a little like that . . . twice.

Two perfect, unleashed moments when she thought she'd tasted his heart. Her eyes burned, but she blinked and turned to Luka. "Yes, but no. It's . . . beautiful and big and rugged, and yes, it can be dangerous, but also . . . it's a place to restart your life . . . maybe find yourself."

He considered her. "You were flying search and rescue, correct? On some team?"

"Did my mother tell you that?"

"I believe it was your friend Shep."

She frowned. "I don't—when—"

"He made quite a ruckus at the castle during our gala. I think your mother is still trying to sort it all out with my mother."

Her mouth opened. "You . . . what? What do you know about that?"

He frowned. "My father may be the sovereign, but he's delegated management of Cryptex to me. So yes, I am aware of his attempted breach of our complex."

His attempted breach. "Shep?"

"Oh." He grimaced. "I've let the cat out of the bag, haven't I?"

"What cat? What bag?"

"So the fact is, I saw your friend Shep that night, after you disappeared."

Correction—*after I was kidnapped.* But she didn't say that. Who knew how much—

"He told me you were abducted by some bad players. The Russian Bratva? You had me quite worried, but he said he and his team would find you. That's when I realized that your friend . . . well, I don't know how to tell you this, Delaney, but I believe your friend Shep is a spy."

Oh. She managed to keep her face unmarked by the revelation.

"Let's just say that he told me he had a plan to upload a virus into your Cryptex account. I think he feared that he'd gotten you somehow caught up in his clandestine game."

Right. He probably had to say *something* about the blackout and the sirens, so . . . And the best way to lie was to tell the truth, right? "I see."

"I spoke to him briefly during the panic, after the lights were restored. It was then that he mentioned that you might have been abducted. Later, he found me—he said you'd been taken into the mountains and they were going to find you. And then he told me the entire story, about how the Bratva wanted to steal your money and was coercing you to give it to them."

"He told you that?"

"Said that he was trying to stop an international terrorist plot and that he'd developed a virus that could track the money if they stole it from you. He gave me a drive and told me to upload it and attach it to your account, in case it got accessed. I had my people look at it—and confirmed it was a tracker. It could follow the Cryptex NFT throughout the blockchain. So I had them upload it and attach it to your account."

She just stared at him.

"I know. I hate to be the one to tell you this. People are not always what they seem."

Oh, that was just it. Shep was *exactly* what he seemed.

Her hero. For as long as she could remember.

"So, did they get it?" he asked.

She frowned.

"The money. Did they get into your Cryptex wallet?"

She sighed. "Yes. The money is gone. It was moved—"

"Which means it can be tracked."

And just like that . . . with his words, it was over.

Her orders changed. Or maybe she was simply released from duty. Sure, she heard her father's words from just a few days ago, the ones that seemed pinned to her soul— *"You are who you are, Laney. And you can't change that"*—and maybe he was right. She couldn't change it. But she could be *more* than that.

The journey was the point. As was the changing and growing and becoming.

She sat, looking at Luka as he sipped his tea, and heard her mother's words from days ago. *"I want you to be happy. To find a man who sets your heart on fire. With whom every day is a new adventure. And who makes you feel adored. Like a princess."*

A man like Shep.

"Have you ever heard of a black swan, Luka?"

He set down his cup. "Yes. It's an unexpected event. Something completely out of the ordinary that has great impact. But also something that should be obvious to everyone in hindsight. Like your 9/11 attacks."

"Indeed."

"Or I suppose your sudden desire to return to Alaska?" He smiled then and raised a regal eyebrow.

She smiled back. "Did you mean it when you said you'd do anything in your power for me?"

"As if you were a princess. However, I do think you're about to break my heart."

She bowed her head, then met his eyes. "How do you feel about lending me a plane?"

How Moose loved it when everyone came home safely.

Moose walked across the tarmac to the Tooth after moving the chopper into the Air One Rescue Quonset hut, the memory of the James family's reunion at the Anchorage hospital still warm in his mind.

Yes, this was how it was supposed to turn out—happy endings. No more lawsuit. And Shep seemed better as he talked with Axel at the hospital. Something about Axel and Shep's new dog and his condo—

Maybe Shep would be okay. And Boo and Oaken seemed on their way to the altar, and . . . and maybe he should just stop worrying about everything.

Start savoring the fact that every day, God carried him through the valley to the next mountain.

Moose walked inside, and everything seemed brighter when he

spotted Tillie. She wore her jacket, her beautiful black hair pulled back, boots, and a smile that went right to his soul.

Yes, he loved it when everyone came home safely.

She was hugging Boo, then showing her the ring as the door closed behind him.

"Moose. You didn't say anything," Shep said, walking over to him. He grabbed Moose's hand, slapped him on the arm.

"I was waiting until we got the ring sized," Moose said.

"I just picked it up," Tillie said, coming over to him. She put her arms around his neck and then, in front of everyone, kissed him.

Oh. Well, then.

Just a short kiss, but that was enough right here, right now. "Can we get married tomorrow?"

She laughed, patted his cheek. "Absolutely."

He held her in the circle of his arms. "I was thinking maybe . . . a party? At my place? Tonight." Despite the pitch darkness outside, the night was still early, plenty of time for steaks on the grill.

"There's a Blue Ox hockey game on tonight," said Axel. "I recorded it."

"I need to run home and check on my dog," Shep said. "But if I can bring Caspian, then cool."

"Aw, too bad Hazel isn't here." Tillie said. "She loves dogs." She put her hands on Moose's chest. "I dropped Hazel off at Roz's. She never gets to see her anymore, what with my not needing Roz to babysit. How about if I pick up a pie?"

"I need to go home, shower, and change," Boo said. "I'll ask Oaken to pick me up. We'll meet you there."

"I can drive you," Tillie said. She looked at Axel. "Thanks for the use of your wheels."

"No problem, Til."

"I'll get my gear," Boo said and went into the locker room.

Axel and Shep followed her, and Moose stood out in the foyer with Tillie. Pulled her back to himself and lowered his voice. "I wasn't kidding about tomorrow."

She put her hands on his chest, running them over his jumpsuit. "Give a girl a few days to find a dress."

"You could get married in a burlap bag for all I care." He kissed her again, this time slower, savoring her, drinking in the mystery of how suddenly the world seemed right and perfect, untouchable.

Boo came out of the locker room. "Whoops—"

Tillie untangled herself from his embrace, laughing.

Laughing.

He could live forever in that laugh. Rare and beautiful. It wrapped around him and sent heat through him to his bones.

"C'mon," Boo said, heading toward the door.

"See you at the house," he said as they left.

Shep came out next, also holding his gear. "I'll be there in an hour or so."

"Perfect. I'll get the steaks seasoned up."

Shep left and Axel came out. "I called Flynn. She's just finishing up her shift. Said she'd connect with Tillie and ride with them." He clamped his hand on Moose's shoulder. "We'll call this an engagement party."

"I can live with that," Moose said. He went into the locker room, changed out of his jumpsuit. Came out to see Axel texting. "What's up?"

"Flynn said that Dawson called her—has news about Tillie's house fire." He pocketed the phone. "Said she'd talk to us when she got there." He picked up his bag. "Let's go."

They were walking out of the Tooth when a Porsche Cayenne pulled up. The window slid down.

"Hey, Oak," Axel said. "Nice wheels."

"Thought I'd need something sturdy for Alaska."

"Couldn't have gone with a Ford?" Axel said. "Just sayin'."

"Leave the rock star alone," Moose said.

Oaken smiled, shook his head. "I was coming to meet Boo, but she texted to say we're meeting at your place?"

"Engagement party," said Axel.

"About time," Oaken said. He stuck his hand out the window, grabbed Moose's in a handshake.

So maybe it hadn't been a terrible idea to say yes to the reality show last fall. Yes, it had had some serious ripple effects—like Tillie's ex tracking her down, and maybe London's past also finding her. But it had also given Boo a future, and they'd tracked down a serial killer, and Axel had miraculously found someone who could put up with him. Okay, that wasn't fair—Axel was a catch. He just needed the right person.

They all did.

"I'll follow you to the house," Oaken said.

Moose headed over to his truck and threw his bag in the back. Axel had gotten into the passenger seat. The lights of the city shone upon wet pavement, a slight wind off Cook Inlet sprinkling snow like fairy dust into the air.

"I think Shep might be leaving us," Axel said quietly as they drove up the highway. "He offered to sell me his condo."

Moose looked at him. "Really? I thought he'd taken it off the market."

Axel lifted a shoulder. "I don't know. He seemed pretty jazzed about it, so maybe he's headed back to Montelena?"

"He's been in love with London for years, I think. I don't know why I didn't see it before, but yeah, once you find the one . . . well, if I were him, I would do anything to be with the woman I loved."

"Even give up Air One?"

Moose looked at Axel. Frowned. "What are you saying?"

Silence.

They turned off the highway onto Moose's road.

"Are you thinking of leaving too?" The question sat in Moose's gut.

"What? No. Just thinking about how life can turn, just like that. And what you do when it does."

"I think you stand on what you know. Circumstances and even life plans aren't your foundation, right? God is," Moose said. "So I guess, yes, I'd give up Air One if I had to. But I think Tillie is happy in Anchorage, so . . ."

They'd turned down Moose's driveway, dark, the trees hovering overhead. It occurred to him as they drew closer to the house that the motion lights hadn't flicked on. Maybe a fuse was out.

He pulled up, Oaken's headlights behind him, and then Oaken pulled up next to him. The house sat in darkness, the front porch light off.

"The power out?" Oaken said as he got out. He'd turned his cell phone light on.

"Guess so. Happens sometimes after a storm." Moose grabbed his gear. "I'll check on the fuses in the garage before the ladies get here."

He walked up the front steps, pressed the key code for the door, and let himself in, followed by Axel and Oaken.

He missed Hazel's cheery voice greeting him when he walked in the door. Tomorrow wouldn't be soon enough.

He tried the light. Nothing. *Weird.* "The house is off too."

"Where's the fuse box?" Oaken said. "I'll take a look."

"It's in the basement. I'll go," Moose said. He dropped his gear, pulled off his boots, and hung his coat, and the guys did the same.

Axel followed him downstairs to his domain.

He could have flicked on his cell phone, but Moose let his memory lead him through the dark basement. Just the moonlight off the river, shining into his sliding-glass-door walkout, gave him light into the theater room with the flatscreen and big sectional. Axel grabbed his cell phone and flicked on his flashlight as they walked into the room with the hot tub and sauna attached. Moose had thought he knew this place inside and out until London had sneaked in through said sauna over a week ago via Pike's secret lair.

He'd have to board that up. Now, he went to the electrical panel in a nook next to the sauna and opened it. Shone his cell phone flashlight on it.

The main breaker had blown. He turned it back on, and lights flushed through the entertainment area. "You left the light on when you left for the callout," he said to Axel.

"Add it to my tab."

The television also flicked on in the entertainment area. Moose gave him a look as he turned.

And stopped.

"Just slow your roll there, Moose," said Harry Benton, standing with a small Glock pointed at Axel, who now raised his hands.

Harry wore an army-green jacket, boots, and carried a backpack.

And behind him, another man. *Right*—Liam Grant. He held a shotgun, trained on Moose.

Moose drew in a breath. He wasn't close enough to grab either gun—not that he knew how he would do that—but the impulse shot through him along with the punch of shock.

He raised his hands. "Listen, guys—"

"Shut up," Harry said. Not a big guy, really, but the man was burly enough to suggest he wasn't someone that would go down easily. And behind him, Liam looked a little unhinged. From the snow on their jeans, it looked like they'd trekked here from the woods.

Except, how had they—

Oh. His thoughts went back to Hazel, seeing someone on the deck. And how he'd stepped out to see and then gone back inside—and had he locked the door?

Maybe. But it had been days since then and . . .

Maybe it didn't matter how they'd gotten in. Just, "What do you want?"

Harry motioned for them all to move into the theater room. Liam backed up, his gun following them.

These guys had probably thought this out while he'd been off flying around Europe.

A chill went through him at how he'd left Tillie and Hazel here alone.

"Get on your knees," Harry said.

Moose didn't move.

"Hey, Moose, the lights came on upstairs, so—"

Oaken came down the stairs, hit the landing, and before Moose could shout, a shot exploded, ricocheting through the house.

Oaken jerked back, shouted, then fell the final few steps.

"Hey! Stop!" Moose said.

"Don't move!" Liam, now turning back to Moose.

Definitely unhinged.

Oaken had gotten up, now backpedaled to the wall, blood spurting out of a shoulder wound, running down his arm. A groan pulsed out of him. "You shot me! Why'd you shoot me?"

Moose glanced at Liam. Maybe the idiot had shot Oaken by accident, a reflex, but now his gaze hardened, and he narrowed his eyes.

"Because you deserve to die." The cool voice of Harry Benton, taking over.

A frozen silence slithered through Moose, and maybe Axel too, because he drew in a breath.

Oh. No.

Oaken's gaze hardened into recognition. "Benton."

"Get him over here," Benton said to Axel, and motioned with his handgun. Axel helped Oaken over to the main area, in front of the sofa.

"Now get on your faces."

Aw. Moose didn't move. "C'mon, Benton. You want me, not the team. It was my fault we didn't go back out. My call—"

Benton turned his gun to Axel.

"Okay, okay . . ." Moose lay down, his face into his carpet, fighting off words.

"Tie him up," said Benton to Axel, and tossed him the backpack.

Axel pulled a zip tie from the bag. Swallowed.

Benton turned his gun on Moose.

"Just take a breath there, Benton. I gotta figure out how to work these." Axel stepped over Moose. "Sorry."

Moose looked at him, his jaw tight. Met his eyes.

Axel nodded.

Another shot—and this time, the television shattered over them, careening off the wall. Axel caught it a second before it landed on Moose, and pushed it away.

"Next one goes into your brother," said Benton, and Axel held up his hands in surrender.

Moose let Axel bind him.

"Tighter," said Benton.

Yeah, that worked. The tighter the better.

"And his feet."

Axel tied Moose's feet.

"Now the movie star."

Moose closed his eyes, listening to Oaken grunt. He lay on the floor, also face down, bleeding into the carpet.

Liam came over and put the end of his shotgun against Moose's head.

"Now you, hotshot," said Benton.

Axel landed on the floor next to Moose, his forehead into the carpet, a muscle pulling in his jaw.

From somewhere, Moose's cell phone buzzed, and he realized he'd dropped it near the sauna.

Liam went to get it, came out with it still ringing. "It's someone named Hot Hot Babydoll."

Axel looked at Moose. "Really?"

"She typed in her own name," he said with a growl.

"Decline the call. She'll worry." Benton crouched in front of him. "Then text her and tell her that he's tied up but to hurry. Then go upstairs and pull the gas line from the stove. We want everything to be ready when they get here."

Moose froze. "You burned down Tillie's house."

"You should thank me. She and her cute daughter moved in here to play house. Your happy little family." Benton stepped back. "I told you someday you'd know how it felt to lose someone. How about your entire team?" He took another step back. "Now you'll know how it feels to wait, knowing every minute brings you closer to the death of the people you care about."

Moose swallowed. Closed his eyes. Thank God Hazel wasn't here.

But he lay there, and all he could think was . . .

Please, Tillie, don't come home.

FOURTEEN

THE TOOTH WAS DARK.

London didn't know exactly what scenario had lodged in her brain over the past twenty-some hours, but maybe, just a little, she'd hoped the team might be . . . what? Waiting for her? With open arms?

"You getting out?" This from her Uber driver.

"No. Can I add an address?"

Probably better to go back to her old house, see if Boo might be there. She owed Boo an explanation anyway.

"Sure," Uber man, a guy named Felix, said. She told him the address and he keyed it in, and the additional fare came up on her phone.

They drove away from the Tooth, into the night, the lights of Anchorage glimmering against the faraway mountains.

So, okay, perhaps her decision to return to Alaska might be more celebrated in her head than in reality, especially since she'd so dismantled Shep's hopes and sent him away dark and wrecked.

Who knew what he'd said to Moose and Axel? Although, as Felix drove through the neighborhoods toward her rental home, she dismissed the accusation. Shep wasn't a guy to bare his pain to his buddies.

Even to her, really.

In fact, the guy was, and had always been, so solid, so put together that she hadn't really realized how much she'd hurt him over the years until he'd left her in Montelena.

Okay, she'd had a glimpse of the depths of his love when he'd kissed her, but . . .

Yes, the man was a well of emotion behind that steadfast exterior.

And she'd torn him apart. No wonder he'd given up.

Hopefully, those emotions wouldn't make him turn her away, too angry with her to give her a second—no, probably this ranked as fifth—chance.

"This one?" said the man, and London nodded as he pulled up to the small bungalow that overlooked Cook Inlet. Of all the places she'd lived, this was one of her favorites, the view through the trees of the water, the piney smell that surrounded the yard. Boo's Rogue sat in the plowed driveway. Another car was parked behind it, a Yukon, and she recognized it as Axel's car.

Huh.

She grabbed her bag, got out, and confirmed the payment, added a tip, then headed to the door.

Okay, deep breath. Yes, her roommate knew she was alive, but . . . well, that conversation hadn't quite gone down yet between them, so . . .

She opened the door.

Stepped inside.

Tillie sat on the sofa in the family room, frowning at her phone. She looked up, and her mouth opened. "London?"

London dropped her bag in the entryway. "Hey." She shut the door. "What's going on?"

"London!"

She followed the voice to see Boo on the stairs, wearing a pair of leggings and an oversized sweatshirt.

"Hey, Boo—"

But Boo had rushed down the stairs. "I know I saw you in Montelena, but . . . sheesh, you walked away before I got . . . well, this." She pulled London hard into her embrace.

"I'm sorry." Wow, she'd been selfish, and Shep's words about being cruel rushed back to her. London's throat thickened, her chest knotted, and *shoot*, now her eyes filled. "I'm sorry I lied to you."

Boo held her away. Met her gaze, her own eyes watery. "No, I get needing to hang on to secrets, even wanting to leave the past behind." She raised an eyebrow. "But that's over, right?"

Oh, she hoped so.

Boo hugged her again. "I'm just glad you're back. When Shep came home alone . . ." She let her go again. "Okay. See, everything's good. The team's back together. And"—she glanced at Tillie—"we're heading over to Moose's because Tillie and Moose are engaged."

"What?" London turned to Tillie, who'd stood up, still frowning at her phone. Now she pocketed it.

"Yeah. Moose finally asked," Tillie said. "Long story."

London crossed the room. "Yeah, but an easy ending. We all know he's been in love with you for years."

Tillie met her hug. Behind them, a knock on the door, and London turned to see Flynn walk in.

"Hey, London," Flynn said. "I didn't know you were back. Are you going to Moose's?"

And just like that, everything was back to normal. Her, back with the team. *London Brooks, pilot.*

Laney Steele, long gone.

"Yeah." She swallowed. "Um, is Shep going?"

A couple smiles, one from Flynn, the other, Tillie.

"He went home to get his dog," Boo said. "But he said he'll be there."

His dog. London had forgotten about the animal, and, well, *Jasmine*. Her gut tightened. Maybe he deserved a woman like Jasmine, someone who was there to meet him when he came home. Steady, dependable.

Whatever. London could be steady and dependable.

"Moose just texted and said to hurry," Tillie said. "Weird."

"Let's go," Boo said.

"Ride with me," said Tillie. "Then Shep will have to give you a ride home." She winked.

"I'll go with you too," said London.

"I'll ride with you guys," Flynn said. "We need to talk about your house anyway."

They got into Axel's SUV, and Tillie cranked up the heat as she pulled out. "So, Montelena. Was it beautiful?"

"Gorgeous."

"I looked it up," Flynn said. "It has a castle."

"It does. And a king. And a royal family. And it's one of the wealthiest countries in the world."

"Glad you're home," said Boo, touching London's shoulder with hers in the back seat. "The team was a little lost without you."

Silence, and Tillie met London's gaze in the mirror. "I just feel better knowing that Moose has you for his copilot."

Sweet. But the sense of all of it swelled up inside her. Home. Belonging. She could go all in on being London Brooks, no problem.

They got on the highway heading northeast, toward Moose's place.

"Okay, so Dawson called me," Flynn said. "The fire report came back. They're not sure it was arson, but the gas line on your stove had been cracked, filling your house with gas."

"I smelled gas," Tillie said. "I couldn't figure out where, so I went outside."

"Through the garage?"

"Yes."

"Because that's where the fire ignited. Their guess is that the gas from the house seeped out and connected with the pilot light of your furnace. And since the gas from inside had escaped, it took some time to engulf the entire structure."

"It caught fire not long after I crossed the street," Tillie said. "Sheesh, if I had stayed inside—"

"But you didn't," London said. "You can't what-if. It'll take your breath away. You're here now, and safe, and all you can say is, 'Thank You, God.'"

Tillie nodded, and London looked out the window. *Thank You, God, for showing up, so many times.* Prince Luka's words returned to her. *"The journey—not the ending—is the point of the story. It's how the characters change and grow and become, right?"*

Yes. And all the what-ifs that *hadn't* happened were part of the twists in the story. And evidence of the hand of God with her, whether she'd been Princess Delaney, Laney Steele, or London Brooks.

"So, do you think it was an accident, or arson?" Boo asked, leaning up.

"The house was empty a long time while I was in Florida. Maybe the hose just got cold and cracked," Tillie said.

"Or someone broke in?" This from Flynn.

Tillie's hands whitened on the steering wheel.

"Axel told me what happened at the courthouse, with Harry Benton," Flynn said.

"Harry Benton? Why do I know that name?" London leaned forward in her seat.

"His daughter, Grace, was the one who died in the blizzard at the Copper Mountain ski resort last spring."

"Right. I remember now. She was attacked by the Midnight Sun Killer."

"And left out in the cold to freeze to death," Boo said. "Poor Oaken still has nightmares sometimes of leaving her behind."

"The coroner said she might have been dead before they quit the search," Tillie said. "It's the reason why the lawsuit was dismissed."

"But Benton believes differently. And that's why he threatened Moose," said Flynn. "At least, according to Axel."

"Oh, the man—and Grace's fiancé—definitely threatened him. Told him that someday he'd watch the people he loved die."

Wow, London had been out of the loop while chasing her shadow. Through the rearview mirror, she saw Tillie's mouth tighten.

"I'm so tired of unhinged, angry people taking out their pain on others," Tillie said quietly.

London nodded, along with Boo.

"Yeah. It got me worried," Flynn continued. "So I did some sleuthing on Benton. He's a contractor. And Liam Grant works for him, a mechanical engineer. They own a building company."

Silence.

They'd turned off the highway, toward Moose's place.

"So they'd know all about gas lines?" Boo said. "Right?"

"Maybe," Flynn said. "I checked and there's no record of Benton or Grant leaving Alaska after the trial. They did check out of their hotel two days later, but their rental car hasn't been turned back in. . . ."

"So they could still be in Alaska?" said Boo.

"Starting gas fires?" London added.

"Dawson put out a BOLO on the car and the men," Flynn said. "The rental is a Kia Sorrento and has Washington State plates."

"Like that one?" Boo said, and Tillie touched her brakes. The car sat on the side of the road, dark and lightly dusted with snow, as if it had been sitting for a while.

Tillie slowed and then pulled up in front of it. Flynn got out and shone her light on the plates, came back, her expression haunted. "The plates say Montana, so it might not be them."

"Or they changed the plates," London said.

"How far are we from Moose's place?" Boo asked.

"Maybe a quarter mile," London said, her mind on her own not-too-distant hike through the woods. She reached for the door handle. "I'm getting out. Just in case."

"I'll go with you," Flynn said. She turned to Tillie. "Maybe it's nothing. But watch yourselves, ladies. We'll meet you at the house."

Tillie pulled away, and London shoved her gloved hands into her pockets. "Are we overreacting?"

"Dunno," said Flynn. "I came from work, so . . ." She opened her jacket, revealing where she wore a shoulder holster, her issued Glock tucked away.

"Let's hope you don't have to use that," London said. "I'd suggest we use our cell phone lights, but I don't want them to see us coming. We'll have to go by starlight." Moonlight shone through the trees, upon the glistening snow. Tillie's taillights had disappeared, probably down Moose's driveway.

"We'll take the drive in, then cut around to the back of the house, see if we can see anything through the back windows." She took off toward the driveway at a light run.

The motion-sensor lights had flickered on, a couple of them fading to dark with the passing of the SUV.

"Let's get off the drive," she said, and they cut a path at the edge of the trees, down to the house.

"I texted Axel on our drive up, but he didn't answer," Flynn said now.

Their feet crunched through the snow, faster now as London picked up her pace despite the deep snow. Flynn followed her, and they skirted the edge of the forest all the way along the property line of Moose's place. His house rose large and impressive in the night, dark save for the light streaming from the basement walkout sliding door.

"The guys said they were going to watch the hockey game," said Flynn quietly.

London grabbed her arm. "Let's just . . . take a look." She kept low, running from one stand of trees to the next, then finally hunkering down beside the woodshed.

From here, she got a good view of the horror inside.

"Is that Benton?" asked Flynn.

"Yeah, I think so." London blew out a breath at the sight of Moose and Axel on the floor, two men standing near them, holding weapons. "Call Tillie, tell her not to go in."

Except, too late, because Tillie and Boo came down the stairs. *Oh no.*

Tillie put her hands up, and Boo ran over to someone—*ah*, Oaken on the floor too.

Moose was shouting, making a ruckus.

"We need to get in there before Benton shoots them all."

"I'll call Dawson, get the APD out here."

London got up. "Do it right now."

Then she went into the shed, opened the root cellar door, and climbed down the stairs. She opened the hidden door and keyed in the code. The last time she'd tried, she'd broken the latch inside. The door didn't budge.

Think.

She climbed up to the woodshed and found the maul for chopping wood on a nearby stump. She grabbed it and the sledgehammer.

"What are you *doing*?" Flynn said, following her back to the root cellar.

"This is the tunnel to the house."

London shoved the maul between the frame and the door. She picked up the sledgehammer. "Stand back."

Then she slammed the hammer into the maul. It made a terrible clang, enough to carry to the house, but the door ripped open.

Flynn shone her light down the tunnel, but London knew the way and ran through it, the air still as clammy and rank as before. She keyed in the code at the far door, then opened it and found herself back in the office.

For a moment she debated turning on the power and lighting up the screens, but she'd seen the situation just fine already. Still, maybe there were more attackers—

"Is this the tunnel to the sauna?"

She nodded, and Flynn headed in, so London followed her up.

They came out into the sauna room just like before, but now Flynn crept into the box, London behind her. The light from the other room didn't reach the sauna but illuminated the horror in the entertainment area.

Boo was bleeding from the mouth, and blood covered her hands and shirt. She knelt above Oaken, who had rolled over onto his side, his hands tied behind him. He bled from a shoulder wound.

Axel lay on his side, as if he had tried to get up and had been kicked, given the welt on his jaw. He glared at Benton, the man's back to London.

Moose, however, was still struggling, shouting. "Stay away from her. She's not a part of this! She's not even a part of the team!"

Maybe he was referring to Tillie, who had her hands up, the other man—*right, the fiancé, Liam Grant*—holding a shotgun to her chest.

London and Flynn crept out of the sauna into the pool room, huddled in the darkness under the pony wall.

"Can you get a shot off, take down Grant?" London said. Benton stood closest to the door. "I can get to Benton."

Flynn nodded. "Except Grant is looking pretty spooked. He's not a criminal—"

"Now he is."

"Yeah, but mostly he's desperate. And that's—"

"Dangerous. People do stupid things when they're desperate," London said. *Like faking their own deaths and forgetting who they are.*

But London knew *exactly* who she was. London, Laney, Delaney—but most of all, the woman who loved her team.

"I'll provide the distraction—you shoot as soon as the door is open." London hustled to the door.

Moose was still shouting. "Let her go! Just let her go!"

"Get on your face!" Benton said to Tillie.

As London watched, Moose rolled onto his back, and suddenly, his hands came free. He launched himself at Benton's feet.

She threw open the door, let out a roar, and dove at Benton.

Behind her, a shot erupted, but she'd already taken Benton down to the floor, pinning him.

"Tillie!"

The shout from Moose nearly shook her hold free, but she closed her eyes and hung on. *Focus, London.*

Moose was on the man, wrestling with his gun, and she boxed Benton's ears.

Another shot, and Moose fell back, shouting.

Benton rolled then, and a pain seared through her leg. She jerked, and Benton wrenched free. Heat pooled, and as she rolled, she realized he'd stabbed her. Maybe with a piece of broken television.

Benton hit his feet and headed for the sliding door.

Moose had the gun, rolled, and took a shot.

The door window shattered.

Benton ran straight through it.

Oh no—he wasn't going to get away to show up and terrorize them another day. London rolled to her feet and took off after him through the shattered door, into the night.

Shep hadn't meant to be a jerk. Jasmine was a sweet girl, but when she'd brought pork dumplings over along with Caspian and offered to stay and heat them up for him, he'd had to tell her the truth.

Now he turned to Caspian, who sat shotgun in the front seat, staring at him with those big brown eyes. "I know she's nice to you, pal, and frankly, knows you better than I do, but . . . the thing is, I don't belong to her. I belong to London, right?"

Caspian definitely looked better-fed, his dark coat shiny, and he seemed to understand. He lay on the seat now and put a paw on Shep's leg.

Shep rubbed the dog behind his ears. "But I am going to have to figure out what to do with you. I'm not sure that spy life agrees with having a dog."

Caspian whined.

"I know. I am hoping that Hazel and Tillie fall in love with you."

He'd showered fast, and even though he'd found Jasmine in his kitchen with dinner when he came downstairs—note to self, change the door code before he sold the condo to Axel—he'd only be a little late for dinner at Moose's. Maybe an hour behind everyone, but with Boo and Tillie going to Boo's house, the party wouldn't start for a while anyway.

Although, how he was going to tell Moose he was leaving . . . Yeah, here he was, right back to where he'd been a month ago when he'd thought London might be dead.

But she's not dead, and he was going to make sure she stayed *not dead.* And home could be wherever she wanted it to be.

As long as it was with him.

His stomach growled. He'd missed Moose's steaks, for sure. And maybe he should call London just to . . .

What? Apologize? Yes, probably. But also, just to tell her . . .

Shoot. He should have had the courage to stand in faith that God could give him the right happy ending.

Even if it looked different from the one he'd expected.

He looked at Caspian. "Hard to belong to someone who doesn't seem to want you." But maybe that was a lie. Wow, he hoped it was a lie.

She'd never said she loved him, though.

Aw. This might be another colossal mistake. But it didn't feel like a mistake, and maybe that's what faith was . . . moving forward, trusting God, even when it didn't make sense.

He pulled up to the house and parked his Tahoe next to Axel's Yukon and a shiny Porsche.

Probably Oaken's.

Caspian jumped out the driver's-side door.

The front light flicked on when Shep climbed the steps and opened the door, expecting a kitchen full of his team.

Shouting from downstairs, and Caspian ran past him, barking.

He followed him in and then—

A gunshot. He froze.

The door to the basement stood open, and Caspian ran down the stairs to more shouting, a scream, the crash of glass—

Shep scrambled down the stairs after the dog.

The sight stopped him. Tillie, going mano a mano with a burly guy, dodging a punch, landing an uppercut on his chin, then sweeping out his legs and pouncing on him, trapping his arms.

Only then did he see the blood cresting down her face onto her shirt. But the woman seemed unfazed, and she hit the man just as Flynn ripped flex cuffs from Axel's wrists with a piece of glass from the shattered television.

Axel rolled to his feet. "Help Tillie!"

Flynn grabbed the angry man by one arm, and Axel was right there, grabbing the other arm.

Tillie hit him again, and this time the man stopped struggling.

Boo had picked up Oaken, sat him up against the wall, had shoved a pillow into his shoulder. Blood saturated his shirt.

And Moose had completely lost it, ripping at his leg ties.

Only then did Shep see the shattered glass door.

Moose looked up at him. "She's out there!" He pointed to the door. "She went after him."

Caspian, as if understanding completely, took off into the night.

Shep came into the room, slowing. "Who?"

"London!"

He stalled for just a second. *London?*

Of course, London. Showing up, unexpected. Completely changing his world.

Then he looked at the shattered door and took off.

Bloody footsteps shone in the snow in the pool of light from the house. The illumination reached out enough to show two figures fighting in the night.

London—seriously? But he could recognize her anywhere, fast and tough as she dodged a man swinging at her. She returned a blow and staggered.

Staggered? Oh no. Her blood darkened the snow.

The man rounded on her, and Shep's entire body nearly exploded when he connected, a right hook to her face.

Her gorgeous, beautiful face—

Shep tasted only justice as he roared, running full-out toward them.

The man tripped her up, and even as she rolled, landing on her back, he was on her.

Hands to her throat, pushing her into the snow.

Shep's feet crashed through the broken snow, but Caspian reached them first. He caught the man's jacket, growling.

The man punched the dog, who let go, whining.

And that turned Shep to fire.

He launched himself at the man, caught him, and they rolled through the snow.

The man hit him, but Shep was right there with years of bottled-up anger, the violence banked for this exact moment.

One punch and the man staggered back.

Shep hit his feet. Then charged. The hill caught them, and suddenly they were sliding toward the river.

The roiling, dark, lethal river. Shep pushed the man away, rolled onto his stomach, kicked hard into the embankment.

The man kept sliding, shouting—

He splashed into the river.

Shep rolled over, breathing hard.

The current grabbed the man, and he shouted, panicking as the cold shocked him.

Shep got up, scrambled down to the edge. Icy chunks settled near the shore, but the man had fallen deeper, floating now some ten, then fifteen feet away.

"Help!" he shouted at Shep. "Help!"

Shep turned back to the house, to London and his team. They'd spilled out of the house, Flynn with London.

"Help!"

He glanced at the man in the water. *Shoot*—

"Swim!" Shep plunged into the water, the temperature like knives to his skin, and *oh, this was stupid, stupid*—

"Shep!"

He turned and spotted Axel, now wading out into the water, his arm outstretched.

The man was swimming now, fighting the current. He made it to a boulder, clinging hard. Shep grabbed Axel's hand, and in a moment, Moose ran up.

He stood on the shore. "What the—"

"He's going to drown," said Shep, and for a second, he saw that truth play in Moose's eyes.

But Moose was built like Shep, and after a moment, his mouth tightened and he walked out into the water, grabbing Axel's arm, making a human chain. Shep went deeper, up to his thighs now, Axel's grip on him an anchor. The man was only feet away, clinging to the boulder, the water rushing over him, shaking him. He stared at Shep, not reaching for him.

"C'mon, dude. I'm not letting go of my teammate, so you're going to have to decide whether you want to live or die."

The man gasped, fighting for breath in the tumult of water.

Shep leaned out for him, his hand splashing down in the water.

"C'mon, Benton!" Moose shouted from shore. "Don't let your pride kill you! Grab on!"

The man clung to the rock, his gaze on Shep, then Axel and Moose. And then Shep could almost see it in his eyes. The grief, swelling up to crash over him, overtake him.

"I . . . I'm not going to let you save me."

"Benton!" Moose shouted even as the man let go.

Shep lunged for him, but Axel grabbed him back. The man went spinning out into the current, going down, splashing up, and then disappearing.

Shep let out a word, hitting the water.

Axel yanked him toward shore. "You can't save someone who doesn't want to be saved."

He stared at the darkness. Maybe. But it was his job to try.

Always, to try. So maybe he was walking, a little, in his old man's shoes.

He struggled out of the current, Moose reeling them in, and then landed on shore, shivering, frozen. "We should look for him."

"I'm not endangering my team," Moose said. "Besides . . ."

Caspian's barks lifted into the air.

London.

Shep pushed past Moose, already heading toward the chaos, running hard through the slick, sharp snow.

London lay in the snow, Boo beside her and shoving snow into the wound in London's leg. It saturated the white, red and shiny. Tillie had run out, breathing hard, her own head wound bandaged with a towel. She held another towel and gave it to Boo.

Shep dropped to his knees beside London, reaching for her. "What—what are you—"

"I'm sorry," she said, grabbing his hand. Her eyes had turned glossy. "I should have followed you. Chased after you. Because you're right—you know me. You know all of me—"

"Okay—yes, I do, but let's get you sorted—"

"I choose you, Shep."

Oh. "Listen, London—Lacey—whoever you want to be—I'm in. I've always been in." His grip tightened on hers.

"We need another towel, and where is that ambulance?" Boo said from somewhere behind him.

"I shouldn't have made you choose. You be who you want. I'll be—"

"My hero."

He made a face. "Seriously?"

"It felt right." She grinned, tears cresting down along with a groan as Boo tightened the towel around her leg.

"I was going to say, I'll be here. Still holding on."

"I love you, Shep. I always have—and I always will—"

Aw, and he didn't have a hope of stopping himself from leaning in and unleashing a little of the emotion inside.

"Hey—let's not get the heart pumping any more than necessary here," Boo said.

Shep pulled away, met Boo's eyes. "How bad is it?"

"I don't think it nicked the artery, but she's bleeding pretty good," Boo said.

Moose had Tillie in his arms, holding her, and Axel had fallen to his knees, breathing hard. He looked like he might throw up even as Flynn ran outside.

"Cops are here. They've called an ambulance."

London turned to Shep, grabbed his shirt. "Shep, if you want to stay here and build a life in Alaska, I'm in. Or wherever—"

"Yes," he said. "*Wherever*. Because wherever is always home with you."

"Wow," Axel said. "That's . . . Shep, I'm impressed."

"Guys, she's not going to *die*," Boo said. "I just want to get her stitched up."

"Besides, been there, done that. Not recommended. Zero stars," London said.

"What she said," Shep said, and picked London up, easy, into his arms. "Let's get you to a hospital."

"And Oaken—he was shot too," Axel said.

"He'll be okay," Boo said. "It nicked his shoulder."

"I have to say this is the worst engagement party I've ever been to," Axel said.

No one smiled.

"Really? C'mon, that was funny."

London looked at Shep, grinning. "It sort of was."

Moose and Tillie headed to the house. Shep followed them, carrying London, Caspian barking at his feet, running in circles.

Inside, Dawson Mulligan had finished cuffing Grant, who sat on the sofa, his jaw tight as Dawson read him his rights. The man looked away, his eyes distant. As if his world had exploded and he didn't know how to put it back together again.

Shep remembered Grant having that same sort of look back when his fiancée went missing, and later, when they'd found her body. So maybe he'd never recovered. Maybe this was what grief looked like when pain turned to vengeance.

And it occurred to Shep that this could have been him—minus the shooting, but still, a hollowness, even a terrible sense of unfairness that could have dogged his every thought.

Unless.

Unless he hung on to faith. To believing that God was bigger than his grief. And in the end, God had surprised him with so very much.

"London—what—I thought you were dead," Dawson said.

"Surprise," she said, her arms looped around Shep's neck.

Shep shook his head.

Dawson looked at Flynn. "Hello?"

"Sorry," Flynn said.

"So, what exactly went down here?" Dawson indicated for another officer to haul Grant up.

Moose opened his mouth, closed it. Sighed. "My team . . . got ambushed." He suddenly seemed taken apart. "I can't believe . . . Guys, I'm so sorry."

"He might be going into shock," Boo said. "Get him some water."

"Seriously? Look at you all," Moose said. "This is all my fault."

He gestured to Oaken, who sat with the pillow to his shoulder, and Tillie, with her sodden towel over her head, and Axel, a little beat up, standing with his hands on Flynn's shoulders, and London, bleeding in Shep's arms—

"What are you talking about?" Shep said.

"If I hadn't said yes to that stupid reality show—"

"Stop," Shep said. "If it weren't for that show . . . well, we'd all still be . . . maybe less bloody, but God had a plan, even in the crazy. Even when"—he looked at London—"when life seemed unhinged and out of control."

"Out of bounds." She smiled at him.

"Moose and Tillie got engaged," Axel said. "So that's a win."

Moose smiled.

An EMT appeared on the stairs. "Where's the injured?"

"Here," Boo said.

"Me," Oaken said.

"Right here," said Moose.

"London first," said Shep and carried her up the stairs.

Outside, light bathed the yard, and he walked her right down to the open doors of the ambulance. Set her on a gurney. "She needs some fluids and painkiller, and stitches," he said to the EMT who'd followed him out.

Shep climbed in behind her.

"Sorry, sir, you'll have to ride separately," the EMT said. Not a big guy, but sturdy enough.

Shep looked at London. "I don't think so."

"That's against the rules."

Shep turned and gave the man a look. "I see this going one of two ways. You could try to drag my body out of here—and you could probably give it a good go—but I promise you, it won't go well. And in the end, I'll be the one still standing."

The man's eyes widened.

"Or you could close those doors and drive us to the hospital."

"Let him go," said Dawson, coming off the front steps. "He's a rescue tech. He knows what he's doing."

The EMT raised his hands.

From the house, Caspian ran out barking, circling Dawson. "Hey, buddy," he said and rubbed the dog's ears. "Who do you belong to?"

"He's mine," said Shep. "Can you watch him for me?"

Dawson nodded. "No problem." He crouched in front of the dog, who licked his chin.

Huh. Maybe the dog didn't belong to Shep after all.

The EMT shut the door. Then he went around to the front seat and climbed in.

Shep sat down on the bench.

"You were a little scary there," London said. "Sounded like you might actually hit him."

Shep shrugged. "I said I wasn't a man of violence. I never said I wouldn't use it."

She smiled, her eyes warm in his. "You saved my life."

"Of course I did." He caught her hand. "Where you go, I go, London. Or Laney, or whoever you decide to be."

"Just yours, Shep. Just yours." Then she reached out and grabbed the front of his shirt, pulled him down, and kissed him. Sweetly, surrendering, giving herself over to him as he wrapped his arms around her and held her.

And right there, right then, he knew what it meant to fly.

EPILOGUE

"HAS IT STARTED YET?" FLYNN'S VOICE PRE-ceded her down the stairs to Moose's basement. The smell of popcorn followed her, emanating from the bowl she held along with a handful of napkins.

"Not yet," Axel said and picked up the remote to turn on the television, the brand new one that hung on the wall in Moose's repaired basement. That and a new sectional and new carpet—he'd given the entire thing a makeover in the last couple weeks.

He blamed it on Axel moving out, having purchased a town-home in Anchorage. But Shep had no doubt it had to do with wanting to scour away the memories of trauma or anything that might scare Hazel.

He'd also opened up the sauna and installed a new code on the doors leading through Pike's tunnel to the outside world. "Just because you never know when you need to escape," he'd said to Shep as they'd worked on the door in the firewood shed.

Yes, well, Shep wasn't going anywhere, at least for right now.

But he could see the future in London's eyes, the unfinished business with Tomas. However, she'd promised not to leave in the middle of the night, day, or any other time without letting him tag along.

Because that's what it was like to be in love with a spy, apparently.

For now, however, London had shed her Swan persona, and sat with him on the sofa, reaching for the popcorn bowl as Axel pressed play on the flatscreen.

"You sure your agent got this right?" This from Moose, who sat next to Hazel, tucked into him and eating popcorn. He addressed his question to Oaken.

"I don't know. She told me to watch, so here we are." He leaned a hip against the pool table, his arms around Boo, who stood in front of him.

"I think we're a shoo-in," said Boo, glancing up at him. "Have you see the TikToks?"

"I hate social media," said Oaken.

"I know. I keep deleting my app. Then adding it again."

He grinned at her, shaking his head.

"Hazel—it's past your bedtime." Tillie had come downstairs.

"Mom—it hasn't even started yet. Please—"

Moose looked over at Tillie, gave her a smile.

Tillie. She wore a black Iron Maiden Training T-shirt, a group she'd just started for young women who wanted to get fit. "Oh, for crying out loud—okay. But I reserve the right to change my mind."

"I just know you're going to win," Hazel said to Moose.

"It's not an awards show yet, pumpkin. It's the just the International Emmy World Television Festival—where they announce the nominees for the awards."

Tillie leaned down and kissed the top of Moose's head. "Dawson just got here."

Shep could have figured that out by the way Caspian got up then and wagged his tail. Maybe he should give the dog to the cop, or at least share custody. Caspian trotted over as Dawson came down the stairs. He wore a slick of snow in his dark hair and crouched, and Caspian gave him a kiss.

"Wow. Clearly you need a girlfriend," Flynn said over her shoulder from where she'd settled next to Axel, under his outstretched arm.

"Funny," Dawson said, but he glanced at Moose, then away, and deep in Shep's mind he remembered a story, maybe, of Dawson and Moose, and an accident and a woman who'd died. Maybe a woman Dawson had loved.

But then the show came on, and all he cared about was here, now, and the fact that everyone was safe and home and not out in the blizzard forming in the northern mountains. No doubt tomorrow they'd have calls.

In fact, if they stayed too late, they'd all have to bunk down here, in Moose's massive house. Like a giant slumber party.

"Any word from your parents?" London said quietly.

He glanced at her. "No. I called all their regular skiing haunts. I even called Harrington Bly, one of my old teammates down in Montana. He's going out to check on their last known camping location. But I'm thinking I might need to get on a plane to Montana."

Never mind that they'd dropped off the planet without telling him. Apparently, he'd always be the one left behind on the slope.

"Please be back by my wedding," Tillie said.

"Three weeks!" Hazel said, holding up her fingers. "And I'm a bridesmaid!" She clapped her hands, and Caspian barked.

"Okay, okay," Moose said. "Here come the nominations."

"I can't hear," Oaken said. "Turn it up, Axel."

Axel picked up the remote, aimed it at the television. Nothing happened.

"Oh, sorry—the awards are online. It's streaming from my computer," he said and pushed himself up from the sofa. The computer sat on a TV stand next to the flatscreen, an HDMI cord coming from the back.

"You need an upgrade, bro," Moose said. "Something made in this century, with Bluetooth."

"What can I say?—I spent all my dough on the down payment." He glanced back at Flynn and winked.

Which only caused him to trip backward, stumbling over the dog. Caspian jumped up, began to bark, lunged at Axel.

Who backed away into London, who sat up and caught him but only managed to push him away, where he tripped over Shep's feet.

Axel's arms windmilled as his feet caught, and he headed toward the floor, reaching out to catch himself—

On the HDMI cable.

Attached to the back of the television.

Which yanked it free from the wall.

Shep and Moose weren't fast enough to catch it from crashing onto the floor, and Axel covered up, his arms over his head as the monster 85-inch bounced off him.

Sparks and the shattering of the screen crashed through the silence.

Then, "Axel, what the—" Moose started, but Flynn pushed past him.

"Are you okay?" she crouched next to him.

He had already pushed the television off himself. "Whoops."

Moose closed his eyes, shook his head.

"Does that mean we don't get to see if you win?" Hazel, her eyes wide.

Shep looked at London, who was stifling a grin.

"Let's see if we can pull it up on Moose's computer," Tillie said, and held out her hand to Hazel.

Dawson followed her up, Caspian on his heels.

Shep stepped over Axel and lifted the end of the television, Moose on the other as they set it up against the fireplace.

"This show will never stop giving me grief," Moose said.

London had helped pick up the popcorn spilled when Flynn got up. Now she stood with Flynn, bowl in hand, her gaze on Shep. "I think it gave us all a fresh start." She smiled.

His entire body filled with heat and hope and joy. Yeah, he didn't care where he lived, as long as it was with London.

"I, for one, am grateful for the show," Oaken said. "In fact . . ."

Shep had nothing when Oaken stepped in front of Boo.

And then everyone went quiet as Oaken knelt in front of Boo Kingston, whose eyes had widened.

"Brontë Kingston, you are the best thing that ever happened to me. You're the one I want to write songs for and sing them onstage to, it's your voice I long to hear after a long day on the road. You're the reason I want to come home, because you are my home. You're so brave, and smart and . . . you get on my nerves in the best of ways, and . . . I've been trying to figure this out for a while, and I just can't take waiting one more second. Please . . . will you marry me?"

He even had a ring, the box pulled from his pocket.

Boo's eyes had filled.

"I know I shouldn't have asked in front of everyone—"

"Why not?" Boo said. "They're family." Then she caught Oaken's face in her hands. "And they already know my answer. Yes, Oaken Fox. Of course I'll marry you. Where you go, I go. I was just hoping you'd ask." She leaned down then and kissed him, and Shep turned to London and, shoot, just had to kiss her too.

She wound her arms around his neck, kissed him like she meant it. Leaned back. "Where you go, I go."

"Even to Montana?"

"It's one of my favorite places."

Footsteps on the stairs, then, "Are you kidding me? I missed it again? Sheesh, you guys, I leave the room for one minute and the whole world changes."

Tillie, on the stairs, shaking her head. She looked at Moose. "I found the site on the computer and set it up in the kitchen, on the island."

Then she smiled at Boo and Oaken. "I think I have some congratulatory pie in the refrigerator."

Of course she did.

Shep followed London and the rest upstairs to where Hazel sat on one of the stools, staring at the screen. Dawson sat beside her.

"What is this show?" London said.

"It's a convention. The nominations are live-streamed at a gala event at the end of the convention."

"They just did the animation nominations," Hazel said.

Tillie opened the refrigerator.

Moose leaned over the counter, listening. Axel pulled out a chair, Flynn next to him. She set the popcorn bowl on the island.

"It's really coming down," Oaken said, standing at the sliding glass door, his hand in Boo's. "Good skiing this weekend."

"All I see are accidents," Boo said.

Tillie pulled out an apple pie and set it on the island.

"The reality show category is up," Axel said.

Lights cascaded across the entry windows. Moose looked up, frowned, then headed to the front door.

Shep stepped up behind Axel, watching the announcer.

"Turn up the volume, honey," Tillie said to Hazel.

"Uh, Shep, can you come here?" Moose's voice, and Shep turned.

Moose stood in the doorway, looking over his shoulder. Shep frowned. Headed to the door.

Moose held it wider as he approached, and Shep slowed.

In the driveway, the engine still humming, a thirty-five-foot sleek and modern Winnebago Adventurer.

What?

And as he stood there, the passenger door opened. A woman, late fifties, wearing a ski hat and jacket, mukluks, dropped down into the gathering snow. She looked up at the porch, smiled. "Wow, it's a long way up here."

"Hello, Mrs. Watson," Moose said, heading outside. He'd already slipped on boots.

"That's Edie to you, Moose. We talked about this on the phone." She held her arms open to hug him.

Shep blinked, then grabbed a pair of boots by the door and followed Moose out. His father rounded the front of the RV. "Shep!" He came up, and before Shep could find words, pulled him into a hug. "You're a sight for sore eyes!"

What was going on?

And there was Moose, grinning at him like, like . . . "Did you do this?"

He frowned. "Do what?"

He fielded a hug from his mother while Moose shook his father's hand. "Daniel."

"Moose."

They were all one big happy family, it seemed.

Without him.

"What's going on?"

His father smiled. "We saw the show, son. And I thought . . . what better place to spend the winter than Alaska? Took a while to get here—we left Montana a couple months ago and worked our way north. Stopped in Banff for a few weeks—led three people to the Lord in one day!"

London had come out onto the porch, wearing oversized boots and his jacket.

"But I've been trying to call you."

"Oh." He glanced at his wife. "Our cell phone gave up the ghost on the road." He laughed. "I picked up a pay-as-you-go phone. It's a little spotty, but it gets the job done."

Hardly.

"The problem is, your dad can never remember anything, and he forgot your number!"

He didn't know why the words came as a punch. Of course he had.

"But he remembered the Air One outfit and called the office yesterday, and Moose picked up. Told us you'd be here."

He looked at Moose then, who was grinning. Shep hardly recognized him.

He turned back to his parents. "I still don't understand. You came . . . here?"

"We missed you," his mother said.

The words simply undid him.

London slid her hand into his. "Hey, Mrs. Watson. Remember me?"

A blink, a frown, then, "Wait. Delaney, right? Sam and Pete Brooks' cousin from England?"

"Close enough," she said and gave her a hug. "But your son calls me London."

Shep turned to his father. "You really came all this way to spend the winter in Alaska?"

His father frowned. "Son. I came all this way to spend winter with you."

Oh. His chest webbed. He opened his mouth, but his throat had tightened.

He looked away, his jaw tight.

London stepped up and gave his father a hug. "Nice to see you again, Mr. Watson."

"Call me Daniel," he said, and winked. "Moose, can I bother you to park my wheels in your driveway? Just until the blizzard dies. Then we'll find a campground."

"You can park here all winter long if you'd like," Moose said.

"Oh no. We need to be near the ski hill," his mother said.

Of course.

"Because that's where Shep lives, right?"

He looked at her. She smiled. Aw, and now his eyes wettened. London's hand slid into his, squeezed.

"Moose—Uncle Moose!" Hazel's voice on the front porch made them turn. She wore her socks, her hands fists, and she pumped them hard. "You're nominated! *The Sizeup* is nominated for best reality television!"

She wrinkled her nose. "I just know you're going to win!"

Moose had climbed up the steps and now picked her up. "Aw, Hazel. Don't you know? I've already won."

She threw her arms around him, and he gave her a kiss on the cheek as they went inside.

"What he said," London whispered into Shep's ear, then kissed him and headed inside.

Which left him to stand in the cold with his parents.

Who were here, in Alaska,

Just because.

No, just because they wanted to see him.

He let out a long breath and watched it gather, a storm in the night, then float away.

"Would you like some pie?" he said.

His father grinned, nodded as they turned to the house. Held open the door for his wife as she went inside, but stopped Shep with a hand to his chest. "I just have one very important question, son."

Shep stilled.

"Can she ski?"

A beat, and then Shep laughed. Loud and full, and his father did too. Shep put his arm around his shoulders. "Oh, Dad, you have no idea."

And then they went into Moose's warm home to celebrate.

Have you read the epic homecoming of the Kingston Brothers in the best-selling Sky King Ranch series?

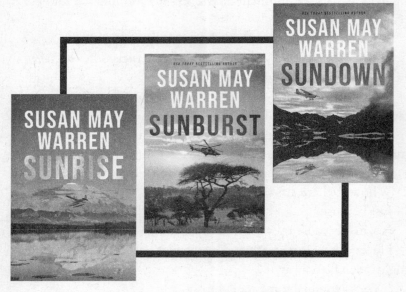

When their father is seriously injured in a bush pilot accident, three estranged brothers must make their way back to Sky King Ranch in Copper Mountain, Alaska to face the past that tore them apart. But trouble is waiting for this former military heroes, the kind of trouble that might just cost them the future they've been fighting for. Read the epic trilogy today!

Find out more at susanmaywarren.com.

Note to Reader

Thank you again for reading One Last Stand! I hope you enjoyed the epic finale, along with a few visits from old friends!

Stay tuned for more Air One Alaska stories coming in 2026!

If you did enjoy One Last Stand, would you be willing to do me a favor? Head over to the product page and leave a review. It doesn't have to be long—just a few words to help other readers know what they're getting. (But no spoilers! We don't want to wreck the fun!)

I'm genuinely overwhelmed with gratitude for the incredible team that surrounds me. A sincere thank you to my editors, Anne Horch and Rel Mollet, for their impeccable and invaluable feedback. Your unique touch truly enhances the stories I tell, and I am so appreciative of your efforts.

A warm embrace to my writing partner, Rachel Hauck, and to Sarah Erredge, who are always ready to explore new ideas with me, no matter how many questions I may have. Your support is priceless, and I cherish it deeply.

A heartfelt acknowledgment to my husband, Andrew, for all the technical support behind the scenes. You ensure everything operates seamlessly, and I simply couldn't manage this without you.

Cheers to Emilie Haney for her stunning cover designs that create the perfect initial impact for my books, and to Tari Faris, who makes the interiors just as captivating.

Thank you, Katie Donovan, for your meticulous proofreading skills, especially when we're up against tight deadlines.

I am deeply thankful to each of you for your contributions. Together, we form a team whose collective efforts and dedication are reflected in every story we share. A special mention to Andrea Doering and the team at Revell for their partnership and faith in my work. My heart overflows with gratitude because of all of you!

To my dear readers, thank you for embracing my books. It's my sincere hope that the time you spend with my characters enriches your life in some way. I'm eager to hear your thoughts—not just about this book, but about any characters or adventures you'd like to explore in future stories. Feel free to reach out at susan@ susanmaywarren.com. And for a glimpse of what's coming next, please visit www.susanmaywarren.com.

If you're interested in news about upcoming releases, exclusive freebies, and sneak peeks, I invite you to sign up for my weekly newsletter at susanmaywarren.com, or simply scan the QR code provided.

Onto the next adventure!

XO!
Susie May

More Books by Susan May Warren

Most recent to the beginning of the epic lineup, in reading order.

ALASKA AIR ONE RESCUE

One Last Shot
One Last Chance
One Last Promise
One Last Stand

THE MINNESOTA MARSHALLS

Fraser
Jonas
Ned
Iris
Creed

THE EPIC STORY OF RJ AND YORK

Out of the Night
I Will Find You
No Matter the Cost

SKY KING RANCH

Sunrise
Sunburst
Sundown

GLOBAL SEARCH AND RESCUE

The Way of the Brave
The Heart of a Hero
The Price of Valor

THE MONTANA MARSHALLS

Knox
Tate
Ford
Wyatt
Ruby Jane

MONTANA RESCUE

If Ever I Would Leave You (novella prequel)
Wild Montana Skies
Rescue Me
A Matter of Trust
Crossfire (novella)
Troubled Waters
Storm Front
Wait for Me

MONTANA FIRE

Where There's Smoke (Summer of Fire)
Playing with Fire (Summer of Fire)
Burnin' For You (Summer of Fire)
Oh, The Weather Outside is Frightful (Christmas novella)
I'll be There (Montana Fire/Deep Haven crossover)
Light My Fire (Summer of the Burning Sky)
The Heat is On (Summer of the Burning Sky)
Some Like it Hot (Summer of the Burning Sky)
You Don't Have to Be a Star (Montana Fire spin-off)

THE TRUE LIES OF REMBRANDT STONE

Cast the First Stone
No Unturned Stone
Sticks and Stone
Set in Stone
Blood from a Stone
Heart of Stone

A complete list of Susan's novels can be found at
susanmaywarren.com/novels/bibliography/.

About the Author

Susan May Warren is the USA Today bestselling author of over 95 novels with nearly 2 million books sold, including the Global Search and Rescue and the Montana Rescue series. Winner of a RITA Award and multiple Christy and Carol Awards, as well as the HOLT Medallion and numerous Readers' Choice Awards, Susan makes her home in Minnesota.

Visit her at www.susanmaywarren.com.